TRESS
OF THE
EMERALD SEA

BOOKS BY
BRANDON SANDERSON®

THE COSMERE®

THE STORMLIGHT ARCHIVE®

The Way of Kings
Words of Radiance
Edgedancer (novella)
Oathbringer
Dawnshard (novella)
Rhythm of War

THE MISTBORN® SAGA

THE ORIGINAL TRILOGY

Mistborn
The Well of Ascension
The Hero of Ages
Mistborn: Secret History (novella)

THE WAX AND WAYNE SERIES

The Alloy of Law
Shadows of Self
The Bands of Mourning
The Lost Metal

COLLECTION

Arcanum Unbounded:
The Cosmere® Collection

OTHER COSMERE NOVELS

Elantris
Warbreaker
Tress of the Emerald Sea

ALCATRAZ VS.
THE EVIL LIBRARIANS

Alcatraz vs. the Evil Librarians
The Scrivener's Bones
The Knights of Crystallia
The Shattered Lens
The Dark Talent

WITH JANCI PATTERSON
Bastille vs. the Evil Librarians

OTHER NOVELS

The Rithmatist
Legion: The Many Lives of
Stephen Leeds

THE RECKONERS®

Steelheart
Firefight
Calamity

SKYWARD

Skyward
Starsight
Cytonic

WITH JANCI PATTERSON
Skyward Flight: The Collection

TRESS

OF THE
EMERALD SEA

BRANDON
SANDERSON

TOR

TOR PUBLISHING GROUP
NEW YORK

TRESS OF THE EMERALD SEA

Copyright © 2023 Dragonsteel Entertainment, LLC

Symbols and illustrations by Howard Lyon
Copyright © 2023 by Dragonsteel Entertainment, LLC

All rights reserved.

A Tor Book
Published by Tom Doherty Associates / Tor Publishing Group
120 Broadway
New York, NY 10271

www.tor-forge.com

Tor® is a registered trademark of Macmillan Publishing Group, LLC.

The Library of Congress Cataloging-in-Publication Data is available upon request.

ISBN 978-1-250-89965-1 (hardcover)

Our books may be purchased in bulk for promotional, educational, or business use. Please contact your local bookseller or the Macmillan Corporate and Premium Sales Department at 1-800-221-7945, extension 5442, or by email at MacmillanSpecialMarkets@macmillan.com.

First Tor Edition: 2023

Printed in the United States of America

0 9 8 7 6 5 4 3 2 1

FOR EMILY,

Who has all my love

CONTENTS

ACKNOWLEDGMENTS

What a ride.

When I sat down to write this book on a whim, I had no idea where the whole project would end up going. (Be sure to check out the postscript at the end of the book, where I talk about my inspirations for it in ways that might be a little too spoilery to put up front.)

I envisioned something special for the four books from the 2022 Secret Projects Kickstarter campaign, but my team has gone above and beyond. This turned out to be an absolutely gorgeous volume. I know that many of you will be listening to the audiobook, which certainly has its own special artistry—but if you get a chance, make sure you leaf through the premium print edition. Because wow.

It's fitting, therefore, to start off our thank-you with Howard Lyon. I envisioned these books being kind of an "artist's showcase," where we picked an artist and let them go a little wild with what they wanted to do in creating the book. Howard did so much on this book. The cover, the endpapers, the interior illustrations—but really, the entire design owes a lot to him. Thank you, Howard, for being willing to take on this huge project. You did an amazing job.

Isaac Stewart is our art director at Dragonsteel, and was essential in making this all come together. Rachael Lynn Buchanan was our art assistant. Bill Wearne at American Print and Bindery really came through for us to get the premium edition printed, considering shortages. Many thanks, Bill. And I'd also like to thank all the people in the supply chain, from the paper mills to the cover and foil material suppliers, the press, the bindery, and the delivery drivers.

At Dragonsteel, our COO is Emily Sanderson. Our Editorial department is Peter Ahlstrom, Karen Ahlstrom, Kristy S. Gilbert, and Betsey Ahlstrom. Kristy Kugler was our copyeditor. Our Operations department is Matt "Are you going to do this in every book, Brandon?" Hatch, Emma Tan-Stoker, Jane Horne, Kathleen Dorsey Sanderson, Makena Saluone, and Hazel Cummings. Our Publicity and Marketing department is Adam Horne, Jeremy Palmer, and Taylor Hatch.

These folks don't get enough credit for all the wonderful things they do to make my projects happen. In particular, with this Kickstarter campaign, I needed their enthusiasm and their wonderful ideas. (For example, the original idea for a subscription box was Adam's several years ago.) It was a lot of work to get all of this put together and executed, so if you have a chance, thank my team in person.

And, of course, we need to give an extra special thanks to my Fulfillment department. Kara Stewart's team worked long hours to get the premium books to you all. They deserve a round of applause, and include Christi Jacobsen, Lex Willhite, Kellyn Neumann, Mem Grange, Michael Bateman, Joy Allen, Katy Ives, Richard Rubert, Sean VanBuskirk, Isabel Chrisman, Tori Mecham, Ally Reep, Jacob Chrisman, Alex Lyon, and Owen Knowlton.

I'd like to thank Margot Atwell, Oriana Leckert, and the rest of the team at Kickstarter. In addition I'd like to thank Anna Gallagher, Palmer Johnson, Antonio Rosales, and the rest of the BackerKit team.

At the JABberwocky literary agency, Joshua Bilmes, Susan Velazquez, and Christina Zobel have done an excellent job placing this book at publishers worldwide. For the trade release at Tor in the US, I would like to thank Devi Pillai, Tessa Villanueva, Lucille Rettino, Eileen Lawrence, Alexis Saarela, Rafal Gibek, Peter Lutjen, Heather Saunders, and Hayley Jozwiak. In the UK I'd like to thank Gillian Redfearn, Emad Akhtar, and Brendan Durkin at Gollancz, as well as my UK agents, John Berlyne and Stevie Finegan at the Zeno Agency.

We had a special sensitivity reader help us with this book—Jenna Beacom—and she was incredible. If you ever need someone to give you help on a book in regards to Deaf representation and how to write a deaf character, go straight to Jenna. She'll help you get it right.

Our alpha readers for this project were Adam Horne, Rachael Lynn Buchanan, Kellyn Neumann, Lex Wilhite, Christi Jacobsen, Jennifer Neal, and Joy Allen.

Our beta readers were Mi'chelle Walker, Matt Wiens, Ted Herman, Robert West, Evgeni "Argent" Kirilov, Jessie Lake, Kalyani Poluri, Bao Pham, Linnea Lindstrom, Jory Phillips, Darci Cole, Craig Hanks, Sean VanBuskirk, Frankie Jerome, Giulia Costantini, Eliyahu Berelowitz Levin, Trae Cooper, and Lauren McCaffrey.

Gamma proofreaders also included Joy Allen, Jayden King, Chris McGrath, Jennifer Neal, Joshua Harkey, Eric Lake, Ross Newberry, Bob Kluttz, Brian T. Hill, Shannon Nelson, Suzanne Musin, Glen Vogelaar, Ian McNatt, Gary Singer, Erika Kuta Marler, Drew McCaffrey, David Behrens, Rosemary Williams, Tim Challener, Jessica Ashcraft, Anthony Acker, Alexis Horizon, Liliana Klein, Christopher Cottingham, Aaron Biggs, and William Juan.

Last but not least, I need to give a special thanks to all of you who backed the Kickstarter project. I wasn't gunning for the number one spot—let alone double that. I just wanted to do something different, something interesting, and something cool. Your support continues to mean so very much to me. Thank you.

Brandon Sanderson

PART
1

1

THE GIRL

In the middle of the ocean, there was a girl who lived upon a rock.

This was not an ocean like the one you have imagined.

Nor was the rock like the one you have imagined.

The girl, however, *might* be as you imagined—assuming you imagined her as thoughtful, soft-spoken, and overly fond of collecting cups.

Men often described the girl as having hair the color of wheat. Others called it the color of caramel, or occasionally the color of honey. The girl wondered why men so often used food to describe women's features. There was a hunger to such men that was best avoided.

In her estimation, "light brown" was sufficiently descriptive—though the hue of her hair was not its most interesting trait. That would be her hair's unruliness. Each morning she heroically tamed it with brush and comb, then muzzled it with a ribbon and a tight braid. Yet some strands always found a way to escape and would wave free in the wind, eagerly greeting everyone she passed.

The girl had been given the unfortunate name of Glorf upon her birth (don't judge; it was a family name), but her wild hair earned her the name everyone knew her by: Tress. That moniker was, in Tress's estimation, her most interesting feature.

Tress had been raised to possess a certain inalienable pragmatism.

Such is a common failing among those who live on dour lifeless islands from which they can never leave. When you are greeted each day by a black stone landscape, it influences your perspective on life.

The island was shaped rather like an old man's crooked finger, emerging from the ocean to point toward the horizon. It was made entirely of barren black saltstone, and was large enough to support a fair-sized town and a duke's mansion. Though locals called the island the Rock, its name on the maps was Diggen's Point. No one remembered who Diggen was anymore, but he had obviously been a clever fellow, for he'd left the Rock soon after naming it and never returned.

In the evenings, Tress would often sit on her family's porch and sip salty tea from one of her favorite cups while looking out over the green ocean. Yes, I did say the ocean was green. Also, it was not wet. We're getting there.

As the sun set, Tress would wonder about the people who visited the Rock in their ships. Not that anyone in their right mind would deem the Rock a tourist destination. The black saltstone was crumbly and got into everything. It also made most kinds of agriculture impossible, eventually tainting any soil brought from off the island. The only food the island grew came from compost vats.

While the Rock did have important wells that brought up water from a deep aquifer—something that visiting ships required—the equipment that worked the salt mines belched a constant stream of black smoke into the air.

In summary, the atmosphere was dismal, the ground wretched, and the views depressing. Oh, and have I mentioned the deadly spores?

Diggen's Point lay near the Verdant Lunagree. The term "lunagree," you should know, refers to the places where the twelve moons hang in the sky around Tress's planet in oppressively low stationary orbits. Big enough to fill a full third of the sky, one of the twelve is always visible, no matter where you travel. Dominating your view, like a wart on your eyeball.

The locals worshipped those twelve moons as gods, which we can all agree is far more ridiculous than whatever it is you worship. However, it's easy to see where the superstition began, bearing in mind the spores—like colorful sand—that the moons dropped upon the land.

They'd pour down from the lunagrees, and the Verdant Lunagree was visible some fifty or sixty miles from the island. That was as close as you ever wanted to get to a lunagree—a great shimmering fountain of colorful motes, vibrant and exceedingly dangerous. The spores filled the world's oceans, creating vast seas not of water, but of alien dust. Ships sailed that dust like ships sail water here, and you should not find that so unusual. How many other planets have *you* visited? Perhaps they all sail oceans of pollen, and *your* home is the freakish one.

The spores were only dangerous if you got them wet. Which was rather a problem, considering the number of wet things that leak from human bodies even when they're healthy. The least bit of water would cause the spores to sprout explosively, and the results ranged from uncomfortable to deadly. Breathe in a burst of verdant spores, for example, and your saliva would send vines growing out of your mouth—or in more interesting cases, into your sinuses and out around your eyes.

The spores could be rendered inert by two things: salt or silver. Hence the reason the locals of Diggen's Point didn't terribly mind the salty taste of their water or food. They'd teach their children this ever-so-important rule: salt and silver halt the killer. An acceptable little poem, if you're the sort of barbarian who enjoys slant rhymes.

Regardless, with the spores, the smoke, and the salt, one can perhaps see why the king who the duke served needed a law requiring the population to remain on the Rock. Oh, he gave reasons that involved important military phrases like "essential personnel," "strategic resupply," and "friendly anchorage," but everyone knew the truth. The place was so inhospitable, even the smog found it depressing. Ships visited periodically for repairs, to drop off waste for the compost vats, and to take on new water. But each strictly obeyed the king's rules: no locals were to be taken from Diggen's Point. Ever.

And so, Tress would sit on her steps in the evenings, watching ships sail away as a column of spores dropped from the lunagree and the sun moved out from behind the moon and crept toward the horizon. She'd sip salty tea from a cup with horses painted on it, and she'd think, *There's a beauty to this, actually. I like it here. And I believe I shall be fine to remain here all my life.*

2

THE GROUNDSKEEPER

Perhaps you were surprised to hear those last words. Tress *wanted* to stay on the Rock? She *liked* it there?

Where was her sense of adventure? Her yearning for new lands? Her wanderlust?

Well, this isn't the part of the story where you ask questions. So kindly keep them to yourself. That said, you must understand that this is a tale about people who are both what they seem and *not* what they seem. Simultaneously. A story of contradictions. In other words, it is a story about human beings.

In this case, Tress wasn't your ordinary heroine—in that she was in fact decidedly ordinary. Indeed, Tress considered herself categorically boring. She liked her tea lukewarm. She went to bed on time. She loved her parents, occasionally squabbled with her little brother, and didn't litter. She was fair at needlepoint and had a talent for baking, but had no other noteworthy skills.

She didn't train at fencing in secret. She couldn't talk to animals. She had no hidden royalty or deities in her lineage, though her great-grandmother Glorf had reportedly once waved at the king. That had been from atop the Rock while he was sailing past, many miles away, so Tress didn't think it counted.

In short, Tress was a normal teenage girl. She knew this because the other girls often mentioned how *they* weren't like "everyone else," and after a while Tress figured that the group "everyone else" must include only her. The other girls were obviously right, as they all knew how to be unique—they were so good at it, in fact, that they did it together.

Tress was generally more thoughtful than most people, and she didn't like to impose by asking for what she wanted. She'd remain quiet when the other girls were laughing or telling jokes about her. After all, they were having so much fun. It would be impolite to spoil that, and presumptuous of her to request that they stop.

Sometimes the more boisterous youths talked of seeking adventure in foreign oceans. Tress found that notion frightening. How could she leave her parents and brother? Besides, she had her cup collection.

Tress cherished her cups. She had fine porcelain cups with painted glaze, clay cups that felt rough beneath her fingers, and wooden cups that were rugged and well-used.

Several of the sailors who frequently docked at Diggen's Point knew of her fondness, and they sometimes brought her cups from all across the twelve oceans: distant lands where the spores were reportedly crimson, azure, or even *golden*. She'd give the sailors pies in exchange for their gifts, the ingredients purchased with the pittance she earned scrubbing windows.

The cups they brought her were often battered and worn, but Tress didn't mind. A cup with a chip or ding in it had a *story*. She loved them all because they brought the world to her. Whenever she sipped from one of the cups, she imagined she could taste far-off foods and drinks, and perhaps understand a little of the people who had crafted them.

Each time Tress acquired a new cup, she brought it to Charlie to show it off.

Charlie claimed to be the groundskeeper at the duke's mansion at the top of the Rock, but Tress knew he was actually the duke's son. Charlie's hands were soft like a child's rather than callused, and he was better fed than anyone else in town. His hair was always cut neatly, and though he took his signet ring off when he saw her, it left a slightly lighter patch of skin that made it clear he usually wore it—on the finger that marked a member of the nobility.

Besides, Tress wasn't certain what "grounds" Charlie thought needed keeping. The mansion was, after all, on the Rock. There had been a tree on the property once, but it had done the sensible thing and died a few years earlier. There were some potted plants though, which let him pretend.

Grey motes swirled in the wind by her feet as she climbed the path up to the mansion. Grey spores were dead—the very air around the Rock was salty enough to kill spores—but she still held her breath as she hurried past. She turned left at the fork—the right path went to the mines—then wove up the switchbacks to the overhang.

Here the mansion squatted like a corpulent frog atop its lily. Tress wasn't certain why the duke liked it up here. It was closer to the smog, so maybe he liked the similarly tempered company. Climbing all this way was difficult—but judging by how the duke's family fit their clothing, perhaps they figured they could use the exercise.

Five soldiers watched the grounds—though only Snagu and Lead were on duty now—and they did their job well. After all, it had been a horribly long time since anyone in the duke's family had died from the myriad of dangers a nobleman faced while living on the Rock. (Those included boredom, stubbed toes, and choking on cobbler.)

She'd brought the soldiers pies, naturally. As they ate, she considered showing the two men her new cup. It was made completely of tin, stamped with letters in a language that ran top to bottom instead of left to right. But no, she didn't want to bother them.

They let her pass, although it wasn't her day to wash the mansion's windows. She found Charlie around back, practicing with his fencing sword. When he saw her, he put it down and hurriedly took off his signet ring.

"Tress!" he said. "I thought you wouldn't be by today!"

Having just turned seventeen, Charlie was two months older than she was. He had an abundance of smiles, and she had identified each one. For instance, the wide-toothed one he gave her now said he was genuinely happy to have an excuse to be done with fencing practice. He wasn't as fond of it as his father thought he should be.

"Swordplay, Charlie?" she asked. "Is that a groundskeeper's task?"

He picked up the thin dueling sword. "This? Oh, but it *is* for gardening."

He took a half-hearted swipe at one of the potted plants on the patio. The plant wasn't quite dead yet, but the leaf Charlie split certainly wasn't going to improve its chances.

"Gardening," Tress said. "With a *sword*."

"It's how they do things on the king's island," Charlie said. He swiped again. "There is always war there, you know. So if you consider it, it's natural the groundskeepers would learn to trim plants with a sword. Don't want to get ambushed when you're unarmed."

He wasn't a good liar, but that was part of what Tress liked about him. Charlie was *genuine*. He even lied in an authentic way. And seeing how bad he was at telling them, the lies couldn't be held against him. They were so obvious, they were better than many a person's truths.

He swiped his sword in the vague direction of the plant once more, then looked at her and cocked an eyebrow. She shook her head. So he gave her his "you've caught me but I can't admit it" grin and rammed the sword into the dirt of the pot, then plopped down on the low garden wall.

The sons of dukes were not supposed to plop. One might therefore consider Charlie to have been a young man of extraordinary talents.

Tress settled in next to him, basket in her lap.

"What did you bring me?" he said.

She took out a small meat pie. "Pigeon," she said, "and carrots. With a thyme-seasoned gravy."

"A noble combination," he said.

"I think the duke's son, if he were here, would disagree."

"The duke's son is only allowed to eat dishes with names that have weird foreign accents over their letters," Charlie said. "And he's never allowed to stop sword practice to eat. So it is fortunate that I am not him."

Charlie took a bite. She watched for the smile. And there it was: the smile of delight. She had spent an entire day in thought, contemplating what she could make with the ingredients that had been on sale in the port market, hoping to earn that particular smile.

"So, what else did you bring?" he asked.

"Charlie the groundskeeper," she said, "you have just received a very free pie, and now you presume to ask for more?"

"Presume?" he said around a mouthful of pie. He poked her basket with his free hand. "I know there's more. Out with it."

She grinned. To most she wouldn't dare impose, but Charlie was different. She revealed the tin cup.

"Aaah," Charlie said, then put aside the pie and took the cup reverently in both hands. "Now *this* is special."

"Do you know anything about that writing?" she asked, eager.

"It's old Iriali," he said. "They vanished, you know. The entire people: poof. There one day, gone the next, their island left uninhabited. Now, that was three hundred years ago, so no one alive has ever met one of them, but they supposedly had golden hair. Like yours, the color of sunlight."

"My hair is not the color of sunlight, Charlie."

"Your hair is the color of sunlight, if sunlight were light brown," Charlie said. It might be said he had a way with words. In that his words often got away.

"I'd wager this cup has quite the history," he said. "Forged for an Iriali nobleman the day before he—and his people—were taken by the gods. The cup was left on the table, to be collected by the poor fisherwoman who first arrived on the island and discovered the horror of an entire people gone. She passed the cup down to her grandson, who became a pirate. He eventually buried his ill-gotten treasure deep beneath the spores. Only to be recovered now, after eons in darkness, to find its way to your hands." He held the cup up to catch the light.

Tress smiled as he spoke. While washing the mansion's windows, she'd occasionally hear Charlie's parents berate him for talking so much; they thought it silly and unbecoming of his station. They rarely let him finish. She found that a shame. For while yes, he did ramble sometimes, she'd come to understand it was because Charlie liked *stories* the way Tress liked *cups*.

"Thank you, Charlie," she whispered.

"For what?"

"For giving me what I want."

He knew what she meant. It wasn't cups or stories.

"Always," he said, placing his hand on hers. "Always what you want,

Tress. And you can always tell me what it is. I know you don't usually do that, with others."

"What do *you* want, Charlie?" she asked.

"I don't know," he admitted. "Other than one thing, that is. One thing I shouldn't want, but I do. Instead, I'm *supposed* to want adventure. Like in the stories. You know those stories?"

"The ones with fair maidens," Tress said, "who always get captured and don't get to do much besides sit there? Maybe call for help now and then?"

"I suppose that does happen," he said.

"Why are they always fair maidens?" she said. "Are there maidens that are unfair? Perhaps they mean 'fare,' as in food. I could be that kind of maiden. I'm good with food." She grimaced. "I'm glad I'm not in a story, Charlie. I'd end up captured for certain."

"And I would probably die quickly," he said. "I'm a coward, Tress. It's the truth."

"Nonsense. You're merely an ordinary person."

"Have you . . . seen how I respond around the duke?"

She grew silent. Because she had.

"If I weren't a coward," he said, "I'd be able to tell you things I cannot. But Tress, if you did get captured, I'd help anyway. I'd put on armor, Tress. Shining armor. Or maybe dull armor. I think if someone I knew were captured, I wouldn't take the time to shine the armor. Do you think those heroes pause to shine it, when people are in danger? That doesn't sound very helpful."

"Charlie," Tress said, "do you *have* armor?"

"I'd find some," he promised. "I would figure something out, surely. Even a coward would be brave in the proper armor, right? There are lots of dead people in those types of stories. Surely I could get some from one of—"

A shout sounded from within the mansion, interrupting the conversation. It was Charlie's father grousing. So far as Tress had been able to tell, yelling at things was the duke's one and only job on the island, and he took it very seriously.

Charlie glanced toward the sounds and grew tense, his smile fading.

But when the shouts didn't draw near, he looked back at the cup. The moment was gone, but another took its place, as they tend to do. Not as intimate, but still valuable because it was time with him.

"I'm sorry," he said softly, "for bringing up silly things like fare maidens and robbing armor from dead people. But I like that you listen to me anyway. Thank you, Tress."

"I am fond of your stories," she said, taking the cup and turning it over. "Do you think any of what you said about this cup is true?"

"It *could* be," Charlie said. "That's the great thing about stories. But look at this writing—it says it did once belong to a king. His name is right here."

"And you learned that language in . . ."

". . . gardening school," he said. "In case we had to read the warnings on the packaging of certain dangerous plants."

"Like how you wear a lord's doublet and hose . . ."

". . . because it makes me an excellent decoy, should assassins arrive and try to kill the duke's son."

"As you've said. But why then do you take off your ring?"

"Uh . . ." He glanced at his hand, then met her eyes. "Well, I guess I'd rather *you* not mistake me for someone else. Someone I don't want to have to be."

He smiled then, his timid smile. His "please go with me on this, Tress" smile. Because the son of a duke could not *openly* fraternize with the girl who washed the windows. A nobleman pretending to be a commoner though? Feigning low station to learn of the people of his realm? Why, that was expected. It happened in so many stories, it was practically an institution.

"That," she said, "makes perfect sense."

"Now then," he said, retrieving his pie. "Tell me about your day. I must hear."

"I went browsing through the market for ingredients," she said, tucking a stray lock of hair behind her ear. "I purchased a pound of fish—salmon, imported from Erik Island, where they have many lakes. Poloni marked it down because he thought it was going bad, but that was actually the fish in the *next* barrel. So I got my fish for a *steal*."

"Fascinating," he said. "No one throws a fit when you visit? They don't call their children out and make you shake their hands? Tell me more. Please, I want to know how you realized the fish wasn't bad."

With his prodding, she continued elucidating the mundane details of her life. He forced her to do it each time she visited. He, in turn, paid attention. That was the proof that his fondness for talking wasn't a failing. He was equally good at listening. At least to her. Indeed, Charlie found her life *interesting* for some unfathomable reason.

As she talked, Tress felt warm. She often did when she visited—because she climbed up high and was closer to the sun, so it was warmer up here. Obviously.

Except it was moonshadow at the moment, when the sun hid behind the moon and everything became a few degrees cooler. And today she was growing tired of certain lies she told herself. Perhaps there was another reason she felt warm. It was there in Charlie's current smile, and she knew it would be in her own as well.

He didn't listen to her *only* because he was fascinated by the lives of peasants.

She didn't visit *only* because she wanted to hear his stories.

In fact, on the deepest level it wasn't about cups or stories at all. It was, instead, about gloves.

3

THE DUKE

Tress had noticed that a nice pair of gloves made her daily work go so much better. Now, she meant the *good* kind of gloves, made of a soft leather that molds to your hands as you use them. The kind that—if you oil them well and don't leave them out in the sun—don't ever grow stiff. The kind that are so comfortable, you go to wash your hands and are surprised to find you're still wearing them.

The perfect set of gloves is invaluable. And Charlie was like a good set of gloves. The longer she spent with him, the more *right* their time together felt. The brighter even the moonshadows were, and the easier her burdens became. She did love interesting cups, but a part of that was because each one gave her an excuse to come and visit him.

The thing growing between them felt so good, so wonderful, that Tress was frightened to call it love. From the way the other youths talked, "love" was dangerous. Their love seemed to be about jealousy and insecurity. It was about passionate shouting matches and more passionate reconciliations. It was less like a good pair of gloves, and more like a hot coal that would burn your hands.

Love had always frightened Tress. But when Charlie put his hand on hers again, she felt heat. The fire she'd always feared. The coal was in there after all, just contained—like in a good stove.

She wanted to leap into his heat, all logic discarded.

Charlie froze. They'd touched many times before, of course, but this was different. This moment. This dream. He blushed, but let his hand linger. Then he finally raised it and ran his fingers through his hair, grinning sheepishly. Because he was Charlie, that didn't spoil the moment, but instead only made it more sweet.

Tress searched for the perfect thing to say. There were any number of lines that would have capitalized on that moment. She could have said, "Charlie, could you hold this for me while I walk around the grounds?" then offered her hand back to him.

She could have said, "Help, I can't breathe. Staring at you has taken my breath away."

She could even have said something completely insane, such as "I like you."

Instead she said, "Huuhhh. Hands are warm." She followed it with a laugh that she choked on halfway through, exactly mimicking—by pure chance—the call of an elephant seal.

It might be said that Tress had a way with words. In that her words tended to get in her way.

In response, Charlie gave her a smile. A wonderful smile, more and more confident the longer it lasted. It was one she'd never seen before. It said: "I think I love you, Tress, elephant seal notwithstanding."

She smiled back at him. Then, over his shoulder, she saw the duke standing in the window. Tall and straight, the man wore military-style clothing that looked like it had been pinned to him by the various medals on the breast.

He was *not* smiling.

Indeed, she'd seen him smile only once, during the punishment of old Lotari—who had tried to sneak off the island by stowing away on a merchant ship. That seemed the duke's sole smile; perhaps Charlie had used the entire family's quota. Nevertheless, if the duke did have just one smile, he made up for it by displaying far too many teeth.

The duke faded into the shadows of the house, but his presence loomed over Tress as she bade farewell to Charlie. On her way down the steps, she expected to hear shouting. Instead an ominous silence followed her. The tense silence that came after a lightning flash.

It chased her down the path and around to her home, where she murmured something to her parents about being tired. She went to her room and waited for the silence to end. For the soldiers to knock, then demand to know why the girl who washed the windows had dared to touch the duke's son.

When nothing like that came, she dared hope that she was reading too much into the duke's expression. Then she remembered the duke's singular smile. After that, worries nipped at her all night.

She rose early in the morning, wrestled her hair into a tail, then trudged to the market. Here she'd sort through the day-old goods and near-spoiled ingredients for something she could afford. Despite the early hour, the market was abuzz with activity. Men swept dead spores off the path while people gathered in chattering knots.

Tress braced herself for the news, then decided nothing could be worse than the awful anticipation she'd suffered all night.

She was wrong.

The duke had sent out a declaration: he and his family were going to leave the island that very day.

4

THE SON

L eave.
　　Leave the island?
　　People didn't *leave* the island.

Tress knew, logically, that wasn't explicitly true. Royal officials could leave. The duke left on occasion to report to the king. Plus he'd earned all those fancy medals by killing people from a distant place where they looked slightly different. He'd apparently been quite heroic during those wars; you could tell because a great number of his troops had died, while he lived.

But in the past, the duke had never taken his family. "The ducal heir has come of age," the proclamation announced, "and so we shall present him for betrothal to the various princesses of the civilized seas."

Now, Tress *was* a pragmatic young woman. And so she only *thought* about ripping her shopping basket to shreds in frustration. She merely *deliberated* whether it would be appropriate to swear at the top of her lungs. She *barely considered* marching up to the duke's mansion to demand he change his mind.

Instead she went about her shopping in a numb haze, using the familiar action to give her suddenly crumbling life a semblance of normality. She found some garlic she was certain she could salvage, several potatoes that hadn't withered too badly, and even some grain where the weevils were large enough to pick out.

Yesterday, she'd have been pleased with this haul. Today she couldn't think of anything but Charlie.

It seemed so incredibly unfair. She'd only *just* acknowledged what she felt for him, and already everything was turning upside down? Yes, she'd been told to expect this pain. Love involved pain. But that was the salt in your tea—wasn't there also supposed to be a dab of honey? Wasn't there supposed to be—dared she wish—*passion*?

She was to receive all of the detriments of a romantic affair with none of the advantages.

Unfortunately, her practicality began to assert itself. So long as the two of them had been able to pretend, the real world hadn't been able to claim them. But the days of pretending were over. What had she *thought* was going to happen? That the duke would let her marry his son? What did *she* think she could offer someone like Charlie? She was nothing compared to a princess. Think of how many *cups* they could afford!

In the pretend world, marriage was about love. In the real world, it was about politics. A word laden with a large number of meanings, though most of them boiled down to: *This is a matter for nobles—and (begrudgingly) the very rich—to discuss. Not peasants.*

She finished her shopping and started up the path toward her home, where at least she could commiserate with her parents. But it appeared that the duke was wasting no time, for she saw a procession snaking down toward the docks.

She turned around and walked back via a different path, arriving right after the procession—which began to load the family's things onto a merchant ship. Nobody was allowed to leave the island. Unless they were, instead, somebody. Tress worried she wouldn't get a chance to speak with Charlie. Then she worried that she *would*, but he wouldn't want to see her.

Mercifully, she caught him standing at the side of the crowd, searching among the gathering people. The moment he spotted her, he rushed over. "Tress! Oh, moons. I worried I wouldn't find you in time."

"I . . ." What did she say?

"Fare maiden," he said, bowing, "I must take my leave."

"Charlie," she said softly, "don't try to be someone you aren't. I *know* you."

He grimaced. He was wearing a traveling coat and even a hat. The duke considered hats improper wear except during travel. "Tress," he said, softer, "I'm afraid I've lied to you. You see . . . I'm not the groundskeeper. I'm . . . um . . . the duke's son."

"Amazing. Who would have thought that Charlie the groundskeeper and Charles the duke's heir would be the same person, considering they're the same age, look the same, and wear the same clothing?"

"Er, yes. Are you angry at me?"

"Anger is in line right now," Tress said. "It's seventh down, sandwiched between confusion and fatigue."

Behind them, Charlie's father and mother marched up onto the ship. Their servants followed with the last of the luggage.

Charlie gazed at his feet. "It seems I am to be married. To a princess of some nation or another. What do you think of that?"

"I . . ." What should she say? "I wish you well?"

He looked up and met her eyes. "Always, Tress. Remember?"

It was hard for her, but after groping around for a moment, she found the words hiding in a corner, trying to avoid her. "I wish," she said, seizing hold of them, "that you wouldn't do that. Get married. To someone else."

"Oh?" He blinked. "Do you really?"

"I mean, I'm sure they are very nice. The princesses."

"I believe it's part of the job description," Charlie said. "Like . . . have you heard of the things they do in stories? Resuscitate amphibians? Notice for parents that their children have wet the bed? One would have to be relatively kind to do these services."

"Yes," Tress said. "I . . ." She took a deep breath. "I would still . . . rather you didn't marry one of them."

"Well then, I shan't," Charlie said.

"I don't believe you have a choice, Charlie. Your father wants you married. It's *politics*."

"Ah, but you see, I have a secret weapon." He took her hands and leaned in.

Behind, his father moved up to the prow of the ship and looked down, scowling. Charlie, however, smiled a lopsided smile. His "look how sneaky I am" smile. He used it when he wasn't being particularly sneaky.

"What . . . kind of secret weapon, Charlie?" she asked.

"I can be *incredibly* boring."

"That's not a weapon."

"It might not be one in a war, Tress," he said. "But in courtship? It is as fine a weapon as the sharpest rapier. You know how I go on. And on. And on."

"I *like* how you go on, Charlie. I don't mind the on, in fact. I sometimes quite enjoy the *on*."

"You are a special case," Charlie said. "You are . . . well, this is kind of silly . . . but you're like a pair of gloves, Tress."

"I *am*?" she said, choking up.

"Yes. Don't be offended. I mean, when I have to practice the sword, I wear these gloves and—"

"I understand," she whispered.

From atop the ship, Charlie's father shouted for him to be quick. Tress realized then that—like Charlie had different kinds of smiles—his father had different kinds of scowls. She didn't much like what the current one implied about her.

Charlie squeezed her hands. "Listen, Tress. I promise you. I'm *not* going to get married. I'm going to go to those kingdoms, and I'm going to be so *insufferably* boring that none of the girls will have me.

"I'm not good at much. I've never scored a single point against my father in sparring. I spill my soup at formal dinners. I talk so much, even my footman—who is *paid* to listen—comes up with creative reasons to interrupt me. The other day I was telling him the story of the fish and the gull, and he pretended to stub his toe, and . . ."

The duke shouted again.

"I can do this, Tress," Charlie insisted. "I *will* do this. At each stop, I'll pick out a cup for you, all right? Once I've bored the current princess to death—and my father has decided we need to move on—I'll send you the cup. As proof, you see." He squeezed her hands once more. "I'll do it, not only because you listen. But because you know me, Tress. You've always been able to see me when others don't."

He began turning to finally respond to his father's shouts. Tress held on, clinging to his hands. Unwilling to let it end.

Charlie gave her one last smile. And though he was plainly trying to act confident, she knew his smiles. This was his uncertain one, hopeful but worried.

"You are my gloves too, Charlie," Tress said to him.

After that, she had to let go so he could jog up the plank. She'd imposed enough already.

The duke forced his son belowdecks as the ship slipped off the dead grey spores nearest the Rock and into the true verdant ocean. Wind caught the ship's sails and it struck out toward the horizon, leaving a wake of disturbed emerald dust behind it. Tress climbed up to her house, then watched from the cliff until the ship was the size of a cup. Then the size of a speck. Then it vanished.

After that, the waiting began.

They say that to wait is the most excruciating of life's torments. "They" in this case refers to writers, who have nothing useful to do, so fill their time thinking of things to say. Any working person can tell you that having time to *wait* is a luxury.

Tress had windows to wash. Meals to cook. A little brother to watch. Her father, Lem, had never recovered from his accident in the mines, and though he tried to assist, he could barely walk. He helped Tress's mother, Ulba, knit socks all day, which they sold to sailors, but with the expense of yarn they turned only a meager profit.

So Tress didn't *wait*. She worked.

Still, it was an enormous relief when the first cup arrived. It was delivered by Hoid the cabin boy. (Yes, that's me. What tipped you off? Was it perhaps the name?) A beautiful porcelain cup, without even a single chip in it.

The world brightened that day. Tress could almost imagine Charlie speaking as she read the accompanying letter, which detailed the affections of the first princess. With heroic monotony, he had listed the sounds his stomach made when he lay in various positions at night.

As that hadn't been quite enough, he'd then explained how he kept his toenail clippings and gave them names. That had done it.

Fight on, my loquacious love, Tress thought as she scrubbed the mansion's windows the next day. *Be brave, my mildly gross warrior.*

The second cup was of pure red glass, tall and thin, and looked like it could contain more liquid than it actually did. Perhaps it came from a particularly stingy tavern. He'd put off this princess by explaining what he'd had for breakfast in intricate detail, as he'd counted the pieces of the scrambled egg and categorized them by size.

The third cup was an enormous solid pewter tankard with heft to it. Perhaps it was from one of those places Charlie had made up, where people always needed to carry weapons. Tress was reasonably certain she could knock out an attacker by swinging the tankard. The latest princess hadn't been able to withstand an extended conversation about the benefits of various punctuation marks, including a few Charlie had invented.

The fourth package's card included no letter, only a small drawing: two gloved hands holding to one another. The cup had a painted butterfly on it with a red ocean underneath; she found it odd that the butterfly wasn't terrified of the spores. Maybe it was a prisoner, forced to fly out over the ocean to its doom.

The fifth cup never arrived.

Tress tried to play it off, telling herself that it must have been interrupted in transit. After all, any number of dangerous things could happen to a ship sailing the spores. Pirates or . . . you know . . . spores.

But the months stretched long, each more tedious than the one before. Every time a ship arrived at the docks, Tress was there asking for mail.

Nothing.

She did this for months on end, until an entire year had passed since Charlie had left.

Then, finally, a note. Not from Charlie, but from his father, sent to the entire town. The duke was returning to Diggen's Point at long last, and he was bringing his wife, his heir . . . and his new daughter-in-law.

5

THE BRIDE

Tress sat upon her porch, leaning against her mother, and watched the horizon. She held the last cup Charlie had sent. The one with the suicidal butterfly.

Her lukewarm tea tasted of tears.

"It wasn't very practical," she whispered to her mother.

"Love rarely is," her mother replied. She was a stout woman, with a cheerful kind of girth. Five years ago, she'd been thin as a reed. Then Tress had learned her mother was giving up a portion of her food to her children—from then on, Tress had taken over shopping and had made their money stretch further.

A ship appeared on the horizon.

"I've finally thought of what I should have said." Tress pushed her hair out of her eyes. "When he left. I called him a glove. It isn't so bad as it sounds. He'd just called me one, you see. I've had a year to think about it, and I realized I could have said something more."

Her mother squeezed her shoulder as the ship drew inevitably closer.

"I should have said," Tress whispered, "that I loved him."

Her mother joined her as she marched, like a soldier on the front lines facing cannon fire, down to the docks to greet the ship. Her father, with his bad leg, stayed behind—which was good. She feared he'd make a scene, the way he'd been grumbling about the duke and his son these last few months.

But Tress could not find it in herself to blame Charlie. It wasn't his fault that he was the duke's son. It could have happened to anyone, really.

A crowd had gathered. The duke's letter said he wanted a celebration—and he was bringing food and wine. Whatever else the people thought of getting a new future duchess, they were not going to miss a chance at free alcohol. (As it has ever been, gifts are the secret to popularity. That and having the power to behead anyone who dislikes you.)

Tress and her mother arrived at the back of the crowd, but Holmes the baker waved them up on his steps so they could see better. He was a kind man, always saving the ends of loaves, then selling them to her for pennies.

So it was that Tress had a good view of the princess as she appeared on the deck. She was beautiful. Rosy cheeks, shimmering hair, delicate features. She was so perfect, the finest painter in the seas couldn't have made improvements in her portrait.

Charlie had at last been able to become part of a story. With effort, Tress was happy for him.

The duke appeared next, waving his hand so the people knew to cheer for him. "I present," he shouted, "my heir!"

A young man stepped up onto the deck beside the princess. And it was most definitely *not* Charlie.

This young man was around the same age as Charlie, but he was six and a half feet tall and had a jaw so straight it made other men question if they were. He bulged with muscles—to the point that when he lifted his arm to wave, Tress swore she could hear the seams on his shirt begging for mercy.

What under the twelve moons?

"After an unfortunate accident," the duke proclaimed to the hushed crowd, "I was forced to adopt my nephew Dirk and appoint him as my new heir." He gave a moment for the crowd to take that in. "He's an excellent fencer," the duke continued, "and responds to questions with single-sentence answers. Sometimes using only one word! Also, he's a war hero. He lost ten thousand men in the Battle of Lakeprivy."

"Ten thousand?" Tress's mother said. "My, that's a lot."

"We shall now celebrate Dirk's marriage to the princess of Dormancy!" the duke shouted, raising his hands high.

The crowd remained quiet, still confused.

"I brought thirty kegs!" the duke shouted.

They cheered. And so, a party it was. The townspeople led the way up to the feast hall. They remarked on the princess's beauty and marveled that Dirk managed to balance so well while walking, considering his center of gravity must have been located somewhere around his upper sternum.

Tress's mother told her she would get answers, and followed the crowd. However, when Tress came out of her shock, she found Flik—one of the duke's servants—waving to her from near the bottom of the gangplank. He was a kindly man, with wide ears that looked as if they were waiting for the right moment to bolt and fly away.

"Flik?" she whispered. "What happened? An accident? Where is Charlie?"

Flik glanced up at the train of people walking to the feast hall. The duke and his family had joined them, and were far enough away that any scowls would lose their potency due to wind resistance and gravitational drop.

"He wanted me to give you this," Flik said, handing her a small sack. It tinkled as she took it. Inside were broken pieces of ceramic.

The fifth cup.

"He tried so hard, Miss Tress," Flik whispered. "Oh, you should have seen the young master. He did everything he could to put those women off. He memorized eighty-seven different types of plywood and their uses. He told every princess he met—at length—about his childhood pets. He even talked about *religion*. I thought they had 'im at the fifth kingdom, as that princess was deaf, but the young master went and threw up on her at dinner."

"He *threw up*?"

"Straight in 'er lap, Miss Tress." Flik looked both ways, then waved for her to follow as he carried some luggage off the docks, leading them to a more secluded location. "But his father got wise, Miss Tress. Figured out what the young master was doing. The duke got right mad. Right mad indeed."

He gestured to the broken cup she was carrying in her sack.

"Yes, but what happened to *Charlie*?" Tress asked.

Flik looked away.

"*Please*," Tress asked. "Where is he?"

"He sailed the Midnight Sea, Miss Tress," he said. "Beneath Thanasmia's own moon. The Sorceress took him."

Those names sent a chill through Tress. The Midnight Sea? The domain of the *Sorceress*? "Why would he ever do such a thing?"

"Well, I right think it's because his father forced him to," Flik said. "The Sorceress isn't married. And the king has long wanted to try to make her less of a threat. So . . ."

"The king sent *Charlie* to try to *marry* the *Sorceress*?"

Flik didn't respond.

"No," Tress said, realizing it. "He sent Charlie to die."

"I didn't say anything like that," Flik said, hurrying off. "If anyone asks, I didn't say *anything* like that."

Numb, Tress sat down on one of the dock pillars. She listened to the spores stirring, a sound like pouring sand. Even on an out-of-the-way island like hers, they knew of the Sorceress. She periodically sent ships in to raid the borders of the Verdant Sea, and it was incredibly difficult to fight her. Her stronghold lay hidden somewhere in the remote Midnight Sea, most dangerous of them all. And to get to it you had to cross the Crimson Sea, an unpopulated sea that was only slightly less deadly.

Finding out Charlie had been captured by her was like finding out he'd gone up to one of the moons. Tress couldn't just take one man's word. Not on something like this. She didn't dare bother others with questions, but she listened as the servants talked in hushed tones to inquisitive dock workers, eager to get the ship unloaded so they could join the party. They all gave similar answers. Yes, Charlie had been sent to the Midnight Sea. The duke and the king had decided it together, so it must have been a good idea. After all, someone had to try to stop the Sorceress from raiding. And Charlie, of all people, was . . . erm . . . the obvious choice . . . for . . . reasons.

The implications horrified Tress. The duke and the king had realized Charlie was being difficult, and their solution had been to simply get rid of him. Dirk had been instated as heir within hours of receiving word that Charlie's ship had vanished.

In the eyes of the nobles, this was an elegant result. The duke got an heir he could finally be proud of. The king got an advantageous marriage alliance in Dirk's bride from another kingdom. And everyone got to blame another death on the Sorceress, building public opinion toward another war.

After three days, Tress at last dared impose on Brunswick—the duke's steward—with a plea for more information. As he liked her pies, he admitted that they'd received a ransom letter from the Sorceress. But the duke, in his wisdom, had judged it to be a trick to lure more ships into the Midnight Sea. The king had declared Charlie officially dead.

Days passed. Tress lived them in a daze, realizing nobody cared. They called it *politics* and moved on. Though the new heir had the intellect of a soggy piece of bread, he was popular, handsome, and very good at getting other people killed. While Charlie had been . . . well, Charlie.

Tress spent weeks gathering her courage, then went to ask the duke if he'd please pay the ransom. Such a bold move was difficult for her. She wasn't a coward, but imposing upon people . . . well, it simply wasn't something she did. But with her parents' encouragement, she made the long trek and quietly made her request.

The duke, in turn, called her a "hazelnut-haired strumpet" and forbade her from washing windows anywhere in town. She was forced to begin knitting socks with her parents for greatly reduced pay.

As the weeks passed, Tress fell into a lethargy. She felt less like a mere human being, and more like a human who was merely being.

Life on the Rock for everyone else returned to normal, easy as that. Nobody cared. Nobody was going to do anything.

Until it was, two months after the duke's return, that Tress made her decision. There *was* somebody who cared. Naturally, it would be up to that person to do something. Tress couldn't impose on anyone else.

She was going to have to go rescue Charlie herself.

PART
2

6

THE INSPECTOR

Once Tress made the decision, a knot came undone within her—like she'd finally worked a tangle out of a stubborn lock of hair.

She would do it. She had no idea *how*, but she *would* find a way to get off the island, cross the terrible Crimson Sea, enter the Midnight Sea, and rescue Charlie. Yes, each of those problems seemed equally impossible. But somehow less impossible than imagining the rest of her life without him.

First though, Tress went to talk to her parents. (Something more people in stories such as this should do.) She sat them both down, then explained her love for Charlie, her realization that no one would help him, and her determination to go find him—though she expressed worry that her absence might cause them hardship.

Both listened quietly as she spoke. This was, in part, because she'd baked them quail-egg pies. It's more difficult to object to your daughter's temporary insanity when your mouth is full.

Once she'd finished, Lem asked for seconds. It was a two-pie type of predicament. Ulba only finished half of her meal, sitting back and leaving the rest untouched. It was also a half-pie type of predicament.

Tress's father ate his second pie with deliberate care, digging down from the top, then eating outward, saving the crust for the end. Finally, he crunched through that. Then he stared at the plate for a long, uncomfortable moment.

Was it . . . perhaps . . . a *three*-pie predicament?

"I think," he said at last, turning to Ulba, "we are going to have to let her do this."

"It's lunacy!" Tress's mother said. "Leave the island? Travel to the Midnight Sea? Steal a prisoner from *the Sorceress*?"

Lem felt at his mustache bristles with his napkin, cleaning out remnants of the meal. "Ulba, would you say our daughter is more practical than we are?"

"Yes, I would normally say that," Ulba said.

"And would you also say she is more thoughtful than we are?"

"She is always thinking," Tress's mother agreed.

"How often does she impose upon people or ask for what she wants?"

"Almost never."

"With all that in mind," Tress's father said, "it must be the right decision for her to leave. She will have considered all other options. Leaving the island to rescue the man she loves might sound like lunacy, but if every other option has been discarded as impossible, then insanity might—in this case—be *practical*."

Tress felt a small thrill inside. He agreed?

"Tress," her father said, leaning forward, resting his once-powerful arms on the tabletop, "we can care for your brother and ourselves if you go. Please do not worry about us; you are too accommodating in this regard. But neither of us can go with you. You understand this?"

"Yes, Father," she said.

"I had always wondered if this island would prove too small for one such as you."

This made Tress frown.

"Why do you act like that?" he asked her.

"I don't want to be rude."

"Then I demand you tell me, so that not speaking would be even more rude."

Her grimace worsened. "Well, why would you say the island is too small for me, Father? There's nothing extraordinary about me. If anything, I am too small for it."

"Everything is extraordinary about you, Tress," her mother said. "That's why nothing in particular stands out."

Well, parents have to say things like that. They're required to see the best in their children, otherwise living with the little sociopaths would drive a person mad.

"I have your blessing then?" Tress asked them.

"I still think this is a terrible idea," Ulba noted.

Lem nodded. "It is. But a terrible idea executed brilliantly has to be better than a brilliant idea executed terribly. I mean, look at pelicans."

"True," Tress's mother said. "But are we capable of *either* kind of brilliance?"

"No," Tress said. "But maybe we can take a whole lot of little steps that, when looked at together, might seem brilliant to somebody who doesn't know us."

And so, they set to work. Tress was keenly aware that Charlie might be suffering, but she resolved to take her time. If she *was* going to do something as stupid as leave the island, she figured she should be meticulous about it. Perhaps that would dilute the stupidity with time, like how good flour could dilute the stale and improve the bake.

She took to knitting socks at the cliffside so she could watch the ships that came and left. Her mother began to make stockings at a table near the dock so she could take notes. They compared their findings each night, with Tress's father listening and offering his thoughts.

Though Tress had always possessed a curiosity about the mechanics of shipping, she now had a motive to learn the details. There were two types of people who regularly left the island. The first was, of course, the crews of the various ships. When they landed, they'd come ashore to shop or visit the local taverns. The Rock didn't have much to recommend it, but Brick's ale was known as some of the best in the region. Plus, with enough of it in you, the rest of the amenities looked a whole lot better.

The second type of people who left the Rock were government officials. Not only the duke and his family, but other royal administrators, such as tax collectors, royal messengers, and cargo inspectors. They were allowed to leave when they saw fit. Members of the nobility who visited could also leave—and they usually did so quickly, after realizing their awful mistake.

Tress's biggest challenge would be the current cargo inspector. The severe woman authenticated the writs of visiting merchants, then examined cargo for stowaways. For a place where no one wanted to live, the Rock certainly had lots of *things* people wanted. Salt from the mines, Brick's ale, even down and feathers from the gulls.

The townspeople couldn't sell these things except to ships that had a writ of commission from the king. The cargo inspector oversaw it all. When the current one had arrived earlier in the year, she'd refused to give her name, insisting they simply call her "Inspector." She claimed she wouldn't be remaining on the Rock long enough for names to matter.

Tress couldn't remember an inspector who had been more strict. This woman was always watching, swinging the rod she carried, searching for any excuse to deliver a punishment. She seemed too stern to be fully human. As if instead of being born, she'd been spawned—and instead of growing up, she'd metastasized.

Tress and her mother spent hours covertly studying how the inspector searched outgoing shipments. Bags of feathers were weighed, while barrels of salt were stabbed, to search for possible stowaways. But some things being shipped—like large kegs of the local brew—couldn't be opened without spoiling them. What if a person were to hide in a keg? Could they fill it with something like salt to make it weigh and balance correctly?

Unfortunately, the inspector had an answer to such potential escape plans. When examining kegs, she employed a special listening device, like the ones physicians used for hearts. The inspector would linger on each keg, listening for someone moving or breathing inside. Reportedly, the inspector had extremely good hearing and could detect the very heartbeats of stowaways.

Was there a way around this? A way to exploit the situation?

One night, two weeks after she'd first decided to leave, Tress sat up with a notebook full of ideas. The Emerald Moon shone bright as always, stoic and immobile in the sky. Spores poured downward in the distance, like crystalline moonlight.

Her father limped over, settled down, then waved for her to show him her plans. He read them carefully, then nodded. "This could work."

"It *could*," Tress said, yawning. "But I don't think it will. I might be able to fool a bunch of sailors, but I'd never fool Brick, Gremmy, or Sor. They will know that something is wrong." She rubbed her eyes. She'd been going without sleep, fraught as she was. (Worry, it might be said, is the carrion feeder of emotions. Drawn to other, better emotions like crows to a battlefield.)

"Perhaps you don't have to fool them," her father said. "Perhaps they would be willing to help."

"I couldn't ask that of them," Tress said. "What if the inspector catches me? The others would get into too much trouble."

Her father nodded again. That was, of course, the sort of thing Tress would say. So he suggested she go to bed. Tress looked as if she were about to fall asleep in the middle of the conversation—which was saying something, considering how many of Charlie's stories she'd survived without so much as a yawn.

After she went upstairs, Lem retrieved his cane, put on his coat, and went out to do some advanced fathering.

7

THE FATHER

Lem was not a poor man.

Now, you might say to me, "Hoid, this entire story has shown me the opposite. Lem's family is always scrimping to survive." And I would reply, "Please stop interrupting."

Lem was not poor, he simply didn't have a lot of money.

That night as Tress slept, Lem limped down the long road to Brick's tavern. He knew for certain that Gremmy and Sor would be there. After all, the tavern didn't close until two.

Lem hobbled in. It was still early enough that the place was happy and boisterous. Evenings at the tavern, as you know, are like fires in a hearth. They live two lives.

There's the part where they're roaring, festive, and cheerful. Then the evening begins to drift. The tavern becomes colder, darker, and quieter. Those who populate the tavern during its second life don't want companionship. Just company.

That was a few hours away, so Lem passed laughing miners sharing rounds and chatting about their boring boring. He spotted Gremmy and Sor together, as they often were. The dockworker and the dockmaster looked like opposite ends of a tack. Gremmy—with his squat body and flat head—had a haircut that said, "What's the cheapest?" Sor was ostensibly Gremmy's boss, but rarely brought the matter up, in case it might accidentally sound like he was offering to pay the tab. He sat tall and straight, and sipped at a beer because he didn't want to be seen drinking the wine that he could afford.

Brick, of course, was behind the bar, standing on his stool to be at eye height to his patrons. Tress needed all three men's help, but Lem didn't approach any of them. Instead he took up position near the dartboard. Jule was playing, and offered Lem the next game, which he happily accepted.

Lem threw the first dart several feet below the board, hitting the wood there on one of two knots that bore holes from a large number of darts.

Jule eyed it approvingly and took his own throw, hitting near Lem's.

"I heard," Lem said, taking his second throw, "you helped Gremmy with his tab again. Right nice of you, that was."

Jule nodded in appreciation.

Next game was against old Rod, the innkeeper. Lem missed his first two throws, unfortunately. One was so off, it hit the dartboard. The third hit far beneath it though.

"Nice," Rod said. "Does that cane help with your balance, Lem? I swear you've gotten better at darts since the accident."

"Having a cane doesn't help with darts, Rod," Lem said. "Havin' nothing to do though . . ."

Rod grunted.

"You still help Brick with the brewing on weekends?" Lem asked.

"More often than not," Rod said, and took his throws. After that Rod moved off, making way for another game, and another. As men came to play Lem, they read the unspoken script of his questions.

They remembered that time when Rod had been drunk, and Lem had helped him home. And Jule, when he'd lost his roof during the windstorm, Lem had helped build a new one. There were dozens of similar stories. Lem was the human equivalent of a deep, pure well, always full of water when you needed it. He'd offer what you needed and ask nothing in return. In fact, he'd never bring it up again.

Unless it was urgent.

Unless it was important.

In those cases, well, Lem might have been poor in the kind of currency that paid taxes. But he was downright *wealthy* when it came to the kind of currency that mattered.

Word got around that night. Lem needed something, specifically from Gremmy, Sor, and Brick. Lem—the man with no debt—needed this favor so badly, he almost *asked* for it. In the language of men like these, that's the equivalent of begging.

Lem continued playing darts, and scored quite well. If you're wondering at the odd targets they used, it should be noted that—one evening a couple years earlier—someone had noticed that a group of knots high on the wall looked an awful lot like a face. The duke's face, in fact, if you imagined the grain of that wood as his hair, and the dart board as the family insignia on his chest.

And, well, somewhere below that were two prominent knots in the wall. Right above where the legs would have been.

Lem threw, and nearby men winced. "Nice," one noted.

As the night progressed, quiet, invisible ledgers were tallied. Decisions were reached, but not spoken. They didn't need to be, for the next morning—too early for any of them—Tress found the barkeep, the dockmaster, and the dockworker on her doorstep. They *demanded* to help her in whatever she was doing.

So it was that a little over a week later, a large keg was deposited on the dock for inspection. Gremmy pushed it up alongside five others.

The perfect ship had arrived for executing Tress's plan, a vessel known as the *Oot's Dream*. It needed to be a ship with a crew that didn't often visit Diggen's Point, and it needed a king's writ authorizing the purchase of Brick's ale.

The sailors of the *Oot's Dream* nearly took the kegs on board without inspection, but the captain had read the terms of his writ. "There is supposed to be an inspection, is there not?" he demanded. "We cannot leave port until it has been done."

So, the inspector was summoned. She arrived with a scowl that could have killed spores, her rod held at the ready to deal out justice. She examined the first keg, then used her listening device on it.

Nearby, Sor peered at his pocket watch, counting the seconds, his heart thumping. Gremmy mopped his head as the inspector moved down the line of kegs. Brick nudged him, trying to urge him to not look so suspicious.

Finally, the inspector listened to the last large keg. Just big enough for a girl to curl up inside, it was. The inspector listened closely, and found . . . nothing.

She waved for the cargo to be loaded. The three conspirators exchanged glances. Until the inspector paused and turned back. Then in a sudden motion, she kicked over the last keg.

It went *thump*.

Then it went *ouch*.

"I thought so!" the inspector said, grabbing a crowbar from the dock, then prying the keg's top free to reveal the truth—a raven-haired young woman hiding inside, trying to sneak off the island. "Feathers as insulation!" the inspector cried. "You thought that would muffle the sounds enough to fool *my* ear?"

Well, after that, things went downhill at speed. "This couldn't have been managed without help!" the inspector snapped at the dockmaster. "This couldn't have been managed without a *conspiracy*!"

Poor Gremmy couldn't take it, and started bawling right there. Brick tried to quiet him, while Sor wondered out loud if maybe he could order Gremmy to take his punishment for him.

"The king has worried about your disloyalty," the inspector said with a sneer. "He warned me about the people of this town. He will be told of this, that you all worked *together* to circumvent his laws. Pay for only five kegs, Captain."

The other five kegs were loaded onto the ship, and the ship took off toward the Emerald Sea's Core Archipelago to deliver the ale. The inspector went with them—leaving her assistant to watch the docks—declaring she would tell the king personally of the betrayal at Diggen's Point.

Now, you might have noticed that the young woman in the barrel was not Tress, and you might think she was actually in one of the other kegs. She was not.

Tress was not hiding in some other piece of cargo.

Tress was not hiding at all.

Tress was the inspector.

8

THE STOWAWAY

Tress thought she could see the real inspector arriving on the docks in the distance. A tiny irate figure who gestured in anger at the fleeing ship. She would be told that the captain had insisted on leaving without inspection. By now, Gret—the dockmaster's daughter—would have climbed out of the hollow keg and left. There would be no other witnesses left on the Rock except for Brick, Gremmy, and Sor—whose debts had now been paid.

Just like that, Tress was free. This time, Diggen's Point was the thing that grew smaller and smaller in the distance. Practically everything and everyone that Tress had ever known lived on that island. And soon she wouldn't even be able to see it.

Leaving didn't feel exciting. It felt heavy. Every child looked forward to the day when they could choose a different path from the one their parents were on. Tress sincerely hoped she hadn't decided on one that led straight off a cliff.

But she *was* free. She'd escaped without a hitch. She wondered if maybe her other tasks would be accomplished with similar ease. She could wonder this because—lacking formal training in the arts—Tress had no concept of dramatic irony.

She turned her gaze to the sky. It was so *blue* out here, away from the mining smog. That felt immoral somehow, as if she were seeing the sky without its clothing. The air smelled . . . not of salt anymore, but pure and clean. And dangerous. No salt meant free spores.

Fortunately, the deck's railing was lined with silver. And surely people wouldn't travel the Emerald Sea if it weren't *reasonably* safe. The ship's sails billowed and shook as the vessel turned, sailors calling to one another as they worked. They'd been forced to take her; the king's writs of purchase obligated captains to ferry government officials who required passage away from the Rock.

So the crew left Tress alone as she stood at the back of the ship, on the quarterdeck, near the wheel where the captain chatted with the helmsman. Tress wore an inspector's uniform, with a bright red and gold coat going down past her knees. They'd stolen it the night before; it was the spare one from the inspector's closet. Tress's mother had altered it perfectly to appear as if it had been made for Tress. And, of course, a "mistake" on the dock register in the inspector's room had indicated the wrong time for the *Oot's Dream* to leave the Rock, so she'd shown up late.

The only things Tress had brought with her were a small bundle of clothing and a bag of cups. Her favorite among them was the fourth cup that Charlie had sent. The one with the butterfly on it. Something about the simple design struck her.

She was glad the sailors ignored her, because it was difficult to cover up how much she gawked at the green spore ocean. Tress wasn't aware of the science of what made the ship float, but it's actually rather interesting. Vents deep below on the ocean floor sent up bursts of air. With this agitation, the spores became as liquid. The phenomenon is possible on any world, including your own. Fluidization, it's called. Pump air up underneath a box of sand, and you'll see something similar to what Tress was watching.

Bubbles burst from the spores all around, making the ocean churn and undulate. It slapped the ship's hull and flowed away, splashing, making waves. It wasn't *quite* like water; it was too thick, and the tips of the waves broke apart into puffs of green spores. In fact, the sea was wrong in the way that solely something almost right can be. Familiar, yet alien. As if it were liquid's disrespectful cousin who told inappropriate jokes at Grandma's funeral.

The ship sailed like any ship would on water. But it could move only as long as the air bubbled up from below; the people on Tress's world called this phenomenon "the seethe." It came and went randomly, fluidizing entire oceans for days at a time. Periodically it would cease—stranding all the ships sailing upon it. Interruptions were usually short, but occasionally lasted hours or even days.

A wave broke high against the side of the ship, tossing up a burst of spores. Tress cried out despite herself and backed away, but the spores turned grey, dying.

"Haven't sailed much, eh?" the captain asked from nearby. He had terrible breath, a crispy tan complexion, and stringy, matted hair. Imagine him as the answer to the question: "What if that gunk from your shower drain were to come to life?"

Still, he was the best option Tress had found in her weeks of watching, so she wasn't going to complain. Even if he did laugh at her again the next time the spores surged.

"We have silver enough," the captain said, waving toward the trim on the railing and built into the wood of the deck. A line of it ran up the mast. "Kills any spores that come too close, Inspector. You're safe."

Tress nodded, trying to look as if she didn't care. But she kept her coat buttoned up tight and found herself breathing shallowly and wishing for a salted mask.

Instead, she brought out her notebook and worked on her plan. She'd made it off the island. Next, she needed only to wait. The vessel would deliver her to the king's island in the Core Archipelago. From there, Tress had to find her way into the palace so she could get a copy of Charlie's ransom note.

That would be the easiest way to free him. Yes, paying off a ransom herself would be next to impossible, but it *did* seem easier than sneaking across the Midnight Sea to confront the Sorceress. Hopefully if she could find a way to pay—or persuade the king to pay—Charlie would be delivered to her, safe.

The deck creaked as the captain stepped nearer. "You have beautiful hair, Inspector," he said. "The color of a good cup of mead!"

Tress snapped her book closed. "Perhaps I will retire to my cabin now."

He smiled. The man was exactly the sort of person who thought every woman in the room was thinking about him. Which they were, as each desperately hoped he would head the other direction. He waved for Tress to join him in walking down from the quarterdeck toward the cabins below it.

Thankfully, the captain left her without needing to be ordered. The room was small but private, and the door locked. Tress felt a great deal better once she was safe inside. She poured some water into her butterfly cup and settled onto the bunk to think.

It all felt so much more *real* now. Was she really doing this? Had she *really* left her home? What were those strange colorful pigeons, and why were they talking to her?

This last part was a side effect of the poison the captain had ordered put in Tress's drink. There are, unfortunately, no talking pigeons in this story. Merely talking rats.

9

THE RAT

Tress awoke. That was nice.

Tress very much approved of not dying on the first day of her adventure. However, she had a pounding headache, and all she could see was blackness. Did one see blackness, or was it the mark of not seeing? Can you hear silence? Taste nothing?

Well, judging by the creaking of the wood, she was in the ship's hold. She groaned and sat up, then felt around. Her fingers met bars. She was in a cage.

"You won't find a way out," said a quiet voice. It sounded male, but had a pinched quality to it, like someone had taken the speaker's words and was squeezing out the juice.

"Who are you?" Tress asked softly.

"A fellow prisoner. I heard them talking about you. You're an inspector?"

"Yes," Tress lied. "For the king. I can't believe they'd dare assault me."

On the inside, Tress was panicking. The captain must have figured out her ruse. The ship would be returning to Diggen's Point to find the real inspector, and everything would fall apart.

No. It had *already* fallen apart.

She sat down, her back to some bars.

"Lunatic choice you made, Inspector," the voice said. "You boarded the ship alone? How did you *think* this would play out? Were you planning to take them all on your own?"

"Take them?" Tress asked. "Where?"

"You . . . don't know?"

In case you're new to this, nothing good ever follows a question like that.

"This is a smugglers' vessel," the voice explained. "They *forged* mercantile writs from the king. It lets them buy and sell goods without paying tariffs."

Tress groaned, thumping her head against the bars. "And they thought I was suspicious of them. They thought *that's* why I got on their ship."

"It wasn't?" the voice said, then started laughing. Or rather, Tress thought it was laughter. It came out as a high-pitched series of squeaks— like the sound of a hyperventilating donkey. "It was completely coincidental? Oh, you poor woman."

Tress folded her arms tight in the darkness, suffering the mockery. At least she wasn't going to be taken back to Diggen's Point to be turned in to the duke. Instead the smugglers would undoubtedly murder her and dispose of the body.

She decided not to cry. Crying would be utterly impractical. So it was settled. Absolutely no crying.

Her eyes vetoed the resolution.

"Hey," the voice said. "Hey, it's all right. At least you got off the Rock, right?"

"You know about the Rock?" Tress asked, wiping her eyes. Stupid things. Probably just wanted something to do, with the not seeing and all.

"I was on my way there for a visit," the voice said, "before the sailors found me out. Locked me in here."

"Why would you *visit* Diggen's Point?" Tress demanded.

"I have my reasons," the voice said. "My kind are mysterious like that."

"Your kind?" Tress asked.

"Here, let me show you. Might want to shade your eyes."

A moment later light poured into the chamber, spilling from a small hole in the hull. Tress blinked, pushing her frazzled hair out of her eyes as she made out her surroundings. She was in a cell built into part of the ship's hold, maybe four feet on each side and not much taller.

Across from her, lashed on top of some boxes, was a much smaller cage. In it sat a common black rat. He'd pulled a cork from the hole with his little paws.

"I keep this thing plugged," he said, "so they don't know about it. Don't want them to move the cage, you know? I . . ."

The rat trailed off as he turned and saw her for the first time, then cocked his head.

"What?" Tress asked.

The rat was silent. The only sounds came from the ship rocking in the spores and the boots thumping on the deck above. Tress pulled back. She didn't like the way the rat stared at her with those beady little eyes.

"*What?*" she demanded.

"Didn't get a good look at you when they brought you down. I didn't realize . . . didn't expect you to be so young. You're no royal inspector."

"I have a young face."

"I'm sure," the rat said. He moved to the edge of his cage and sat on his haunches, leaning forward, tiny paws together. It was a very ratlike pose, which Tress supposed made sense.

"You're sneaking off the island," he said. "Why under the moons would you do that?"

"I told you," Tress snapped. "Nobody *wants* to be on Diggen's Point. Anyway, the sailors bought my act, so you don't need to keep staring at me like that. My escape plan worked."

"Save for the whole 'accidentally frightening a bunch of smugglers' part, I assume."

Tress wiped her eyes once more. "Can we maybe backtrack on this conversation? It looks like we missed the main roadway. I don't mean to be rude, but *you* are a *rat*."

"Seems self-evident."

"But you're talking."

"Again, self-evident."

"Yes, but . . . but *how*?"

"With my mouth," he said. "Also, reference my previous answer."

She bit her lip. It was a testament to her state of mind that she'd pushed him that far already. Was asking a talking rat why he could talk impolite? She probably would have been offended if someone had asked *her* why she could talk.

The rat moved to pick up the cork. "There's a story behind how I can talk, I suppose. It's not one I'm interested in telling."

"Huh," Tress said.

"What?"

"It's just . . . I'm not used to people saying things like that."

The rat nibbled a bit on the cork, then moved it toward the hole.

"Could you leave the hole open?" Tress asked. "A little longer?"

The rat sighed, as he nearly had the cork positioned. But he lowered it to the cage floor again. The boots up above were stomping around quickly. Perhaps they were changing course?

"So . . . smugglers," Tress said.

"Smugglers," the rat agreed, sniffing the air. "Got caught chewing on their rations, and had to either give up my secret and talk, or get tossed overboard as a pest. Turns out they think a talking rat might be worth something. I considered warning them I didn't have anything interesting to say, then thought it unwise to give them reason to doubt my value." The rat gnawed more on the cork. "Because of the impending war, every second captain is a smuggler these days. So you shouldn't feel too bad for falling in with some."

"The war?" Tress asked.

"With the Sorceress," the rat said. "She's been sending more ships in to raid, and the king has been building up his forces—commandeering merchant vessels like a child reaching for treats. Seeing how easily you can find yourself conscripted these days, it's no wonder so many sailors are having a bout of prolapsed morals, so to speak."

"Do you think I could deal with them?" Tress said. "Explain that I'm not actually an inspector?"

"Oh, suddenly you aren't?"

"I'm whatever gets me out of this cage. A friend of mine is in trouble, and I need to rescue him."

"Him?" the rat said. "You left your home for a man?"

Tress remained silent.

"Hon, no man is worth getting killed over," the rat said. "If you manage to escape, you should head on home to your rock."

"He's not just any man," Tress said. "And—"

She cut off as a loud *pop* sounded somewhere outside. Tress cocked her head. What an odd noise to hear out on the ocean. Whatever could it be?

Fate answered her by sending a cannonball, priority delivery, right through the ship's hull.

10

THE SPROUTER

The cannonball crashed through the far wall and soared across the center of the hold. When it hit the opposite wall, it burst into shards of wet ceramic and what looked like metal beads. Those scattered to the floor, mixing with splinters of broken wood. The deck above clamored with the sounds of scrambling feet and screaming men.

"What's happening?" Tress shouted toward the rat.

He'd pulled back against the far corner of his cage, cringing and shivering. "We're being attacked!"

"I mean," Tress said, "what can you see out there? Go look through your hole!"

Though the cannonball had left a rather large second hole, it wasn't close to Tress and didn't let her see much of the outside world. Unnervingly, each time the ship crossed a wave, the new hole sank low enough to let spores spill in. She could see *those* just fine.

"I spot one other ship," the rat said. "Can't see a flag."

"Pirates?" Tress asked.

"Pirates shouldn't be firing, at least not without demanding surrender first," the rat said. "What's the good of sinking all your potential booty under an ocean of spores? Must be a royal ship who found out this lot were smugglers, and decided to deal with them the civilized way."

"Civilized?" Tress screamed as another shot sounded outside. This one appeared to miss, fortunately.

"Takes a civilization to build a cannon. What? You think there are forests out there growing them spontaneously?"

Each pop of the cannon made her wince, but the immediate danger was those spores. As the ship rocked, more and more of them flooded the hold, covering the floor, spreading toward her in a green pool. Some of the spores died, turning a dull grey, but the silver in the deck above was far enough away that many survived. Inching closer to her cage each time the ship climbed a wave and tipped the floor in her direction.

Though sometimes described as dust, aether spores are thicker—more like fine sand. So they don't float around in the air like dust does, without a strong breeze. Tress pulled her shirt collar up over her mouth anyway, watching with terror.

For the spores were rolling toward the fragments of the broken cannonball—and the water it had sprayed all over the wall. In that moment, Tress was given a crash course in naval warfare upon the spore seas. Yes, the enemy *could* have used uninteresting metal cannonballs. Instead they used ones designed to blast open and dump water—making each shot far more interesting. (Assuming you, like me, find creative deaths interesting.)

Some living spores finally touched the water.

They grew in a flash. Imagine lightning, but made of vines. They burgeoned, sweeping around one another, almost instantly growing into a jagged pattern some ten feet tall. Within moments a snarl of vines—vaguely shaped like a tree—had grown in the hold, with vine "roots" cracking the wood underneath and vine "branches" pushing up to bow the deck above.

Tress couldn't help imagining some of those spores growing in her mouth or nose. She got a few things wrong, but she understood the basics.

In case you have a more limited imagination, it begins with a feeling like hands forcing your jaws apart. Then vines fill your throat, growing wherever they can find space, snaking down into your lungs. They knock loose teeth, and drill up through your soft palate and into your sinuses. They don't usually reach your brain though, so you get the pleasure of suffocating to death as you feel the vines rip your eyes out of their sockets.

You're welcome.

Fortunately for Tress, a sailor soon stumbled down the steps with a lantern, wearing a cloth mask and bearing some odd equipment. Among it was a strange device called a splintbox. (A device which—I happen to know by pure coincidence—is exactly the right size to carry a human head.)

The sailor held the splintbox up beside the hole in the hull, then carefully poured a few drops of water in the top. A sheet of reddish-pink stone grew out the front of the box. Translucent, like cloudy crystal, the stone fused with the wood on the sides, plugging the hole.

The sailor cut the sheet off the front of the box with a silver knife. Every ship on Tress's world had at least one sailor trained to handle and use spores, known as a sprouter.

Tress watched in amazement. She'd heard of that substance: roseite. It grew from the pink-red spores of the Rose Sea, which bordered her own Emerald Sea. Unlike the Crimson Sea or the Midnight Sea, the Rose Sea was inhabited—which meant its spores weren't *quite* as deadly as others'. Still, it seemed plenty dangerous to her. Growing vines in your mouth was bad enough. Crystals sounded even worse.

Yet the sailor had casually used them to *repair* the ship, leaving the roseite on the hole like a bandage.

You could *use* spores? For practical purposes?

Just like that, Tress's lesson in naval warfare was shoved aside by a lesson in utilitarian economics.

With the hole patched, the sprouter unslung the device he'd been carrying over his shoulder; it looked like a pole with a plate on the bottom end. When he waved it over the floor, the remaining green spores turned grey. The plate, Tress realized, had to be made of silver.

He gave the vine growth a quick glance, but apparently decided it wouldn't do more harm for the moment, and so left it and walked toward the steps to the upper deck.

"Wait!" Tress called to him, grabbing the bars at the front of her cage. "That has to be a royal ship out there, right? If it's firing on us, rather than demanding ransom or surrender? They're here to exterminate some smugglers."

"Better hope they don't!" the sailor said to her. "You'll go down with us, inspector or not." He made a rude gesture toward her, which on their planet involved flipping his fingers in her direction, as if flinging water.

"That's my exact point!" Tress said. "If they knew there was a royal inspector on board, do you think they'd be so eager to fire on us?"

The sprouter stared at her a long moment, then scrambled to grab the keys to her cell.

11

THE THIEF

The sight that confronted Tress as she emerged from the hold could have unnerved a dragon. The ship that had been firing on them was far closer than she'd expected—close enough that she could make out the sailors on the deck.

The enemy ship had two cannons, one on the foredeck, one aft. Now, you might have heard stories of great sailing ships with a dozen or more guns on each side. They hadn't reached such heights on Tress's world; many ships had only one cannon, and they kept them on swiveling platforms. Often a ship's crew had a cannonmaster in charge of aiming.

The *Oot's Dream* had a single small cannon on the foredeck. At the moment, the smuggler ship was heeling hard as part of a weaving maneuver, rather than firing.

Tress didn't know sailing mechanics; she simply saw the enemy ship looming and watched with a slack jaw as their front cannon lobbed a shot toward the *Oot's Dream*. It hit the spore sea starboard amidships, and—unlike the cannonball that had broken through the hull earlier—this one smashed on first impact, releasing its cargo of water into the spores.

A treelike burst of vines exploded into existence inches away from Tress. More twisted than a librarian's love life (trust me, they're a strange bunch), it writhed with overlapping tendrils. It reminded Tress of her hair most mornings, before she got out her brush.

The gnarled vines grabbed hold of the ship, latching onto its gunwale. The vines that strayed near silver greyed and died, like spores did, but they held on tight nonetheless. It seemed this method of bombardment could rip a ship apart, silver or no silver. Either that or the vines would get a good hold and strand the ship in place, leaving it easy pickings.

Tress was shoved aside as sailors with axes rushed over to attack the vines in an attempt to cut the ship free. "That was too close!" the captain said, shouting to the helmsman. "Keep weaving, Gustal!" He stood nearby, and Tress could—regrettably—smell his breath as he spun on the sailor who had pulled her up the steps. "What under the moons are you doing with that woman, Dorp!"

"She's a royal inspector, Cap'n," Dorp said, gesturing to Tress. "I figured maybe if they saw 'er, they wouldn't be so keen on sinkin' us. Cap'n, sir!"

The captain's expression turned from angry to excited. "Dorp, that's the first good idea you've ever had. Drag her to the quarterdeck. Hoist her up high, if you have to, and let's pray to the moons it gives those yaldsons pause!"

Tress bore the treatment with as much dignity as she could manage. They soon had her standing up on the rim of the quarterdeck, waving for everything she had, hoping that the red coat would persuade them to hold their fire.

Unfortunately, the attacking ship either didn't see or didn't care, because the next cannonball hit the quarterdeck bulkhead, smashing through and causing quite a clutter in the captain's cabin.

The sprouter cursed. "What a stupid idea," he snapped, dragging Tress by her collar as he went belowdecks again to check for more leaks and return her to her cage. Unexpectedly, a second after they reached the hold, the ship lurched.

It was so jarring that Tress tripped and fell face-first into the dead spores that covered the floor of the hold. She scrambled to her knees and wiped away the spores with frantic hands, panicking. What if a few live ones remained?

The sprouter had let go of her collar. "No," he said, turning to stare up the steps. "No, no, *no.*"

The ship groaned around them, sliding to a halt. Then it fell quiet. Even the footsteps stilled—and it took her a moment to realize what had happened. The seethe—the bubbles that fluidized the spores—had stopped.

The ship had essentially run aground on the ocean itself. Until the seethe began again, they'd be trapped. Stuck in one place.

"Nononono!" the sprouter cried, forgetting Tress and running up the steps.

The reason for his panic occurred to Tress almost immediately. The enemy cannon was already pointed straight at them. And they were no longer moving.

A second later, a cannonball blasted through the aft hull, ripping a wide hole. Tress screamed and covered her head as the cannonball soared over her and crashed right through the front of the ship, never shattering as it was supposed to.

Tress cowered on the floor, awaiting the next inevitable shot. Then, through the terror, her practicality asserted itself. She turned, shifting wood debris off her back, and looked out through the large new hole in the hull. Across the ocean at the enemy ship, which was also stuck in place several hundred feet away.

The sea had become, essentially, solid. At least as solid as a sand dune. It was made of deadly spores, but it could be walked on. And while the people on that enemy ship *might* wish her harm, those on the *Oot's Dream* most certainly did.

It didn't take long for her to make the decision. She threw herself to her feet and pushed past the vine growth in the hold, making for the hole.

"Watch out!" the rat said from behind as something dropped on her. The sprouter, seeing her move, had leaped off the broken steps above to tackle her.

"Here now," he said. "That's a right good idea. You're gonna give me that coat, and I'm gonna go plead for my life with those fellows." He began to rip at her clothing, and she frantically felt around for a weapon. Her fingers latched onto something metal and she swung it up, clocking the sailor on the head. He dropped like a streaker's trousers.

Tress gasped, panting on the floor, then glanced at what she'd grabbed. A pewter cup.

Wait, *her* pewter cup.

Huh, she thought. *Didn't expect to be right about that.*

She searched around and spotted her things nearby, along with some other items that had been tossed around in the explosion. Then she cried out as another cannonball hit the ship somewhere above, making men scream.

She grabbed her sack, then stumbled over to the rat's cage. "Almost forgot about you," she said. "Sorry."

"It's a common human failing," he said. "Don't get me started on the way your people talk about my kind."

"Brace yourself," Tress said. "I don't have anything to cut that cage free, so . . ." She raised her heavy metal cup, then swung it down and broke off the little lock.

The rat shoved out with his snout, then leaped onto her arm and climbed up her shoulder. She supposed that, with spores all over the floor, she didn't blame him for getting up high.

"The name is . . ." The rat coughed. "The name is . . . Huck. That'll do, as I don't think my real name will work."

"Something in rat language that a human couldn't say?"

"Basically," he said as she turned and walked over to the hole in the ship. "You?"

"Tress," she said.

"Well then, Tress," Huck said, "you ready to do something absolutely insane?"

"Such is, unfortunately, becoming a theme to my life," Tress said, then stepped out onto the spores.

12

THE CROW

The spores scrunched under her feet.

Tress tried to breathe slowly and shallowly. Even with her shirt once more pulled up over her mouth, she felt exposed. All it would take was a single spore.

Another cannonball *whooshed* overhead, crunching through the ship. However, she walked carefully, slowly, to keep from kicking spores up into the air. Steady and deliberate, that was the way. Despite her entire body being taut with anxiety, knowing that at any moment the seethe could start again—and she'd sink to her death.

"Now that's a sight," Huck said softly from her shoulder.

Tress risked a glance back. For some reason, a flock of seagulls was beginning to gather around the *Oot's Dream*. Several sailors had been wounded in the most recent shot, and one man had fallen off the side of the ship.

He was bleeding.

The poor man thrashed and screamed, spraying blood across the spores—which grew in bursts, undulating and latching onto the ship like enormous tentacles from some unseen leviathan. The sailor disappeared in the contorted explosion of vines, but she could hear him screaming in there somewhere as he was crushed, more and more blood leaking out to feed the hungry ocean. Gulls dived at the vines and attacked them with apparent gusto. What was that about?

Tress turned forward and continued, step after step, toward the enemy ship. Though it had seemed close from the hold, out here it felt miles away.

"I've never done this before," Huck said from her shoulder. "You know. Walked out on it."

"Me either," Tress said, trying to prevent herself from hyperventilating.

Keep. Moving. Forward.

"I don't mean to alarm you," Huck said, "but the seethe will probably start up again any minute now . . ."

Tress nodded. She knew the basics. There were long stillings now and then, maybe every day or two, when the seethe stopped for several hours. There were times when it would stop for a day or more, though those were rare.

Most stillings were only a few minutes long. As if the seethe were some singer deep under the ocean, pausing briefly to draw in another breath.

She tried to pick up her pace, but the spores were deceptively difficult to walk on. Her feet slid, and moons above, she hadn't laced her boots tight enough. She could feel spores getting into her shoes, slipping between the fibers of her socks and rubbing against her skin.

How much sweat would it take to set one off?

Just keep moving.

Step. After. Step.

She heard scrunching noises approaching and glanced behind her. One of the smugglers had seen what she was doing, and was running toward the enemy ship. He was kicking up so many spores. She tensed, bracing herself, worried that—

Snap. A mess of vines burst from his eyes, and he dropped, writhing, making more grow up around him. Tress kept going, but another sailor passed her, walking with a confident steady stride. Faster than she dared.

They were over halfway to the other ship.

Please, Emerald Moon, she prayed. *Please. Just a little more time.*

She could see sailors gathering on the foredeck of the other ship. They'd stopped firing. They didn't need weapons any longer. The smuggler ship cracked and popped in the distance as an overwhelming number of vines grew up on the side where the bleeding sailor had fallen.

Tress felt the eyes of the enemy sailors on her. One figure in particular—standing right at the prow of the ship, wearing a hat with a tall black feather—looked ominous. The shadowed figure raised a long musket and aimed straight at Tress.

Then the figure turned slightly. The musket shook, and the crack sounded a fraction of a second later. The sailor who had been striding toward the ship in front of Tress dropped, his blood starting another eldritch spire of twisting vines.

Tress stopped, then braced herself for a second shot. When it didn't come, she started forward again. It was too late to turn back, and certain death lay that direction anyway.

So she pressed forward, feeling an awful tension, like a bowstring being drawn farther, and farther, and even farther. She kept waiting for that crack, or for the ground to start trembling beneath her feet. Or for a spore to slip into her nose or to touch one of her eyes.

When she at last reached the shadow of the grounded enemy ship, it felt like she'd been walking for an eternity with a knife right at her throat.

Sailors gathered at the ship's rail and stared down at her. She spotted no uniforms, except maybe on that figure in the center. With the black-plumed hat, their face was lost in shadow as the sun shone from near the horizon, silhouetting them.

No one said anything. The sailors didn't offer Tress a place on their ship, but they didn't shoot her either. So, lacking any other options, Tress tied her sack of cups to her belt and tried to find a way to climb up. Unfortunately, the keel and hull of the ship were of smooth brown wood, and after a few attempts Tress knew that scaling it would be impossible.

"I'm sorry," Huck said. "I think I must have been wrong. Those don't look like the king's people up above, Tress. I wish . . . I wish that I . . ."

Tress gave their situation a moment of thought. Then she wiped her finger to remove any spores before putting it to her mouth. She got some spittle on her fingernail, took a deep breath, and flicked it toward the spores a few feet away.

A midsized vine "tree" grew from the spores, curling around itself and reaching into the sky. Tress grabbed it, feeling the rough coils beneath her fingers, like rope.

Then she climbed.

"That's it!" Huck said, scrambling off her shoulder and up higher along the vine. "Come on, Tress. Hurry!"

She did her best, pulling herself up some ten feet until she could barely reach a porthole on the side of the ship. Huck leaped onto her shoulder again as she grabbed ahold and clung to the hull. She could see the ship's name there, painted in golden letters. The *Crow's Song*.

Up above, some of the sailors were laughing, chatting with a jovial nonchalance about her struggle. Spores streamed from her boots as she hung there, scrabbling for a foothold on a small ledge running along the outside of the ship below the portholes.

"There it is," Huck said. "Listen."

It started as a low humming that vibrated the ship. Moments later the spores began churning, air rising up through them. The ship lurched— nearly shaking Tress free. Orders above led to unfurled sails.

Tress's vine ladder slipped away, sinking into the suddenly fluid ocean. She glanced at the *Oot's Dream* as it listed to one side, dragged down by the many vines that wrapped it. The entire thing bobbed, then capsized, before finally sinking entirely.

Vines mushroomed up around the vanishing wreck as men screamed, giving their water to the ocean, and the flock of gulls scattered. Tress's current ship sailed past the wreck, but the *Oot's Dream* was gone before they arrived. Just three lonely crewmembers remained. Two on pieces of wreckage, one in a small lifeboat. All three wore scarves over their mouths, their eyes squeezed shut.

Two shots sounded from the deck, killing the two on the wreckage. For some reason, the *Crow's Song* left the man in the lifeboat alive. The sole remnant of the smuggler crew. An . . . ignoble end to Tress's first voyage.

She clung to the hull of the *Crow's Song*. Her fingers began to burn, her arms to ache. But there were no handholds above—plus, the side of the deck and gunwale extended out there. She doubted she had the strength or skill to get up over that, if she could even reach it.

So she hung on. Tight as she could, as the ship rocked and swayed.

Faces periodically appeared above, glancing down to see if she was still there. Then they'd call out to their fellows to relay her status.

Still there.

Still there.

"Go," she whispered to Huck. "You're a rat. You can climb that."

"Doubt it," he said.

"You could try."

"That's a fact. I could."

Together they clung there. For what seemed like an eternity. Finally she started to slip. Her aching muscles screamed, and—

A rope slapped the wood next to her. She stared at it, numb, wondering if she had the strength to climb it. Instead she snatched it, hung on, and tucked her head against her arm.

Blessedly, the rope began to move, pulled up by several of the sailors above. When she was high enough, an enormous man with his black hair in dreadlocks reached down and grabbed her under her arms, then dumped her onto the deck. The last spores on her clothing died as the silver in this ship's deck killed them.

"Captain Crow said we could pull you up if you lasted fifteen minutes," another sailor said, a shorter woman. "Can't believe you did. You're a strong one."

Tress coughed, lying on the deck, her exhausted arms pulled against her. Fifteen minutes? That had been only *fifteen minutes*? It had felt like hours.

"Not strong," Tress said, hoarse. "Just stubborn."

"That's even better," the sailor said.

Huck wisely kept quiet, though he snapped his teeth at a sailor who tried to grab him.

"What are you?" Tress said to the sailors. "King's men? Privateers?"

"Neither," said another of the sailors. "We'll put up the king's colors soon, but that's a lie. It's our pretty face. Doug's sewing us a proper flag so it will be ready for next time. Black on red."

Black on red? It was pirates after all. Was that an upgrade or a downgrade from being among smugglers? And why had they sunk that other ship, never asking for loot?

A stout figure pushed through the sailors. Captain Crow—judging by the plume in her hat—had harsh lines for a face, with tan skin and a scowl deep as the ocean. Crow was . . . well, I've known a few people like her. She seemed too harsh. Too full of anger. She was like the first draft of a human being, before softening effects like humor and mercy had been added.

"Throw her overboard," the captain said.

"But you said we could haul her up!" said the short woman.

"That I did, and that you did. Now toss her."

No one moved to obey.

"Look at how scrawny she is," the captain snapped. "An inspector? I've known a few of those—they pick the job for its ease. She'll have never worked a day in her life, and there's no place for anyone without a use on the *Song*."

The pirates still appeared reluctant. Why would they care about her? But their hesitance was an opportunity. So Tress—dizzy with exhaustion— pulled herself across the deck and struggled to her knees. She'd spotted a bucket and brush here, and she methodically—as fast as she could make her aching arms work—took out the brush and started scrubbing the deck.

Captain Crow eyed her. The only sounds were the seething spores and the brush scraping back and forth.

At last, the captain pulled a canteen from her belt and took a long drink. It did look like a nice canteen. With leather up the outsides that had feather patterns imprinted on it. Even when exhausted, Tress appreciated a good drinking vessel.

Crow stalked off—and gave no further orders to deal with Tress. The pirates retreated to their posts, and no one tossed her.

She kept working anyway. Scrubbing as Huck whispered encouragement in her ear. She worked well into the night, until—numb with fatigue—she finally curled up in one corner of the deck and fell asleep.

PART

3

13

THE CABIN BOY

Tress awoke the next day with a face full of hair. She felt stiff, like a washrag that was long overdue for a turn in the laundry. She unfolded herself from the deck, trying to tie back her hair, and vaguely remembered being kicked during the night and told to move so she wouldn't be underfoot. She'd done it, but had been kicked awake again for the same reason on two separate occasions. There didn't appear to be any place on the deck where she *wouldn't* be underfoot.

Her next thought wasn't for food. It wasn't for something to drink, or other biological needs.

It was for Charlie.

Never had Tress felt so naive. She'd thought she could simply leave her home and rescue someone? Even though she'd never set foot on a ship before? She felt a fool. Worse, she felt pain for Charlie, who must be somewhere frightened, trapped and alone. His agony was her agony.

It might seem that the person who can feel for others is doomed in life. Isn't one person's pain enough? Why must a person like Tress feel for two, or more? Yet I've found that the people who are the happiest are the ones who learn best how to *feel*. It takes practice, you know. Effort. And those who (late in life) have been feeling for two, three, or a thousand different people . . . well, turns out they've had a leg up on everyone else all along.

Empathy is an emotional loss leader. It pays for itself eventually.

That wasn't of much comfort at the time for Tress, miserable on the deck, realizing that—before she could even think of helping Charlie— she was going to have to find a way to save herself. She huddled against the gunwale, and heard someone belowdecks yelling that "first watch" could come to mess.

Huck whispered something to her and scrambled off to investigate. Tress's grumbling stomach reminded her that the last thing she'd had to eat or drink had been the water that made her see pigeons. So, aching, she climbed to her feet. "Mess" meant food on a ship, right? Maybe they wouldn't notice if she . . .

A lanky figure in an unbuttoned military coat stepped in front of her. Bald, with scruff on his chin, the fellow wore a sword at his side and had two pistols tucked into his belt. Laggart, the cannonmaster, was the ship's first officer. He had wiry muscles, and that long neck and bald head hinted he might have a buzzard somewhere in his family tree.

He looked Tress up and down. "First watch can eat," Laggart said. "Those are the men and women getting ready to take over sailing for the day. Are you going to be working the sails or the rigging today, honey-hair?"

". . . No," Tress whispered.

"Second shift will eat next," Laggart said. "They worked all night, and can eat as soon as their replacements arrive."

"And . . . what watch am I?" Tress asked softly.

"Captain says you're third watch," Laggart said, then smiled as he left.

Eventually second watch was called, and the sailors exchanged places. Tress waited, groggy and stiff. And she waited. And waited. One might say she was quite the waitress that morning.

Third watch was never called. Tress suspected she was the only one "assigned" to it. So she did her best to ignore her stomach, instead observing the pirates at work. Maybe if she learned their tasks, she'd be able to anticipate how to keep out of their way.

She spent the morning so occupied, and fortunately most of them didn't seem bothered by her. They weren't a jovial crew, but they were apparently a dedicated one. A few times, Tress caught Captain Crow watching her from the side while drinking from her canteen. Her glare made Tress feel like a stubborn spot on a window.

Best to put herself to work. She rummaged in her sack, checking on her cups, then took out her hairbrush. After beating her hair into submission and locking it away in a braid, she picked up her bucket and floor brush—then realized she didn't have any more water or soap.

She stood there looking foolish before someone approached with a fresh bucket for her. She thanked him, then—with a start—realized she recognized him. It was Hoid, cabin boy of the *Whistlebow*. There was no mistaking his gangly figure and his pure white head of hair. Though everyone called him "boy," he appeared to be in his thirties and evidently of sound mind—until he opened his mouth.

"My gums sure do like a lickin'!" he said to her, then walked away with a bowlegged gait that made him wobble like a drunk penguin.

Yes, that's me.

No, I don't want to talk about it.

As I wandered off to go stuff shoelaces up my nose, Tress moved up to the quarterdeck, as it had less traffic. Here she set to work again. Turned out, Tress was quite good at scrubbing decks. It was like scrubbing windows, except you didn't need to be able to see through them at the end. In fact it was too easy, perhaps demeaning of her washing talents. Like hiring a world-class surgeon to cut the crust off your sandwich.

During her breaks, she watched the crew. She was able to pick out other faces that—like Hoid—she knew, if only vaguely. Often ships passing the Rock would unload a few crewmembers. These would get a pass from the inspector and would be hired on by another visiting vessel.

This didn't seem to be a notably rough lot—it was a mixed crew, with a variety of ethnicities and nearly as many women as men. That wasn't uncommon in the spore seas. You took whoever was willing. Sexism interfered with profits.

How had such a *normal* crew ended up as pirates? And not merely ordinary pirates, bloodthirsty ones who would sink a ship without asking for plunder?

They didn't even cover up the name of their vessel, Tress thought. *And they left one sailor alive.* Something was strange about this ship.

"I've been wanting to gargle my shirts!" I said, walking past. I pointed at her with both hands and winked. "But I ate them last week."

Tress cocked her head, watching me wander away. As she did, Huck scampered across the deck and up onto her shoulder.

"What is wrong with that guy?" the rat asked softly.

"I'm not entirely certain," Tress whispered. "I've met him before though. He's nice. If . . . weird."

"People who collect stamps are weird, Tress. That man is a few eggs short of a dozen—and he doesn't realize the other ten he collected are actually rocks."

Sigh.

All right, so here's the thing. I'd had an encounter—well, more a collision—with the Sorceress a few years before. Let's just say she had something I needed, but liberating it from her proved more difficult than I'd assumed. The end result? The Sorceress gave me one of her famous curses. Look, even the most graceful dancer trips once in a while.

My curse took away my sense of taste and, well, my other four senses as well.

"What did you find out?" Tress asked the rat.

"I snatched some food," Huck said, "but could only get rat-sized portions. Sorry. Also, they really are sewing a pirate flag. I'd guess they're new to this. Maybe that's why they accidentally sank the other ship."

"No," Tress whispered, returning to her scrubbing. "They left one sailor alive on purpose, and didn't cover their ship's name. They didn't sink that ship because of inexperience . . ."

". . . they did it to declare themselves," Huck agreed. "The pirate version of sending out a crier to announce a sale at the cobbler's shop. Moonshadows. They killed almost *thirty people*."

Tress looked up across the crew working at their posts. Earlier, she'd read intent and focus in their movements. Now she saw something else. A kind of acute desire to lose themselves in work. Perhaps to avoid having to think about what had happened the day before.

Something is very wrong on this ship, she thought again.

Unfortunately, before she could think more on that, other matters— of a more scatological nature—demanded her attention.

14

THE DOUGS

The *Crow's Song* was a much larger ship than Tress's previous one. *Oot's Dream* had been a two-masted vessel, similar to what you might call a brigantine. The *Crow's Song* was instead a full four-masted vessel, built for speed but with a spacious cargo hold and multiple decks. It was the equivalent of what you'd call a small galleon—and it had a rather large crew for Tress's world, consisting of sixty people.

I'm not going to ask you to remember them all. Mostly because *I* don't remember them all.

Therefore, for ease of both narrative and our collective sanity, I'm going to name only the more important members of the *Crow's Song*. The rest, regardless of gender, I'll call "Doug."

You'd be surprised how common the name is across worlds. Oh, some spell it "Dug" or "Duhg," but it's always around. Regardless of local linguistics, parents eventually start naming their kids Doug. I once spent ten years on a planet where the only sapient life was a group of pancake-like beings that expressed themselves through flatulence. And I kid you not—one was named Doug. Though admittedly it had a very distinctive smell attached when the word was "spoken."

"Doug" is the naming equivalent to convergent evolution. And once it arrives, it stays. A linguistic Great Filter; a wakeup call. Once a society reaches peak Doug, it's time for it to go sit in the corner and think about what it has done.

Anyway, there was at least one woman actually named Doug on the *Crow's Song*, but I can't remember which one she was—so for the purposes of this story, they're all Dougs.

Tress approached one and asked—hesitantly—where the toilet was. The Doug pointed her toward the stairs down, explaining that the "middle deck head" was for low-ranking crew.

With Huck on her shoulder, she began to explore. The ship had four levels. The Dougs called the top one—which was exposed to the sky—the "upper deck." The "middle deck" contained places like the mess and the armory, and small rooms for officers. The "lower deck" was a cramped place where most of the sailors made their bunks.

Beneath that was the hold, a cavernous space for the copious loot the pirates would surely acquire once they figured out how to stop sinking it all to the bottom of the ocean.

There were several toilet rooms, with working plumbing, thank the moons. She peeked into an unoccupied one and saw a toilet, but no bath. How did the crew bathe? She desperately wished she could, as she kept finding dead spores in the folds of her clothing. It made her skin writhe to think how much of it must have gotten on her.

She did her business in the cramped chamber with only a tiny porthole in the wall for light. Huck politely waited outside without being prompted, proving quite gentlemanly for a rat. Feeling a little better, Tress slipped out and let him hop back onto her shoulder. What did they do with human waste, out here on the ocean? Save it all up for composting on islands? What about on long voyages? Dumping it overboard seemed dangerous, not to mention gross. Dangergross?

On her way back to the upper deck, she heard a voice coming from a room near the head. She lingered, peeking in to see a man behind a counter—the large man with dreadlocks who had hauled her onto the deck. Now, when I say "large," you might have imagined him as heavyset, or perhaps beefy. He was both, yes, but neither word did justice to Fort, the ship's quartermaster.

Fort wasn't large like, "Hey, eat a salad" or even large like, "Hey, do you play sports?" He was large like, "Hey, how did you get through the door?" It wasn't that he was fat, though he did carry a few extra pounds. More, he looked like a person built using a different scale from the rest of humanity. One could imagine that the Shards, after creating him, had said, "Maybe we went a little far in places," and decided to cut ten percent off all other humans to conserve resources.

Fort was holding up a ceramic cannonball that was small in his hands. His fingers on both hands were gnarled, either from some old injury or a congenital disease. The condition had to affect his dexterity.

He was with a gangly woman in a vest and trousers, her hair cut very short. Ann (the ship's carpenter) had a nose like a dart and carried not one, not two, but *three* pistols strapped to various places on her person.

Fort handed Ann the cannonball, and although it looked light in his grip, the way she hefted it indicated otherwise. Then he picked up what appeared to be a wooden sign with a black front. Maybe two feet across and somewhat less tall.

"You examined each one in the armory?" Ann asked.

Fort glanced at the back of his wooden board and nodded.

"You didn't find any others that were defective?" Ann asked.

Fort tapped the back of the wooden sign, and words appeared on the front.

Not a single one, the sign said. **Each one I inspected has a proper fuse, timed to explode before it sinks a ship, so it can be captured and looted.**

Ann thumped the ball onto the counter. "Well, if none of the others are defective, we shouldn't have to worry about sinking someone else by accident."

Fort again tapped something on the rear of the board using his index knuckle. As he did, the words changed.

I don't like this, Ann. We were supposed to launch cannonballs that only incapacitated the ship, not sank it. I hate that we ended up killing those people, and I really don't like how the captain acted afterward. It doesn't make sense.

"What are you saying?" Ann asked.

I'm saying I don't like this at all. It's not the kind of piracy we signed up for.

"I don't like it either," Ann said. "But it's too late to change our minds. This is better than getting conscripted, at least."

Is it though? Is it really? I didn't want those people's deaths on my shoulders, Ann.

Ann didn't respond. Finally, she stood up straight and walked toward the door. Tress felt a moment of panic, not wanting to be discovered eavesdropping, and scurried back into the head.

Tress listened to Ann leave up the steps outside. "What do you make of that, Huck?" she whispered.

"Don't know," he said. "Sounds like they didn't intend to sink the *Oot's Dream*, which makes sense. But after the first cannonball broke through the hull and started the ship going down, the pirates must have decided to finish the job."

Tress nodded, although she didn't know what to think about all of this.

"They're still culpable though," Huck added. "What did they think would happen, turning pirate and attacking? They can't simply decide to be sad for killing someone *after* trying to rob them. These pirates are outlaws now, Tress."

"Doesn't sound fair," she said. "The king would hang the quartermaster even if he didn't fire the cannon?"

"The law is clear. Felony murder rule, to be precise. Commit a crime and someone dies? That's murder. Even if you weren't intending it. The royal navy will be hunting this lot—and we'd best not be on board when they get caught. Just in case the officials don't believe you're a captive."

It was a wise suggestion. This ship was a death trap—either the captain would eventually tire of her, or she'd end up dead in the inevitable fighting. She had a job to do in saving Charlie, and couldn't waste time.

But how to escape? She couldn't exactly jump overboard. Plus, her dry throat warned her that she had other more immediate concerns. If the captain wouldn't let her eat, she wouldn't live long enough to escape.

She snuck over to the quartermaster's room again and glanced in to see that the large man had turned his back toward the door. He was arranging things in his many trunks and boxes behind the counter. Could she steal something to eat? Or perhaps Huck could do it for her? She glanced at him.

"What?" he asked loudly.

Tress glared at him, making a shushing motion.

"I think he's deaf," Huck said. "When I was prowling earlier, I heard someone mention that the quartermaster couldn't hear."

Indeed, Fort continued his work, still facing away from them. He didn't notice them talking.

"I met a deaf human once," Huck said. "She was a dancer, and one of the best under the moons—best I'd seen, anyway. I was enjoying the time with her, but it ended up getting interrupted in a rather abrupt way. Which is a shame, but things happen. I also couldn't afford to talk to her, since—you know, things relating to who and what I am. Didn't want to reveal myself."

"Maybe," Tress suggested, "this would be another good time to not talk. Unless you want one of the pirates to realize they have a potentially sellable loquacious rat on board."

"Yeah, good point," he said. "It's just, I spent all those weeks hiding on the smuggler ship before they grabbed me. Got kind of lonely. It's good to have someone to chat with . . ."

She glanced at him.

". . . which I'll stop doing now."

Tress moved to leave—but as she did so, one of the boards creaked underfoot. Fort spun immediately in her direction, then narrowed his eyes as he saw her. He might not have been able to hear, but every quartermaster I've ever known has a kind of sixth sense for when people are sneaking around near their goods.

Beneath the enormous man's glare, Tress felt like bolting. But he *had* been the one who'd pulled her up onto the deck. She stood in place instead, until he raised his strange board from the counter.

Come here, girl, it read.

It wouldn't do any good to run. So, feeling like she was entering the dragon's den, Tress entered the room.

15

THE QUARTERMASTER

Fort looked her up and down, rubbing his chin with thick fingers. Finally, he tapped the back of his board and words appeared for her.

You have a name?

"Tress, sir."

And are you truly a royal inspector?

"I . . ." Tress swallowed. "No. The coat doesn't belong to me. I stole it."

You're a pirate now, Fort wrote. **What you steal IS what belongs to you.**

"I'm not a pirate," she said.

You are so long as you want to keep breathing, Fort wrote. **Don't tell anyone you don't intend to join us. That sort of talk gets a person tossed overboard.**

Tress nodded. "Thank you, sir."

Don't call me sir. I left that title behind a long time ago. My name is Fort. Anyone feed you yet?

In response, her stomach growled. She shook her head.

Fort leaned below his counter, then came up with a plate, the thin ceramic edge held between the first two fingers of his hand. Earlier, she'd thought he would lack dexterity due to his fingers—which looked like they'd each been broken in several places, then allowed to heal without splints. Yet he managed quite well. Some actions took more effort, and his hands did tremble, but he was obviously capable, even if he had to do things differently from other people.

After placing the plate before her, he pulled out a pot, scraped at the bottom, and slopped some crusty hash browns onto the plate. He followed that with some watery eggs.

Leftovers from breakfast, Tress thought. *The dregs the others didn't eat.*

She waited, with difficulty, before eating anything. He watched her, then dropped a fork onto the plate. She took this as permission and dug in.

It was awful.

The overcooked hash browns had the consistency of beetle shells—complementing the eggs, which were reminiscent of what might have been found *inside* those beetle shells. You didn't have to be a master cook to tell this food was awful, but to someone like Tress it was worse. Feeding *her* cold and crusty leftovers—the bits that hadn't gotten any spices on them—was like locking a master pianist in a room by themself, then piping in off-tune kazoo renditions of great masterpieces.

Tress didn't complain. She needed to eat, and she wasn't going to reject the only thing she'd been offered. Despite it tasting less like food and more like what food turned into.

To take her mind off the "meal," Tress nodded to the board that Fort used for communicating. "That's an odd device."

He handed her a cup of water (a nice bronze one that lacked ornamentation, but shone when it caught the light). The water at least tasted pure and clean. She drank it down eagerly.

It is, isn't it? Fort wrote. **Your words appear for me on the back as you speak. It can even differentiate voices, and puts a mark before them to indicate someone new is talking.**

"Wow," Tress said.

Now, you might be wondering why Fort didn't read lips. I, like many hearing people, once assumed this was the magical solution for people navigating the hearing world. But in case you haven't heard—pun intended—reading lips doesn't work like it does in stories. It's a messy business, full of guesswork, and is extremely taxing. Even for experts.

Fort used to rely on it anyway, enduring its low accuracy. Until he was able to find his way to this device. It had many functions—including some he didn't know yet. For example, the words would appear larger if he wrote fewer of them, taking up all the space on the board. But when he wrote longer messages, the words shrank to fit more.

It's wonderful, Fort said. **I got it from a wizard a few years ago.**

"A wizard?" Tress said.

From beyond the stars, Fort said. **A very strange fellow. He used it to translate words to our language. I traded hard to get it. It seemed to surprise him when he realized how much it would help. It's hard for me to write the usual way for hearing people, since I can't make some of the shapes.**

That "wizard" from the stars wasn't me, by the way. I've always wondered who traded the device to Fort. That's Nalthian tech, with Awakened predictive Connection circuits.

Fort turned the board around and showed her the back, where he could tap letters and bring down lists of common words. The board anticipated his needs, giving likely options. It worked with supernatural speed, seeming to anticipate his very thoughts.

I have to leave it out in the sun once a week, or it stops working, Fort wrote. **And its magic won't respond to anyone other than me. So don't think about stealing it.**

"I wouldn't dare," Tress said with a start. "I mean . . . you've been so kind to me."

It isn't kindness, Fort wrote. **It's a trade.**

"For what?"

Haven't decided yet, Fort said. **Go back to your food, girl.**

She did. Unfortunately.

As she tried valiantly to keep eating, another of the sailors walked in. This was the shorter woman who had stood up to the captain the day before. Her black hair was in tight curls. She strode in and slapped something on the counter, barely giving Tress a glance.

How to describe Salay, the helmswoman? She was the same ethnicity as Fort, and like him was from the Islands of Lobu in the Sapphire Sea, where the zephyr spores release a burst of air when watered. She had delicate features, but wasn't the least bit fragile.

"All right, Fort," she said. "I'll give you three."

She'd deposited three small earrings onto the table.

I told you, Salay, Fort wrote. **I have no use for earrings. They make my ears itch.**

"Four then," Salay said, placing another on the counter. "I won them off a Doug at cards, but it's all I have. They're solid gold. You won't get a better deal anywhere."

At the word "deal," Fort perked up visibly. He inspected the earrings.

"Come on, Fort," Salay said. "I need to get back to duty."

Fort rubbed his chin, then scratched at his dreadlocked head. Then he took something from below the counter and set it out for her: a pocket watch.

"Finally," Salay said, slipping it off the counter and hurrying out.

Fort inspected the earrings one at a time, smiling. It was true that he had no use for earrings, but . . . it *was* a good deal. And good deals, to Fort, were their own reward.

Tress managed to choke down the last of the food. She felt she deserved a medal for that. Fort merely gave her another cup of water, then shooed her away—but not before he wrote, **Come back after everyone else has had supper. Maybe I'll have something for you to eat.**

Tress nodded in thanks. On her way out, she passed me skipping a little as I went in to settle on a stool before Fort's counter. The quartermaster brought out some more of the "food" and gave it to me.

"My favorite!" I said.

Don't try to eat the plate this time, please, Fort wrote.

I dug into the food, humming to myself at the flavor.

What? Yes, I could taste it. Why wouldn't I be able . . .

Oh, the five senses? Yes, I said I lost my sense of taste to the Sorceress's curse. You thought . . . you thought I meant *that* sense of taste? Oh, you innocent fool.

She took my *other* sense of taste. The important one.

And with it went my sense of humor, my sense of decorum, my sense of purpose, and my sense of self. The last one stung the most, since it appears my sense of self is tied directly to my wit. I mean, it's in the name.

As a result, I present you with Hoid, the cabin boy.

Anyway, that rounds out the people you need to remember for now. Captain Crow. First officer (and cannonmaster) Laggart. Fort the quartermaster, Ann the carpenter, and Salay the helmswoman. Everyone else was a Doug, I think . . .

Oh, right. I nearly forgot Ulaam. But seeing as he was dead, he barely counted.

16

THE CORPSE

With her stomach full of "food," Tress was able to return to the top deck and resume her scrubbing with renewed vigor. She didn't know how long it had been since someone had properly washed this deck, but it was coated with a layer of dead spores that had turned black with grime. It took real work to get down to the actual wood, and so her progress was slow.

"Wow," Huck said from her shoulder, comparing the dark grimy wood ahead to the vibrant brown planks she'd cleaned, silver lines sparkling between many of them. "That really makes a difference."

"Spore scum sticks to basically anything," she said, scrubbing hard. "I've never found a better remedy than soap and effort. This wood is going to need some pitch when I'm done though."

Tress knew quite a lot about sailors for someone who knew next to nothing about sailing. She had listened to many a man or woman complain about the life, which—to hear them talk—was an existence full of drudgery. Many an off-duty sailor in the tavern had been assigned scrubbing duty before, so Tress knew that pitch on the boards would seal them and fill the gaps—plus it made them far less slippery. And you always scrubbed *across* planks, never along them, so you didn't wear grooves down the centers.

Her head was full of wisdom like that: the wisdom of complaints. It also taught her the hierarchy of a ship's crew. Most of the sailors would be equals, save for the officers. She'd met all of those except two: the ship's surgeon and the ship's sprouter. She'd never understood that last term, not until she'd seen the man use the spores on the previous ship.

She passed midday, and ignored her stomach as it started to growl again. It should have known better, after what she'd done to it at breakfast. Fortunately, she found out where to get new water—from barrels in the hold—and she was allowed a cupful to drink each time she went to refill her bucket.

Otherwise, she scrubbed. Tragically, this work—like washing windows—was great thinking work. And her mind was, as I believe we've established, often full of thoughts.

That is one of the great mistakes people make: assuming that someone who does menial work does not like thinking. Physical labor is great for the mind, as it leaves all kinds of time to consider the world. Other work, like accounting or scribing, demands little of the body—but siphons energy from the mind.

If you wish to become a storyteller, here is a hint: sell your labor, but not your mind. Give me ten hours a day scrubbing a deck, and oh the stories I could imagine. Give me ten hours adding sums, and all you'll have me imagining at the end is a warm bed and a thought-free evening.

Tress's mind spun around what the quartermaster had said about the cannonballs. What had gone wrong? She was so intrigued that when she picked her next section to scrub, she placed herself near the forward cannon.

Moments later, a Doug called to her. "Hey, you!" he said. "New girl! Yes, you. Come on now, I need your help!"

Concerned, but too polite to object, Tress stowed her bucket and brush. She dusted off her knees, then followed after the Doug as he led her down to the hold. Here he gathered some cannonballs from a bin.

"Carry that," he said, pointing to a small keg near the wall.

Tress hesitantly picked it up, finding it lighter than she'd expected. "What's this?" she asked.

"Zephyr spores," the man said. "From the Sapphire Sea."

She nearly dropped the keg in shock. Spores? An entire keg of them?

She could see why he'd demanded her help. Indeed, he eagerly chose to carry the much heavier cannonballs, leaving her the task of lugging the spores.

"Why," she said, "do we have a small keg of spores?"

"For firing the cannons," the Doug explained. "Can't just drop a cannonball in! You need something to go *poof*, send the ball flying."

Spores? They used *spores* to fire the cannons? She carried the keg more gingerly as they started up the steps.

"Normally," the Doug said, "this would be old Weev's job, seein' as how it involves spores and all."

"Weev? Is he the ship's sprouter?"

"He *was*." The Doug's expression fell. "Nice fellow. Liked having him around. He was terrible at bluffing, you know, so I always beat him at cards."

"What happened?"

"Didn't want to become a pirate."

"So he got off at port?"

"Oh, he got off," the Doug said. "But there wasn't no port . . ." He glanced toward Captain Crow, who stood on the quarterdeck sipping at her canteen, wind blowing the black feather in her hat.

"Captain killed him?" Tress whispered.

"He was the only one who stood up to her," the Doug said, "when she proposed this new occupational direction. Well, Weev is occupyin' the bottom of the ocean now. Sprouters are a crazy lot, always spendin' more time than's right around spores. But he didn't deserve that. Just for askin' questions we was all thinkin.'"

He fell silent. At least she now knew why she hadn't met the ship's sprouter yet. And now you know why I didn't tell you to remember his name. Also, no, he's not the corpse. Well, he's *a* corpse. But he's not *the* corpse on the ship. There's another. Try to keep up.

The Doug led Tress to the cannonmaster's station. Laggart wasn't there at the moment, and the forecannon was lashed in place with its paraphernalia. The Doug began unloading cannonballs into a bin.

"All right," he said to Tress. "I'm going to go get a few more cannonballs to refill the stock. See that big barrel there? It's lined, like that keg you're holding, with stuff that protects spores from our silver. We need spores alive for shooting cannonballs at other folks.

"The cannonmaster though, he needs those spores in little pouches he can stuff into the cannon easily during a fight. You'll find empty pouches in the barrel. What you need to do is pour those spores into the pouches—without spilling any—and tie them off. Also, you got to do your pouring *inside* the larger barrel, because of the lining that protects the spores."

The Doug shifted uncomfortably on the deck, his hands in his pockets, looking at her.

"Very well," Tress said.

"No complaints?" he asked.

She shook her head. She'd rather not do the work, as she was terrified of spores. But she also couldn't let that fear inconvenience the others. After all, she was newest on the ship. It made sense that she should do the dangerous work no one else wanted.

Tress moved over to the barrel and took off the lid. At the bottom were some filled pouches; a bunch of empty ones were in a little net attached to the outside.

"You're . . . really not going to complain?" the Doug asked. "I complained when they made me do it."

"You're probably smarter than I am," Tress said. "Any tips?"

"There's a funnel, some goggles, and a mask. Other than that . . . try not to worry. This ain't the most dangerous type of spores. You should be fine."

Many perils could fit between the sounds in "should be." But Tress was alive because the crew had resisted tossing her overboard when the captain had demanded. It seemed best to stay in their good graces. So Tress simply nodded and got to work.

17

THE CARPENTER

The blue spores fascinated Tress. They were the first spores from another moon, another sea, that she'd seen up close. They were beautiful, almost crystalline. The fact that they could likely kill her with ease only made them more captivating. Like an expertly forged sword crafted with love, dedication, and sweat by a smith so that some-day you could do the most ugly things possible in the most beautiful of ways.

She sent Huck away with a quiet word, to not put him in danger. Then she whispered a prayer to the moons and thought of Charlie. Getting the crew to trust her was the best way to further her goal of reaching him. Doing the work they didn't want to do themselves was bound to lead her toward opportunities. Even washing windows had led her to opportunities. The most important one being when she met Charlie in the first place.

All that in mind—and with the mask over her mouth and the goggles over her eyes—she felt only *slightly* terrified as she lowered the small keg into the larger barrel. There were hooks on the side where she could affix it, and the spigot at the bottom of the keg—like for pouring beer—let the spores drain out at a careful rate. Her hand still shook as she held the funnel and filled up the first pouch with the radiant blue spores.

She tied it and set it carefully on the bottom of the barrel near the other pouches. She fell into a rhythm, filling them, taking care not to spill a single spore. It was tense work, far worse for thinking than cleaning the deck. But Tress—being Tress—couldn't avoid thoughts entirely.

She wondered exactly what the spores did that made the cannon fire. She wondered if there were other types of spores being carried in the ship's armory—and who managed them, if the crew's sprouter was dead.

Also, she wondered why the large barrel had a false bottom.

She recognized it easily. After all, she'd spent several weeks becoming an expert on barrel contraptions and how to hide things in them. On one of the devices she'd prepared for leaving the Rock, they'd installed a secret latch hidden right about . . . there.

She found it near the barrel's banding. A little piece of metal she could wiggle. When she moved it, a hole—little larger than a fist—opened in the bottom of the barrel. A few pouches of spores dropped in, and her breath caught. When she reached in to pull them out, her fingers brushed something else.

A cannonball. Hidden in the cavity beneath the barrel's false bottom. There was room for three or four of them inside.

She quickly pulled the pouches out and reset the device. As she returned to her work, her hands trembled even *more*. Her mind raced so fast, it would soon need a new set of tires.

She could see it. She knew what had happened.

The cannonmaster was in charge of loading, aiming, and firing the weapon. He'd be given a rack of cannonballs, but who would be watching to see if he grabbed one from this secret compartment instead? Probably no one.

She bet those hidden cannonballs wouldn't pass Fort's inspection—they wouldn't be rigged to incapacitate the target with vines. Laggart, the cannonmaster, had *deliberately* sunk that other ship.

But why? The entire situation didn't make sense for a multitude of reasons. It wasn't just the lack of plunder. Why bother *hiding* the fact that they were going to sink the ship? Why the subterfuge?

It only made sense if . . .

"So, zephyr spore duty," a voice said behind Tress. "I wondered who the Dougs would force to do it, now that Weev is dead."

Tress turned to see the lanky, sharp-nosed woman with the short hair who had been talking to Fort earlier. Ann, the ship's carpenter.

Every ship needs a good carpenter. Oh, a sprouter can patch up a hull with a quick burst of spores—but silver erodes even fully hardened roseite over time. Doesn't take a man long at sea to start contemplating how thin the barrier is between him and certain death. Just a plank. If you ever want to have a good face-to-face with your mortality, you'll find the opportunity on the deck of a ship at night, staring at the endless darkness beyond you—when you realize the darkness beneath is somehow even more heavy, more vast, and more terrifying.

That's when you realize that having a good carpenter on board is worth paying them a double share of wages. In fact, it's quite the steal.

"I don't mind the duty," Tress said, making another pouch. "I'd do it again if they asked." Inwardly, she was uneasy with how Ann walked next to the cannon, trailing her fingers on the metal. She'd been talking to Fort about the cannonballs. What side was she on? How many sides were there? What had Tress gotten herself *into*?

Sadly, she didn't know the half of it yet.

"Don't say things like that, Tress," Ann said. "Sailors don't *volunteer* for duty. It's downright untraditional."

"You know my name?" Tress said.

"Things get around on a ship," Ann replied. "I'm Ann. Ship's carpenter. Assistant cannonmaster."

Assistant to Laggart? Tress licked her lips, nervous—then stopped. Licking anything was *not* a good idea when handling spores. She made another pouch.

Had Ann seen her find the hidden chamber?

"What do you think?" Ann said, settling on a box nearby, a hand on one of her pistols as if taking comfort in it. "You're a pirate now, Tress. An unexpected sideways turn in life."

"Better than an unexpected turn downward," Tress said.

"Aye," Ann said. "That it is."

Tress wanted to ask more questions, but it felt like too much of an imposition. These people had spared her. Who was she to be making demands of them? So instead she said, "You all seem to be adjusting well to being pirates."

"Adjusting well? What kinda talk is that?" Ann leaned forward. "You want to know why, don't you? How we ended up this way?"

"I . . . yes, Miss Ann. I do."

"Why not ask?"

"I didn't want to be impolite."

"Impolite? To *pirates*?"

Tress blushed.

"I don't mind talkin' about it," Ann said, staring out over the sea. Before them the ship's prow cut a path through the spores. "The cap'n spun it well. We could either end up fighting in the king's coming war, or we could strike out on our own, throwing away all the laws about writs and tariffs. Plus, the cap'n said we'd be doing a noble and important duty."

". . . Important?" Tress asked.

"A vital part of the economy."

". . . Um, I see."

"Do you?"

"Actually, no," Tress admitted.

"Then why not say so, girl?" Ann said, shaking her head. "Anyway, our job is important. You know how rich folk are—they make all this money off people sailing around, selling and buying for them. Then what're they gonna do with the money? Lock it away. What good is *locked away* money? Ain't nobody going to enjoy it if it's trapped in a vault with Granna's wedding ring.

"So we've gotta take some. Inject it back into the economy, as a stimulus. To help local merchants, the small folk who are just tryin' to live. We do an important service."

"By . . . stealing."

"Damn right." Ann sat back, shifting her hand on her pistol. "Least, that's what it was supposed to be like. We weren't supposed to be dead-runners. I guess we all knew the risk. Didn't expect to fail so hard on our first act of piracy though."

Tress cocked her head, barely resisting the urge to scratch at the place where the goggles met her face. Despite the silver on the deck, spores on her fingers could live long enough to do damage.

"I'm . . . confused," Tress said. "Deadrunner?"

"You don't know?" Ann said. "What kind of sailor are you?"

"The kind that . . . doesn't know what a deadrunner is?" She felt profoundly annoyed at being berated for withholding questions, then being mocked when she didn't.

"There are two varieties of pirates, Tress," Ann explained. "There's the ordinary kind, then there's the deadrunners. Regular pirates rob, but don't kill unless they're fired upon. You sail well enough to catch the ship you're chasing, and they surrender their ransom price. Then *they* sail away with their lives, while *you* sail away richer.

"That's how it's supposed to work. It becomes a contest, see? A race, with a little extortion to keep it interestin'. The king's marshals, they keep records. So long as you let folks go, so long as you don't murder crews . . . well, if you get caught, they lock you up. But they don't hang you."

"That sounds remarkably civilized," Tress said.

Ann shrugged. "Civilization exists because everyone wants to keep their innards in'r innards. You don't punch a fellow when you first meet him, 'cuz you don't wanna get punched each time *you* meet someone. The king knows this. So long as he gives pirates a *reason* not to go all the way, they'll hedge.

"Besides, who *wouldn't* rather have a chase than a battle? The poor sods on merchant ships don't want to lose their lives over their master's money. The masters don't want their ships being scuttled or stolen. And you don't last long as a pirate if'n you've gotta wipe the deck with your blood every haul. Except, you know, if you kill someone by accident."

"Or an entire ship's worth of people," Tress said.

Ann nodded. "Then you become a deadrunner. No mercy for you if caught. Even other pirates will hate you. Nobody will take crew from a deadrunner ship. You're left to make your way, lonely as the single bean in a poor man's soup."

By the moons, it made sense. Tress revised her opinion of Ann. That forlorn expression, that regret . . . it meant whatever conspiracy there had been to sink the smuggler ship, Ann hadn't been part of it.

Laggart *had* been though. And likely the captain. They'd *wanted* to become deadrunners. Hence the hidden cannonballs, the sinking of the *Oot's Dream*. Why else would the captain leave one of the sailors alive to spread the word?

Tress was so absorbed by these thoughts that she forgot herself and absently scratched at the itch by her goggles. She froze as she was doing it. *Moonshadows.*

Well, at least—

That was when Tress's face exploded.

18

THE OTHER CORPSE

Tress found herself lying on the deck, the goggles blown free of her face. What was that sound? Screams of pain?

No. Laughter.

Ann was laughing uproariously. Tress immediately put her hand up to her cheek. It was sore, but fortuitously still attached to her face. She'd gotten a mote or two of zephyr spores under the rim of her goggles, where they had touched a bead of sweat. Mercifully, that tiny amount of spores didn't pack enough of a punch to kill her.

"It isn't funny," Tress said, sitting up.

(She was right. It was *hilarious*.)

"Come on, spore girl," Ann said, helping Tress up by the arm. "Let's have the surgeon look you over." She shouted toward the Doug who had made Tress do this work, and told him to clean up. Then Ann helped the disoriented Tress down to the middle deck.

"You really work with that stuff?" Tress asked Ann. "As assistant cannonmaster?"

"Well, when they let me," Ann said.

"Why don't the cannons explode?"

"They do. That's what makes the cannonballs shoot out."

Tress determined to give that some thought later, as it didn't make sense yet. Washing windows, it should be noted, is not an occupation that offers a thorough education in ballistics.

Over from the mess, near the prow, was a door that had been closed when Tress had investigated earlier. Now Ann pushed it open and steered Tress inside. There she found a man dressed in a sharp suit of a cut she'd never before seen. It was somehow less ostentatious but more elegant than the uniforms the duke and Charlie had worn. Pure black, with pressed lines and no buttons on the front.

He had jet-black hair, and features that looked too sharp to be real. Like he was a painting, or a drawing. His skin was an ashen grey, his eyes bloodred. If the underworld had legal counsel, it would have been this man.

Tress should have been frightened of him, but instead she was awed. What was a creature like this doing on a pirate ship? Surely this was a divine being from beyond space, time, and reality.

In a way, Tress was correct.

And no, he still hasn't given me my suit back.

"My!" Dr. Ulaam said with a refined but excitable voice. "What have you brought me, Ann? Fresh meat?"

"She was loading the zephyr pouches," Ann explained, leading Tress to a seat at the side of the small chamber, "and some got underneath her goggles."

"Poor child," Ulaam said. "New to the ship, hmmmm? You have very nice eyes."

"If he asks to buy them," Ann whispered, "haggle. You can usually get double his first offer."

"My eyes?" Tress said, her voice rising. "He wants to take *my eyes*?"

"After you are dead, naturally," Ulaam said. This room was filled with cabinets and drawers. He unlatched one and took out a small jar of salve, then turned toward her. "Unless you'd rather do it now? I have several fine replacements I could offer. No? What about just one?"

"What . . . what *are* you?" Tress asked.

"He's our zombie," Ann said.

"Such a crude term," Ulaam replied. "And not terribly accurate, as I've told you."

"You ain't got a heartbeat," Ann said. "And your skin is cold as a wet fish."

"Both adaptations reduce my required caloric intake," Ulaam said. "My method is efficient. I think everyone will be going around without a heart, once I solve the problem of how lacking one kills humans." He offered Tress the salve. "Put this on your skin, child, and it will help with the pain."

Tress accepted it, and timidly put a dab on her finger.

"She took it easily," Ulaam said. "Is she brave or stupid?"

"We haven't figured out yet," Ann said.

"I . . . gather this must be some kind of hazing," Tress said, "from the way Ann keeps grinning. So I might as well get it over with. If any of you wanted me dead, I'm as good as tossed overboard anyway."

"Ooo," Ulaam said. "I like her. I'm going to have to keep an eye on you, girl. Here, hold this."

He dropped something into her other hand.

It was a human eye.

She squealed and dropped it, though Ulaam caught it with a quick snatch. "Be careful! It's one of my favorites. Observe the deep blue coloring. It would look wonderful exchanged for your left eye—you'd be heterochromatic blue and green. Quite striking."

"I . . . No thank you?"

"Ah well," Ulaam said, putting the eye away. "Perhaps another time. Use the salve; there is no prank involved. I'm probably the least dangerous thing on this ship."

"You literally eat *people*, Ulaam," Ann said.

"Dead ones. My! How dangerous! Like the mighty worm of the earth or the bacteria of decomposition. They are my colleagues."

Hesitant, Tress touched the salve to her cheek. The pain vanished immediately. Startled by the efficacy, she rubbed it around her cheek. When Ulaam held up a hand mirror, her skin wasn't even red, and there was no sign of a wound.

"There's a reason we keep 'im around," Ann said. "Even if he's weird as a two-headed snake."

"As the only true source of modern medicine in this backwater land," he said, "I find your vivid simile inaccurate; incomplete axial bifurcation is far more likely in reptiles than other animals, so if you *wish* to call me odd, pick a two-headed bird or a mammal for full effect."

Both women stared at him, trying to parse that sentence.

"I've eaten several two-headed snakes," Ulaam noted. "And mimicked their forms. So rather than being as *odd* as one, I've literally *been* one. Alas, I couldn't divide my consciousness and think twice as quickly. Wouldn't that have been fun?" He took the salve back from Tress. "Anyway, try to avoid blowing yourself up in the future, hmmmm? It mangles the corpse and gives it a metallic taste."

If you're wondering, I have it on good authority that Ulaam was *enjoying* himself during my regrettable period of indisposition. He made no move to break my curse, and instead wrote some extremely embarrassing accounts of my actions and sent them to several good friends of ours.

Granted, the rules of the curse prevented me from giving any direct explanations of how to break it. But I really expected more from him. As it stands, after coming to find me and then discovering my . . . ailment, he'd just taken up residence on the ship. He'd always fancied becoming an explorer. "For the sense of adventure, hmmmm?" he'd said.

The crew hadn't known what to make of him at first. Captain Crow shot him a few times, an experience he reports as being "invigorating." Members of his species are virtually impossible to kill. Other than the eating corpses part, they can be handy to have around—as the crew soon discovered.

From then on, they simply dealt with him. Rather like a rash that occasionally rescues one from life-threatening wounds. He didn't ask for payment aside from the occasional otherwise-useless corpse. It's gruesome, yes, but you'll find you're able to put up with quite a bit of eccentricity in a person who can literally work miracles on your behalf.

Tress—understandably left numb by her first interaction with the ship's surgeon—was deposited on the deck near her bucket and brush. Ann went off to do some other work, so Tress—prodding at her completely healed cheek—decided to go back to scrubbing.

She hadn't made much progress before Huck came scampering up. "Something's happening."

"What?" Tress asked. "An attack?"

"No, no. See, you sent me away, so I figured I'd go sneak some food. I'd already eaten, but you never can have too much, right? I was down in the hold where—I'll have you know—there's nothing really accessible without nibbling through sacks. And people *hate* when we nibble through sacks. If they hate it so much, why not leave them untied for us? Then no sacks are harmed, you see, and—"

"What did you want to tell me, Huck?" Tress asked. "What's happening?"

"Right, I was getting to that. Laggart was down there looking through the storage. And Tress, he fetched a couple of cannonballs. I saw him sneak them into his pack."

Interesting. It was time to test her theory.

She positioned herself to scrub near the forward cannon station. Not too close, but close enough to watch. Then she became a waitress again for a short while, watching for Laggart.

It didn't take long.

THE CANNONMASTER

L aggart swooped over to the cannon and craned his long neck over
the barrel, eyeing the bundles of spores. He eventually declared the
work well done, praising the Dougs.

At that moment they discovered the wonders of outsourcing: the luxury of taking all the credit, doing none of the work, yet reserving someone
to blame just in case. Tress didn't mind. She'd rather not have Laggart
paying attention to her.

The Dougs hopped off to other duties, and Laggart made quite the
show of cleaning the cannon himself—something he never left to another's care.

Tress scrubbed the deck nearby, invisible in plain sight. Whenever Laggart turned her way, her head was inconspicuously down in her work. Yet
she watched closely, and spotted it as he stealthily took a fist-size cannonball from his pack and hid it in the false bottom of the barrel.

She had been right. He kept rigged cannonballs in the hidden compartment. Cannonballs designed to sink ships. But why? It was so much
more dangerous to be deadrunners, and it denied them loot. Wasn't that
the one essential thing that defined pirates? Other than, you know, the
boats and stuff?

He *wanted* the crew to become deadrunners. Against their wishes or
knowledge.

Laggart finished his work, shouted at a few nearby Dougs for being lazy, then hauled his pack to his shoulder. He strutted off toward the captain's cabin, where Crow let him in—and posted a sailor at the door before closing it. The heavyset Doug didn't look much like a guard, but the way he lingered reminded Tress of how Brick's cousin stood watch by the tavern door on nights when people were expected to get rowdy.

"I need to know what they're talking about in there," Tress said.

"Yeah, that would be great, wouldn't it?" Huck said from her shoulder. "I'll bet it's very secretive."

"I need someone to slip in," Tress said.

"Maybe we could ask one of the Dougs?" Huck said.

"Someone," Tress said, "who is *small, quick,* and who *won't be noticed listening.*"

"Dang," Huck said. "Don't know if the Dougs will be sneaky enough. Have you *heard* the way they tromp around on the deck? I was trying to sleep last night, and I'd swear they have lead in their shoes. It . . ." He trailed off, noticing her glaring at him. "Oooooohhhhh. Rat. Right, right. Got it."

He hopped off her shoulder and scuttled over to the gunwale, then scrambled along it in the shadows over to the captain's cabin. The Doug watching didn't notice as Huck slipped along a small ledge on the outside of the ship and went in the captain's window.

Perhaps you're wondering why Huck had so quickly fallen in with Tress. Well, there are a lot of things I could tell you here—but suffice it to say that in the short life of Huck the rat, every human he'd met had tried to kill, capture, or sell him. Every human but Tress. He didn't know a lot about people, having spent most of his life isolated—but he did like Tress. He would rather she not die. So, spying it was.

Tress began scrubbing furiously to work out her anxiety. Minutes passed with the weight of hours, as she worried about sending Huck into danger to satisfy her curiosity. That wasn't something she would normally have done. Life as a pirate was already affecting her.

Yet Charlie was out there somewhere, afraid, hurting. She had to find a way to escape, then continue her quest. So maybe learning to impose on people a little was all right.

"Hey," Huck said, scampering across the railing next to her, "you got anything to eat? Spying is hungry work."

Tress glared at him as her stomach growled.

"Just asking," Huck said. "Moons, girl, no need to look at me like I ate the center of the loaf and left you the heels."

"Did you hear anything?" she asked.

Huck twitched his nose in a way he seemed to think she would understand, then he hopped down and scurried over to a more sheltered section of the deck. She followed, her back to the Dougs. To anyone watching, she'd simply be doing her thing, scrubbing away. They wouldn't be able to see Huck.

"All right," the rat said from the deck in front of her. "I'll tell you what they said. Let me get into character."

". . . Character?" Tress said.

Huck went up on his hind legs, holding his little ratty paws before himself with his nose up in the air. "I am Captain Crow," he said in a surprisingly good approximation of her aristocratic accent. "Hip, hop, do as I say. My, this canteen water is tasty. Laggart, what news of the cannon? Is everything ready?"

Tress waited, her head cocked.

"You be Laggart," Huck hissed.

"I wasn't there! I don't know what he said."

"You'll do fine." Huck waved his paw at her. "Go ahead. Be Laggart."

"Uh . . . the cannons are . . . ready?"

"Voice needs more crust to it," Huck whispered. "And stretch out your neck like his. It will help you get in character."

"But—"

"Excellent, Laggart," Huck said in his captain voice. "But I have unfortunate news via a raven from my contact in Kingsport. The remnants of the ship we sank have been found, but there were no survivors, just a single corpse. That man we left alive appears to have rejected my bountiful generosity and done me the insult of dying from wounds we didn't realize he had."

"She said that?" Tress whispered. "Those exact words?"

"It's a dramatic recreation," Huck hissed. "What, you think I wrote it down? With these?" He waved his paws at her. "That's as close as I can remember. Now do Laggart's part."

"Um . . . that's sad?" Tress said.

"Tress, that's not what he said. He said, 'All that work for *nothing*? We'll have to sink another then!'" He waved a paw for her to continue.

Tress sighed. "All that work for nothing. We'll have to sink another then."

"Moonshadows, could you put *less* emotion into it?" Huck said. "I feel like you're not taking your role seriously."

"I don't—"

"This is a problem, Laggart," Huck said in his captain voice, falling to all fours and stalking back and forth with his nose in the air. "The crew is upset. I'm worried about some of them running off."

"But *why*?" Tress said.

"We're getting there," Huck said. "Look, why don't I just do Laggart's part too? You take a break. Memorize your lines next time, all right?"

"But—"

Huck stretched out his neck and spoke with a creepy, scratchy voice. "As well you should, Captain," he said. "Fort is brewing trouble, and maybe Salay too. We need blood binding them to this ship if we're going to do what you want."

Huck moved over to be the captain again, standing up on his hind legs with his front paws on the gunwale, as if mimicking the captain gazing out the window. "The crew will never follow us to dangerous seas unless they have no other choice. Unless they're desperate. We will sink another ship, Laggart, and leave *a couple* sailors alive this time."

Huck turned to her and settled into a more ratlike posture. "And that's it."

"Dangerous seas," Tress whispered. The Verdant Sea was one of the *safer* ones, but apparently Captain Crow wanted to leave such spores and head toward a place the crew wouldn't go unless they had no other choice.

"So, what do you think?" Huck asked. "She's got some kind of special curse for the crew, eh? Blood binding them to the ship?"

"No curse," Tress whispered, continuing to scrub so she wouldn't appear suspicious.

"But Laggart said—"

"It was a metaphor, Huck," Tress said. "Don't you see? The captain isn't certain of her crew's loyalty. She wants to sail dangerous seas, but is worried they'll desert her if she tries to make them do that. So . . ."

"So she turns them to piracy, then 'accidentally' sinks a few ships," Huck said. "Making them into deadrunners. Chased by the law, ostracized by other pirates, they'll have no choice but to follow her orders." Huck twitched his nose, which seemed to be his version of nodding in agreement. "I can see that. Yeah, you're probably right. You . . . look morose though."

"Not morose," Tress said. "Merely distracted."

"Why?"

"Because," she said, "I've just figured out a way for us to escape this ship."

20

THE HELMSWOMAN

C aptain Crow soon emerged from her cabin, leaving Laggart to strut across to the bow while she climbed up to the quarterdeck. Tress went down to refill her bucket and left Huck to forage for some more food. Returning to the upper deck gave her an excuse to reset her location, so she moved to the quarterdeck, near where the captain stood next to Salay—the helmswoman who had traded Fort those earrings earlier.

Tress didn't want to act suspicious, so she didn't execute her plan at first. She scrubbed, feeling the boat rock upon the spores. Listening to the Dougs calling to each other and the planks creaking. There's a certain *freedom* to the sounds of a ship at sea. The feeling of motion, of going somewhere. On an ocean—even a spore ocean, so long as the seethe holds up—it's hard to sit still. You're either bending the waves and wind to your will, or you're being bent to theirs. Usually it's a careful grapple between the two.

As Tress stood up to stretch, she gazed across the vibrant green sea. It was odd because the moon was in the wrong place—always before it had been almost overhead, but they'd sailed far enough that it was several degrees lower.

She couldn't help but remark upon the sea's beauty. Spores, vibrant in the sunlight, shimmered as they seethed. An endless expanse of lush death, waiting to explode with life. Like with the zephyr spores earlier, this beauty transfixed her. Our minds want dangerous things to be ugly, yet Tress found those rolling waves *inviting*. In the moment, she imagined those rippling spores upon her skin, but rather than cringing, she was curious.

Danger doesn't make a thing less beautiful—in fact, there's a magnifying influence. Like how a candle seems brightest on the darkest night. Deadly beauty is the starkest variety. And you will never find a murderess more intoxicating, more entrancing, than the sea.

"North," the captain said, holding up a compass. "North, Salay. Toward the Seven Straits."

"Into the shipping lanes?" Salay asked.

"Best place to find our next target," the captain said, tucking away her compass.

Tress sensed her opportunity. She settled down, scrubbing hard, then muttered, "You'll kill more, will you?"

She heard the captain shift behind her. Tress kept her head lowered. After a moment though, she muttered, "They were good people you killed. Poor Kaplan. And Marple. And Mallory. Fed to the spores."

The deck creaked as Captain Crow stepped over. This was a dangerous ploy, but . . . well, Tress was surrounded by pirates sailing the spore sea. She hadn't grown up knowing danger, but they were quickly becoming acquainted.

"You muttering something, girl?" Crow asked. "Ungrateful, maybe, for the kindness this here crew showed you?"

Tress froze as if frightened, and dropped her brush as she looked up. "Captain! I didn't know you . . . I mean . . ."

"Are you *ungrateful*?" Crow asked.

"I appreciate my life," Tress whispered, her eyes down.

"But?"

"But that ship carried my family, Captain. I loved them."

"You're a royal inspector. Why were you traveling with your family?"

"That?" Tress scoffed. "An inspector left this coat at a tavern we stopped by, and I started wearing it because it made my family laugh. And now . . . now they're all dead . . ."

She let it linger. Then she glanced up and saw thoughtfulness on the captain's expression. Understanding.

No, you didn't kill everyone *on the* Oot's Dream, Tress thought. *You left one alive. And if she were to escape, then tell everyone how the* Crow's Song *killed her family . . .*

The captain turned toward Salay and unscrewed her canteen. According to what Tress had overheard from the crew, it was common water, which explained why the woman wasn't drunk all the time.

"Changed my mind, Helmswoman," Crow said, then took a drink. "Take us east, toward Shimmerbay. We should restock on water."

"If you say so, Captain," Salay said. "I thought we had enough though."

"Never can have enough water," the captain said. "Can't let my canteen go dry, can we? Besides, we've got rats on board. Need to pick up a ship's cat."

Quick as that, Salay called orders to the crew in the rigging and spun the ship's wheel, and they turned toward freedom. Tress felt a surge of excitement.

Now, most people would agree that humans are not telepathic. We can't directly send our thoughts or emotions into the minds of others. Nevertheless, you can hear my story and imagine the things I describe—the same as I picture them in my own mind. What is that, if not a form of telepathy?

Beyond that, there are those among us who have the uncanny ability to read another's emotions. Not through magic, or mystical Connection, or any such figgldygrak. No, they are simply students of human nature. They can pick up on people's moods through subtle cues of body language—in the way their eyes move, the way their muscles twitch.

Some of these are doctors interested in healing the mind. Others find their way to the clergy, in search of ways to help the human soul. Then there are the ones like Captain Crow, for whom their ability to read others provides a . . . different kind of advantage.

That moment on the deck, a part of Crow's mind picked up that Tress was excited. That Tress was *happy* the ship had turned toward Shimmerbay. Crow wasn't conscious of what she knew, or how she knew it, but—like one might feel an oncoming bout of indigestion—she knew that she wasn't pleased and that Tress was the reason. If you want to ruin Captain Crow's day, point out that she made someone happy. If you want to ruin her entire week, point out that she did it by *accident*.

Crow didn't reconsider her decision to sail for the port. She wasn't the type to second-guess herself. Instead Crow just pulled her foot back and planted a solid be-booted *kick* right in Tress's stomach.

The unexpected blow left Tress groaning, tears leaking from her eyes as she curled up in a puddle of soapy water. Crow sauntered off, whistling casually and screwing closed the top on her canteen. She was, it might be noted, a perfect example of why the word *jerk* needs so many off-color synonyms. One could exhaust all available options, invent a few apt new ones, and still not be able to completely describe her. Truly an inspiration to the vulgar poet.

Salay now, she was another story. People considered the short helmswoman stern, but she'd been on the business end of a few unearned kicks herself. After barely a moment of thought, she locked the ship's wheel in place—something she wasn't supposed to do save for emergencies—and stepped over to check on Tress.

"Hey," Salay said softly, rolling Tress to her side. "Let me feel at it. If you've cracked a rib, we'll want to take you to visit the ship's surgeon."

"No!" Tress said. "He wants to cut pieces of me off!"

"Nonsense. Ulaam wouldn't hurt a dove."

". . . He wouldn't?"

"Nope. They don't have hands he can embalm." She winked at Tress, who—after a moment—managed a grin despite the pain.

Salay prodded at Tress's lower ribs and listened to Tress explain what hurt and what didn't. That persuaded both that the kick hadn't broken anything other than Tress's mood, so Salay returned to her post and unlocked the wheel.

She continued to watch Tress sitting in a morose lump on the deck. Eventually Salay called, "You ever worked a ship's wheel before?"

Tress hesitantly stood and looked over at her, questioningly. Salay stepped back and gestured to the wheel.

Now, I know that on your planet, steering a ship isn't that big a deal. In many places, they'll hand the ship's wheel to any kid with a standard number of fingers and a habit of leaving at least one out of their nose for extended stretches of time. But on the spore seas they treat it differently. Guiding the ship is a privilege, and the helmsperson is an officer tasked with a serious duty.

So even if Tress had often been on ships—as she'd been pretending—it was likely she wouldn't ever have taken the wheel. Awed, she stepped over, double-checking with Salay before fixing her hands on the wheel in the positions the helmswoman indicated.

"Good," Salay said. "Now, hold it firm. You feel those vibrations? That's the seethe shaking the rudder. You need to be careful to not let that shake the entire ship. Hold the wheel firm, and take any movements slowly and smoothly."

"And if the seethe stops?" Tress asked.

"Turn the wheel to straighten out the rudder, so the spores don't rip it free. But again, you need to be *careful*. A sudden motion from the helmswoman can send sailors tumbling from the rigging."

Tress nodded, wondering if maybe it wasn't the best idea to entrust such an important duty to *her*. Salay, however, was a little like Captain Crow—in that she was the opposite of the captain in the way that only someone very similar could be.

Salay also had an instinct for what people were feeling, and she'd noted Tress's dedication to her scrubbing. A woman who did such a simple duty with exactness . . . well, in Salay's experience that sort of thing scaled upward. Same way you would be more likely to lend your best flute to someone who treated their own battered one with respect.

Tress held firmly to the wheel, feeling the chaotic churn of the spores beneath travel up the tiller ropes, through the wood, and into her arms. She felt a deeper connection to the sea when standing there, and—if not a power over it—an ability to ride it. There was strength in being the one who steers. It was a freedom she had never before known, and had never before realized she needed. One of the great tragedies of life is knowing how many people in the world are made to soar, paint, sing, or steer— except they never get the chance to find out.

Whenever one does discover a moment of joy, beauty enters the world. Human beings, we can't create energy; we can only harness it. We can't create matter; we can only shape it. We can't even create life; we can only nurture it.

But we *can* create light. This is one of the ways. The effervescence of purpose discovered.

Then Tress saw the captain stalking across the deck, and the pain in her stomach—including some not directly caused by the kick—returned. "Won't the captain be mad if she sees me up here?"

"She might," Salay said. "She couldn't do anything about it though. Traditions as old as the seas say the helmsperson decides who steers the ship. Not even Crow would dare imply otherwise. If I wanted, I could keep the wheel from *her*."

As if to prove her point, Salay showed Tress the ship's compass and sky chart, both kept in a cabinet next to the helm. She had Tress correct the ship's course by a few degrees, taking them to the east of a group of large rocks jutting from the ocean ahead.

"It's the helmswoman's job," Salay said, her expression distant, "to protect the ship. Keep a steady hand, steer clear of danger. Out of storms, away from spore explosions. Keep them safe somehow . . ."

Tress followed Salay's gaze. She was staring down at Captain Crow.

"She is pushing the crew," Tress said, cautiously choosing her words, "to go further than they want."

"We all decided this together," Salay said. "We're responsible for our actions."

"She's more reckless than the rest of you," Tress said. "She . . ." Tress almost explained what she'd discovered about the captain and Laggart, but thought better of it. Making such an accusation didn't seem prudent. She barely knew Salay or anyone else on this crew.

"Crow is a harsh one," Salay said. "That's true. That might be what this crew needs though. Now that we're deadrunners."

Those were Salay's words, at least. The way she glared at the captain wasn't so respectful.

"I don't understand why you've all done this," Tress said softly. "Becoming . . . what you have."

"It's a fair question," Salay replied. "I guess we all have our own reasons. For me, it was either this or give up sailing. Maybe I should have done that. It's just . . . there's something about standing on a ship, holding the wheel. Something special. Moons, I sound like a lunatic talking like that. I—"

"No," Tress said. "I understand."

Salay regarded her, then nodded. "Anyway, I have someone to find out here on these seas. Sooner or later I'll sail into a port and discover my father is there. I can pay his debts and bring him home. Surely it's the next port . . ." She lifted her compass, then stared off toward the horizon.

Tress felt a sudden stab of shame, though she couldn't place the reason. Yes, she understood something in Salay's voice—that longing for someone in trouble. That determination to do something about it since no one else would. But there was no reason to feel *ashamed* of—

The wheel lurched in her hands, and the entire ship began to shake. Tress gripped tight, then—terrified she'd drop the sailors from the rigging—eased the wheel to the right, straightening the rudder. The *Crow's Song* stopped quivering, and—as Tress fought the wheel—slowly glided to a halt. The seethe had stilled.

Sweating, gasping, Tress looked to Salay. The helmswoman, ever stoic, merely nodded. "That could have been worse," she said. Then, noticing how the sudden halt had panicked Tress, she added, "Maybe go take a rest."

21

THE PIRATE

L aggart called for the afternoon watch to go for dinner while they waited out the stilling. Not wanting to draw the captain's ire any further, Tress returned to her work, scrubbing while everyone else relaxed.

As always, she spent the time thinking. I would call the gift of thoughtfulness a double-edged sword, but I've always found that metaphor lacking. The vast majority of swords have two edges, and I've not found them to be any more likely to cut their owner than the single-edged variety. It is the sharpness of the wielder, and not the sharpness of the sword, that foreshadows mishap.

Tress's mind *was* sharp as a sword, which in this moment was unfortunate. Because while she'd identified a path to freedom, she couldn't help listening in as Ann leaned against the mast nearby and spoke to Laggart.

"The one who loaded spores for your cannon?" Ann said, thumbing over her shoulder at Tress. "It wasn't the Dougs. It was her. Thought you should know."

Please don't stick up for me, Tress thought, feeling another stab of guilt. *Please don't remind me how nice you are.*

Night fell and the seethe began again, sending the ship back on course toward its port. Tress tried to scrub away her frustration, but guilt does not clean as easily as spore scum. And soon I came ambling up to her.

"Your coat is nice," I whispered to her, "but it would look better if you painted half of it orange."

"Orange?" Tress said. "That . . . sounds like it would clash."

"Clashing is good fashion, trust me. Oh, Fort says to go see him for food." I winked. "I need to go nibble on my toes for a bit. They taste like *fate*."

Tress tried to ignore the offer, but soon Huck came bouncing up to her. "Hey. You hungry? I'm hungry. We gonna go try to get some food or what?"

With a sigh, Tress let him climb onto her shoulder, then trudged down to the quartermaster's office. There, by the light of a small lantern, Fort handed her another plate of food. It didn't taste quite so offensive as last time—but perhaps that was because so many of her taste buds had committed ritual suicide following the apocalyptic breakfast.

Tress sat on a stool in front of Fort, who insisted—via his incredible writing board—that he wasn't doing her a favor, and this was merely a trade. Tress saw through it. She saw it in the way he refilled her cup (the same bronze one she had used earlier) when it got low, and how he had saved her a bit of cake for dessert. It was awful, old and crusty like the rest, but the thought meant something.

Moons, it *hurt*. Not the food; her own betrayal. She'd known these people only a day, but she still smiled when Ulaam sauntered in and haggled for the gull bones from dinner, which Fort had saved for him. It was not the haggling itself that she smiled at, but the fond way the two sported during it. This ship was a *family*. A doomed family led by a mother who didn't care for them.

Tress had to do something.

"Fort," she said, looking down at her plate and pushing around the last bit of what she *hoped* was gull meat. "I don't think Captain Crow has the crew's best interests at heart."

Fort froze, holding a cup he'd been polishing. A nice pewter mug, with delightful nicks along the rim from repeated use. Tress didn't know if it was from the seventh-century Horgswallow tradition or simply a close copy, but it was an excellent specimen.

"I . . . I listened in on her," Tress said. "When she and Laggart—"

That's enough, Fort wrote. **Anything more will get you tossed overboard, Tress. No speaking mutiny.**

"But Fort," she said, lowering her voice, "you were worried about the cannonballs, and I discovered—"

He slapped the counter to cut her off. Then he very deliberately wrote in large letters, **NO MORE.**

Moonshadows . . . he looked terrified, broken fingers trembling as he tapped on his board.

Captain visited, asked why I was being so nosy. Shouldn't have said anything. Don't you say anything. It's too dangerous. SHE'S too dangerous.

He erased those words quickly, glancing toward the door, sweating as he shook the board and made certain nothing incriminating remained.

Finish your food, Fort wrote.

"Why are you all so scared of her?" Tress said. "She's just one person."

Fort's eyes widened. **You don't know,** he wrote. **Of course you don't. And I won't say; not my place. But she could kill every one of us, Tress. Easy as that. So keep your tongue and LET IT DROP.** He punctuated that by putting the board down and turning away from her.

So much for warning the crew about the captain's plans. She forced herself to eat her last bite of the meal, then slipped out of the quartermaster's office. She lethargically walked back onto the upper deck, her belly full, her feet feeling like they were chained.

"Moons," Huck whispered from her shoulder. "We need to get away from here before the place turns nasty. How are we going to escape? You never told me."

In response, Tress raised a finger and pointed. The Verdant Moon dumped spores far in the distance, but was close enough to illuminate the deck with a green glow. Ahead of the ship, lights dappled a large shadow. Land, and the port city of Shimmerbay. Freedom.

"I could sneak away no problem," Huck said. "But they'll be watching you. Captain will set guards, Tress. They won't let you go."

"Ah, but they will," she said, sick.

The captain ordered the crew to quarters for the night, saying they were making a quick stop and anyone who tried to sneak off would be flogged. Then she set Laggart on watch. But Tress slept on the deck as she had the night before—and with no sailing to be done, there was no one to trip over her.

Around midnight, Laggart wandered off to use the privy. He made certain to clomp loudly on the steps, to wake Tress—who wasn't asleep, though she appreciated the gesture. She stood up, quietly gathered up her sack of cups, then crossed the empty deck.

"Huh," Huck said. "If they didn't want anyone getting off . . . why did they run a gangplank down to the dock?"

"Because," Tress whispered, standing there, "Crow wants me to spread the story of the *Oot's Dream* sinking. Remember, the captain *wants* this crew to be deadrunners. If I am allowed to slip away, she presumes I'll tell everyone.

"Then the crew will be trapped beneath the captain's will. They're too afraid of her to mutiny, and as long as they're too frightened of the law to escape, they'll have to do what she says. Sail dangerous spores, essentially as her slaves."

"Poor lunatics," Huck said. "Well, let's get away before we end up like them."

Tress hesitated at the top of the gangplank. Shimmerbay was a good distance from Kingsport, but she could make her way there. Continue her plan of figuring out what the Sorceress wanted for Charlie, then find a way to free him.

"Tress," Huck said, "I can't help noticing that you aren't *moving*."

"I should stay," she whispered. "And help the crew."

"What?" Huck exclaimed. "No, you shouldn't."

"They've been so kind to me."

"You barely even met them! You don't owe them anything."

"I saved you when I'd barely met you," Tress said. "I didn't owe you anything."

"Well, I mean . . ." The rat rubbed his paws. "Yeah, but . . . well . . . Huh."

She didn't know if she could rescue Charlie. She wanted to so badly, but his pain—though poignant to her—wasn't something she could immediately prevent.

The people of this crew were different.

"Maybe if I can help the crew," Tress said, "they'll take me to the Midnight Sea to get Charlie."

"They're pirates."

"They're a family," Tress said. A plan started to form. A way she could stop Crow in secret. "And I . . . Huck, I need to do what I can. For them."

Decision made, a weight came off her. She wasn't abandoning Charlie. But this *was* something she needed to do.

"Oh boy," Huck said as Tress turned around and walked back to her sleeping spot.

"You should run," Tress said to him. "Get away. I won't blame you, Huck. It's the smart thing to do."

He clicked his teeth together, and she thought maybe that was a ratty version of a shrug. "I have a good feeling about you," he said. "But, I mean, are you *sure* about this?"

Of course I'm not, Tress thought. *I haven't been sure of anything since I left the Rock.*

Something flared in the night. A match. Tress felt a spike of alarm as she saw the light illuminate a figure sitting on the steps up to the quarterdeck. Captain Crow, her face outlined in orange as she lit her pipe.

Had she seen? Had she *heard* Tress talking to Huck? The captain puffed on her pipe and waved out the match, plunging her face into darkness—backlit by the bright, moon-filled sky.

"Captain?" Tress asked.

"You should run, girl," Crow said. "You've proven yourself these last two days, and I judge you worthy of life. So go ahead. Slip away into the night."

"I . . ." Tress took a deep breath. "I want to join your crew."

"Join us?" Crow laughed. "Just earlier today you were cursing us for having killed your family."

"I lied, Captain. I wanted to make you feel sorry for me, so you'd take pity and feed me. I know you saw through that. Your kick proved it. I shouldn't have lied."

"Then that wasn't your family on the ship?"

"I was a stowaway," Tress said. "Didn't belong there any more than I belong in Shimmerbay. I think I might belong here."

Crow didn't reply at first. She unscrewed the top of her canteen, a rattling sound in the night. Tress thought she could track the captain's thoughts. If Tress *hadn't* lost anyone, if she *wasn't* angry at the crew . . .

Captain Crow stood up, a shadow in the night. "Run along anyway. No place for you here. We don't need you scrubbing the deck all day, underfoot. I save that job for punishment, and with you doing it, you've taken away one of my tools for ship discipline. Everyone on this ship must have a place, and you have none. Unless you'd like to take the role of our anchor."

Crow turned toward her cabin, smoke drifting up from her pipe. Tress nearly ran off as she'd been told. And yet . . .

A piece of her hated being bullied. Hated it enough to overcome her reluctance to impose. She'd hated how the duke bullied Charlie. She'd hated how the inspectors bullied the dockworkers. And she hated it more here, facing down a woman who thought she could do whatever she wanted, to whomever she wanted.

"You don't have a ship's sprouter," Tress said.

Captain Crow froze at the door to her cabin.

"He's dead," Tress continued. "You need someone for the job, but the Dougs won't do it. Otherwise you'd have pressed one of them into it by now. They made *me* fill the zephyr pouches. They're frightened of spores."

"And you aren't?" Crow asked from the darkness.

"Of course I am," Tress said. "But I figure a healthy respect for them helps a sprouter stay alive."

Silence. Crow was a shadow in the night, watching her, judging her, smoke puffing up into the emerald sky.

"Aye," Crow said. "You're right on that. Suppose maybe there *is* a place for you here. You did cross the spores on foot. Took a zephyr explosion to the face. Still willing to work with spores, eh? Yes indeed . . . I could make use of you. In fact, I might have the *perfect* place for you."

Tress frowned to herself. Were they participating in the same conversation?

"Welcome to the *Crow's Song* then, ship's sprouter," the captain said, pushing into her cabin. "You'll forfeit your share of loot from our first three plunders, but can take an officer's portion after that. Also, you can't eat with the others. Go to Fort for leftovers. Sprouters are a strange lot, and I don't want you getting spores into the food."

"I . . . Yes, Captain."

"And don't lie to me again. Or we'll be finding out what happens to a human when they swallow a pouch of zephyr spores. Dr. Ulaam has always wondered." Crow raised her canteen to her lips as she shut her cabin door.

Knees soft as lard, Tress flopped down on the deck, then pulled her red inspector's coat tight. She was terrified by what she'd done, but determined. She knew it was right; she *felt* it.

For better or worse, Tress was a pirate now.

PART
4

22

THE IDIOT

The next day, Captain Crow woke Tress with a shout. That should have been Tress's first clue that something was odd, as it didn't involve kicking. Crow passed up opportunities to cause physical pain about as often as banks provide free samples. Instead Crow led Tress through the middle deck to a room with a very large padlock on the door. The type you use to make a statement.

"You really aren't afraid of spores, girl?" Crow said as she counted over the keys on her keyring.

"I said that I am afraid, Captain. It's just that lately, everything and everyone seems inclined to try to kill me. So I guess spores are simply one more, no more notable than the others."

"No more notable?" Crow said, selecting the correct key. "Well, that's an encouraging attitude. Encouraging indeed, my red-coated sprouter."

The click of the key in the lock had an ominous tone. The sound of a trap being sprung. Crow removed the key from her ring and handed it to Tress. "This will be yours now, girl."

Tress took it, but had not missed that the ring held a second key identical to this one. Crow pushed through the door, and Tress glanced down the hall to where several Dougs were watching and whispering to one another. When the door opened, they stepped backward.

Bracing herself, Tress followed Crow into the room. It did not seem so fearsome as to warrant such a reaction from the Dougs. The small chamber, longer than it was wide, had a single porthole at the end looking out at the sea. Spores churned up from the ship's passing, occasionally rising to cover the window, briefly plunging the room into darkness.

It had a bunk on one end that was pure *luxury* to Tress, with a *blanket*, a *mattress*, and a *pillow*. Sure, the mattress looked lumpy, the pillow was small, and the blanket likely hadn't been washed since the invention of vowels. But when you've been sleeping on the deck, you learn to grade on a curve.

Along the wall opposite the bunk was a small worktable. Above it, a set of drawers was built into the wall. The only other item of note was the large mirror hanging above the table, giving the room an open feeling—and revealing to Tress *exactly* how much of a mess her hair was. It evoked the impression of an eldritch horror escaping from its long slumber to stretch tentacles in all directions, disintegrating reality, seeking the lives of virgins, and demanding a sacrifice of a hundred bottles of expensive conditioner.

Crow stepped over to a door nestled in the corner, near the head of the bunk. She pulled that open and gestured inside, revealing a stall—barely tall enough to stand up in, with a floor that lowered two feet down into a basin. With a drain? And a spigot high on the wall?

A *bath*? If the bunk was luxury, the idea of a bath was *paradise*.

"We keep that spigot hooked to a barrel filled with water," Crow said. "Let us know when you want it refilled. Weev always needed a lot of it for his experiments."

". . . Experiments?"

"With spores," Crow said, sighing. "You'll have to keep up, girl, if you're going to train as our sprouter. *Any* time you work with spores, do it in this chamber unless you get *specific* permission from me. I'd even prefer you fill the zephyr spore charges for the cannons in here."

"I understand," Tress said.

"Be sure you do," Crow said. "Your entire chamber is reinforced with aluminum, but there's a silver lining beyond in case something breaks through. Despite all those protections, you could rip my ship apart if you're careless."

Tress nodded.

"You have no idea, do you?" Crow said. "What you're doing? What will be expected of you? You have *no clue* how dangerous your job will be. Do you really want to go through with this?"

"Do I get to sleep in that bed?"

"Yes."

"Then I'm in."

Crow smiled. It would have been *less* unnatural to see those shining teeth and curling lips on an actual crow. "I'll send Ulaam to brief you. But before you grow too fond of your new accommodations, be sure to have a look at the floor."

The captain sauntered off, taking a swig from her canteen. Tress sat on the mattress, trying to discern what the captain had meant by that last comment. The floor looked normal. Wooden planks, though a little dusty, since it didn't appear that anyone had cleaned the room since Weev's death.

As she considered it, that troubled her. Why hadn't anyone claimed this room? A bed, a mirror, and *running water*? The moment Weev died, the sailors should have been fighting for a chance to . . .

Then it struck her. There was no silver in the floor.

She would have seen it sooner, if she'd been more experienced with ship life. Except for one little section near the cannon, all decks—save the hold—of the *Crow's Song* were inset with silver. This was a fine, expensive merchant vessel (they could even afford some aluminum, which wasn't as costly at this point as it had once been, but still pricey), and it was built to keep its occupants comfortable and—most importantly—safe.

Except in here. Where the sprouter needed to work with spores. Tress glanced at the porthole, and the verdant spores rolling past. Each time the ship surged in the sea and the room plunged into darkness, her heart sped up a little.

Moons. No wonder no one else had wanted the room. You'd have to be insane to sleep in here.

Huck found her snoring softly a short time later. One shouldn't blame her. Sleeping on the deck hadn't really involved much sleeping.

"Tress?" Huck whispered. "What's this? Your own room?"

She sat up groggily. "Yup. It's a deathtrap, but a comfortable one. Where have you been?"

"They got a cat, Tress," Huck grumbled, eyeing the door. "An actual *cat*. This is an insult of the gravest kind. As in the kind that leads to my grave . . ."

"Stick close to me," Tress said. "I'll try to keep you away from it."

Huck shivered visibly. "I *hate* cats," he whispered. "Plus, how stupid do you have to be to get a cat because of *one rat*? Like, what is going to eat more of your food? Me, or the thing ten times my weight? Idiot humans. Er. Other humans. Not named Tress."

"I'm my own brand of idiot, Huck," she said. "Considering I'm still on this ship."

With a sigh, she heaved herself off the bed and went above to fetch her sack of cups. She returned to the room, where she began arranging the cups on her worktable, thinking of the stories Charlie had told her when she'd shown him each one.

She felt like a traitor. Staying and helping people she barely knew? Instead of hunting for a way to save him? She whispered prayers to the moons as she arranged the cups, and promised herself that she *would* find a way. If she could help this crew, and they weren't willing to take her to the Midnight Sea in return, maybe they could still help her in some other way? Like gathering money for the ransom?

That made her feel sick. She didn't want to rob people to save Charlie. In that moment, holding the cup with the butterfly, she acknowledged something. She could never pay a ransom—and she wouldn't resort to piracy to do it. She'd have to find some other way to save Charlie.

But how? What could she do?

As she was contemplating this, fighting to keep her tears in check, a peppy voice spoke from the doorway.

"Need a hand? Hmmmmm?"

"You didn't *literally* bring me a hand, did you, Ulaam?" Tress asked.

Ulaam furtively tucked one arm behind his back. "Would I be so crass, Miss Tress?"

". . . Yes? It's why I asked?"

The ashen-skinned man (person? thing?) grinned and stepped

into the room. Behind him, I peeked in—but as Tress didn't have any marmosets, I wasn't interested at the moment.

"You know about all of this, Doctor?" Tress said, waving to the small room with the basin and the spigot. "The captain said it was for experiments."

"Yes, Weev loved the experiment of 'How can I con everyone else into letting me take warm baths?' They keep the water barrel out in the sun; while I doubt your washing will be *toasty*, you also won't be freezing any bits off." He glanced at her. "If you do, be sure to save them for me, hmmmm?"

"So it *is* a bath," Tress said.

"Well, Weev *did* need a room where he could manipulate spores— and sometimes activate them—without posing too much danger to the crew. That required a ceramic basin that would hold water. He merely extrapolated. He was a cunning fellow. Except that part at the end." Ulaam shook his head. "What a waste of a corpse."

"Captain says I'll need to take on some of Weev's duties if I'm going to stay on the ship. Was there more than the work with the zephyr spores?"

"You'll want to practice with roseite, for sealing breaches in emergencies," Ulaam said. "And in growing verdant without breaking anything, as the vines can be emergency food. Yes, they *are* edible. I suppose anything is, if you're optimistic enough!"

"I'm optimistic!" I said, looking in again. "I once ate an entire rock. Had to fight off its family first though." I growled and wandered away.

Tress mostly missed what I said, focused as she was on my ailments. "Do you know what his . . . issue is, Doctor?" she asked.

"Hoid has too many issues to count," Ulaam said, poking through the drawers above her table. "I wouldn't trouble yourself with his situation. He's nearly as deft at untying knots as he is at creating them."

She nodded and eyed her bunk. When Ulaam left, could she take another nap? Or would she be reprimanded for loafing?

"Yes . . ." Ulaam said absently, "Hoid should have known better than to tangle with the Sorceress. In fact, he probably *did* know better. Frightening, how infrequently he lets that influence what he actually decides to *do*."

Tress felt a start that drove away thoughts of sleep. "The *Sorceress*?"

"Hmmmm? Yes, what did you *think* happened to him? He puts on a brave front, pretending to be just an ordinary idiot, but I assure you that he's instead the *extraordinary* kind. Remarkable really. I always say, when trouble troubles you, keep a stiff's upper lip! Or several."

"There's someone on this ship," Tress said, choosing her words carefully, "who *knows the way* to the Sorceress? Who has been there before, and escaped alive?"

"Technically, yes," Ulaam said. "But I haven't the faintest idea how Hoid did it—I found him like this after I arrived on the planet in response to his letter."

"On the . . . planet?" she asked. "Like, you're from the stars?" She'd heard stories of visitors from the stars, but had thought them fancies. Even if there did seem to be more and more of them these days, talked of among sailors.

"Hmm?" Ulaam said. "Oh, yes. Not from a star really, but a planet that orbits one. Regardless, I doubt you'll be able to get anything useful out of Hoid with that curse in place."

She put thoughts of such distant locations—and the cups they must have—out of her mind for now. There . . . there was someone here who could help her find Charlie! Hoid could be her solution! She felt an enormous sense of relief, then a sudden strike of panic. If she had left the ship, she would never have known.

She sat down with a dazed expression, realizing that I was in fact the key she needed. She formed a real plan at last; one she could maybe accomplish. Find out from me how to reach the Sorceress, and perhaps learn how to deal with her.

Still a daunting prospect. But it was better than what she'd had before. And as she sat there, she considered that perhaps this crew—and the kindly people on it, trapped in their own kind of prison—were *exactly* what she needed in order to save Charlie.

23

THE ASSISTANT CANNONMASTER

There are twelve seas," Ann explained as she sat on the railing of the ship, knocking her heels rhythmically on the wood. "And therefore, twelve kinds of spores. How could you not know that?"

"I lived all my life in a little mining town," Tress explained. "Yes, we always talked about there being twelve seas and twelve moons. But I've learned so much in the last few days, I figured I should confirm things like that."

She's right to ask, Ann, Fort said, holding up his sign. **There are, after all, thirteen kinds of spores.**

"No there ain't," Ann said. "Don't you be spreading that lie."

It's not a lie, he wrote. **It's a legend. Different thing entirely.**

"Nonsense is the proper term," Ann said. "People can't even make up their minds on what color 'bone spores' are supposed to be. White or black? Or both? Listen, Tress. There are *twelve* kinds of spores."

Tress nodded. They were at the prow of the ship, on the upper deck, near the forward cannon. Tress hadn't been surprised to find Ann here—the lanky carpenter often hung around the cannon, shooting it glances like a teenager with a crush. However, Tress *had* been surprised to see Fort sitting on deck this morning, darning socks. A part of her had believed him a permanent fixture of his office.

For her part, Tress was carefully counting the pouches of zephyr spores in the gunnery barrel. She'd asked Laggart, and he'd said they should maintain forty on hand. She figured that counting them gave her a good excuse to move them out of the barrel into an aluminum box, where they'd be safe from the ship's silver.

"Twelve seas," Tress said. "How many have you seen, Ann?"

"Three," she said proudly. "The Emerald Sea, the Sapphire Sea, and the Rose Sea."

Impressive, Fort wrote.

"I know, isn't it?"

I've been to ten.

"What?" Ann sat up straight. "Liar."

Why would I lie?

"You're *literally* a pirate," Ann said. "Everyone knows you can't trust those types."

Fort rolled his eyes expressively, then turned back to his work on his socks. Tress hesitated, looking at her box of pouches. Had that been the twenty-second or twenty-third she'd just counted? With a soft groan, she piled them all back into the barrel and started again.

"Which two?" Ann asked, tapping Fort to make him look up. "Which ones haven't you been to?"

Not hard to guess, Fort wrote.

"Midnight and Crimson Seas?"

He nodded.

"The Midnight Sea," Tress said as she counted. "That's where the Sorceress lives."

"Yeah," Ann said. "And the Crimson Sea is the domain of the dragon. But that's not why people don't sail them. It's the spores, Tress. You need to know this stuff, if you're gonna sprout. Most types of spores are deadly, but two are downright catastrophic. Stay away from crimson spores and midnight spores, all right?"

"All right," Tress said. "You have to go through the Crimson though to get to the Midnight, right? So I'm unlikely to ever do that." She frowned. "Why do you have to go through one to get to the other? Can't you just sail around the Crimson to get to the Midnight?"

"Not unless you can sail through several mountain ranges," Ann said.

"I suppose you could sail all around the world, then come upon the Midnight from behind."

It's one of the reasons the Sorceress set up there, Fort explained. She controls trade through the region—the passage that connects the planet. Only her ships can sail the Midnight.

"Been years," Ann noted, "since there was any trade though. The king doesn't want to pay tariffs, and so it's war instead."

As if he thinks he can beat her, Fort said, shaking his head. He can't even get a proper fleet through the Crimson. Too dangerous.

Tress nodded. These seemed like things she probably should have known already. She was playing catch-up, but for a second time she was glad she hadn't left these people. She realized that only one member of the crew likely had experience with the Sorceress personally—but all of them had information that could help her.

"There are twenty-five pouches here," she said, finishing. "So I need to make fifteen more."

"Without blowing off your face this time," Ann said.

"I didn't blow it off."

"Technically, I'm sure *some* pieces of it were removed," Ann said. "Too bad you got that salve. You'd look badass with a scar or two on your face."

Tress gave a noncommittal shrug to that. Then, as Ann returned to pestering Fort, Tress quietly undid the latch that opened the false bottom of the barrel and counted. Five hidden cannonballs, each a little larger than her fist.

With Huck acting as lookout, she'd retrieved some ordinary ones from the ship's hold. No one guarded them. Who would steal them? But now, trying to keep herself from sweating at the subterfuge, she began slipping them from her sack and swapping them for the ones in the barrel's false bottom.

She was certain she'd be noticed at any moment. But people rarely watch you as much as you think; they're too busy worrying whether you are watching *them*. So Tress was able to, one at a time, replace Laggart's secret cannonballs with ordinary ones. Then she latched the hidden bottom and replaced the twenty-five zephyr spore pouches.

The swap performed, she pointedly dried her hands and did *not* poke at her mask. Anyone can blow their face off by accident—I mean, who hasn't—but if you do it twice in a row, you look really silly.

Tress cinched closed her sack. She still didn't know what she'd do with those sabotaged cannonballs. Hide them in her cabin? Drop them off the boat in secret?

"Hey Tress," Ann said. "When you're making charges, you think you could maybe whip me up a few extra? So I can practice?"

"Don't see why not," Tress said. "Assuming the captain says it's all right."

"Yeah," Ann said. "Of course." Though there was something in her tone, reminiscent of how you might talk about that project you've been planning to finish "tomorrow." She wandered off, but only after trailing her fingers along the length of the cannon.

Fort had been focused on his work, and had therefore missed the conversation. While his condition leads to plenty of difficulties, I will say I've always envied his ability to—by looking away—completely excise from his life most of the stupid things people say.

Tress settled down on the deck in front of him, catching his attention. "What's up with Ann and the cannons?" Tress asked. "I thought she was the ship's assistant cannonmaster."

Suppose she still is, Fort wrote. **Didn't ever officially get removed from the post. She won't be firing guns anytime soon though.**

Tress's breath caught. "What did she do?" she whispered, leaning in.

Are you whispering? Fort wrote back.

"Um . . . yes."

That's cute.

"Ann. Are you going to tell me about her or not?"

What will you trade me for the information?

"Do we *have* to negotiate every time, Fort?" Tress asked. "Can't we just chat like friends?"

But the negotiation is the fun part! he wrote. **It's what tells me about you. What you're willing to give up, what you value. Come on. Doesn't it excite you to try to find the best deal?**

"I . . . don't really know."

What will you tell me to get me to talk about Ann? Information

for information. You're distracting me from repairing these socks, you know. I can't sew and watch the board at the same time. So you owe me.

"But I don't know anything interesting to trade."

Oh? And why are you here? What possessed a nice girl from a small town to steal an inspector's coat and go out pretending to be a pirate?

She leaned in, speaking softly despite what he'd said before. "My ignorance is *that* obvious?"

Girl, if you'd been sailing the spore sea for longer than a week before we found you, I'll eat my own cooking. So why are you out here?

"I'm looking for someone," she said. "Someone dear to me."

Ah, Fort wrote. So you're searching the seas, like Salay. Hoping that at each new port, you'll at last find the sock that . . . He deleted that part. Sorry. Board isn't always good at predicting. You're hoping to find that PERSON you've lost.

Tress glanced across the ship toward the helmswoman, who stood as sturdy as the masts, fixed in her place on the quarterdeck, both hands gripping the ship's wheel. As usual, her dark eyes were fixated on the horizon with the kind of intense expression people reserved for only the most important of tasks, like finding the last piece of unopened candy in a bag full of wrappers.

She hunted relentlessly for her father. In the face of Salay's confident determination, Tress's own quest seemed laughable.

"It's . . . not really the same," Tress told Fort. "Salay has no idea where she'll find her father. I know exactly where Charlie is."

Fort nudged her a moment later. Oh? he'd written. Just need to save up some money to get to him, then?

"It's worse than that, I'm afraid," she said. "The Sorceress has him. Attacked his ship. Took him captive."

Fort's shoulders slumped. Oh, he wrote. I'm sorry.

"Yeah. I barely have any idea what I'm doing, Fort. But I have to reach him." She grimaced. "I said I'll likely never reach the Midnight. That was kind of a lie. I'm determined to get there. Somehow."

If the Sorceress attacked his ship, he's dead. I'm sorry. You should probably move on.

"He's alive," Tress said. "She asked for a ransom from the king to free Charlie. I thought . . . maybe I could make enough money to convince the king to pay it."

Tress, Fort wrote, **the Sorceress doesn't ask for money as ransom. She asks for souls, usually from the royal bloodline. Mere money would never satisfy her.**

Tress blushed, feeling like an utter lunatic. She'd already realized that she wouldn't be able to pay his way free, but still, the depth of her ignorance was disturbing. Like a fish trying very hard to jump out of its tank in order to escape, she'd been trying to solve a problem before stopping to wonder if she even understood her situation.

Look, if this Charlie was kept for ransom, he's likely a nobleman. Right?

"Yes," Tress whispered.

That lot don't care about people like us, Fort wrote. **I'm sorry, but it's the truth. You'd best move on.**

"Maybe," Tress said.

Well, you gave me information. Only fair that I give you what you wanted. I can tell you about Ann.

"I didn't tell you anything important, Fort," Tress said. "You don't have to take that in trade."

Ah, he wrote. **But the information about Ann is barely worth anything. Everyone knows it. You'd have found out soon anyway.**

"You acted like it was some big secret!" Tress said.

No. I just asked what you wanted to trade. He grinned, poking her in the arm with a knuckle, then continued writing. **Don't look indignant. Revealing your emotions makes it easier for people to get a good deal out of you. That one is free.**

Ann was given the job of assistant cannonmaster because she asked for it after the last one died. But no one thought to have her fire one of the blasted things first.

"And . . . ?" Tress asked.

That woman has worse aim than a drunk man riding a three-legged llama, Fort wrote. **She once fired a pistol at a target, but managed to nearly hit ME—and I was standing next to her. The first time**

she manned the cannon, her aim was so far off, the only thing NOT in danger was her target.

"Moons," Tress said. "Maybe . . . she just needs more practice."

I'll let you teach her, then. I'll be safely boarded up in my room, maybe with some armor on. Fort eyed her. Some things aren't meant to be, girl. Sometimes you simply have to accept that.

"You're talking about me. And Charlie."

Maybe. Listen, Tress. Even if he's still alive, the Sorceress will have cursed him like poor old Hoid. She uses a lot of different types, but she always puts one on her captives, to keep them pliable.

"How do you know so much about it?" Tress asked.

Captain told me, Fort explained. When she had me trade to get Hoid on our ship.

"The captain *specifically* wanted Hoid on the ship?" Tress asked. "Why?"

Don't know. She heard about his curse and his trip to the Sorceress. Getting him was a poor deal, since his former shipmates were happy to be rid of him. Captain insisted though.

Fort shook his head, considering the damage to his reputation once people found out how much he'd traded to get a lunatic to be their cabin boy.

Tress's interest deepened, however. Captain Crow had manipulated the crew into becoming pirates, then forced them to become deadrunners—because she wanted them to sail dangerous seas. And she'd specifically been watching for someone cursed by the Sorceress?

Could the captain be looking to visit the Sorceress herself?

Tress looked toward Crow. And then, Tress took the singular step that separated her from people in most stories. The act, it might be said, that *defined* her as a hero. She did something so incredible, I can barely express its majesty.

I should consider this more, Tress thought to herself, *and not jump to conclusions.*

THE CURSED MAN

Perhaps you are confused at why I, your humble storyteller, would make such a fuss about this. Tress stopped, wondered if she'd jumped to a conclusion, and decided to reconsider? Nothing special, right? Wrong. So very, soul-crushingly wrong.

Worldbringers like myself spend decades combing through folk tales, legends, myths, histories, and drunken bar songs looking for the most unique stories. We hunt for bravery, cleverness, heroism. And we find no shortage of such virtues. Legends are silly with them.

But the person who is willing to reconsider their assumptions? The hero who can sit down and reevaluate their life? Well, now *that* is a gemstone that truly glitters, friend.

Perhaps you would prefer a story about someone facing a dragon. Well, *this* isn't *that* kind of story. (Which makes it even more remarkable that Tress still does that eventually. But kindly stop getting ahead of me.) I can understand why you would want tales of people like Linji, who tried to sail around the world with no Aviar.

I, however, would trade a dozen Linjis for one person who is willing to sit down for a single blasted minute and think about what they're doing. Do you know how many wars could have been prevented if just one person in charge had stopped to think, "You know, maybe we should double-check; perhaps blinking twice *isn't* an insult in their culture"?

Do you know how many grand romances would have avoided tragedy if the hero had thought, "You know, maybe I should ask her if she likes me first"?

Do you know how many protracted adventures might have been shortened if the heroine had stopped to wonder, "You know, maybe I should look extra carefully to see if the thing I'm searching for has been with me the entire time"?

I'm drowning in bravery, cleverness, and heroism. Instead, kindly give me a little common sense. At that moment, Tress was downright majestic.

I need more information, Tress thought. *Before I decide that I know what the captain's plan is. I need to find a way to spy on her. Maybe I can use Huck again.*

She nodded—and in that moment, Tress saved herself a huge amount of trouble. The captain's plan had *nothing* to do with the Sorceress, after all, but *everything* to do with why the crew were so frightened of her.

Tress picked up her sack—pretending it wasn't full of cannonballs, which was as hard as it sounded—and carried it to the aft cannon, which was set up on the quarterdeck. She performed a similar swap there (placing the cannonballs she took in a separate bag within her larger one) while counting zephyr spore charges.

Then she hauled her bag belowdecks, where she stowed it in her room. From there she went looking for me. Now, normally this would also have been a shining example of common sense on her part. Everyone can use a little more Wit in their lives. Except me. I could stand to lose a pound or two.

Unfortunately, I wasn't exactly in the best state of mind during this voyage. She found me playing cards with a group of the Dougs. I was wearing a shoe around my neck, tied by the laces, as I'd decided it was certain to be the absolute *soul* of fashion the following season. I'd forgotten to wear pants, as one does, and my underclothing needed a good washing. Actually, all of me did.

I was trying to play a game I'd invented called "Kings" where everyone held their cards backward, so you didn't know what you had but everyone else did. I can imagine several interesting applications of this now—but back then the only interesting part was how easily the Dougs won my wages off me, followed by my shoe.

I still have no idea what I did with the other one.

Once the Dougs were finished taking me for what little I was worth, they scrambled off to find some other victim. I sat there, wondering if perhaps I should start wearing a sock around my neck, until Tress settled down beside me.

"Would you like to play Kings?" I asked with a grin. "I still have some undershorts I can bet!"

"Um, no thanks," Tress said. "Hoid, I know you visited the Sorceress. Do you . . . remember anything about it?"

"Yup!" I said.

"Great! What can you tell me?"

"C . . . c . . . c . . . can't!" I said, tapping my head. "Words don't work that way, kiddo. She makes them into something else!"

"I don't understand," Tress said.

"Neither do I!" I replied. "That's the problem! Can't say anything at all about what you might think! It's p . . . p . . . p . . ." I shrugged, unable to form the word.

"Your . . . curse forbids you from talking about your curse?" Tress guessed.

I winked. Mostly because I had something in my eye. But in this case, Tress had guessed correctly. The Sorceress was quite specific with each geas: if you tried to talk about it, you'd stutter or the words would die halfway out of your lips. You couldn't even tell people you were cursed unless they already knew.

"So," Tress said, "if I want you to lead me to the Sorceress, I have to find a way to break your curse—without knowing anything about it. Plus, I have to do that without any help from you whatsoever."

I took her hands in mine. I looked her in the eyes. I took a deep breath, trembling.

"I once ate an entire watermelon in one sitting," I told her. "And it gave me diarrhea."

Tress sighed, pulling her hands free. "Right, right. I guess finding a way to break your curse is *slightly* less impossible than finding my way to the Sorceress on my own. That's something, at least."

There *was* still a part of me—deep down—that knew what was going on. The Sorceress was cruel like that. Sure, turning a man into a simpleton is fun—but *true* torture lies in letting him remain just aware enough to be horrified.

That sensate part of me scrambled to find some way to help. Ulaam had been useless, of course. That's the problem with immortals—they get used to sitting around waiting for problems to work themselves out.

But here was someone willing to help. What could I say? What could I do? Only a sliver of me was still awake, and it had almost no control. Plus, every time I tried to say anything about my specific predicament, the curse would activate, driving me back and prompting me to do something monstrous, like wear socks with sandals.

That glimmer of awareness started to fade. And I seized upon that. My own stupidity. The curse, like many magics of its ilk, depended on how the subject thought—on their Intent. I could use that, I knew.

The spark flared up, like a midnight fire as the coals shifted. I reached toward Tress and blanked my mind as I forced out a string of words.

"Listen, this is important," I said to her. "I promise. You must bring me to your planet, Tress. Repeat that."

"Bring you . . . to my planet?"

"Yes, yes! I can save you if you do that."

"But you're already here!"

"Here what?" I said, having deliberately forgotten what I'd said. "Planets don't matter. For now, look for the group of six stars, Tress!"

Tress hesitated. Six stars? Unfortunately, in that exclamation, my strength was spent. I sat back, adopted a goofy grin, and decided to do some empirical research regarding the flavors of different toes.

With a sigh, Tress returned to her quarters. She'd left the door open for Huck, and so wasn't surprised when she arrived and found . . .

Whimpering?

She burst into the room to find the ship's cat—Knocks—crouched and staring under the bed, tail waggling. Tress threw the thing out the door and slammed it, and in the silence that followed she could distinctly make out the sounds of a hyperventilating rat.

"Huck?" she asked, getting down on her hands and knees, peering beneath the bed. She made him out in the corner, squeezed into the space between the wood of the bed's leg and the wall. As he saw her, he came timidly toward her, and she scooped him up, feeling him tremble in her hands.

"It's gone," she said. "I'm sorry, Huck."

He didn't speak—a rare occasion where he seemed completely without breath or words. He just cringed there in her hands, looking more . . . well, like a rat than he ever had before.

Finally he spoke, his voice trembling. "Perhaps you can leave the door locked from now on. There's a crack in the floor, and I can squeeze in that way, after climbing the post in the hallway below."

"All right," Tress said. "Are you . . . going to be okay?"

Huck glanced at the door. "Yeah, sure," he whispered. "Give me a little time. I . . . still can't believe they got a cat."

"You're intelligent, Huck," Tress said. "You can handle a common cat."

"Sure. Yeah. No problem. But Tress . . . I don't know. It's always watching. Prowling. Cats are supposed to sleep twenty-six hours a day. How can I use my intelligence, how can I plan, knowing it's *watching*?"

After a few minutes, he seemed to relax. He nodded to her, so she set him on the footboard, then lay back on the bed, staring at the ceiling—which was the upper deck of the ship. She could hear sailors crossing it, feet thumping. Wood creaking as the ship rocked. Spores made a constant low, hushed sound as they scraped past. Like a whisper. Someone had carved parts of the ceiling with a knife. Crude little patterns of crossing lines.

"I hope your day has been better than mine," Huck said, perched on the footboard of the bed. The entire thing had a nice railing to keep her from rolling out as the ship swayed.

"It's been somewhat frustrating," Tress said. "But not life-threatening." What she wanted wasn't nearly so important as what he needed, and she felt guilty for focusing on herself. "Your problem with the cat is more pressing. Maybe we could keep it extra well fed, so it doesn't want to hunt you?"

"Cats don't stop hunting because they're full, Tress. They're like people in that regard."

"Sorry," she said. "We don't have cats on the Rock."

"Sounds like a wonderful place."

"It was sweet and tranquil," she said. "And though the smog above town is pretty terrible, people tend to treat one another well. It's a good place. An honest place."

"I'd like to go there someday. I know you're thirsty for adventure, but I've had plenty."

"You could go," Tress said. "You don't need to stay with me, Huck."

"Tired of me already?"

"What!" she said, sitting up. "That's not what I meant!"

"You're too polite, girl," he said, twitching his nose. "I'll assume that you know less about rats than you do about cats. Try to imagine what it's like to be roughly the size of a sandwich, and to have most of the world consider you as tasty as one. Trust me, you'd do what I have."

"Which is?"

"Find a sympathetic human and stick close to them," Huck said. "Besides, I have a good feeling about you, remember?"

"But you've got to have family somewhere."

"Yeah, but they don't much care for me," he said.

"Are they . . . like you?"

"You mean, can they talk?" Huck said. "Yes." He paused, his head cocked, as if searching for the right way to explain. "I come from a place a lot like the one you came from. My kind has lived there for generations. But my kin, they thought it was time to go. See the world. They dragged me off for my own good. *That* didn't go well.

"They wouldn't much like me hanging around with you. I'm not supposed to talk to your kind, you see. Still, like I said, I've got a good feeling about you. And so, I'm staying close. But I certainly wouldn't mind if *you* decided—of your own free will—to head someplace less exciting . . ."

Tress tried to imagine it. A land full of talking rats? It sounded exotic and interesting. The twelve seas were a strange and incredible place, full of wonders. Huck kept talking, telling her about life as a rat. And there was a calming sense to his voice. It soothed her, and she found herself relaxing, her eyes tracking the carvings on the ceiling. Someone—perhaps her predecessor—had taken a lot of time to carve them. In fact . . . did those bursts of crossing lines look like . . . stars?

Tress sat up, cutting off Huck. He scampered along the bed railing over beside her. "What?"

Stars. Carved in little bursts. A single star there, then two stars close together next to it. Then three . . . all across the wood of the ceiling, as if someone had stood on the bed with a knife and used the point to scrape them.

No groupings of six stars, she thought.

"What?" Huck said. "What are you staring at?"

"Nothing," Tress said, flopping back down. "I thought, for a moment, that Hoid had said something important."

"You've been listening to *him*? Tress, I thought you were smart, for a human. Hoid is . . . you know."

"He said something about six stars," Tress said. "But there are no bunches of six."

"I can see that," Huck said. "I told you he's a lunatic, Tress. No use in trying to figure out what he means."

"I suppose," she said.

"Besides," Huck noted, "those look more like explosions. The stars are under the bed."

Tress froze, then leaped off the bed and pulled herself underneath. The bottom of the bed frame was carved as well—and with patterns that were indeed more starlike. There was one patch of six stars. Feeling like she might be submitting to lunacy herself, Tress pushed it.

Something clicked, and a small latch opened on the side of the frame. Inside, Tress found a small aluminum container the size of a matchbox. Huck climbed onto her shoulder as she pushed it open.

In it she found midnight-black spores.

25

THE PREY

So how did I know?

Well, I believe you've been told. I'm an expert at being places I'm not supposed to be. I have an innate sixth sense for mystery. In my current state, I might have thought vests with no shirt underneath to be the absolute height of fashion, but I was still fully capable of a little constructive snooping.

Tress's breath caught. Huck hissed softly.

Midnight spores. Somehow, Weev had gotten ahold of midnight spores. She was reminded of what the captain had said, that all sprouters were—to one extent or another—crazy.

Weev, she thought, might have been a little extra so. (Tress was being generous. I'd have called him crazier than a nitroglycerin smoothie.)

"Put those away," Huck said. "No, better, spread them over the silver. Kill them, Tress. Midnight spores are dangerous."

"In what way?" she asked. "What do they do?"

"Terrible things."

"All spores do terrible things," Tress said. "What do these do *specifically*?"

"I . . . don't know," Huck admitted. "But I feel like you're *way* too relaxed about holding them."

Perhaps she was. But danger is like icy water; you can get used to it if you take it slowly. She tucked the little box of spores safely back in its hidden compartment. She'd have to see if Ulaam knew—

She jumped as the bell rang up above. Three quick peals, a warning to everyone on board. A ship had been spotted in the distance, and the captain had decided to pursue.

Tress scrambled out of her room, but then stood in the hallway, not wanting to crowd the Dougs as they hastened to the top deck. It was excruciating to wait, as she didn't want to miss anything.

She needn't have worried.

When she finally reached the deck, she found the Dougs clustered anxiously near the railing, looking out at a distant ship. As usual, the *Crow's Song* flew a royal merchant's flag. They wouldn't announce their pirate nature until the proper dramatic moment. Like the third-act twist of a play, only with the added bonus of grand larceny.

What followed was an extended chase that took five hours.

The *Crow's Song* was faster than most ships, particularly after it dropped the ballast it used to sit lower in the spores, mimicking a merchant ship fully laden with goods in the hold. But "speed" is a relative term at sea— particularly the spore sea, when the seethe could stop or start at any moment.

Tress hadn't realized how unusual it had been for her first vessel to be caught by surprise. This second pursuit required exacting work from the crew and the helmswoman, who slowly but surely ran down their prey.

The hours made Tress's tension mount. This was it. The final test of her plan to swap the cannonballs. She grew increasingly certain she had failed. Surely someone had discovered what she'd done. Surely she wasn't clever enough to trick seasoned killers like Laggart and the captain.

Her heart nearly leaped from her chest when Crow shouted the order. "Forward cannon to bear! All sailors, take arms!"

The Dougs ran for their muskets—though the ship they were chasing was still far away. Tress didn't try to arm herself. Considering how she'd fired a musket precisely zero times in her life, she figured the best way to keep her digits attached was to continue that perfect record.

She did, however, position herself near the prow, where she could witness Ann begging Laggart to let her have the first shot. He chewed her out and sent her to stand with the others—where one of the Dougs pointedly took the pistol from her hand and put a cutlass in it instead. Ann had another pistol out a moment later, slipped from the holster on the back of her belt.

"Warning shot, Cannonmaster!" Crow shouted.

Tress held her breath. Laggart swiveled the cannon with a crank, then sighted with his spyglass before using another lever to raise the cannon's barrel a few inches. He continued this process, exacting and precise, making adjustments. Finally, he pulled a wet firing stick from the bucket of water at his station.

He touched it to the firing pan, setting off the zephyr spores with a raucous explosion. The ball soared *directly* at the fleeing ship. This was no warning shot; it would be another "accidental" direct hit—intended to sink, not frighten. Tress heard Ann mutter nearby as she watched the cannonball's trajectory.

Tress steeled herself, her panic mounting as she thought of the poor sailors on that ship.

Then, with what seemed like only moments to spare, the cannonball exploded. Set to detonate like a mortar, it sprayed water across the side of the prey ship—but left the hull unharmed. The sea's response was, of course, immediate. Enormous tentacles of vines erupted from the spore sea, wrapping around the wet side of the ship, gripping the vessel in a deadly embrace. Even from a distance, Tress was certain she could hear the planks groaning.

But the ship's hull did not crack. The precision shot immobilized the ship instead of destroying it.

Though the crew cheered—this meant easy plunder—Laggart cursed softly, his face going red. The shade of a forge the moment before you remove the iron and proceed to lay into it with everything you have.

Captain Crow marched across the deck to the cannon station. Her glare could have skinned a cat, but out loud she said, "Not exactly what I'd call a warning shot, Cannonmaster. But that was . . . a very clean capture."

"Thank you, Captain," Laggart said. "I apologize for failing you in your request." He punctuated each syllable, as if he were whipping the sounds for coming from his lips.

Tress nearly started hyperventilating from the anxiety. Was Laggart looking at her with a more-surly-than-normal expression? Did he know? If he suspected foul play, there was only one rational culprit.

The captain seemed like she wanted to order another shot, but then she glanced at the cheering Dougs. Even in the twisted lump of smoldering coal that was her heart, Crow understood she needed good morale on her vessel. A quick and easy haul here would accomplish that.

"Run up the pirate's flag, seaman Doug," she said.

In response, their prey fired a flare bright in the air. Surrender. The Dougs cheered again. Tress started to calm down. It . . . it was working.

Unfortunately, as the *Crow's Song* drew close to the captive ship, the seethe stilled. The *Crow's Song* lurched to a halt, and this instantly dampened everyone's enthusiasm. Tress looked at the Dougs, worried. What was the problem? There were interruptions like this every day.

"Ann?" Tress said, sidling up to her. "What's wrong?"

"The ship surrendered," Ann said, her voice tense, "'cuz they knew they were beaten. With them held by vines, we could maneuver, an' they could not. But now we're both of us stuck. The sea just evened this match. An' they gotta be asking if maybe they shouldn't just . . ."

She trailed off as a blue puff of zephyr spores rose from the other ship's aft. Followed by a crack.

Followed by a whistle and a *crash* as a cannonball hit the *Crow's Song* right at the prow, where spores met wood.

26

THE SHARPSHOOTER

Dougs shouted and went scrambling. Ann cursed something incredibly vile relating to what comes out of the business end of a seagull.

"Damn fine shooting," Laggart muttered. "Hit us first shot? They've got quite the cannonmaster."

Crow shoved aside a few Dougs, then calmly raised her weapon. It looked . . . sleeker than the older muskets the Dougs carried, and had a different sight.

Though the *Crow's Song* had shortened the distance to the other ship, Tress was still amazed as the captain trained her musket toward the enemy, closed one eye, and fired. A man on the distant ship—the one holding the water firing stick as his assistants reloaded the cannon—dropped in a spray of blood.

"Well," Laggart said, "I guess they *had* a damn fine cannonmaster."

"Carpenter and sprouter," the captain said loudly as she lowered her musket and began to reload, dropping a small pouch of zephyr spores down the muzzle. "We've been hit. When the seethe comes again, we'll scoop up half the sea—and everyone on this ship will find out what spores taste like. Perhaps you'd like to do your jobs and prevent that."

"Right, Cap'n!" Ann said, raising her pistol. "Let me just get off one shot before—"

At least a half dozen Dougs grabbed her arm, wrestling for the pistol. The captain ignored them, sighting once again, then dropped the sailor who had been hefting a cannonball to load into the enemy's cannon.

It was the best shooting Tress had ever seen. It was the only shooting, granted. Nevertheless, I'll admit Crow was one of the best shots *I'd* ever seen. And considering that primitive muskets handle like a snake being electrocuted, that is saying something.

"To work, Ann," the captain said, calm—yet somehow threatening, ice crusting her voice. "Or my next shot won't have to travel to another ship."

"Moonshadows," Ann said, stumbling over to Tress. "Those Dougs *really* wanted a chance to use my pistol, eh? Well, let's be on with the cap'n's order. Stop delaying, Tress!" She scrambled belowdecks, Tress following.

"You have your tools?" Ann asked as they reached the middle deck.

"What tools?" Tress asked. "Ann, I only became ship's sprouter this morning! I have no idea what I'm doing."

"Right, right," Ann said, wiping her brow. Above, a cannon shot sounded from their ship. "We need rose spores. There should be a whole bunch of them in Weev's room."

Tress nodded. She led Ann to the room, though the carpenter hesitated at the threshold. Tress continued inside, then pried off the top of a small barrel full of rose spores.

"Get some of those," Ann said, "and put them in one of the metal boxes. The kind you can transport spores in? Yeah, that. Um . . . I saw Weev use some other equipment too. I don't really know a lot about this, kid."

Tress finished filling the metal box with spores. Then she pulled open the closet, revealing an array of metal tools hanging from pegs on the inside of the door. She didn't see *anything* like the box the sprouter had used on the other ship. Weev, it should be noted, was a *purist*. He preferred the classical tools of the trade, not the modern ones.

"Any of these look right?" Tress asked.

"Oh!" Ann said. "That one with the flat side, like a plate. And that trowel. Grab those."

The second tool did indeed look like a small shovel, but the first one looked less like a plate to Tress and more like a shield. A little round shield—flat on the front, with a handle on the back to hold it.

The tools had clips on them for hanging from a belt, but there wasn't time for that. Tress gathered them up, along with the spores and an eyedropper bottle of water, then stumbled out to meet Ann—who backed away, hands up.

"Righty-o," Ann said. "Normally, I'd let the sprouter handle the initial patch while I gathered lumber, but I think maybe you could use a little help, eh?"

"Thanks," Tress said, letting Ann lead the way down to the hold. Bright sunlight bathed the normally dim confines, shining in through a hole near the ceiling. The hold was taller than the other decks, putting the hole some nine feet up in the air.

"I'll get a ladder," Ann said. "So, what you need to do is grow some spores in that hole. It don't have to be pretty—I'll do the pretty part with wood over the next few days. We just need that hole filled. Roseite is good at resisting silver, and can last quite a while once in place. So it makes a great plug, assuming you . . . ya know . . . don't kill yourself first."

"Any advice on avoiding that last part?" Tress asked, her voice growing more shrill.

"Wish I did, kid. Those are the right two tools, but I stayed real far away whenever Weev broke out the spores. That guy was nuttier than squirrel droppings. No offense."

Ann set up the ladder, then backed away. She didn't offer any further help, but Tress was thankful nonetheless. She climbed to the top of the ladder and looked out at the ocean of spores.

At the moment they were calm, flat, stable. But the instant the seethe started, the ship would move forward—and the verdant spores would come flooding through the gap. Even if the hold had a silver lining, the ship would quickly take on too much weight and stop floating.

Tress didn't hear any more shots from above. She pretended that was a good sign as she set her equipment on a nearby shelf for sacks. Last of all, she opened the aluminum box of spores. They looked like grains of pink salt. Trembling, she tipped the box until a few of them dribbled out onto the edge of the broken wood.

Unfortunately, by the time she had the dropper open and the water ready to squirt, the spores had turned a dark grey. Dead from the silver in the deck just above. Feeling stupid, she closed the box—but not before a number of those inside had died also.

She took a few deep breaths. Then, forcing herself to keep trying, she put some water on the wood first—then opened the box. Leaning back and shielding her face, she sprinkled a few spores onto the water.

It was a commendable execution of a terrible plan.

The rose spores burst into thick roseite crystals—like big chunks of quartz. While they weren't sharp, some broke up into the ceiling and another shot diagonally past Tress's head—nearly smashing her in the face.

It didn't plug the hole—the crystals left far too much space between them, and their weight caused them to rip off the wood and tumble down: half out into the sea, half down to the bottom of the hold. Tress gasped, belatedly.

"Tress!" Ann said. "Be careful!"

Moonshadows . . . what was she *doing*? The entire ship was depending on her, but she knew as much about this as she did about weaponized vexillology. (Watch out for the solid-colored flags. They'll getcha.)

You saw that sprouter on the Oot's Dream, *she reminded herself. He sealed the hole. The tools were different, but you know what the patch is supposed to look like.*

As she fumbled with the tools, she noticed something. The roseite was still growing. When the large crystals had broken free, they'd left small bits attached to the hull—and those, touching water, were expanding slowly. Like a creeping mold.

Did the same thing happen with verdant spores? Did the vines keep growing if you added more water? She didn't know. But she added some water to the growing roseite spores. And yes, although the growth was slow, they did continue to expand.

Far too slowly to fill the hole, she thought. Still, like the proverbial politician in a dumpster, it was a good start.

She took the tool that resembled a shield and pressed it to the roseite. The crystals responded immediately, pulling toward the metal, which (from the slate grey color) seemed to be simple iron. The other tool, the trowel, made the crystals grow away from it. It was of polished silvery metal. (Steel, for those who compulsively track these things.)

Right, so each tool influenced the growth of the spores. That made sense. Perhaps—

A low, rumbling noise came from outside the hull. A reverberating horror. The sound of spores churning. The seethe was beginning again.

"Tress!" Ann shouted.

No time for contemplation. If those spores flooded in, Tress would be the first to go. She took the shield-tool in her left hand and pressed it to the hole. With her other hand, she grabbed a tiny pinch of two or three spores—no time to worry if her hands were dry enough—and dropped them in the water on the rim of the broken wood.

They exploded, but were pulled to the shield—and it prevented them from going in unexpected directions. The force of it did nearly shove her off the ladder. Ann cried out and grabbed the base of it to steady her, which helped.

As roseite crystals began to grow around the edges of the shield, Tress grabbed the trowel and pushed them away. She was able to angle them to grow toward the sides of the hole, like using mortar that grew as she directed.

Wind in the sails made the ship rock backward, lifting the prow. Tress barely got the crystals to seal the final edge of the hole as the ship crashed forward. Her plug shook and cracked. There had been water on the other edge, but the vines that grew because of it didn't break through—and there wasn't enough water for them to grow big enough to trap the ship.

The moment stretched, pulled taut with anxiety, trembling and holding its breath.

The patch held.

"Oh, moons," Ann said. "You actually did it. Can you . . . maybe put another layer on, or . . ."

"Let's not tempt fate," Tress said, trying to pull her shield tool free. It was overgrown with the roseite and affixed in place. "I'll probably need a silver knife to cut this off. Maybe we should try that when we're docked someplace safe."

"Yeah, all right," Ann said, holding the ladder as Tress climbed down.

"I'm just glad you were here. Until you took the job, it would have been my duty to patch that. I would've used wood, and that pause in the seethe was short enough that I wouldn't have had nearly enough time."

Another crack sounded above. Gunfire.

"This isn't over yet," Ann said. "Merciful moons, I hope that patch holds. Come on."

THE SPORE EATER

Tress made a brief stop in her room to stow the box of spores and her remaining tool—reassuring Huck, who was hiding under the bed again—then hurried up the steps. By the time she arrived, the *Crow's Song* was getting dangerously close to their target.

Three bodies lay bleeding on the deck of the merchant ship. The rest of the crew held up their arms, no visible weapons drawn. It looked like Laggart had tried another cannon shot—because another burst of vines covered the ship's aft section, many of them overgrowing the enemy cannon.

Another of Tress's swapped cannonballs had exploded instead of sinking the ship, but it might not be enough. The merchant vessel had given Crow plenty of excuses to be angry; Tress worried she would order the crew to slaughter everyone aboard that poor vessel. The pirates would have their treasure, and Crow would have her reputation as a deadrunner.

As the *Crow's Song* slowed, several Dougs threw hooks with ropes over to the merchant vessel. Another dropped the anchor. Nervous, Tress looked to the captain, who stood with her musket at the ready.

"All crew," Crow said, "swords out. Prepare to board."

Tress felt a sudden spike of panic. No! After all she had done to protect those—

"Captain!" a voice called. Sharp, commanding.

Everyone turned toward the quarterdeck, where Salay stood, one hand on the ship's wheel. She locked it in place, now that the ship was anchored, then walked to the steps.

"By tradition," Salay called, "the duty to engage the captain of a captured ship falls to me, does it not?"

The Dougs kept their weapons trained on the merchant vessel, but none spoke. They knew someone was very likely to be shot in the next few minutes, and didn't want to seem like they were volunteering.

Crow turned to face Salay straight on, musket held in a loose grip. The helmswoman did not back down, and Tress found herself praying to the moons.

"We have subdued them," Salay said loudly. "They have surrendered. We became pirates for the freedom. Nothing more." She stood firm, and her posture made her intent clear. She would *not* stand by and let the merchant crew be slaughtered.

If Crow wanted a massacre today, she'd have to start by killing Salay. Crow could do it; she'd done it to Weev. But how many crewmembers could Crow lose and still have a functioning ship?

"As you say," Crow finally announced. "Let them know I do not . . . appreciate the bilging my ship received after they sent up the flare of surrender. That sort of . . . indiscretion costs lives."

"They'll pay more than the normal bounty," Salay said. "I'll make sure of it, Captain."

Tress let out a held breath. Sailors started moving again, throwing more boarding hooks to keep the ships from drifting apart. Salay was the first to hop over to the merchant ship.

Tress sat down on the steps to the quarterdeck, worn out, now feeling like the washrag you find at the very bottom of the bin—the one that had been wadded up, then pressed flat for weeks by the pile.

A shadow fell over her. "We didn't sink," Crow said. "That means you did your job."

Tress nodded.

"She was great, Captain," Ann said from behind. "A natural, I'd say. Sealed that hole on her second try. Barely seemed terrified by the spores."

"Indeed," Crow said, her expression unreadable as she continued looking at Tress. "Ann, don't you think you should be fitting planks? In case this . . . expert work by our new sprouter isn't as durable as it might seem?"

"I suppose." She moved off.

"Ann," the captain said, holding her hand out.

Ann sighed and handed over a pistol she'd found somewhere, then vanished belowdecks.

Crow moved over to watch the merchant ship as Dougs began appearing from its hold bearing rolled rugs—the ship's cargo. The group of merchant sailors huddled on deck, where their captain spoke softly with Salay. He had a squeezed face, with too much forehead and chin, like you were seeing it reflected in a spoon.

Everyone had calmed down save one man: a sailor who knelt on the deck apart from the others. Something about his posture bothered Tress, so she climbed the steps to get a better look through the overgrown vines. Yes, the man was cradling the corpse of one of the people Crow had shot. A friend? Family member?

The weeping man looked up. Reckless, dangerous. Tress opened her mouth to call out a warning, but the man lurched to his feet and pulled a pistol from his belt. With a quivering hand, he pointed it across the gap between ships toward Crow.

Again, everyone froze. Everyone but Captain Crow herself. She stared down that barrel with indifference.

"Smocke!" the merchant captain yelled. "Don't be a lunatic, man! You'll get us all killed!"

The man, Smocke, stood up—stained with his friend's blood—but didn't lower the gun. He also didn't pull the trigger. Captain Crow raised the pistol she'd taken off Ann and pointed it at the man.

Then Crow turned the pistol around and shot herself in the head.

Immediately, *vines* erupted from Crow's skin. They split her cheek and wormed out around her eyes, writhing and twisting. One *caught* the bullet. The skin of her face and hand rippled, as if she had serpents for muscles. The vines wriggled, then withdrew, slithering back into her body.

A drop of blood leaked from the corner of Crow's eye, and a bit more seeped from a rip in her cheek, but otherwise her face appeared untouched. She lowered the pistol, then took a long pull on her canteen. Finally she waved Smocke forward—as if demanding he try shooting her too. Several of his crew members tackled him, and the shot went off into the air.

"I expect my ship to sail in under an hour," Crow said loudly, "laden with more riches than she should rightly carry." Her eyes lingered on the other ship's captain, who still stood near Salay. "If it is not done, I shall visit your fine vessel and teach *each* and *every* one of you what it means to cross Captain Crow. If you doubt my sincerity, ask the crew of the *Oot's Dream* how much they're enjoying life at the bottom of the Verdant Sea."

The captain disappeared into her cabin. Tress slumped on the steps again, trembling, burdened by the terrible sight of those vines bursting from Crow's body.

What was she?

28

THE EXTRA
GOOD LISTENER

The captain is a gestator for the verdant aether," Dr. Ulaam said, holding up a narrow bottle containing something uncomfortably reminiscent of a kidney floating in solution.

"She just ate *what*?" Tress asked, sitting in his exam room.

"Not just ate. Gestate. It means to incubate. Crow is host to an aggressive strain of the verdant parasite. Your lore calls people like her spore eaters, though I find that an imprecise term. Tell me. Where do spores come from?"

"The moons," Tress said.

"Ah, yes," Ulaam said. "The moons. As food comes from the kitchen, or pottery comes from the Zephyr Islands. There couldn't possibly be another step involved, hmmm? These things just magically appear?"

"So . . . you mean how do the spores *get* to the moons?"

"Rather," Ulaam said, "what on the moons produces them? Hmm?"

"I . . . have no idea," Tress said. It was a realization she probably *should* have made before.

Ulaam knelt beside her, holding the kidney up to her side. He shook it, then raised his eyebrow. "Trade?" he asked. "This one will make your urine smell of lilacs."

"Um . . . no thank you."

"Would you sell one?" Ulaam said.

"Again, no."

"Selfish," Ulaam said. "You don't need two."

"And how many do *you* have?"

Ulaam grinned. "Touché."

"To say what?"

"No, it means you have successfully rebutted me." He stood up, shaking his head. "Regardless, your moons are home to a group of voracious entities known as aethers. Though the true aethers on other worlds have a symbiosis with people, the ones on your moons have become insatiable, aggressive, and fecund."

"I'm not allowed to say that word," Tress said.

"No, it means . . . actually, that word means something very close to what you think it means, but it's a more polite way of saying it. Anyway, the aethers up above are rampantly self-propagating, and each is connected to a primal element. Vegetation, atmosphere, silicate . . ."

"This alone is dangerous, but your varieties are also highly unstable. The tiniest hint of a catalyst—water, in this case—and they pull Investiture directly from the Spiritual Realm to explosively germinate. It's a remarkable process."

Tress considered this, and found herself with a dozen more questions. Once, she might have been too polite to ask them, as he didn't owe her explanations. But there was something about Ulaam that invited such conversation. Surely that was it, and not that she was changing.

"So . . ." Tress said, "how did the captain get that thing inside of her?"

"I've been unable to find a satisfying answer," Ulaam said, pulling out a rack full of bottled kidneys, then putting away the one he'd been holding. "Some say it randomly happens to people who fall into the sea, while others claim you have to ingest a very special kind of spore."

"So she *did* eat it," Tress said. "Maybe."

"Maybe," Ulaam said, pulling back the sleeve of his suit to reveal a grey-skinned forearm.

With an ear growing out of it.

"You have an ear on your arm!" Tress said.

"Hmmmm? Oh, yes."

"But . . . why?"

"Because when I put it on my inner thigh," Ulaam said, "I kept hearing my clothing brush across it in a most distracting way."

"Isn't your head a better location?"

"I already have two there," Ulaam said. "Did you not notice them? Earregardless, your captain's affliction is a dire one. She is connected *directly* to the prime verdant aether growing on the moon. It needs water to survive, and the moon has none. So it somehow infects people on the planet.

"The vines inside Captain Crow are exceptionally thirsty, and they constantly drain her of liquid. Somehow, they use that liquid—along with that from other spore eater hosts around the world—to feed the enormous overgrown aether on the moon. I've been unable to discover the mechanism."

"The vines keep her alive though," Tress said. "They saved her from that bullet."

"Yes," Ulaam said. "The aether protects itself by protecting her, but it's rabid. Insatiable. Incapable of rational thought, it is sucking her dry. The affliction is progressive, taking more and more from its host. I'm told it is exceptionally painful, and it is *always* fatal."

"Merciful moons," Tress whispered. "That almost makes me feel sorry for her."

"Yes, well, most terrible mass murderers like Crow *do* tend to be well acquainted with tragedy. It makes you wonder who the *true* monster is: the killer, or the society that created them?"

Tress nodded.

"That was a trick question," Ulaam said. "The true monster is the one in that drawer next to you. I gave it seven different faces."

Tress glanced at the drawer in the small end table beside her seat. It rattled. She pretended not to notice.

"At least now I know why the crew is afraid of her," Tress said. "They don't dare mutiny because that thing inside her would protect her from them."

"Indeed," Ulaam said. "I have little doubt the captain could kill each and every person on this ship without suffering any ill effects. Other than, you know, no longer having a crew. Temporary immortality does not make one able to trim the sails all by one's self, as the old adage goes."

"That's an old adage?"

"Odd," Ulaam said. "I meant odd. I think the tongue I've been using is wearing out. It used to be able to roll marvelously. Did you know that ability is genetic? One in four tongues can't manage it." He looked closely at her mouth.

Tress pointedly did not attempt to roll her tongue. Instead she tried to figure out Captain Crow's goals. The woman wanted to push the crew, make them desperate. To sail dangerous waters, because she was dying? And wanted to get in as much living as she could before she went?

"How long," Tress said, "do you suppose Crow has left?"

"Hard to say," Ulaam said. "I hear the malady usually plays out in under a year, but I gather she's had it longer than that. She is lasting remarkably long, but at this point I doubt she has months left. Weeks, maybe days. I've noticed she needs to drink nearly constantly to prevent herself from dehydrating and withering away."

It was another piece of the puzzle. Unfortunately, Tress had no idea how many pieces she needed—or what that puzzle would look like when assembled.

"Was there anything else you wanted?" Ulaam asked. "I have acquired an eighth face, you see, and I think there might be space to graft it on the underside of the thorax."

"What do midnight spores do?" Tress asked.

Ulaam frowned. He quietly rolled down his sleeve, then stepped closer to Tress, leaning over and studying her with one eye. "Hoid!" he called.

The cabin boy wandered in. Tress hadn't realized I'd been outside.

"Did you give Tress midnight spores?" Ulaam asked.

"Nope!" I said.

"Good," Ulaam replied. "I was worried that—"

"I gave them to Weev!" I said, excited. (In my defense, I'd thought them a kind of licorice.)

Ulaam sighed, folding his arms. Tress couldn't help wondering if that squished the ear on his forearm, and what it felt like.

"Tress," the surgeon said, "midnight spores are a very different kind of dangerous from the others. They need a persistent living source of water—in the form of the one who germinates them."

"Like what has happened to the captain?"

"Yes," Ulaam said. "But temporary, in this case."

"But what do they *do*?"

"They create midnight aether," Ulaam said. "Also called Midnight Essence: a blob of goo that will imitate a nearby object or entity. The aether stays under your control for as long as you sustain it. It is more practical than many of the other spore creations—but also more nefarious. If you practice with it . . ."

He paused, eyeing her. "*When* you practice with it, have a great deal of water nearby to drink, along with a silver knife. Most sprouters use midnight aether for spying, but be careful of creating a blob larger than about the size of your fist. So, four or five grains maximum. If your creation is too large, it is more likely to escape your control."

"I . . . barely understood half of what you said, Ulaam," she said.

"Half? Why, I knew you were smart. Your brain—"

"—is not for sale," Tress said.

"Oh!" I said. "You can have mine! It keeps trying to tell me that dirty socks aren't an acceptable strainer for pasta, and if that's true, I do *not* want to think about it."

Ulaam grinned, then plucked a little notebook from the inside pocket of his suit coat and began writing. "I'm recording the most embarrassing ones," he said at Tress's confused glance, "to share with him once he's better. I suspect I can milk this for *decades*."

He did.

"Hoid," Tress said, "I need to find out how to get to the Sorceress. You were there, with her. Can you guide me, or tell me how to cross the Midnight Sea?"

"He's not going to be of any help as long as he's under that curse, Tress," Ulaam said. "You'll need to break it."

"But how?" she asked. "You don't know. Who would?"

My face grew thoughtful. During that time period, normally that would mean I was contemplating whether occasionally biting my cheek technically made me a cannibal. But today I was actually thinking about what Tress was saying.

For once it managed to sink in.

"I can talk," I told her softly, "but I can't *say* anything. I can tell you that you should always wear white to someone else's wedding."

"Which is talking but saying nothing. Nothing relevant, at least, about the curse."

"Right! Now, this is important. You need to find someone who can talk *and* say things."

"That describes a lot of people," Tress said.

It was a struggle. The curse tied my tongue and brain in knots. I literally couldn't say too much.

"Find . . . a person . . . who isn't a . . . a person," I said. "And can talk . . . when they . . . should not."

Tress cocked her head. Ulaam stepped closer. "That was more coherent than anything he's managed in months, Tress. I believe he's saying something important."

"It sounds like gibberish. I think he's toying with me."

"Hmmm. If that's so, then it's remarkably like he used to be. A person who isn't a person? And who can talk when they should not . . ."

Tress frowned at me, pondering with that blessedly thoughtful mind of hers. Then it clicked. "A talking animal?" she guessed.

I flopped to the ground, letting out a relieved sigh. I was soon lost in thought, trying to decide if cobblers were *also* good at making desserts, or if that was merely a coincidence.

"Ah!" Ulaam said, clapping his hands—then cringing at the sound so close to one of his ears. "That must be it. He's telling you to locate a familiar."

"A what?"

"Powerful users of Investiture—magic, if you prefer—are often associated with talking animals. I've noticed you have similar lore in your world. Is it not so?"

"I suppose," Tress said, thinking back to nursery stories.

"I'll admit," Ulaam said, rolling up his sleeve again and getting out a scalpel, "that on some worlds, my own species is the cause of these rumors. I don't think that is the case here, however, nor do I think they are the result of an Awakener's arts. Likely, the Sorceress and others like her have found ways to Invest common animals to enhance their cognitive abilities."

"Are you even speaking Klisian?" Tress asked.

"Technically yes, though I'm using Connection to translate my thoughts, which are in a language you've never heard of. Regardless, Hoid seems to think you'll be able to find a familiar—a talking animal, if you will. Such an animal would very likely be connected to the Sorceress in some way. Familiars are usually small creatures, used in spying. Birds. The occasional feline . . ."

"Or a rat," Tress said softly.

"Indeed." Ulaam proceeded to cut the ear off his forearm.

Tress was out the door before he could offer it to her.

THE FAMILIAR

She found Huck in her cabin, sitting on the bed, alternating between chewing on a stale crust of bread and reading one of Weev's books: a notebook detailing the use of verdant spores. She'd left it on the bed, and it looked like Huck had nibbled on the corner of the book between bites of crust—though whether that was intentional or due to some ratty instinct, she could not guess.

"You've been lying to me," Tress said, shutting the door.

Huck crouched down, his eyes darting from side to side, seeking the best place to hide.

"Why didn't you tell me you were a familiar?" Tress demanded.

"Uh . . ." Huck said.

"Were you a companion to the Sorceress? Do you know about her? About how to reach her island? Have you been hiding that all this time?"

"Huh." Huck sat up on his haunches, nose twitching. "I am . . . yes, I am a familiar, which is why I can talk. How did you find out?"

"Hoid," Tress said, gesturing in the direction of the ship's surgery. "It was difficult for him to speak through the curse, but he gave me enough clues to put it together. Huck, why didn't you *tell me*?"

"I didn't want to lead you into danger," Huck said. "The Sorceress is a horrible person, Tress. You shouldn't want to know anything more about her, and you *definitely* shouldn't be trying to get to her island."

Tress stalked over to the bed and knelt beside it, at eye level with the rat. "You," she said, "are going to tell me *everything* you know about the Sorceress. Or else."

"Or else what?" he squeaked.

"Or else"—she took a deep breath, nervous, as she'd never made a threat as dire as this in her life—"I will stop talking to you."

". . . You won't throw me overboard or something?"

"What?" she asked, horrified. "No! That would be awful!"

"Tress, you make a terrible pirate."

"Please, Huck," she said, "tell me what you know. Can you guide me to the Sorceress's island?"

He considered, then began to speak, but cut off. He rubbed his head with his paw. "No," he said. "I can't, Tress. I'm not what you think I am. I'm . . . not a familiar. Well, I guess I kind of am, but not in the way you're thinking. My whole family can talk. I grew up on a lonely island far, far from the Sorceress's realm."

"So you're what? A descendant of familiars?"

"A good explanation," he said, then sighed. "If you really want to get to the Sorceress, your best bet *is* to break Hoid's curse. I can't lead you to her. About that, I'm telling you the truth. I promise."

"Can you at least help me break Hoid's curse?"

He thought for a moment. "I . . . Maybe? I mean, I'm not supposed to talk about this. But so long as it's about Hoid . . . All right, so here's the problem. The Sorceress's magic forbids a person from talking about the specifics of their curse."

"I knew that already," she said.

"But I've heard—from my family, you see—that one can sometimes get a cursed person to reveal things anyway. The curses aren't alive; they are static, like the rules in a contract. That means, despite how much work the Sorceress puts into them, every curse has holes."

"I don't understand," Tress said, still kneeling beside the bed.

"All right," Huck said, "let's pretend you had a friend who was cursed. If you went to them and said, 'Are you cursed?' they wouldn't be able to say yes. But the fact that they can't is itself kind of a confirmation, you know? So in a way, you've tricked the curse into giving you new information."

"But how does that relate to *undoing* the curse?"

"Every cursed person hears the spell being said, and therefore knows the method of their salvation. The Sorceress . . . Tress, she's evil. Sadistic. When she curses someone, she *wants* them to know the path to their freedom, then not be able to tell anyone."

"That sounds horrendous," Tress said, again glancing toward where she'd left Hoid.

"Yeah," Huck said. "I warned you. Look, even *talking* about her is dangerous. You shouldn't keep trying to get to her."

"I'm going," she said. "So I can either go armed with your information, or I can go ignorantly and be more likely to die. Your choice, Huck."

"Ouch. No need to step on the trap after it's already around my neck, Tress. I'm *trying* to help, but there's not a lot I can say. You have to find a way to circumvent the curse. Like . . . assume you asked that friend, 'How do I undo your curse?' once you know there is a curse. That friend won't be able to tell you.

"But say you told your friend a story about someone else who was cured of their curse, and asked, 'What do you think?' They might be able to talk to you about the story, since it's about someone else—and therefore not about their *specific* situation. You might be able to sneak useful information out."

"That sounds like it would involve a lot of guesswork," Tress said. "And confusion."

"And frustration. And pain. Yeah. But it's all I have for you, Tress. I'm not an expert. I think you should focus on keeping yourself alive, not on this mad quest to visit the Sorceress. Crow has it in for you. I can feel it."

"I thought that at first too," Tress said, letting herself be distracted. She needed time to process what he'd said before pushing him further anyway. "But Crow has turned around. She seems happy to have me on board."

"And that doesn't worry you *more*?" Huck asked.

"Now that you mention it . . . I should be suspicious, shouldn't I?"

"Sporefalls, yes," Huck said. "I mean, Crow eats bullets, hates everyone, is determined to give her own crew a death sentence. Yet she—casually—has decided she wants you to stay on board. For reasons."

Tress shivered. "We might need you to spy on her again."

"Uh . . ." Huck wrung his paws a little, then started nibbling on the book again.

"Stop that!"

"Sorry," he said as she snatched it away. "Chewing makes me feel better. I will spy on her if you want, Tress. But . . . I mean, I don't think I'm very good at it. Last time I'm sure they spotted me. That porthole has been kept tightly closed ever since. Plus there's the cat . . ."

Tress tapped her finger on the book. The captain was wily, and even Hoid—an obvious idiot (ouch)—had figured out Huck was a familiar. A girl spending time with a rat that seemed too well-trained? Crow probably had her suspicions as well.

But perhaps there was another way. What was it Ulaam had said about midnight spores? They were useful in spying . . .

She was interrupted by a knock on her door. Tress glanced at Huck, who—with an abundance of caution—grabbed his bread crust in his mouth and hid under the bed. When Tress answered the door, she found Salay standing outside.

"Tress," the helmswoman said, "we need to talk about who you *really* are."

30

THE KING'S MASK

Salay wanted to know who she really was.

Unfortunately, that was a topic of some confusion to Tress herself. In her youth, she'd *thought* she understood who she was. Now she was sailing with pirates and learning to use *spores*. She found herself demanding answers of Ulaam, and not caring if it was polite.

She wasn't even certain she was Tress anymore, or if she'd become someone else. You could say, in other words, that her state at the moment was *dis*tress.

"Well?" Salay asked.

Tress didn't have a lot of experience with lying, but paradoxically, the ones who are most successful at it are those who don't do it very often. So when Tress remained quiet but stepped back and gestured for Salay to come in, it was exactly the right thing to do.

Salay hesitated. Despite her no-nonsense attitude, she was nervous about entering a sprouter's room. You got used to the idea of silver being around. It let you ignore, to some extent, the spores—like how you can usually ignore your nose always being in view. Or like how people ignore the existential horror that comes from knowing their body is slowly deteriorating every day, time itself marching them toward oblivion to the cadence of their beating hearts.

However, although Salay might have been short of both stature and temper, she wasn't short on grit. She stepped into the room and shut the door, heroically enduring the chill that ran up her spine and the goose-bumps that rose on her arms.

"Would you like some tea?" Tress said, getting out two cups. A charming matched pair of a light pale porcelain with silver on the rims. "It's delightfully lukewarm."

"Er, no," Salay said. "Look, I know you aren't who you're pretending to be."

"I'm just a girl trying not to get tossed overboard."

"Yeah, no," Salay said, folding her arms. "I'm not buying the act any longer, Tress."

This made Tress a little annoyed. "What do you want me to say?" Tress asked, in a rare bout of pique. "I've already admitted that I stole this coat. Other than that I'm an insignificant girl from an insignificant island. There's nothing remarkable about me."

"Oh? An 'unremarkable' girl who just *happens* to be unafraid of spores? Who just *happens* to be made our sprouter after only a couple of days on the crew?"

"I'm terrified of spores!" Tress said, for once not caring if she was being discourteous. "I needed a job on the ship, and this was the only one available!"

Salay leaned forward, studying Tress. "Moon of veils, you're so *good* at this. I don't see a hint of a tell that you're lying."

"Because I'm not lying! Look, if you don't believe me, then what *do* you think I am?"

"A royal inspector," Salay said, "in disguise."

"This," Tress said, gesturing to her inspector's coat, "is a disguise?"

"It's a clever plan, I'll admit," Salay said. "You knew we'd instantly suspect a newcomer. But of course, an inspector would be the *last* person to wear one of those! Except when they're being an inspector. So you knew by wearing it, we'd naturally assume you weren't one."

"That is," Tress said, "an interesting thought process . . ."

"Yes," Salay said. "I'll admit, I wouldn't have pieced it together if I hadn't discovered that Crow gave you a chance to flee the ship, and you didn't take it."

Oh. "About that," Tress said, "I simply didn't want to abandon you all. Look, I'm *not* lying. I'm *not* an inspector."

Salay narrowed her eyes. "Yeah? And what about what you did to the cannonballs?"

Tress froze.

"Aha!" Salay said. "You didn't expect me to know about that, did you? I watched Laggart's reaction when that ship didn't sink today. He *wanted* to kill those people, though I haven't figured out why. I *do* know you're the only one who had access to his munitions to sabotage his attempt."

Moon of mercy, Tress thought. *If she figured it out . . . maybe Laggart and Captain Crow have as well.* She should have known she couldn't fool such an experienced crew.

Tress sat down on her bed, disturbed. Salay was wrong about her, but the helmswoman . . . she'd stood up to Captain Crow. She'd prevented a massacre. If Tress was going to trust anyone on this ship, she decided, it should be Salay.

"I found out the captain wanted to sink ships," Tress said, "to make you all into deadrunners. She wants you to obey her unfailingly. Even with her powers, she must fear a mutiny."

Salay leaned down, small tight curls of black hair falling around the sides of her face. "A common girl—as you're pretending to be—*figured out* Captain Crow's plot?"

"By accident," Tress said. "Really, Salay. I have no idea what I'm doing."

"Let's assume I believe you," Salay said. "And accept that you're not an inspector. Can you *prove* what you said about the captain?"

"There are false bottoms in the gunnery barrels," Tress said. "Laggart keeps sabotaged cannonballs in there. I swapped them for ordinary ones so he couldn't sink any more ships. I have the ones I took out, but I don't know if that will prove anything. It's my word against his."

"I don't need you to confront him about it," Salay said, beginning to pace. "We merely need to get others in the crew to agree to take action. I've organized a meeting with Ann and Fort later tonight. If you brought one of those cannonballs, that might be proof enough for them. They're already suspicious of the captain's motives, and . . ."

Salay stopped, then walked back to Tress. "And you just manipulated me into telling you about our secret meeting! *Damn* you're good."

Tress sighed.

Salay held her eyes again. "Cold as ice. With a heart of unyielding steel."

"Really?" Tress asked. "*That's* what you get from my expression?"

"Indeed," Salay said. "Behind the fake fear and confusion you're trying to use to distract me. But I believe you on one thing: you're no royal inspector."

"Oh?"

"You're far too clever for one of them," Salay said. "You must be a *King's Mask!*"

Oh. That explained everything. Or, Tress assumed it would, if she knew what on the twelve seas a "King's Mask" was.

"Everyone knows the King's Masks *must* lie when asked what they are," Salay said, putting her hands on her hips. "To protect their secret missions. So I won't try to get you to confirm it. Will you bring one of those cannonballs tonight?"

"If you think it will persuade the others," Tress said, "then I will." She wasn't certain what any of them could do against someone like Crow, but it would be good to talk about the things she'd discovered.

"Great," Salay said. "Meeting is in the quartermaster's room after second evening mess, when night watch is called." She started toward the door, then hesitated. "Please don't assassinate anyone before then."

With that, she was out the door. Tress sat back on her bed, stunned, as Huck emerged.

"So, King's Mask, eh?" he said. "You sure had me fooled."

"I—"

"That was a joke," he said, nibbling on his stale bread crust again. "I'm guessing you don't even know what they are."

"Not a clue."

"Secret assassin group," Huck said. "Maintained by the king to carry out important missions. Supposedly, there are never more than five at a time. They are the elite of the elite."

"And she thinks an eighteen-year-old girl happens to be one."

"The Masks supposedly take youth potions to disguise their ages," Huck said. "But . . . it's possible they don't really exist, and the king encourages the rumors to make people fear him.

"Don't blame Salay. People on ships like this one hover at the edges of the law, even when they're not pirates. Someone like Salay lives her entire life full of suspicion. She's not dumb; she's just not accustomed to dealing with someone so genuine. It's like you speak an entirely different language."

"I'll need to convince her of the truth," Tress said. "Somehow." She found it physically painful to know someone thought she was an assassin.

"I don't know if I'd go to that meeting, if I were you," Huck said. "Captain Crow is suspicious of Salay and the others. I think she's planning to kill them."

"What? How do you know?"

"When I spied on them for you the other day? I caught a little bit about 'secret meetings' and 'being rid of them finally.' That was before they got to the juicy stuff I told you."

That sounded bad to Tress, but also too vague. She stood up again, pacing through her small quarters, listening to the scrape of spores on the hull outside. "We don't know enough, Huck. We don't know *why* the captain wants to make the others into deadrunners. I mean, she wants to order them to do something dangerous, but why?"

"Yeah," Huck said. "I'm baffled too. Reminds me of a friend of mine. He was a character, I tell you. Once, he was offered cheese—by the way, we don't like cheese as much as people think. Wonder how the rumor started. Anyway—"

"I think," Tress said gently, "we should stay focused, Huck. We need more information about the captain."

Huck dropped his crust. "Okay, I suppose," he said. "I mean, if you really want me to . . ."

Tress immediately felt guilty, remembering his earlier objections. She had no right to ask him to put his life in danger.

"Never mind," she said, tucking an unruly strand of hair behind her ear. "I think there's another way." She looked in the secret compartment under the bed, then brought out the little box full of midnight spores.

"Tress . . ." Huck said. "What are you doing?"

"I'm completely out of my element, Huck," she said. "I'm just a girl with a fondness for cups. I have no special training, no special experience. I can't outmaneuver Crow unless I use the resources I have." She held up the box. "My only real advantage seems to be the fact that I'm *slightly* less terrified of spores than everyone else."

"Yeah, but *midnight spores*? Shouldn't we . . . you know . . . work our way up to something like that? You don't *start* by running a full regalthon. You jog a little first."

"A what?"

"Regalthon," he said. "Forty-mile race, held every year on the king's birthday."

"Forty miles?" Tress said, fishing in the various drawers in Weev's cabinet. Hadn't she seen a silver knife in here? "They'd run out of land and fall off the island if they raced that far. Do they go in circles?"

"Oh, Tress," he said, "most islands aren't the size of the Rock, you know."

"Really?" she said. She pulled the knife out of the drawer. "You mean there are some that are *forty miles* wide?"

"And bigger," he said. "I think one over in the Zephyr Sea is sixty miles across."

"Moons!" she said, trying to imagine that much land in one place. Why, in the center, you might not be able to see the sea at all! She shook her head at the crazy thought and pulled out a few waterskins.

After that she knelt by the bed, picked out three black spores, and set them on the mattress. Huck backed away, towing his crust of bread.

She took a deep breath and thought of Charlie. She could do this. For him, and for the people of the *Crow's Song*. Solve the mysteries on this ship, protect the people here, and they would point her in Charlie's direction.

She raised an eyedropper and released a drop onto the spores.

THE MIDNIGHT
ESSENCE

I assume you have no idea what a Luhel bond is. Don't feel bad. At this point in the story, I was concerned with trying to figure out how many different shades of orange I could wear at the same time. So we all have our priorities.

Most aether spores—like the verdant spores and the zephyr spores—don't involve any kind of bond. Using them is a simple matter of cause and effect. Compressed aether drops to the planet in the form of spores, and a little water encourages it to grow in an explosive burst.

Midnight spores are different—in fact, they're closer to how the aethers are *supposed* to work. Bringing midnight spores to life creates a temporary bond, a kind of symbiosis between host and aether. Unlike the Nahel bond, which trades in consciousness and anchoring to reality, the Luhel bond trades in physical matter. In this case, water.

Tress felt it as a sudden thirst, a drying of her mouth. She reached for the waterskin, then paused, transfixed by the motions of the spores.

They bubbled and undulated, melting and then enlarging like an inflating balloon. In seconds the puddle of goo—though it had begun as three tiny spores—was as large as a person's fist. There it stopped growing, blessedly, though it continued to writhe and distort. For a moment a tiny face appeared—stretching out of the black pus. Then it melted back in.

Offer, a thought impressed on Tress's mind. *Trade. Water. Give water.*

Without knowing what she was doing, Tress agreed.

Midnight Essence, in all its different forms, looks for a pattern, a model. It often takes a cue from its creator or host—and in this case Tress glanced at Huck, who had backed all the way across the bed to the far corner, clutching his crust of bread before him like a somewhat-snacked-upon shield.

The Midnight Essence pulsed with purpose, elongating. It formed a black tail. Four paws. A face and snout . . . a body like a deformed tuber. Soon Tress found herself regarding a small creature that looked *almost* like a rat dipped in black paint. Except the hair seemed more a texture to the skin than individual hairs, and there wasn't enough detail on the toes and the face.

It was too smooth. Jet black and glossy, as if made of tar. Or carved from a tub of lard by a talented artist with no other way to express themself. It scurried back and forth across the bed, trying out its legs—and again, the motions were *almost* ratlike.

Though her thirst was increasing—and strangely, her eyes were beginning to feel dry—Tress couldn't stop watching it. She took a drink—and found herself slurping down the *entire* waterskin. She hadn't thought there would be enough room in her stomach, but once she was refreshed, the Luhel bond strengthened. She'd given it what it wanted, and in so doing gained some measure of control over it. She lost sight of the world around her, her vision fuzzing.

Then she *was* the not-rat. She could direct it, see through its eyes, *smell* what it smelled. She immediately made the thing jump toward Huck, who squeaked and ran under the bed. It was fun for reasons she couldn't explain.

But no, she had *work* to do. Yes, important work that involved scampering across the bed and leaping onto the floor. When she hit, her feet squished into her body, and she had to pop them out again. After that, she scrambled to the door and squeezed under, coming out as goo that oozed back into shape.

Shadows. She *liked* shadows. Down here, in these corridors

below-decks, she could move virtually unseen. Even on the steps, the shadows were deep. But up above, the sun was out from behind the moon. Hateful sun, though it was slinking toward the horizon, drowsy, unaware of her. Midnight Tress crouched on the steps, listening to the footfalls of the people, smelling the old leather of their shoes.

There. A shadow from the mast as the ship turned. She leaped into it, then ran along its length—jumping over the veins of silver in the deck. It would hurt her if she touched it, she knew, but she was stronger in this shape than common spores. Mere proximity wouldn't harm her.

She reached the captain's cabin, which occupied the space directly underneath the quarterdeck. She definitely *shouldn't* have been able to squeeze under that tiny gap between door and deck, but she did. The re-inflation took longer this time, but her eyes re-formed faster than the rest of her, and she was able to scan the room.

Crow sat at her desk by the porthole, writing something by the waning light of the setting sun. Her hat hung on a peg by the door, her canteen was open next to her, and she wore her jacket unbuttoned.

As soon as her feet were back, Midnight Tress scrambled into the deeper shadows beneath a bench. Crow smelled wrong. Of rotten weeds, and burning flesh, and something else Midnight Tress couldn't identify. The other humans smelled of sweat and sweet flesh. Not Crow. Crow wasn't a person, not entirely. The parasite was winning.

Midnight Tress realized she should have waited. Waited until Crow and Laggart were meeting. She should have planned. But plans . . . plans were things for people who didn't exist yet. And Tress existed now.

What was that little book Crow was writing in? Midnight Tress inched closer. Could she keep to the shadows enough that she could read the book? She craned her neck, looking up from the floor, trying to see. But the angle was all wrong. Could she . . .

No. No, she'd have to get right up *beside* Crow to look at the book. She felt excited and eager in this body, but . . . but even in darkness, she wasn't invisible.

Just a little closer. She could get a little closer.

With effort, Tress held herself back. It was like trying to keep from eating when ravenous. She *wanted* to do what she *wanted*. Didn't she?

No. No . . .

Crow would leave soon. Evening mess. She'd go like she always did, get food, and then return. Wait.

Wait.

WAIT.

The call went up. Crow shut her book, took a long drink from her canteen, then stood. She took her hat off the peg, went out the door, then locked it behind her.

Now!

Midnight Tress scrambled out of the shadows. She climbed up the table leg with claws too sharp for her otherwise soft and malleable body. Then she sprang onto the top of the table, so eager to reach the book that her feet twisted and distorted as she ran, extra nubs of more legs growing like tumors at her sides.

She reached the book and bit it, pulling it open to the page that Crow had left marked. And inside was . . . words?

Words that smelled of dust. Dusty, dirty, boring, stupid, melty, inky words. Why words? Why had she been so eager?

Words. Read the words.

She didn't want to, but she did anyway, growing her eyes larger until they bulged from her face—taking in more, making the details more distinct. Many of the words looked printed by some device. But written in the margins, in what she assumed was Crow's handwriting, were notes.

A way to be rid of them, finally? the note said. *A way to banish the spores from my blood?*

Curious. Midnight Tress focused on the text.

It is clearly evident that Xisis has the power to cure any disease. In 1104, a supplicant reported being healed of cancerous tumors in a very extreme state of progression. This individual, Delph of the Zephyr Islands, is a well-known and respected scholar—and his word is trustworthy.

We have another extreme example. In 1123, Queen Bek the Fifteenth was cured of her spore gestation, and remains the only person—in thousands of years of recorded history—to survive such an infestation. Xisis was involved.

Stupid words. Stupid sawdust-in-the-eyes words. Why? She should find something to bite, something that bled warmth and liquid salt.

She fought with herself, writhing, her shape bubbling and squirming. She almost ripped herself apart in her anger. But she won, finally, and forced herself into the ragged rat shape. She bit pages, moving back through the book. She passed other notes from Crow, but most didn't draw her attention—until she saw two words that stuck in her mind from what Huck had said earlier.

Secret meetings with Weev indicated there should be a way to find the proper location. Too bad he turned to blackmail. Ah well. At least he showed some spine before I killed him.

That didn't explain what Xisis was. She flipped through more pages to find the start of the chapter. What was this thing that could cure diseases? An herb? A potion?

No, a being.

Xisisrefliel lives beneath the spores in a palace that somehow exists on the bottom of the Crimson Sea. Though his age is unknown, he has lived in that same spot for at least three hundred years.

Many would, very rationally, call him a myth. However, this chapter will establish that he is undoubtedly real, as evidenced by the testimonies of trustworthy supplicants. Granted, traveling the Crimson Sea is not for the faint of heart. Indeed, there are many who would call into question the sanity of *any* who sail those spores. This has repeatedly been the reasoning for dismissing testimonies of the dragon's existence.

My own efforts to locate the dragon have so far failed, but I can prove it wasn't insanity that led them to their course, but desperation. Their words are trustworthy. Unbelievable though it may seem, Xisis the dragon is real.

The dragon.

Crow thought the dragon was real.

And she wanted to force her crew to sail the Crimson Sea to find the dragon and heal her affliction.

It was the first thing she'd discovered about Crow that made perfect sense. Midnight Tress needed to know more. How did one find the dragon? She'd heard he granted wishes—everyone had heard those stories—but surely there was more to it. Was locating the dragon enough, or did you have to pay him?

But no. Words were splinters for the eyes. Stupid, useless, bloodless, saltless, flavorless, screamless words were over. No more.

The fight began again and her form disintegrated. Mush on the desk, slapping itself and writhing.

Footsteps.

Fighting against the one who wanted words and the not of the will of being again the words.

Footsteps *outside*.

No no no no no no no no no obey.

Crow was returning. Key in the lock.

Had to—

In a flash and a burst of black smoke, Tress was cast out into her own body. She found her mouth parched, dry like it was full of sand. She couldn't recognize the feel of her own *tongue*, now like a lump of cloth, and her hands were *withered* before her. She had collapsed sideways on the bed, and when she tried to speak she let out only a croak.

"Tress!" Huck said, squatting before her face. "Tress!" He held the silver knife awkwardly in his paws. "There was a line of darkness coming out of your mouth. I didn't know what to do, but you were coughing and . . ."

"Water," she managed to force out. She reached toward the second waterskin.

Huck scrambled over and grabbed it in his teeth, pulling it toward her. She managed to dump it into her mouth. As soon as it touched her tongue, her mouth *burned*. She kept drinking through the pain, choking on the water, forcing it down a throat that was dry as parchment.

After that she lay on the wet mattress, wheezing. If she had been that dehydrated normally, she would undoubtedly have died, but this was no normal effect. Timely application of liquid reversed the process, reinflating her twig arms as the burning in her mouth and throat faded.

She slumped back, enjoying the sensation of *not* being in pain, and thought about what she'd learned. That led her to worry. Would Crow find remnants of the midnight spores? As Tress had broken free from the bond, she *thought* she'd felt her body evaporating into black smoke. Had that left residue?

"Tress?" Huck asked. "Are . . . you all right?"

"Yes," she said, her voice hoarse. She pushed her hair away from her face, as it had escaped its tail in her thrashing. "You might have saved my life, Huck. Thank you."

"Well, I guess we're even now," he said. "I'd be at the bottom of the Verdant Sea if you hadn't let me out of that cage."

He was still wringing his paws, so Tress forced herself to sit up and show him a smile. But moon of menace, she could feel a monster of a headache coming on. Perhaps she'd be better off leaving midnight spores alone in the future.

Nevertheless, she knew what Captain Crow wanted. And—though she couldn't be certain—it seemed the things that Huck had overheard *hadn't* been about Salay and the others. The "secret meetings" had been with Weev, and "getting rid of them" referred to the spores in her blood.

Perhaps Salay, Ann, and Fort would know what to do. Tress waited to see if Crow would come barreling in, furious about being spied upon. When that didn't happen, Tress took a luxurious bath, then dressed and prepared to attend the secret meeting. Hopefully the others wouldn't be *too* angry at her when they found out she wasn't a King's Mask.

Tress, of course, underestimated the human mind's ability to believe whatever the hell it wants.

THE LIBERATOR

I've found a way for us to escape our predicament," Salay said, then gestured at Tress. "Behold our liberator."

Tress froze, her hand still on the door to the quartermaster's office, which she'd just shut. She hadn't expected to be put on the spot the moment she stepped in. "Um . . ." she began.

"She can't confirm it, of course," Salay said, lowering her voice to a conspiratorial whisper. "But I'm confident she is a King's Mask."

Fort held up his sign. **Not to be a contrarian, Salay, but I sincerely doubt that's the case.**

"Yeah," Ann said. "I'm with him. Tress is great and all, but she's obviously a girl from a backwater island."

"The entire *point* of the King's Masks is that they seem innocent," Salay said. "How many girls from backwater islands have *you* seen walk on the sea? Then cling to the outside of a ship at sail?"

Fort and Ann studied her, and Tress blushed beneath their scrutiny. "I was desperate," she said. "I just did what I had to in order to survive."

It IS a little suspicious, Fort wrote, **how you almost immediately ended up as ship's sprouter.**

"Right?" Salay said. "She's not afraid of spores."

"I'm *very* afraid of spores," Tress corrected.

"And she could have fled the ship at Shimmerbay," Salay said, "but chose to remain so she could keep an eye on Crow. She admitted as much to me earlier."

Tress sighed. "I . . . don't want to impose, Salay. But I think you're misinterpreting what I said."

"Wait," Ann said. "Salay, you're acting like this is a *good* thing. If she *were* a King's Mask, then she'd kill us all. We're outlaws now."

"Ah," Salay said, holding up a finger. "But she *knows* we aren't complicit in killing anyone."

Technically, we are, Fort wrote, looking morose. **We turned pirate, then people died. Doesn't matter that we didn't shoot the cannon. We're responsible for those poor people's deaths.**

The small room grew quiet. Fort sat on his stool behind the counter, shoulders wide enough that they nearly touched both walls at once. He wore suspenders, as the last seven belts he'd tried to wear had given up on the spot—and I have it on good authority he's been ordered by judicial mandate to stay at least thirty feet from any others as a judgment for past brutality.

Ann sat on the counter by the wall, swinging her legs. She seemed intensely interested in a knot in the floorboards, but in reality she was haunted by Fort's words. They were all culpable. Everyone except Tress.

Salay stepped toward the others, away from the door. "See, that's why it's important that she *is* a Mask. The only way for us to survive after being named deadrunners is to have an agent of the king vouch for us." She looked to Tress, pleading in her eyes. "That's why she could be our liberator. She could tell the king we meant well. That we tried to stop Crow. It's a way out. Isn't it?"

Tress had seen Salay as stern, straightforward. Like a firm handshake in human form. But right now, there was fear in her dark eyes. And pain. Moon of mercy, it was difficult to hear her plea and deny it.

Fort and Ann both looked to Tress, a spark of hope in their eyes as well.

Huck was right. These people weren't fools. They weren't idiots for hoping Tress was something more than the girl she appeared to be. They simply wanted there to be a chance.

Tress's mouth went dry again, though not from abusing aethers this time. There *was* a way for her to prove she wasn't a Mask. She merely had to say she *was* one. Incongruently, this would prove she wasn't one, assuming Salay was right and Masks weren't allowed to admit to their station.

But saying that would stomp out their last light of hope. Doing so felt . . . cruel. Like kicking a kitten.

No. Like strapping dynamite to a kitten, then seeing how high you could get the head to fly.

Tress couldn't say it. They wanted it so much. She in turn was desperate for them to *get* what they wanted. So instead she changed the subject. She reached into her satchel and took out a cannonball.

"I took this," she said, "from a secret compartment in one of Laggart's gunnery barrels."

Salay looked to the other two and pointedly folded her arms, as if to say, *See?*

Fort took the cannonball and balanced it in his palm, his curled fingers against it and the other knuckles holding it steady. He rolled it from one palm to the other, then set it on the counter. He got out a chisel and a hammer, holding them each in his unique way, and gingerly tapped the cannonball in a few specific places. He was then able to hold it down with one palm and twist so the two halves came apart.

Inside, normally one would have found an explosive charge of zephyr spores and the fuse system to burst the cannonball. (We'll get to the specifics later.) Each ball had a number printed on the outside, the seconds until the secondary detonation—which would launch out a spray of water.

In this case, the charge had been replaced by a wadded cloth, the water in the hollow center filled with lead shot.

"Rigged," Ann said, "to sink a ship, not capture it. Moon of justice, Salay. You're right. The cap'n made us deadrunners on *purpose*!"

I knew something was off about all this, Fort said, holding up his sign. **You knew it too, Ann.**

"Yeah, but to see it . . ." Ann said. "How'd you get this without getting caught, Tress?"

"It wasn't hard," she said. "Nobody wants to go near the charges."

"But how did you even *find* them?" Ann asked, poking at the dissected cannonball.

"I, um, have experience with barrels and hidden compartments."

Salay gave her a sly glance and a knowing smile.

My question is WHY? Fort wrote. **What does the captain gain by this? We were already pirates. Killing people instead of looting them makes no sense.**

"Yeah," Salay said. "That's the conundrum."

Tress hesitated, then sighed. She had to tell them. "I overheard the captain speaking to Laggart. She was afraid that unless you were wanted criminals—facing death on any island where you tried to flee—you wouldn't be loyal enough."

"Well, she's right about that," Ann said. "Until that ship sank, I was thinkin' about findin' a way off."

You "overheard" the captain speaking to Laggart? Fort wrote. **How? They never speak their secrets out in the open.**

"They weren't out in the open," Tress said. "They were in her cabin." All three looked at her, and she realized her mistake. Moon of mercy. She shouldn't have come to this meeting with a splitting headache.

"You were able to spy on the cap'n," Ann said, "*in* her cabin while she was speaking conspiratorially to her first officer about her secret plans to betray her crew?"

"Er. Yes."

The words hung in the air for a moment before Ann plucked them and chowed down. "Awfully good at espionage for a girl from a backwater island, aren't you?"

"Just lucky," Tress said, then tried to move on quickly. "Look, I'm worried the captain will try to sink more ships. Swapping the cannonballs helped prevent more deaths today, but I think she wants to murder at least one more crew to get you all on board. I mean, metaphorically on board. With her plan. Since, you know." She gestured to the ship.

"I agree with the Mask," Salay said. "Today was too close. We've got enough blood on our hands. We need to find a way to deal with Crow permanently."

That could take time, Fort wrote. **First, I think we should find a way to quench her bloodthirst.**

"She's not exactly the quenchable type," Ann said, "if you haven't noticed. I think we just need to get her away from where she can do damage."

What if, Fort wrote, **we were to persuade her to sail a different sea? One without so many people on it. That way we'd run into fewer innocents she could hurt.**

"True," Salay said, "but we'd have to get to the Crimson Sea or—worse—the Midnight Sea. But there's no way we'd persuade the captain to do that. She wants to be where the ships are plentiful."

"Actually," Tress said, "I'm pretty sure she'd agree to sail the Crimson Sea."

"Nah," Ann said. "The cap'n's got too healthy a sense of self-preservation. We'd never persuade her . . ." She trailed off, looking at Tress, and narrowed her eyes. "At least, no *normal* crewmember could persuade her of such a crazy idea."

"I think it will be easy," Tress said, uncomfortable. "Salay, you should suggest it."

"After what I did earlier?" Salay said. "Captain *wants* an excuse to hang me right now. If I asked her to sail the Crimson, she'd toss me overboard for sure."

"Do you really think you can convince her, Tress?" Ann asked.

Now, Tress *wanted* to tell them about what she'd learned: that Crow planned to sail the Crimson and get herself cured. And . . . it occurred to her that if the captain got healed, everyone would win. The crew wouldn't have to be afraid of a spore eater, Crow would live, and maybe they could all stop being pirates somehow.

But if Tress were to explain how she knew what she knew, she was *certain* the others would be convinced she was a King's Mask. Overhearing the captain was one thing. But admitting to having somehow stolen her private writings?

So, instead of explaining, Tress nodded. "I'll do it. I'm certain I can make her agree to sail the Crimson. The rest of you can focus on the long-term plan: a way to take the ship back from her."

So long as those spores are in her blood, Fort wrote, **she'll be immune to anything we could do to her.**

"Um, pretend she won't have those anymore," Tress said. "Assume her powers will be negated in the near future. By ... um ... something *completely* unrelated to me."

All three of them took another opportunity to stare at her.

"Right, right," Salay said, ushering Tress out the door. "We'll do that. You get her to sail the Crimson. If she agrees to it, I'm confident I can get the Dougs to go along with the idea too. Most of them are as upset at the killings as we are." Then, in a whispered tone, Salay added, "Just remember our deal. Put in a good word for us with the king. Convince him we didn't want any of this and tell him we helped you stop her. All right?"

"Salay," Tress said. "I'm really not—"

"I know," Salay said. "You can't admit it. How about this. If you *happen* to *have* a chance to speak to the king on our behalf, can you promise me you'll take it?"

"I suppose," Tress said.

"Good enough," Salay said. "And good luck."

33

THE LIAR

Tress found the captain on the top deck, leaning against the rail at the bow of the ship as she poured water from her canteen into a nice tin cup and gazed toward the setting sun that seared the horizon. Tress stepped up, and at that moment the seethe stopped. Doug, the night helmsman, called for the furling of the sails, and the ship scraped to a halt. It was a quiet beast, slumbering to the gentle sounds of wind on spore and canvas.

Each time the ship stopped, the world felt suddenly out of step with its own music. There was no motion to compensate for, and the air was too quiet. The gentle grinding of spores was normally so constant that its lack became unnatural. Even the deck grew quiet as the Dougs went below to grab a snack and play cards until the seethe returned.

The captain didn't acknowledge Tress. She drank the water from her cup, then dangled it from her index finger, staring toward the sun. As if she were a celestial executioner, sent to make certain the day rightly expired.

Tress didn't speak up immediately. The captain had made it clear she wasn't to be interrupted when enjoying a drink. Tress just hoped the woman wouldn't toss the cup into the ocean when she was done. Yes, it was utilitarian in design, but so was Tress herself. She'd hate to have either be wasted.

The Verdant Moon watched overhead, covering a good third of the sky. I've often found it odd how little the people of the spore seas look at their moons. When I first arrived on the planet, I couldn't help staring. There is a malevolence to the way they hover so close. Where most planetary moons stick to the walls and wait for an invitation to dance, these are already on the floor—and they are wearing sequins.

"Why are you here, Tress?" Crow finally asked.

Tress deliberated. If she outright *asked* Crow to go to the Crimson Sea, the woman would undoubtedly be suspicious.

"Well," Tress said. "I wanted to discuss something."

"That's not what I meant," Crow said. "I want to know why you are here on these oceans. What do you want?"

As if *that* were a simple question to answer. People generally don't *know* what they want, though they almost uniformly hate being told what it should be. Plus, Tress had lived her entire life feeling she shouldn't ask for the things she wanted.

"I left my island to see the world," she said.

"People often say that about becoming a sailor," Crow said. "It's a pretty little aphorism, isn't it? With a dainty bow. Travel the seas, see a hundred different islands. Problem is, each dockside bar is frighteningly similar—and that's basically all you're going to see."

"At least I'll get to meet a lot of different people."

"Well, yes," she noted. "That is true. Problem is, their insides also all look frighteningly similar. And as a deadrunner, that's basically all you're going to see of *them*."

Tress glanced away from Crow. She wished the ship would move again. All this standing still made her nauseous.

"So that's it?" Crow said. "Just some childish desire to be someplace else?"

"Yes," Tress said.

The captain seemed disappointed. In the distance, the sun finally sank into the sea, fully extinguished. Only the afterglow persisted to give evidence of the crime.

It bothered Tress how much she'd had to lie lately. Certainly, one shouldn't feel bad about lying to someone like Crow. One shouldn't hit people either, but such social conventions don't apply to the tiger gnawing on your leg.

So Tress wasn't worried about *this* lie. She was more concerned by the general density of lies emerging from her. They were all for the greater good, yes, but the aforementioned tiger might also believe that said gnawing was for the greater good. Specifically *its* good.

Tress was coming to realize a discomforting fact: people are not separated into simple groups of liars and non-liars. It is often the situation, and one's upbringing or genetics, that makes the lies—and therefore the liars.

"Actually," Tress found herself saying, "there is more. Someone I love was taken by the Sorceress. I intend to travel to her island and confront her to get him back."

Crow nearly dropped the cup. Tress reached out, anxious.

"The Midnight Sea," Crow said. "*You* intend to travel the *Midnight Sea.*"

"Well, hopefully not alone," Tress said. "Ideally I'd like to do it in a ship."

Crow laughed, and it was not a cheerful sound. Antagonistic and mocking, it was to ordinary laughter what a guard dog is to a puppy.

"*You?*" Crow repeated. "A straggly-haired washer girl from nowhere? *You're* going . . . I can't even say it!"

Something in Tress changed at that sound. It didn't quite *snap*, but it certainly bent—and found that it was able to flex far more than it had in the past. She looked Crow in the eyes and said, "I don't think that's fair. I have gotten this far. My mother always told me that the hardest part of any task is getting yourself to start it."

"As someone who has climbed several mountains," Crow said, "I can confidently say your mother is an idiot."

Tress felt herself flush with anger. Some things were uncalled for, even among pirates.

"Who," Crow said, "did you think would *take* you on this impossible mission?"

"Well," Tress said, "I only really know the crew of one ship right now. I was kind of hoping—"

She was interrupted by another bout of laughter. She had expected this one. She'd provoked it on purpose. Because she was growing less and less embarrassed about lying, at least to Crow.

And she had just thought of quite the majestic one.

"What if I found a way to pay you?" Tress said.

Crow laughed so hard she started coughing. Ulaam even came up and peeked about the deck at the sound, as the sole previous time he'd heard Crow laugh like that was when one of the sailors had managed to spear himself in the crotch with his own boarding hook.

"Even if I wanted to go to the Midnight Sea," Crow said, wiping her eyes, "and even if *you* could pay *me*, the crew would never agree to it."

"You're probably right," Tress said, pretending to think. "I'd have to ease them into it. Send them someplace menacing, but less dangerous at first. What about . . . the Crimson Sea? I'd need to cross the Crimson to get to the Midnight Sea anyway. So we could go there first."

"They'd never agree to it, girl," Crow said. "This crew is as cowardly as the king himself."

"But say I *could* get them to agree," Tress said. "Would you allow it? Very few ships sail the Crimson, so the ones that do *must* be the richest and most valuable to loot!"

That, it should be noted, made about as much sense as assuming people who live in distant kingdoms must be the most fit, since it takes so long to walk to those places.

Crow shrugged. "If you can persuade them, fine. But they won't agree. Not yet. They're not . . . desperate enough."

Tress thanked the captain and excused herself. She didn't want to say anything more, and didn't need to. Because the captain had effectively just been played by a straggly-haired washer girl from nowhere.

Again.

34

THE TOSHER

There's a story from Tress's land that I'm quite fond of telling. You see, in the palace of the king, the lowliest servant is the tosher—the man who goes through the castle's sewage to make certain nothing useful has been lost or discarded.

No one wanted to be the tosher, for obvious odoriferous reasons. Worse, no one listened to the tosher, because wherever he went, people were either too busy moving upwind from him, or they were preoccupied by trying to remember how to get vomit out of carpet. (Soap, vinegar, and warm water.)

The tosher in our story had a great many items to complain about, some related to the lack of fiber in the royal diet. One thing he didn't complain about was his dinner. Each day he got the same thing. A baked potato with lard.

The tosher loved baked potatoes. So much so that he decided to begin asking for a second one at dinner. He was given it, mostly to get him to go away, and then it became a habit. Two potatoes. Each day.

This continued until the lesser servants were instead served something different for dinner: cornbread with lard. And the tosher *hated* cornbread. He waited for the potatoes to return, but they never did.

One day, while doing his daily work—after remarking that someone must have dyed the punch green again at the latest ball—a thought occurred to him. His life in the palace was miserable, but surely he could do *something* to better his station. He determined to speak to the cook and get potatoes for dinner again.

So the tosher set out on a quest. He found the cook, apologized for making the milk curdle, and made his plea. Potatoes, please. Less cornbread.

The cook was sympathetic, judging by the tears in her eyes. But unfortunately, she couldn't change the menu. She explained that the palace butler set the meal plan; the cook simply made the food.

The tosher went to talk to the butler. He found the man in the middle of a strange activity: trying to see how much handkerchief his nostrils could hold. The tosher presented his problem. The butler seemed sympathetic, judging by the way he was biting his lip. Sadly, he couldn't change the meal plan—because he was allocated supplies by the minister of trade, who no longer provided potatoes.

Well, the minister of trade—it turns out—had dropped her ring into the tosher's domain. The tosher recovered it after some diligent searching, though he did wonder why someone as fancy as the minister of trade ate so much corn. He went to return the ring, and the minister honored the tosher by seeing him in person. Outside. In high winds. While it was raining. During allergy season.

The tosher explained his predicament. The minister of trade was sympathetic, judging by the way she almost fainted as he approached, and she listened to his complaint. However, she could not help him; the *king himself* had mandated that only corn be fed to the servants.

Well, the king wasn't the sort of person you could meet every day. Because he wasn't regular, and it was an every-second-day thing for him. On the proper day, the tosher—umbrella in hand—called up. He knew the king would be able to hear, as the tosher had firsthand, empirical evidence of how good the acoustics were in that particular location.

He asked the king if he would *please* give them potatoes for dinner again. He loved them so much, he always ate two. The king was sympathetic, judging by how he stopped giving the tosher new work for a short time in order to answer.

"I can't," the king said. "The entire potato crop succumbed to pests. Also, look out."

The tosher learned two important lessons that day. First, you don't need to lower your umbrella to talk to someone. Second, no one—not even the king—had the power to provide potatoes at the moment.

"You're the one," the king said after doing his business, "who started the two potatoes thing, eh?"

"Um . . . yes?" the tosher called up, then regretted opening his mouth.

"Funny," the king explained, his voice echoing, "I had to stop buying potatoes even before the crop died. Once *you* took two, *everyone* wanted two. Because of the increased demand, potatoes became too expensive. We stopped being able to afford them for servants."

So in truth, there was a third lesson.

Even small actions have consequences. And while we can often choose our actions, we rarely get to choose our consequences.

As Tress walked belowdecks, she felt a certain . . . discomfort. That was a common occurrence. Conversations with Captain Crow tended to leave a person with residual filth. Emotional soap scum.

As Tress saw Ulaam walking away—disappointed that the laughter hadn't been due to any impaled crotches—she hastened after him.

"Doctor," she said, "there's something I wanted to ask you. About . . . the spores I most certainly did *not* try."

"Hush," he said, looking down the corridor. He ushered her toward her room. Once inside, he inspected her closely. "Yes . . . I believe you're still alive."

"I mean, I'm talking to you. And walking around."

"That's not as concrete a set of evidences as you might assume," he said. "But what was it you wanted to ask me?"

"Do midnight spores . . . leave any kind of trace after the bond is broken?" she asked. "Like, say you were using them to sneak into someplace you shouldn't be."

"That is, generally, where people sneak. Hmmmm?"

"Right. But let's say that, um, you were interrupted and someone broke the spell for you so you didn't die."

"It's not a spell, but a complex symbiotic relationship between two entities. Either way, I'd buy the person who saved you a very nice present. Perhaps a spare shoulder."

"Uh . . ."

"People can always use more shoulders. You know, despite people promising me cold ones as gifts on three separate occasions, they've never come through? Humans can be so inscrutable."

"Right. Uh, back on topic? Please?"

Ulaam smiled, fingers laced before him. Strange, how his grey skin and red eyes could seem so . . . quaint once you got to know him. Less demonic. More eccentric. "You won't be discovered," he said, "unless someone actively *saw* the Midnight Essence moving about while you were controlling it. Once the bond breaks, it evaporates into black smoke, which disperses quickly. No residue is left behind."

Tress nodded, relieved.

"Why are you so anxious about this?" Ulaam asked.

"Well, I just had a conversation with the captain," Tress said. "I feel like I got the better of her. And so . . ."

"And so you wisely assume that maybe instead she was secretly manipulating you. Perhaps because she had a clue as to what you were doing, hmmmm? Curious. What, tell me, did you get her to do?"

"Sail us to the Crimson Sea," Tress said. "I know what you're going to say. But I also talked to Fort, Salay, and Ann. They're willing to sail the Crimson too, and think they can make the Dougs agree."

"I don't doubt they can," Ulaam said. "The three of them can be very persuasive. But *why* are we sailing the Crimson? What in the world could make you *want* that to happen?"

"Oh!" Tress said. "Right. Well, that's what I found out when I was spying on the captain. She plans to visit a dragon and make him heal her."

"Xisis," Ulaam said. "She plans to bargain with Xisis?"

"Yes, and so I persuaded her to sail the Crimson."

"Something she already wanted to do?"

"Well, yes, technically. It's more that I persuaded her without her knowing I was persuading her."

"To, again, do something she *wanted* to do."

"It's complicated. But I worry maybe I'm not as clever as I might have thought I was."

"That seems self-evident, child," Ulaam said.

"Well," she said, sitting down on her bed, "wasn't it at least a *little* clever? The captain was going to sink at least one more ship. So getting everyone to go now instead . . . Everyone wins, right? Assuming we can find the dragon, the captain will get healed. No more ships need be sunk. Maybe once she's no longer dying, Crow will let everyone go. And I . . ."

Well, she would be on the Crimson Sea—remarkably, halfway to the Midnight Sea. That would put her closer to rescuing Charlie than she had realistically thought she would get.

"Child," Ulaam said, going to one knee beside the bed, "Xisis is a *dragon*. He doesn't offer boons. He offers *trades*."

"For what? Treasure? You mean we have to rob some more ships first?"

"Xisis has no need for lucre, Tress. He wants for only one thing in order to continue his experiments: servants to do his chores. But seeing as he lives underneath the spores, he requires a very *particular* kind of servant."

"Particular . . . in what way?" Tress asked.

"They can't be afraid of spores," Ulaam said. "That is always the trade. One reasonable boon—a healing would count, I suppose—in exchange for one slave to work for him all their days. The trick is finding him an offering who doesn't panic at being led through a tunnel of spores."

In that awful moment, Tress remembered the captain's eyes when Tress had decided to remain on the ship. When she'd volunteered to become ship's sprouter.

You really aren't afraid of spores, girl? Crow had asked.

Oh, moons . . . Tress thought.

Outside, the seethe started again. The ship lurched into motion a short time later, and she heard the captain calling new orders. They would head to a port and take on extra stores, since they would very soon be going on a long journey . . . without ports . . .

Crow was planning to trade Tress to the dragon. And Tress, in her ignorance, had greatly accelerated the ship toward the event. She might have tricked Crow, but she'd managed to trick herself as well.

She would have no proverbial potatoes. But she certainly was standing in a big pile of the tosher's soil.

PART

5

35

THE LOVER OF TEA

Tress spent the next three days trying to devise a way to escape.
Surely she'd done all that could be expected of her. She'd protected the crew of an entire merchant ship. She'd managed to set
the *Crow's Song* on a course toward a safe reconciliation for everyone
except herself. Surely her conscience would let her flee now.

The ship would stop at port to take on water before sailing the Crimson, and she *had* to find a way off the ship there. Then she could get on
with her real quest, and let the *Song* go without her.

Except . . .

She sat in her room, leaning on her worktable and looking at the cups
Charlie had sent her while traveling. He'd stayed true to her all that time,
going so far as to sail to the Midnight Sea because he refused to take the
easy path and marry one of the women his father wanted him to. He'd
gone to his doom because of . . . because of love. For her.

Could she really run? Hoid was her best lead in figuring out how
to reach the Sorceress. Plus, here on this ship she had a crew that
would sail the Crimson. And could she *really* abandon her friends?
Particularly when they were showing so much faith in her? If she left,
who would the captain give to the dragon? Would Crow be left with no
recourse but to return to the Verdant Sea and continue her pillaging,
murderous ways?

Questions like these burdened her. Worry has weight, and is an infinitely renewable resource. One might say worries are the only things you can make heavier simply by thinking about them.

The day the *Crow's Song* finally pulled into port, Tress was on the deck, wind making a mess of her mane of hair. Again thinking about Charlie. She missed him a frightening amount. She hadn't realized, in their years together, how much she'd come to rely on his presence.

Not that he'd done anything specific. Charlie wasn't really a "do things" kind of person. He was a "be things" kind of person. Making decisions was easier around him—as if he were an emotional lubricant easing the machinery of the heart as it labored through difficult tasks.

Lately, she'd been having trouble picturing him. She could perfectly remember a picture *of* him, hanging above the mansion's hearth. But him? That wasn't so easy, though she loved him. That is not so odd an occurrence. A picture is an object, easy to define and contain, while a person is a soul—and is therefore neither of those things.

The island appeared up ahead, breaking out of the Verdant. Dougs called out, excited to go ashore. Even Hoid seemed to have a spring in his step as he wandered past wearing . . . well . . .

All right, I was wearing black slacks with bright white athletic socks. There. You know my shame. My relationship to fashion was in those days akin to that of a fifteen-pound spiked mace to an unarmored forehead.

Before Tress could decide if she wanted to execute her half-formed plan of escape, Laggart sauntered over and tapped her on the shoulder. He pointed toward the captain's quarters. "Crow wants to see you, girl."

With a sigh, Tress obeyed. Inside, she found Crow at her desk, holding an exquisite porcelain cup with a floral motif painted across the side. The captain sipped at it and waved toward the seat across the small desk.

Tress sat, noticing—but trying not to stare at—the book she'd read earlier. Crow idly tapped it with an index finger as she stared out her porthole.

On deck, Laggart called orders for the Dougs to prepare the ship for docking. The vessel slowed and turned, wooden timbers giving soft groans of exertion.

"That's . . . a nice cup, Captain," Tress finally said, daring to speak first.

"Got it from those merchants," Crow said. "My first official piece of plunder."

"We're pulling into port," Tress noted, as if it needed to be stated. "I am, um, planning to go ashore . . ."

"No you aren't," Crow said.

"I'm not?"

Crow shook her head and took another sip. "You'll join me in conversation here while the crew unloads cargo and reloads supplies. I should . . . enjoy the company."

A tremor went through Tress, an aftershock to Crow's words. Was this proof she had discovered Tress's spying?

Or . . . no, this might simply be Crow being careful with her chosen offering for the dragon. With a sinking feeling, Tress realized that she wouldn't get to decide whether or not to flee. Even if Crow didn't know what Tress was planning, she wasn't taking any chances.

"Do you like tea, girl?" Crow asked.

"I'm fond of it, yes."

"You'd probably love this," Crow said. "Zapriel tea, from the Dromatory Isles. Expensive stuff. Worth more than gold, by weight."

Notably, she did not offer Tress a cup.

"This is how a deadrunner lives," Crow continued. "Frenzied bursts of opulence. Best enjoyed quickly, as our lives are bound to be short. It pleases me that the rest of you get to experience this."

"Being hunted? Being outlaws?"

"Being one step from death," Crow said. "Most people never *live*, Tress, because they're afraid of losing the years they have left . . . years that also will be spent *not* living. The irony of a cautious existence." She took another sip and eyed Tress. "Do *you* feel more alive now? Now that you have joined us in killing, facing the chance to be killed?"

Tress wanted to answer. Because . . . she *had* noticed this. She wasn't so timid about right and wrong, or about propriety, as she once had been. Was . . . something breaking inside her because of this life?

Could she ever fix it?

"You're wrong," Tress said. "Plenty of ordinary people live meaningful, interesting lives without needing someone like *you* pushing them. You shouldn't be so callous about killing good people."

"I am no more callous than the moons," Crow said. "Why, they take young and old, lovers of virtue or vice. Fallen to disease here, famine there. A casual accident inside the safety of one's home. Why should *I* avoid killing good people? I follow the path of the gods themselves by delivering death indiscriminately. To do otherwise would presume I am greater than they."

"You could have gotten what you wanted without killing."

"Yes, but why?" Crow said. "I'm a pirate. So are you, though you make a terrible one. Too merciful. Looking to protect random merchant ships when you *should* be worried about yourself."

Tress fell silent, her breath catching.

Crow took another sip of her tea. "Yes, I know about the cannonballs," she said. Why beat around the bush when there were so many people who *weren't* currently being beaten? "Laggart hasn't figured it out yet, but he has the intelligence of a walnut. There's only one person who could have swapped those balls."

Tress wished she were more coolheaded, so the sweat on her brow wouldn't give her away.

"Don't look so frightened," Crow said, leaning back in her seat. "That was an enterprising move, if misguided. You'd be an excellent servant— rather, sailor—if you could be properly controlled. Anyway, it's over now. We're sailing the Crimson as you wanted. You really think you can save your friend from the Sorceress?"

"I didn't do it solely for him," Tress said, annoyed at how deeply she allowed Crow's words to sting. "I wanted to protect the crew; I didn't want you truly making them into deadrunners."

The captain laughed. "Protect the crew? By persuading them to sail the Crimson? Child, I worried that killing Weev would deprive me of my favorite source of amusement, but you have well and truly taken his place!"

Tress blushed and looked down. She tried to remember how she'd felt so proud of herself a few days ago—but that emotion seemed remarkably naive now.

"Do you even know?" the captain said. "Do you *realize* what the Crimson Sea is like?"

"I . . . I know it's bad . . ."

Crow let out a roar of laughter, loud enough that the moons themselves assuredly heard. She slapped the table, rattling her tea saucer. "You set us on this course, and you *don't even know* what we're sailing toward!"

It occurred to Tress that she absolutely should have asked this question before. "I understand," Tress said, "that there are more dangerous spores than the verdant ones. But I don't see how a sea can be *much* more dangerous—we already *are* careful not to spill water, and we have silver all throughout our ship. So as long as we're careful, we should be fine, right?"

"Oh, girl," Crow said with a chuckle, "it's not the spores that are the problem. It's the rain."

Right. Rain.

I haven't explained rain.

The more meteorologically inclined among you might be wondering about the planet's weather patterns and water cycle. If you're one of those to whom these things are extremely important, you have my sympathies. It's never too late to develop a personality. Maybe go to a party. But try to avoid topics like weather patterns and water cycles. Unless of course you can do it like me.

Rain falls in small localized ribbons on Tress's planet. These vibrant lines of water weave like serpents in the sky. Rain brings death and life, hand in hand—fitting company for the gods.

More isolated squalls than true storms, these resplendent displays are best at night. They shatter the moonlight into a thousand colors. You haven't witnessed the full grandeur of a rainbow until you've watched one explode in rings on the Verdant Sea, haloing a moon big enough to swallow the sky.

Naturally, aethers grow with the rain, springing up behind those ribbons of water. It's as if some celestial being is drawing lines on a map, and fortifications appear spontaneously at their will. Those walls hang there, gasp for life, then collapse into the sea, devoured by the jealous spores.

It's beautiful in a way only something so terrifying can inspire, and terrifying in a way that only something so beautiful can demand. Fortunately, these rainfalls are perfectly predictable. They follow the same routes every time, so constant that rainfall maps from a hundred years before are still accurate.

Except in the Crimson Sea.

"Rain falls unpredictably in the Crimson, girl," Crow said. "Yes, the spores are dangerous—they create red spines, sharp as a needle. But the *real* danger is the rain. Squalls can come upon you at any time, unexpectedly, weaving through the sky in any direction they please. Sailing the Crimson is all about random luck. No preparation can protect you, because the rain kills the clever same as the fool. Just like I do."

Outside the room, Tress heard thumps as the Dougs began to return with barrels of water. "I . . . see," Tress said, her mouth dry. "And the Midnight Sea? Is it the same? Random rains?"

"Oh, no," Crow said, standing up and stretching. "But it doesn't matter, seeing as how midnight spores birth monsters that serve the Sorceress. Rain can fall twenty leagues from you, but you'll still get swarmed by the monsters. There's no escaping them—at least on the Crimson you can get lucky. No one sails the Midnight without being attacked." Crow smiled. "No one." She nodded then, dismissing Tress.

The Dougs had returned, and the ship was stocked. There was no opportunity for Tress to flee now.

36

THE EXPLORER

Crow followed Tress out. It wasn't until the ship was safely away from port—on a heading that would take them straight into the Crimson Sea—that Tress was allowed to go belowdecks.

Trapped. She was trapped on this ship.

They were sailing toward an insane sea where rain fell unpredictably. And if they survived, she would be sold into slavery to a dragon.

Had she really thought she had the upper hand? Had she *really* thought she could rescue Charlie?

Her? Of all people?

The worst part was, he would probably never know what had happened to her. He'd rot alone in the Sorceress's prison. And if by some miracle he *did* get free, he'd find that she'd left the Rock—but her ship had been destroyed by deadrunners.

She drifted down the steps, then down the hallway. Dougs laughed and worked behind her, thumping on the steps to the hold. But she felt alone. Like she was choking at dinner, and nobody could see. Or maybe nobody cared.

She fled to her room as tears threatened to boil free. She doubted that bawling your eyes out was an appropriate pirate activity, so she was glad she was able to get the door shut before she fully lost control.

"Whoa," Huck said. He scampered up onto the footboard of the bed. "Hey, Tress. What's wrong? What happened?"

"I . . . I . . ." She shook her head and gasped for breath, unable to speak. It was all suddenly too much. People are like stomachs, you know. They can process some of what you feed them, but stuff in too much too fast, and eventually it's going to come right back up.

"What did they do to you, Tress?" Huck asked. "I'll get them back. I promise you. I'll bite 'em on the toes."

"On . . . the toes?" she asked through the tears, imagining the ridiculous sight.

"Yup," he said. "It's a very noble thing to attempt, as the toes are the third most stinky part on a human's body. I'd do it anyway, for you."

Tress settled down on the bed, staring up at the ceiling as tears crawled down her cheeks.

"Tress?" Huck said. "Really. What happened?"

"Nothing happened," she whispered. "And nobody did anything to me. *I'm* to blame. For all of this. The captain plans to trade me to the dragon of the Crimson Sea—I'm to be payment for a healing.

"I knew I was in over my head, so why should I be surprised? Why *wouldn't* I end up trapped on a ship captained by a demon, sailing straight toward my own doom? It's what I deserve."

She put the heels of her palms to her eyes, rubbing them. Then she felt a distinct *bite* on her left big toe.

"Hey!" she said, sitting up and looking toward the foot of the bed, where Huck sat.

"Sorry," he said. "But I *did* promise to bite the person who was responsible for you crying. Also . . . um, no offense . . . but *yuck*."

She flopped back down. "Don't make me laugh," she said. "I might shatter like a cold glass dropped in hot water."

He scrambled along the bed, up next to the pillow, watching her tears. Those were quieter now, but still persistent, like the pain itself.

"I . . . went ashore," Huck said. "I hid in one of the bales of cloth the Dougs hauled out, then made my escape while Fort was selling them. He's good, by the way. I've never seen someone haggle like that man. And beyond that, the town was really interesting. Maybe you'd like to hear about it?"

She shrugged.

"When I'm feeling bad, it's nice to think about something else," Huck said, wringing his paws. "So let me know if I'm helping, or if you want me to be quiet. Sometimes it's better if people—and rats—are quiet. I know that. At least, someone told me that once.

"Anyway, I watched Fort haggle, but I was too far away to read his words. I just know he got way more for those bales of cloth than he should have, considering the buyer must have known they were hot. Oh! And afterward he went to meet with a group of Deaf people living on the island. There were a bunch of them, and Fort smiled a lot and used his hands to talk, instead of the board. I wonder if the other islands have groups like that and I never noticed.

"Anyway, the city didn't fly the royal flag. Isn't that interesting? I know we're at the border of the Emerald Sea, but still. The king has always made it seem like there *aren't* any rogue islands. And we just landed on one! I expected a lot of peg legs and eye patches, but the people seemed . . . normal."

"We're pirates now," Tress said, "and there's not an eye patch among us. We're normal too, I guess."

"Kind of funny to think about, isn't it?" Huck said. "That all the pirates in the world were once someone normal." He fell silent, as if uncertain whether he should continue.

Tress, oddly, found that his talking *was* helping. She'd never been one for wanderlust, but she had dreamed of far-off places and their cups. That part of her genuinely wanted to hear about the island.

"You said the town was interesting," she said, turning to look toward Huck. "Interesting how?"

"Oh!" he said. "They have a *bell tower*, Tress! I've always wanted to see a bell tower. I overheard some people talking, and they said it has fifty-three bells. What an odd number, don't you think? I always thought a bell tower would have one bell. It's not a *bells* tower.

"Well, I walked all the way around it and snuck a peek through the window, and they have *ropes* for ringing the bells! You pull on them and make sounds all through town. I doubt they'd let rats pull the ropes though. Even if we could."

Tress smiled. A simple act, but only moments ago it had seemed as impossible as flying. Or as coming up with a rhyme for "bulb." (No really. Try it.)

There was something endearing about the way Huck continued explaining his experiences on the island. He spoke of the most common things. A garden with flowers that smelled good. A pathway where all the cobbles fit together to make a spiral. A drinking fountain that you worked with a foot pedal.

The fact that he found these things interesting enough to talk about was in itself engaging. The topic mattered less than his enthusiasm. And so, Tress smiled. That didn't banish her worries or her sorrow, but it did nudge those dour thoughts toward transforming into other less oppressive ones.

". . . And then the girl got her brother wet," Huck said, "by stomping on the pedal when he bent down to drink. Isn't that delightful? Reminds me of being young. When I wasn't on a pirate ship far from home."

"You could go back," Tress said. "If you want, Huck. You could leave. You should."

"I can't," he said softly. "I can't ever go back to my island, Tress. Because my home isn't there anymore."

That had the markings of tragedy, so Tress didn't press him for details. Plus, she didn't want to think about the fact that—in all likelihood—she wouldn't ever be going home either.

"Does it seem like things were better when you were younger?" Huck asked. "Did life really make more sense then?"

"Yeah," Tress whispered. "I remember . . . calm nights, watching the spores fall from the moon. Lukewarm cups of honey tea. The thrill of baking something new."

"I remember not being afraid," Huck said. "I remember waking each day to familiar scents. I remember thinking I understood how my life would go. Same as my parents'. Simple. Maybe not wonderful, but also not terrifying."

"I don't think things were really better though," Tress said softly, still staring at the ceiling. "We just remember it that way because it's comforting."

"And because we couldn't see the troubles," Huck agreed. "Maybe we didn't want to see them. When you're young, there's always someone else to deal with the problems."

Tress nodded. Beyond that, memories have a way of changing on us. Souring or sweetening over time—like a brew we drink, then recreate later by taste, only getting the ingredients *mostly* right. You can't taste a memory without tainting it with who you have become.

That inspires me. We each make our own lore, our own legends, every day. Our memories are our ballads, and if we tweak them a little with every performance . . . well, that's all in the name of good drama. The past is boring anyway. We always pretend the ideals and culture of the past have aged like wine, but in truth, the ideas of the past tend to age more like biscuits. They simply get stale.

Tress thought through a few of her personal favorite ballads, which thrummed with honey, and love, and other sweet things.

She genuinely felt better. Moons, hearing about bell towers and water fountains had made her feel *better*. For some people, feeling better would have been an excuse to ignore the situation, but Tress preferred to weaponize her mood swings. So, ever pragmatic, she sat up on the bed and confronted her problems.

"I need a way to defend myself," she whispered. "A way to defeat Crow before she sells me to the dragon."

It was fortunate, then, that Tress's room contained five different varieties of the most dangerous substance on the planet.

37

THE SCHOLAR

Tress had given her room a cursory inspection when she'd moved in. She'd sorted through the things Weev had left, mostly to make certain nothing truly dangerous was hiding among them. Those earlier explorations had been the actions of a girl playing a role.

Now she looked again. As a girl trying to save her life.

Where she had read, now she studied. Where she had arranged, now she organized. And where she had accepted, now she experimented. Nothing motivates quite like a deadline. Particularly one that emphasizes the *dead* part.

Tress didn't just pour her whole heart into the activity, she gave it her entire body, for a heart can't accomplish much without a nice set of fingers. Weev had not been an orderly person. Tress had hoped he'd left behind manuals of instructions. Instead she found scraps and scrawled notes, cluttered with collected tidbits and half-finished ideas. The sort of mental detritus that those unacquainted with genius often attribute to unfettered brilliance.

In truth, there was no pattern to such a mess other than the subtle chaos of frustration. Signs of a mind stretching beyond its limit toward ideas *just* beyond its reach. This can happen to a dunce as easily as a genius; it's no proof of capacity, any more than a person being too full for dessert is an indication of their weight. In Weev's case, the scraps were indicative of a mental hoarder: a person who collected ideas like a grandmother collects ceramic pigs.

It was in the middle of realizing this—and coming to understand that she would find no miracle solution—that Tress ran across the first promising scrap. It was a detailed schematic for a cannonball, with a scrawled message at the bottom indicating the captain had wanted Weev to figure out how to make them himself, so the ship wouldn't have to keep buying them at high prices from the zephyr-masters.

This intrigued Tress. She had a casual interest in the mechanics of cannonballs, like the way you might find yourself interested in the cuisine of a culture whose language you'd been learning. What held her attention, however, was the intricate use of spores inside them.

Weev had been stymied. That much she could tell from his scrawled notes, which only served to distort and obfuscate the otherwise orderly diagram. Still, it depicted a sprouting technique she hadn't been aware of.

By now you've seen that a cannonball on Tress's world wasn't merely a lump of metal, but a piece of artillery—one I promised to explain in more detail. You see, each had a timer inside that, after its launch, would lead to a secondary explosion and a burst of water. Yes, you know that part already. But do you know how the timers were made?

It turned out to be quite simple: the timer fuse was a *vine*. From the notes, Tress learned she wasn't the first to discover that applying water to an aether would cause it to continue to grow after its initial burst. The explosive emergence was erratic, but everything afterward was far more predictable. Even precise. An exactly measured verdant vine would grow at an extremely reliable rate when given an exactly measured amount of water.

(Yes, for those of you who care about things like weather patterns, this growth eventually stopped—and a given vine would eventually exhaust all of its growth potential. Otherwise, people couldn't very well eat them. Getting the vines to the end of their growth potential was essential for turning them into emergency food.)

Anyway, the initial explosion that sent the cannonball soaring *also* broke a small glass container of water inside, soaking a clipping of verdant aether. That vine grew—pushing a plug with a bit of silver on the tip—through a short tube toward the central mechanism of the cannonball. This was a charge of zephyr spores surrounding a hollow sphere made of roseite. That roseite, in turn, had wax on the inside—which allowed it to contain, but not touch, a charge of water.

The silver tip pushed through the zephyr spores, killing a small number of them but leaving most unharmed, and then touched the roseite sphere—which cracked from the pressure of the silver. Water flooded out, touched the zephyr spores, and released their explosion—which detonated the entire mechanism violently, shooting out shrapnel and water.

I have seen the modern designs, a note at the bottom said—she didn't think it was from Weev, but the original creator of the diagram—*and agree. Impact detonation charges are the future of artillery.*

She didn't know what that last part meant, but nonetheless she found the diagram ingenious. Here were three different aethers working together. Verdant for the fuse. Roseite for the water container. Zephyr for the explosion. The central sphere didn't break from the initial firing of the cannonball because it was far, far stronger than glass—but it had a built-in weakness, in that silver could damage it. In this design, she also discovered that wax could insulate an aether from water.

She was in awe, and possible experiments ran through her mind. Now, it should be noted that experimenting with zephyr spores was usually an excellent way to be certain you went home in many small coffins, instead of one large one. But, as we've demonstrated previously, Tress possessed a common sense rare to many in her position.

The sprouter profession attracts a self-selecting crowd. Normally this includes uncommon individuals who have somehow survived their natural inclination to jump from idiotic heights into shallow water, or to ride bicycles down mountainsides, or to eat unidentified brightly colored berries.

The human species does need a certain amount of foolhardiness. Without that, people would have been too reasonable to do frightening things—like venture close to that very hot orange stuff that turns wood black and makes Tharg's beard smoke. But evolution is not a precise mechanism, and it has resulted in a certain number of people in the population with more nerve than neurons. Spore sprouting was only the latest in an increasingly shiny set of activities destined to neatly—and violently—cull such individuals from the gene pool.

But Tress hadn't sought out the occupation. She'd fallen into it. She was intelligent enough to understand the charts and thoughtful enough to expand upon the ideas. And what she lacked in formal training, she more than made up for by being the type of person who used oven mitts even when a pot had been given time to cool down.

It was, at that moment, the exact mix that innovation required. In fact, while some might call what happened next dumb luck, I would term it inevitable.

There's no reason, Tress thought, holding up the schematic, *why you couldn't make something like this that was portable.*

Not just a gun. Guns were common, and while useful, not particularly flexible. Could she improve upon that? What would a modular *spore gun* look like?

A note at the bottom of the schematic—again added by the original creator—gave her the last piece she needed.

Reference my schematic for flares, which iterates on this design.

Moon of meanings . . . Flare guns. The first few steps had already been taken. All Tress had to do was—

A knock came at the door.

Such a little interruption. A polite one, of the type Tress associated with her old life. Nonetheless it shattered Tress's concentration like the thunder of a thousand cannons firing at once. She leaped to her feet and threw open the door, uncharacteristically prepared to unleash a stream of verbal abuse upon the one who had so callously interrupted her.

She found Fort standing outside, plugging the hallway, holding a plate covered with a pot lid to keep it warm. He held up his sign.

You didn't pick up evening mess, it said. **Are you all right?**

Tress blinked, then glanced out her room's porthole. It had gotten so dark, she'd been squinting to read without realizing it. Soon, she'd need to light her lamp—a luxury afforded the sprouter that was denied common sailors. She put a hand to her head, pushing back her hair, trying to track the hours. Had she really been *that* enthralled?

Moon of mercy . . . she'd been ready to snap at Fort when he'd been so kind as to bring her some dinner. What had happened to her? Had some kind of spell on those papers made the time vanish? Or had she really been *that* interested? Remarkable. There weren't any cups involved, nor any windows.

"Thank you, Fort," she said, taking the plate. She peeked underneath the cover and found the normal crusted slop leftovers. Today's offering *might* have once been some mashed potatoes and seagull, though it was difficult to tell through the char. She figured the meals probably *weren't* made of sawdust and rocks, despite the flavor, since she hadn't died from malnutrition yet.

You still owe me for all this, he noted. **Captain never did order me to let you eat, despite your new station.**

"When we figure out the right payment," Tress mumbled, "can we maybe start letting me have some that *isn't* scraped off the bottom of the pot?"

Fort frowned. **What? Tress, I save some for you and Hoid first thing, before I let the Dougs at it.**

"You . . . what?"

It hit her like a hammer to the skull.

This wasn't the leftovers.

This was what *everyone* ate.

"Oh . . . oh *dear*," she said.

Fort had the decency to look down and shrug apologetically. **We took turns after Weev died,** he wrote. **I'm the best we have. Ann's concoction left half the crew sick for three days.**

"Is that so," Tress said. "Well, I think I have discovered a way I can repay you—and the rest of the crew—for the kindness you've shown me."

Cooking here isn't easy, he warned, holding up his palm beside the board after he wrote the words. **We only have sea rations—most of it stale, canned, or dried. It's hard to make palatable.**

"I think you'll be surprised," Tress said. "Come get me tomorrow before you start cooking for evening mess . . ." She trailed off as she heard the bell on deck ring out a warning.

That wasn't the three heavy strikes indicating another ship had been spotted. But neither was it the call to mess, which was a constant ringing. It was two strikes, then quiet, then two strikes.

"What's that?" she asked.

Border ahead, Fort wrote, hand moving quickly as he practically bounced with excitement. **Crimson Sea has been spotted. Want to witness the crossing?**

"Absolutely!" she said, joining him in the hall, though she was strangely reluctant to leave her research. That was silly. She had no formal training in academics; her schooling had ended at basic reading and arithmetic. Surely *she* wasn't secretly a scholar. A window-washing girl? If she'd been inclined toward research, she'd have realized it before.

The truth was, she'd simply never encountered a topic interesting enough—or dangerous enough—to engage her.

38

THE APPRENTICE

I'm not sure I can recommend visiting the spore seas. While there are places in the cosmere that are more deadly, few are so casually danger-ous. Other locations will kill you with a roar or a cataclysm. But the spores, they do it with a whisper. One moment you're enjoying a nice book. The next, you take in an unfortunate breath, get a few crimson spores in your system, and suddenly you've turned your skull into a colander.

It doesn't happen often, but when it does, it seems somehow more unfair than dying from a lightning bolt or a hurricane. Nature is *supposed* to announce herself before murdering you. It's only sporting.

That said, the spore seas *do* have some sights to sell.

Fort made room for Tress by the prow, sending a couple of Dougs to watch from the rigging instead. It was evening, and this far away from the lunagree the green dome of the Verdant Moon drooped low on the horizon behind them—a mirror image to the Crimson one ahead. A vast red sphere in the sky, peeking over the horizon, with the sun hovering above it like an eager sibling.

Closer to the ship, just ahead, the verdant spores gradually mixed with the crimson, making a gradient where—from a distance—the cen-ter was a deep brown. The vibrant, shimmering red beyond seemed an ocean of blood, like the Crimson Moon had been shot and the *Crow's Song* was sailing toward its corpse.

Tress hadn't given thought to how *wrong* that color would feel. The Emerald Moon and Sea had, quite literally, colored everything she'd ever seen. It intimidated her to realize she was leaving it and entering that wounded red ocean instead. She'd been watched by the Verdant Moon all her life, and a very small piece of her—irrational though it was—worried she'd vanish the moment it stopped thinking about her.

As they closed the distance, then crossed the border, Fort leaned against the railing and held up his sign. **You're grinning.**

"Sorry," Tress said. "It's just that this is *terrifying*."

You smile when things are terrifying?

"I didn't use to," she said. "I think my brain is intimidated by how insane things are out here on the seas, and is trying to fit in."

Fort rubbed his chin, but didn't write anything else. She knew he was thinking about her supposed role as a King's Mask, and how she wasn't nearly as frightened of spores as she should have been. And again, it *wasn't* that. She *was* afraid.

At the same time, she hadn't realized how terribly beautiful those red spores would be. Nor how strange it would feel to be leaving the Emerald Sea. These were new emotions, and like new flavors, they could be simultaneously terrifying and intoxicating.

What else would she have never known about herself, if she hadn't left her home island? Worse, how many people like her lived in ignorance, lacking the experience to fully explore their own existence? It is one of the most bitter ironies I've ever had to accept: there are, unquestionably, musical geniuses of incomparable talent who died as street sweepers because they never had the chance to pick up an instrument.

The *Crow's Song* continued straight on into the Crimson Sea until one of the Dougs in the rigging called out a warning. The sky had opened up, and death was snaking toward them.

Tress had never seen rain before. On her island, water came from wells. Though she'd been told about water falling from the sky, it had always felt magical, mystical. A thing of stories.

One of those stories apparently wanted to eat her, for the rain came streaking straight toward them: a knot of fast-moving clouds in the sky, trailing an explosion of aether in a line upon the ocean. A vast wall of crimson spikes that grew up and locked together with such force, the clacking sound was audible from a great distance.

Tress stood, mesmerized. Salay, fortunately, had more experience here—and was already turning the ship when the captain called out an order to do so. They veered hard, tacking to port and swerving—lethargically—back into the Verdant.

The rainline didn't give chase, though it did turn upon the border of the seas, racing on ahead, leaving interlocking crimson spines thirty feet tall. Those eventually slumped and sank into the sea, leaving it pristine, calm. Like a child who stuffed the broken cookie jar under the counter and assumed all would be forgotten.

"Moons," Tress breathed. "What if . . . what if the seethe had stilled right then? What if we'd been unable to move . . ."

Fort glanced at his board to read what she'd said. His only response was to shrug. It was the sort of risk they would take, sailing the Crimson.

Tress turned toward the quarterdeck, where Crow stood near the helm station, taking a long pull on her canteen. She lowered it, and seemed thoughtful.

She wouldn't dare press forward, would she? With that rainline slithering through the region?

"Helmswoman," Crow finally said, projecting her voice so everyone could hear. "Kindly take us south a spell, along the border. It seems . . . imprudent to enter the Crimson at the moment."

"As you command, Captain," Salay said.

Crow swooped down to the main deck, then slammed herself into her cabin. Laggart hurried down the steps, nearly stumbling in his haste, then quickly covered the slip by shouting for the Dougs to get back to work. In minutes, they were sailing a leisurely course along the border. Fort excused himself to go scrub some pots, leaving Tress leaning against the ship's rail.

Laggart stomped past Tress, then hesitated. "You," he said. "What do you think of this *now*?"

"I honestly don't know," she replied. "I'm still trying to wrap my mind around it all."

"I can help with that!" Dr. Ulaam's voice called from nearby.

Laggart grunted. Then he gestured for her to follow. Curious, she joined him on the quarterdeck. Behind the helm and the captain's roost was the aft cannon, set out on its own railed platform, like a heavily reinforced balcony sticking out the very back of the vessel.

It was a dangerous section of the ship, as it was away from the silver protections. Spores that somehow leaped the gap between sea and deck here would take longer to die. That, of course, was important for the zephyr spores used as charges.

Laggart rummaged in the gunnery barrel—an action that fortunately caused him to look down. Because if he'd seen Tress's face, he might have noticed her sudden spike of worry. What was he doing? Was he going to confront her with one of the swapped cannonballs?

Moons . . . she would have made a terrible spy. How could Salay and the others possibly think she was a King's Mask? Tress didn't understand that it is quite possible to be so bad at something it seems implausible. In these cases, it stands to reason that such a person is in fact quite competent—because it takes true competence to feign such spectacular *in*competence. It's called the transitive property of ineptitude, and is the explanation for anything you've seen me do wrong ever.

In this case, Tress's transitive ineptitude didn't come into play, because Laggart didn't see how nervous she was—nor did he confront her with a fake cannonball. Instead he selected an ordinary cannonball, then held it up as if admiring a beautiful painting. Or—considering the way his bald head on the end of his toothpick neck made him look—perhaps he was wondering if there was any relation.

"Now that we're proper pirates," he said to Tress, "I figure we ought to have someone on this ship besides me and the captain who knows how to fire a cannon. The rest of the crew are too useless around spores to be trained. Congratulations."

She noticed that, despite his bold words, he reached very gingerly into the gunnery barrel and selected a pouch of zephyr spores—holding it pinched between two fingers. He quickly loaded it into the cannon through a latch on the top.

"Zephyr charge goes in here," he said, snapping the metal lid closed.

"Get them loaded quickly, because even here, the deck's silver is close enough to start killing spores. Inner casing there is lined with aluminum, to block the silver's influence."

He pushed a wad into the cannon and rammed it into place with a rod. "This rag fills up the bore of the cannon," he explained, "keeps the explosion from going around the ball—and puts the full force on the shot." He slid a cannonball down the front of the cannon. It thumped into place. "Cannon can't angle too low, otherwise we'd roll the ball out the front."

"All right," Tress said. "But . . . um, does the captain know you're having me do this?"

"I'm cannonmaster," he snapped. "Captain won't care who I train. You just do as you're told. Besides, a man needs to take care of himself. I don't want to end up wounded, then get sunk because nobody else on this damn ship has the guts to handle zephyr."

So. Laggart didn't know that she was to be sold to the dragon. This struck Tress as odd, since he seemed to know the rest of the plan. But then she realized there was a good chance the captain considered him a backup sacrifice. He *was* one of the crewmembers who was least afraid of spores.

Laggart picked up a small wooden contraption near the railing, then tossed it overboard. It proved to be a kind of small buoy with a flag, tied by a rope to the ship. As they sailed, it trailed along far behind—like the most conscientious of stalkers.

"Take five shots a day," Laggart told her. "The best way to get a feel for a cannon is to practice."

He started to walk away.

"Wait!" Tress said. "You're not going to give me any more training than that?"

"Training would be useless until you know more," he said. "I'm busy. Figure it out and don't bother me with stupid questions. If you sink a buoy, congratulations. There are more in the hold. Come bother me when you can do it in at most two shots, and then we'll talk about some real training."

"All right," Tress said, an idea occurring to her. "But maybe I should start with something less expensive and wasteful than full cannonballs. We don't have a flare gun on board, do we? I could try that out first."

"What kind of a stupid question is that?" Laggart said.

It was, identifiably, the stupid kind of stupid question. Which at least is better than the redundant kind of statement.

"A flare gun is nothing like a cannon," he said. "So just do what I told you, idiot." He continued muttering to himself as he stalked off.

Tress folded her arms. She'd been *planning* to spend the evening either studying or trying to figure out how to crack Hoid's curse. This was an unwelcome intrusion. Still, perhaps there were some advantages. If she was planning to build her own spore-based weapon to fight the captain, there were worse uses of her time than experimenting with a cannon.

It was just that Laggart, by refusing to offer any useful training, had ensured she'd waste hours figuring out the basic mechanics of aiming the cannon. Even with this brief delay at the border, she knew her time was short. Depending on where the dragon's den was in the Crimson Sea, she had anywhere between a few hours and a few weeks to plan.

A solution occurred to her only a moment later. She pushed the cannon forward, as she'd seen Laggart do. Then she smiled, took a firing rod—which had a soaked bit of cloth on the end—and stuck it into the touch hole. A second later an explosion rocked her, knocking the cannon back along its track.

It took less than a minute for Ann's head to pop up behind, wide-eyed and eager.

39

THE CHICKEN KEEPER

Y ou use these two winches," Ann explained, rotating a handle—not unlike the one on a meat grinder—at the base of the cannon. "This one turns it port or starboard. This other one raises it up in the air. See, a cannonball drops as it flies. So you have to aim upward and kind of *lob* your shot in an arc."

She pointed. "The tricky part is to judge the distance. You've got a lot of cannonballs with different fuse lengths. To properly immobilize a ship, you need the ball to explode right before hitting, so it sprays water."

"Seems like there should be an easier way," Tress said, sitting on the gunnery barrel. "Like making a cannonball that explodes when it *hits* something. Then you'd only have to aim for the ship, not judge the distance."

"I suppose," Ann said. "Ain't ever heard of anything like that though."

I have, Tress thought, realizing only now what the diagram in her quarters had been talking about. It had mentioned "impact detonation charges." *Someone's planning weapons like that. Maybe already built them.*

It wouldn't be too hard, would it? What if you somehow made a cannonball that was pointed instead of round, so you could fire it tip-forward like an arrow. You could then make it so when it hit something, that tip was pushed backward into the center to explode the thing.

But a cannonball that wasn't round? Could that even be created? It was kind of in the name, after all . . .

Ann finished cranking the cannon up, then stood, resting a hand fondly on the weapon. Men, what you want to find is a woman who looks at you like Ann looked at that cannon. Because if such a woman exists, you'll want to move to a completely different kingdom, inform the authorities, and watch the post for packages containing random disembodied fingers.

"Pardon if this is intruding," Tress said, "but why are you so . . . um . . ."

"Weird about guns?" Ann asked.

Tress blushed, then nodded.

"Why are you so weird about blushing when you ask questions?" Ann asked.

"I don't want to impose on people."

"You should more often," Ann said. "How else are you going to get what you want?"

"Well . . . I mean, others shouldn't have to think about what *I* want. It . . ." She took a deep breath. "Will you tell me, Ann, why you are so weird around guns?"

"Why do you think?" Ann asked. "Any guesses?"

"No. I . . . did ask Fort, and *he* said he thought you must have been a slave or something when you were a child. He thinks firing guns is about controlling your surroundings. Having access to power."

"Huh," Ann said, settling onto a box of extra cannonballs. "And he's normally so good at figuring people out."

"So you weren't a slave as a child, I take it?"

"Farm girl," she said. "Raised chickens. It was a great life. You know, chickens are really intelligent and make great pets."

"Really?"

"Yeah. It's a bloody shame they're so delicious. Any other guesses about me?"

"Well," Tress said, "I asked Salay, and she figured that you see cannons and firearms as symbols of authority, so you want to be in charge of them because people take carpentry for granted—and you want a more important job."

"Ah, well," Ann said, "that's exactly what I'd expect Salay to say. *She's* always been terrible at judging people. Like, *really* terrible."

"I . . . um . . . might have noticed," Tress said.

"Please tell me you asked Ulaam about me."

Tress blushed more deeply.

"You did!" Ann said, pointing. "What did he say?"

"I didn't really understand his explanation," Tress replied. "It, um, was something about the shape of the guns . . . and cigars for some reason?"

Ann laughed. A raucous, untamed sound, full of genuine mirth. Tress couldn't help but smile as well. That kind of laughter quickly overbooks a person and looks for additional accommodations nearby.

"So what is it really?" Tress asked as Ann's laughter finally died down.

"I just . . ." Ann shrugged. "I think they're nifty."

"That's all?"

"All?" Ann said. "You can basically define someone by the stuff they like, Tress. It's what sets us apart, you know? We talk about how important culture is, but what *is* culture? It ain't government, or language, or any of that hokum. No, it's the stuff we *like*. Plays, stories, marble collections."

"Cups?" Tress said.

"I suppose," Ann said. "Sure, why not? Cups. I'll bet there are a whole ton of people who collect cups. But it's not a cup alone that's interesting."

"It's how one cup is different from other cups."

"Yeah! Exactly." Ann patted the cannon. "And I'm a cup who likes firearms. I love the smell of zephyr puffing out. You know the one? The electric smell of lightning? I love the *challenge* of trying to hit a distant target. Any dumb oaf can hit a bloke who's next to them. But to get one on the next ship over, completely unaware, while he's sipping tea? Bam, now *that's* style."

She looked off into the distance. "I used to listen to the guns fire in the town. Every Twelveday festival. Well, that and the rare times when raiders tried to attack the port. Each time those shots sounded, echoing against the hills, I thought, 'That's going to be me someday.'"

"I'm sorry," Tress said softly, "that you never got the chance."

"Never got the chance?" Ann said. "I enlisted in the militia the day I came of age! Went right into the cannonade crews. Lasted twenty-four days! Right up until . . ." Ann looked at her. "Did you know cannonballs can bounce? It was the most lunatic thing. Still think I'm the only cadet in the militia who ever managed to shoot her own sergeant . . . when he was *behind* her . . . inside the barracks."

"Wow," Tress said.

Ann sighed, heaving herself up onto her feet. "Anyway, you should try shooting like Laggart told you. Try to fire them so they pass over the buoy, using long fuses for now. Then adjust for the next shot down. Even the best cannoneers use an exploratory shot—helps them judge the wind, get perspective, that sort of thing."

Tress stood, and found herself pricked by a certain lunatic sense of guilt. "You want to take a shot now?"

That is probably the craziest, most reckless thing I've ever heard someone say—and I was literally part of a secret plot to kill God.

"Ha ha," Ann said. "You . . . Wait, you're serious?"

Tress nodded. "You seem to miss it so much."

Ann leaned in close, inspecting Tress. "You don't even look afraid. You really *are* one of them."

Transitive property of ineptitude. Trust me.

Ann stepped over and put her hand on the cannon, then glanced at Tress. "Laggart will be mad."

"He told me to figure this out on my own," Tress said. "And not to bother him. That's what I'm doing. Asking an expert for advice."

Ann looked back at the cannon. Then at Tress yet again. "*Really?*"

"I've lost things," Tress said softly. "And it's . . . not going to be easy to get them—him—back. But the thing you want is right here. So, let's make it happen."

Ann smiled again, then glanced at the buoy. She cranked the cannon to the side. Then cranked it some more. Then some more.

"Um, Ann?" Tress said, pointing. "The buoy is *that* way."

Ann followed her pointing, then looked at the cannon—which was *at least* thirty degrees off. "Looks good to me."

"Trust me," Tress said. "Crank it back."

Ann did so reluctantly. She grabbed the firing rod from its bucket. Then—grinning like an undertaker in a war zone—she fired.

Both of them waited, anticipating the worst. And Tress *did* smell a distinctive metallic scent. The cannonball hit the Verdant Sea behind, then vanished. Without harming anyone.

I'll be honest, I was a little surprised myself.

"Thank you," Ann said softly. "*Thank you.*"

"It wasn't really anything," Tress said.

"It was everything," Ann said. "I was beginning to believe, Tress. What they said. About me being *cursed*. I'm not. I just . . . well, I have bad aim." She looked out over the ocean, then wiped her eyes. "Not cursed. You don't understand how much I needed to know that."

"Join me each day," Tress said. "Take a shot with me. We can get better together."

"Deal."

"Oh," Tress said. "One other thing. Do you know if the ship has a flare gun?"

"Of course," Ann said. "You need them if you get stranded, or to surrender to pirates. Oh! Guess we don't need to worry about that anymore. Surrender means death to us. Anyway, you should be able to get one from Fort."

Ann excused herself after that—tears of joy aren't exactly a good match with an unprotected part of the ship. Tress settled down, thinking about people and how the holes in them could be filled by such simple things, like time, or a few words at the right moment. Or, apparently, a cannonball. What, other than a person, could you build up merely by caring?

Eventually Tress fired a few shots of her own. (They all missed too.) As she was cleaning up afterward, the ship finally turned upon the captain's order. This time no rains chased them off as they entered the Crimson Sea.

40

THE CHEF

The following evening, Tress took stock of the ship's cooking ingredients. What she found was not inspiring. Stale flour, very few useful seasonings, rancid oil. And the ship's oven? Fueled by sunlight spores in a way that made the kilnlike device heat in an *impossibly* uneven way. A quick test of wet flour on a baking pan proved that.

No wonder Fort had difficulty cooking anything without burning it. Indeed, it was possible he did it on purpose in order to cover up the awful flavor of the ingredients. She gave him a look with folded arms, and he shrugged. They didn't need his writing board for that exchange.

"All right," she said, handing him the bottle of rancid oil. "Toss *this* overboard. It's too far gone."

He regarded it with a thoughtful eye, the bottle looking much smaller in his enormous hands, held between two curled, broken fingers. He was so big, Tress couldn't help wondering if he was fully human—which was understandable, but all joking aside, Fort was a hundred percent human. Plus at least twenty percent of something else I haven't been able to determine.

"Trust me," Tress said. "We can make something of the flour, but there's no good use for the oil."

That you know of, he wrote. **You'd be surprised at the things people will trade for.** He tucked it away. Together, they occupied the ship's small kitchen, which wasn't much bigger than Fort's quartermaster office—

though this room had counters running all around with cupboards underneath, broken only by the door on one side and the oven on the other.

"Here," Tress said, pushing a small pile of kulunuts across the counter to him. "Mash these."

Mash?

"Yes, and do it in the mortar so you don't lose any of the liquid. Kulunuts have a lot of fat to them, and we're going to need that, since the oil is bad."

He shrugged, doing as she ordered while Tress made some small alterations with pans to turn the oven into a steamer. "For a more even bake," she explained at his curious expression. "Steam is a good conductor."

But aren't we making bread?

"Nut bread," she said, sifting the flour to check for any mold. Old flour she could work with, but moldy flour? That was *far* worse. Fortunately, this seemed dry and pure enough. "We need to avoid basic breads. Old flour has a bad taste, but it won't make us sick. So we need something where taste won't be too noticeable. Kulunut bread should be workable— and we can steam it."

He took her at her word, continuing to mash. Over the next hour, Tress found herself falling back into old routines. How many times had she cooked food for her parents, using whatever they could afford or scavenge? There was a calming familiarity about doing so again, if on a much larger scale.

She hoped her parents were doing all right without her. She'd intended to write to them, but with all that had happened . . . Suddenly she felt guilty for having wished for more letters from Charlie. If his experiences on the seas had been anything like hers, then it was a miracle he'd found time to send her what he had.

Fort didn't fill the time with idle chitchat, and while you might ascribe this to his deafness, I've known more than a few Deaf people who were quite the blabberhands. Fort watched everything she did carefully—and she found his attention difficult to interpret. Was he trying to learn from her? Or was he suspicious of her?

Uncertain, she popped out the first of her test cakes, sliced off a corner, and offered it to him. Fort picked it up between the sides of his hands. He inspected it. Sniffed it. Tried it. Then cried.

This type of response will send any artist into a panic. Tears wash away the middle ground—all the infinite permutations of mediocre are eliminated, and two options remain: one sublime, the other catastrophic. For a moment, both interpretations existed in a kind of quantum state for Tress. And people wonder why artists so often abuse drink.

Fort reached for another bite.

Tress's sigh of relief could have filled the sails. She went back to chopping gull—this, thankfully, was fresh—for the meat pies. But Fort tapped her on the shoulder.

How did you do that? he wrote. **I watched for sleight of hand.**

"What would I use sleight of hand for?"

Secret ingredients. Swapping one cake for another, pre-prepared.

"Are you always this suspicious?"

I'm a quartermaster on a pirate ship, he said.

"Well, there were no swapped cakes," she said. "And no secret ingredients other than practice and resourcefulness."

He reached for a third bite.

"How much," she said as she chopped, "would you say a meal like this each day would be worth?"

Fort stood up straight, then eyed her, smiling slyly. **Oh, I guess that's a matter for debate, isn't it?**

"That third bite you took suggests the debate is already over."

He hesitated, mid-finger-lick. Then he typed, **I thought you said you weren't tricking me.**

"Curious," she said. "I don't remember saying that. I only stated that the bread was genuine. Not that I wasn't trying to trick you. Care for a fourth piece?"

Now, it should be noted that Tress proceeded with this conversation under a slight weight of guilt. She wanted Fort to like her, and she wasn't generally one to demand trades or payments from friends.

Yet she'd watched how he interacted with others. Fort wasn't a selfish man. He'd not only been the one to haul her up that first day, he'd given her food when she needed it. He always seemed to have what people needed, quietly providing medicine, shoes, or even a deck of cards for a Doug in need. And he rarely took something of equal worth in trade.

Yet with people like Ann or Salay, he'd bargain fiercely for the smallest items. Even ones they *should* be able to requisition from the ship's stores. Tress thought maybe he was like her Aunt Glorf, who had always fought for the best deals at the market. She'd been afraid of looking silly by being taken advantage of.

The guess was as wrong as ending a sentence with a preposition. But it worked anyway. Like ending a sentence with a preposition. Because it convinced her to bargain, even when she didn't want to impose.

Do this once for each day I fed you, Fort said, **and our debt will be equal.**

"Now, that *would* seem like a fair deal," Tress said, "if one happened to be using a rotting loaner brain that Ulaam dug out of his bottom drawer. The food you provided me, Fort, was practically worthless. I'd say that one good meal should balance out a few dozen terrible ones."

The food wasn't worthless, Fort said, mashing some more nuts. He could hold the pestle in his curled fingers quite easily, pausing now and then to tap with his knuckles on the top of his board—which, resting on the counter, now displayed the words on the same surface. **Food has a minimum threshold of usefulness, assuming it's not poisonous.**

"It wasn't poisonous," Tress said, "but it sure *tried*."

It kept you alive, and a life is invaluable, I'd say. So my food, provided when you couldn't get any other, was therefore priceless.

"Ah," Tress said as she chopped, "but the captain has repeatedly said my life is worthless. So your food, in turn, is the same."

If you have no value, Fort wrote, mashing nuts with one hand and tapping with the other, **then surely your labor is barely worth anything at all. And hence, I should be able to employ you for a pittance.**

"Well then," Tress said, "I suppose if that's the case, then I'll find some other way to repay you. What a shame." She took the last piece of the test cake before he could grab it, then popped it in her mouth.

Oh *moons*, she'd forgotten what it was like to eat without forcibly suppressing her gag reflex.

Fort rubbed his chin, then grinned. **All right, fine. Each day of work providing adequate meals like this pays off two days of meals I gave you.**

"Five," Tress said.

Three.

"Deal," she replied, "but you can't tell the others that these meals are mine. I can't afford to be roped into cooking breakfast and lunch as well. I have other work to do."

The crew will get suspicious if two meals are bad and one is incredible.

"So the food is incredible, is it?" she said.

He froze, then grinned again. **I underestimated you.**

"Hopefully that's catching," she said. "You're a resourceful man, Fort. You can come up with an excuse to put off the crew. Tell them you're trying new recipes, but only have time to practice one a day. Plus, if we get that oven working, the things you make might not be so . . ."

Unique? he wrote.

"Unrecognizable."

A deal, I suppose. Assuming you agree to make dessert each day as well. The Dougs have been asking for one that doesn't melt the plates before it can be eaten.

"They've been asking for *more* of what you were making? Moons, how many of those bargain bin brains did Ulaam have?"

Fort laughed out loud. It was a full laugh, but not like Ann's raucous one. More unrestrained than uncontrolled. It was the laugh of someone who didn't care how they sounded or looked to others.

I'm wrong, she realized. *He's not worried about seeming silly by being taken advantage of.*

Well? he wrote. **Dessert?**

"I want a flare gun," she said, sliding her chopped meat into a pie tin, "with flares. Without questions."

He eyed her.

Mask business? he wrote.

"Maybe."

Will it help us with our predicament? He pointed upward toward the captain's cabin.

"I hope so."

Then you may have it. In trade for desserts for the rest of the trip.

"Until we reach our destination in the Crimson Sea," Tress said.

I wasn't aware we had one. Curious. Well, so be it. He wiped his hand, then held it out.

She shook to seal the deal.

Thank you, Fort said. Genuinely.

"For the food?" she asked.

For the trade.

"Why *do* you like it so much, Fort?" she asked, leaning against the counter.

I am a hunter by profession, he explained. It is a mark of pride among my people, and my family in particular, to execute an excellent hunt.

"... Hunt?"

Well, we've broadened the definition over the years, he explained. Turns out, a whole society of hunters doesn't scale well. Who's going to make the shoes? Bake the bread? Plan the weddings? He tapped, blanking the board, then continued, So, we choose our hunt when we come of age. This is mine. A worthy hunt, same as my mother. I record each great victory and send them home in letters to be hung in our family hall.

"Wow," Tress said.

You're impressed? Ann laughed.

"I am impressed," she said. "Plus, I have a friend who'd love hearing that story. I hope you can meet him someday. Is ... your trade deal with me today going to go in one of the letters?"

He laughed again. Tress, it would embarrass you to know how successful my hunt just was. Have you eaten my food? The first bite of bread you gave me was worth every meal I gave you in the past. And you have not only promised more, but are going to let me take credit with the Dougs? He winked at her. I'm going to brag about this catch for three pages! Now, hurry up. I want to try one of those pies.

41

THE PHILOSOPHER

Cutting apart a spore-filled flare while distracted wasn't the best of ideas—but admittedly Tress hadn't *decided* to be distracted. It happened naturally, like a case of the hiccups or the inevitable and relentless entropic decay of the universe.

As she pried the stiff wax-paper cap off the flare, she mulled over the pure joy Fort experienced when negotiating. It had always made her nervous to haggle at the market, as she didn't want to make the merchants feel that their goods were worthless or their service unvalued. Yet Fort *loved* the haggling part.

And Ann, shooting the cannon. Tress thought about her while carefully pouring the spores out of the flare. Had Tress ever seen anyone so excited about anything as Ann got? Even Charlie with a freshly cooked pie hadn't looked so content.

Tress tapped the flare carefully, then glanced at Huck, who had insisted on joining her at the worktable—but hid under a large soup bowl, holding it up an inch or so to peek out. He was mostly afraid of the spores at the moment, though she'd caught him hiding a lot more lately. Even when the cat wasn't around.

"What's that?" he asked as a pink stone sphere rolled from the center of the flare.

"The water charge," she explained, holding it up to the porthole to show light through the pink stone. A shadow of water sloshed inside when she shook it. "When this breaks, the water floods out and ignites the spores. In this case, sunlight spores that burn with a bright hot light."

"Oh," he said, lifting the bowl higher. "So those don't explode?"

"Nope," Tress said. "But they could burn us as they create a bright flash and heat." She set a cannonball on the table with a thump. "Now, one of *these* is filled with zephyr spores. So it will explode right good."

Huck pointedly lowered his shield. Tress rolled the little ball of water-filled roseite back and forth on the table. She remembered sermons on the various Moondays, held at the very top of her island. On the Verdant Moondays, they'd been able to watch the alignment of sun and moon. She had always felt she was missing something at those meetings, since the alignment—from their side—looked like any other moonshadow, which happened every day. But apparently the sun centered *exactly* behind the moon only twice a year.

During such an eclipse, the preachers spoke about respecting the moons and about the meaning of life. Except every preacher who visited the island seemed to have a different idea of what the purpose of life was. Even two preachers from the same moonschool would disagree

That part had comforted her. If *religion* couldn't get it together, then she could be forgiven for being a mess herself.

But now—as she dug in the remnants of the flare for the timer—she wondered. Each of those preachers had acted like they had the answer, like there was one purpose in life. All life. She understood the inclination. A single answer would certainly make things *tidier*. Two plus two is four. Water boils at a specific temperature. Also, the purpose of life is to learn to imitate the call of a marmoset. Go.

For Fort, finding a good trade was the purpose of life. While for Ann, the purpose was to learn to fire a cannon without blowing the limbs off her friends by accident. So were there *many* answers? Or were they all the same answer with different applications?

It should be noted that Tress would have made an excellent philosopher. In fact, she had already determined that philosophy wasn't as valuable as she'd assumed—something that takes most great philosophers at least three decades to realize.

She finally pried out the timer, then set it on the table. The flare gun, she noted, worked a lot like an ordinary pistol. You loaded it with a separate charge for firing.

"So . . . what are we doing?" Huck asked.

"Look here," she said, prying a silver bit off the timer. Conical, sharp on one end, like the tip of a pencil. "This is what makes the flare go off. The silver breaks through the roseite core, which is filled with water."

"What I'm going to do is reverse this. I'm going to put this pointed bit on the *top* of the flare, but facing backward. So when the flare hits something, the silver will be pushed back, break the roseite ball, and let out the water."

"I mean, sure," Huck said. "That sounds like it would work. But *why*?"

"I need to find a way to stop Crow," Tress explained. "But as we saw when we attacked those merchants, a normal gun won't hurt her."

"And you're hoping a flare will?" Huck said.

"Not exactly," she said, then began to rebuild the flare. Not only did she put the silver detonator under the cap instead of at the base of the flare, she replaced the sunlight spores with sand and a few grains of verdant spores. She closed the device back up without the timer, then inspected it. "I asked Ulaam earlier today, and he said that the spores living in Crow's blood will protect her from any weapon that tries to break her skin. So I figure I'll stop her without hurting her."

"How on the seas would you do that?"

"Same way we stop ships without sinking them," she said. "I build a flare that explodes with verdant vines, then use those to stick her to the wall or the floor. If I can make this work, I won't have to kill—or even hurt—her. I can immobilize her, then let Salay take over the ship."

"That's brilliant!" Huck said, peeking out farther from beneath his bowl. "Do you think it will really work?"

Tress loaded the flare—along with some zephyr spores—into the flare gun, which had a stubby, oversized barrel. She sighted down it, but didn't pull the trigger—which would inject water into the barrel and launch the projectile. Testing this sort of thing in her quarters didn't seem healthy.

But how *could* she test it? She needed to be able to hit something solid to break the water cartridge, so she couldn't simply fire it out the porthole. But she also didn't want to let Crow know what she was building.

She'd have to find another way. She set the gun down, then glanced to the side as Huck—finally abandoning his hiding spot—came crawling over.

"Hey," he said, "you look sad. It's all right, Tress. You'll find a way out of this. You're good, and you're smart. You'll make it."

"If I do," she said softly, "it will mean consigning Crow to death. Her disease will eat her from the inside if she doesn't make a trade with the dragon."

Huck wrung his paws, his nose twitching. He didn't say the obvious thing: that Crow absolutely did *not* deserve sympathy. Tress knew this already, and he knew that she did.

Unfortunately, sympathy is not a valve, to be turned off when it starts to flood the yard. Indeed, the path to a life without empathy is a long and painful one, full of bartered humanity sold at a steep discount.

To distract herself from what she was planning to do to Crow, Tress inspected the timer that she'd left out in reconstructing the flare. The small device looked exactly like the schematic had described: a bit of verdant vine for a fuse, already grown from spores, and a small glass vial, which—being far more flimsy than the roseite bead—would break upon firing.

She pried out the vine, then—causing Huck to back up in concern—poured a little water on it. The small vine curled and trembled. She watched it for a time, then figured she should practice with her tools.

The vine wiggled a little more vigorously.

Tress hesitated, then leaned down closer. The aether grew steadily, though it was still no longer than her finger. Then the tip—the part that was growing—turned toward her. The little vine crept in her direction.

Tress scooted to the side. The tip of the vine began growing in that direction instead.

Her confusion deepening, Tress scooted her chair the other direction. Again the vine moved, leaving a zigzag in its expanding length as the tip followed her.

It was running out of water, so she wet it again. Then she got down low, watching it creep toward her. Was it . . . looking for something? Back home, she'd found some weeds in a dim shed that had somehow survived the salt. Those weeds had all grown directly toward the single knothole of light in the boards.

"What are you doing?" Huck said, cautiously approaching.

She put out her finger and the tip of the vine grew toward it, then became a little corkscrew as she made a spiraling motion. It responded to her, not Huck.

Because he's a rat? Or . . . because he's frightened of it? But she was scared of spores too, wasn't she?

Except this little vine wasn't dangerous. So . . . no, she didn't feel afraid. Not at the moment.

When she'd used the midnight spores, she'd been attached to the creation. Curiously, she felt something similar at that moment with the vine. A Connection. She thought she could feel it searching. It was empty, but looking. Wanting.

I understand, she thought to the vine, letting it touch her finger and coil softly around it. Fort had his trades, and Ann her guns. But what did Tress have? She wanted to save Charlie, but that wasn't her purpose. That was her goal.

She glanced toward her cups. While she was still fond of them, she had to acknowledge that she really only looked at them these days because they reminded her of Charlie. The cups themselves didn't hold the charm they once had for her. She had seen too much of the world now. Not merely the places either.

The vine ran out of water and stilled, leaving her finger wrapped— but not with a menacing grip. A light touch. Curious, not dangerous.

She found it remarkable. How could this be? The entire world interacted with spores—at least dead ones—every day. People feared them with just cause. Yet this one felt more like a puppy than a deadly force of destruction.

Could the entire *world* have misjudged something so common? Though it seemed unlikely to Tress, it was true—and not that surprising. People consistently misjudge common things in their lives. (Other people come to mind.)

Tress wasn't discovering something completely unknown. Indeed she was realizing why spores and aethers fascinated sprouters. It all had to do with fear.

While a healthy measure of foolhardiness drove our ancestors toward discovery, fear kept them alive. If bravery is the wind that makes us soar like kites, fear is the string that keeps us from going too far. We need it, but the thing is, our heritage taught us to fear some of the wrong things.

For example, to our ancient ancestors, strange and new people often meant new diseases and the occasional spear tossed at our softer bits. Today, the only things new people are likely to toss our way are some interesting curse words we can use to impress our friends.

Fear of something like the aethers? Well, it's as natural as nipples, but nearly as vestigial as the male variety. And when one abandons certain fears and assumptions, an entire world opens up.

THE GUIDE

I love memories. They are our ballads, our personal foundation myths. But I must acknowledge that memory *can* be cruel if left unchallenged.

Memory is often our only connection to who we used to be. Memories are fossils, the bones left by dead versions of ourselves. More potently, our minds are a hungry audience, craving only the peaks and valleys of experience. The bland erodes, leaving behind the distinctive bits to be remembered again and again.

Painful or passionate, surreal or sublime, we cherish those little rocks of peak experience, polishing them with the ever-smoothing touch of recycled proxy living. In so doing—like pagans praying to a sculpted mud figure—we make of our memories the gods which judge our current lives.

I love this. Memory may not be the heart of what makes us human, but it's at least a vital organ. Nevertheless, we must take care not to let the bliss of the present fade when compared to supposedly better days. We're happy, sure, but were we *more* happy then? If we let it, memory can make shadows of the now, as nothing can match the buttressed legends of our past.

I think about this a great deal, for it is my job to sell legends. Package them, commodify them. For a small price, I'll let you share my memories—which I solemnly promise are real, or will be as long as you agree not to cut them too deeply.

Do not let memory chase you. Take the advice of one who has dissected the beast, then rebuilt it with a more fearsome face—which I then used to charm a few extra coins out of an inebriated audience. Enjoy memories, yes, but don't be a slave to who you wish you once had been.

Those memories aren't alive. You are.

Personally, I don't think I gave proper attention to just how beautiful Tress's world was. To me, it was a backwater planet drowning in the dross of the aethers, which are more useful in other incarnations—and far easier to harvest on the moons themselves anyway.

And yet, nowhere else in my travels have I witnessed anything like those spores. As we sailed the Crimson, I felt like a leaf floating on the blood of a fallen giant. The farther we went, the higher the Crimson Moon soared—dark and ominous in the day, often haloed by sunlight. A clot upon the light.

At night, it burst aflame with its own unblinking, preternatural glow. At first we were too far away to see the sporefall, but as we closed the distance, the lunagree appeared. A fountain from the sky, pouring down into the center of the sea. The verdant spores had always looked like pollen in the air, but this felt like a lava flow. Erupting from the heavens to melt away the planet.

I wasn't in my right mind during the trip, but I could still see. And the polished bits of that land in my memory are always striking images. Surreal, spellbinding pictures of magic so dominant it *literally* fell from the sky.

I believe Tress might have been more pleased if the view *hadn't* been so stunning. She'd have had a better chance of keeping my attention.

"Would you *please* focus, Hoid?" the girl asked.

I pointed at the distant red moon, the spores streaming down to fill the sea. "It looks like the moon is throwing up."

Tress sighed.

"Imagine that the sea is the toilet," I said, "and the moon is the face of a god, heaving onto us after a long night of getting spun around and around on a bar stool."

I actually composed a poem about a vomiting god. I'll spare you, though it's the only time I've had an excuse to make a really good rhyme for "scarf."

Finally, after some prodding, I turned from my newfound muse and settled down on the deck near Tress. She would have preferred to work with me belowdecks, out of sight, but I had been stubborn. I'd wanted to watch the moon barf. As one does.

"We need to break the curse," she said.

"Ah yes," I said. Then I leaned in close, speaking conspiratorially. "You know, I have one of those."

"A curse?"

"Indeed."

"I know, Hoid."

"You do?"

"Yes. It's why we can talk about it. If I didn't know, you couldn't tell me."

"I can't tell you something you don't know, but only things you already know?"

"Yes, because of the curse."

"Oh! A curse! I—"

"—have one of those. I know. I need to break yours so you can lead me to the Sorceress. Nobody knows where in the Midnight Sea she can be found."

I fell silent.

"Hoid?" she asked. "Do you understand?"

"I think I understand. But, see, it's hard." I leaned in closer. "I can tell you . . ."

"Yes?"

"Something important . . ."

"Yes?"

"Socks with sandals," I whispered. "The new fashion movement. Trust me. It will be *all* the rage."

She sighed with increasing exasperation.

I'm accustomed to that reaction from people, but I prefer to be *intentionally* irritating. It's against my professional ethics to frustrate people by accident. It's like . . . a construction worker making a new road while sleepwalking. The foreman would have a fit. How in the world does one make a sleepwalker take a union-mandated break? Do you wake them up?

"Look," Tress said, "I have this paper here, see? And I've written down a lot of words that I think would have to do with curses. Are there any you can't talk to me about? If so, that will give me a clue."

It was a workable idea. I would have been impressed, if I hadn't been distracted by wondering whether anyone had made clothing out of napkins yet.

Tress handed me the list of words. I studied them, cocked my head to the side, then nodded.

"Anything?" she asked.

"I," I declared, "have apparently forgotten how to read."

Showing legendary patience, Tress took the list back and read the words to me. I repeated them.

"Well?" she asked.

"I definitely have heard some of those words before," I said. "Now, I forgot the rules. Is this the game where I draw a picture of the word, or is it the game where I act them out?"

She groaned and lay back on the deck, her head thumping the wood. "Could you maybe lead me to the Sorceress *without* getting your curse broken?"

I fell silent.

"Hoid?"

I smiled at her. I'd blacked out one of my teeth to make it seem like it was missing, as I figured that must be quite fashionable. A number of the Dougs were sporting the look, after all.

"Maybe I could say letters to you," she said, "and you could think of the way to break your curse. I could ask you, 'Is this letter in the word?' Theoretically, you won't be able to say yes if it were."

This one wouldn't have worked. It was an easy enough workaround that the Sorceress had thought of it, and had basically "programmed" the curse to forbid the person from confirming words this way.

In addition, in this specific instance . . . well . . .

"Letters," I said. "Spelling words. Reading . . ."

"Right," Tress said. "Right. You never answered my question, though. Could you lead me to the Sorceress? Even without being uncursed?"

I fell silent.

A part of me was hoping she'd notice how loud that silence was.

"Wait," she said, sitting up. "Every time I talk about sailing to see the Sorceress, you get quiet."

"Do I?" I asked.

"Those are the only times when I've been around you that you haven't had anything to say . . ." Her eyes widened. "Hoid, you can't talk about the Sorceress or her island, right?"

I, notably, was unable to answer.

"Hoid," she said, "can you talk about the king's island?"

"I've been there once!" I said. "Have you heard the story about the king's tosher? I don't really remember it, but it has poop in it, so it *must* be funny!"

"Talking about visiting the king's island didn't make you shut up," she said, "but talking about the Sorceress's island did . . ." She stood up. "I need a map."

And there. After only a few days of trying, she'd discovered more about helping me than Ulaam had in our year together. That stupid shapeshifter was *enjoying* this. I swear, they've all been getting weirder ever since Sazed released them.

Anyway, Salay was at her usual post, guiding the ship deeper into the Crimson. She didn't have a map of the Midnight up there, but—upon Tress's request—she sent a Doug to fetch one from her quarters. It wasn't particularly detailed; none of the maps of the Midnight Sea are. Fortunately, the *shape* was roughly correct, since all of the seas are basically pentagons.

Tress started pointing to places on the map and asking, "Hoid, I'd like you to guide us here. Could you do that?"

Each time, I told her some terribly interesting fact about a place—such as having walked there wearing butter instead of shoes. Until she reached a specific point.

When she asked about that one, I fell silent.

When I stop talking, people often act happy. It's a hazard of my profession. But this time it was different. Tress pulled the map to her chest, her eyes watering.

She knew where the Sorceress's island was. Near the border of the Midnight Sea and the Crimson Sea, perhaps half a day's sail inward.

It was the first concrete piece of information she'd found. The first real step toward rescuing Charlie. It was a beautiful moment that was ruined as a sudden line of rainfall appeared on the horizon—then shot straight for our ship.

43

THE MUSICIAN

I know that sailors fear storms on your planet. It's common among all seafaring cultures I've met. Interestingly, most also ascribe—or in their past used to ascribe—volition to storms. They never simply *are*. They *want something*.

The weather patterns on Tress's world aren't specifically Invested—so they aren't self-aware. But you wouldn't have known that from the way the rain came straight toward the *Crow's Song*.

Tress stared at it, growing numb, the joy of her grand discovery fading. It could all end right here, couldn't it? All her struggles, her preparations . . . it could simply end. The *Crow's Song* could vanish in the rain, speared through at a hundred different angles, then pulled into the deep.

And Tress was powerless to do anything about it.

Moments like these bring wind and rain to life. We need purpose; it's the spiritual conjunction that glues together human existence and human volition. Purpose is so integral to us that we see it everywhere.

Sky gods, making thunder with their shouts or causing lightning to fall with their steps. Winds named and granted different intentions and motives, depending on the direction they blow. Rains withheld, granted, or sent to destroy, depending on the turning of celestial moods.

A storm is not an object like a box or a tree. Even to the more scientifically-minded, storms are more notion than numbers. When does a drizzle become a downpour, and when does a downpour become a storm? There's no firm line. It's about how you feel.

A storm is an idea. It's much more powerful that way. Watching the rain bear down on her—crimson spikes marching behind it like the crossed spears of royal guards—Tress *wanted* it to be a deliberate act of the moons. She didn't want her death to be meaningless.

The ship lurched to the side, making Tress stumble. She cried out and grabbed the rail, then quickly snatched the map of the Midnight Sea before it could blow away. Another lurch of the ship sent her stumbling the other direction. It seemed random to her, but Salay was calling orders nearby, and the Dougs obeyed, managing the sails.

Salay didn't particularly care if her death was meaningless *or* deliberate. Provided it was a long time coming.

As I mentioned, on your planet, you may be accustomed to the helm position on the ship being relatively unimportant. Not so on the spore seas. The ship lurched again, wood groaning, canvas rattling. A sailing ship isn't like most vehicles; it takes time and effort to change its momentum. Tress hung on, eyes wide, as *Captain Crow* caught a dropped rope and pulled it tight. Even she obeyed Salay's orders in this moment.

Nearby, three Dougs rushed to the wheel, helping Salay heave to the side, bending hundreds of tons of wood to her will. The *Crow's Song* veered right to the side of the line of rain, skirting so close to the wall of aether that a few of the crimson spears *scraped* the hull. Salay called for the sailors to steady and slow, for a reason Tress didn't understand—until she saw that the giant snarls of interlocking spikes were sinking.

The aethers emerging from their spores had set the sea rippling, and their retreat doubled that, making it billow and quake. You don't normally get true waves on the spore seas—not like you do on liquid oceans—but when you do, they're extremely dangerous.

The *Crow's Song* shook like the ice in a good cocktail, then tipped to the side like the person who's enjoyed too many. Tress immediately felt sick to her stomach, then panicked at the thought of what vomit would do on a deck in the middle of the spores. She managed to find a bucket, her first job on the ship proving useful in an unexpected way.

Through it all, Salay kept shouting orders. It was almost as if she kept the ship from capsizing through sheer force of will. She moved the vessel at times against the waves, but at others she spun the wheel to flow with the pattern. In those few moments, the ship was a giant musical instrument, and she played it as a master, steering us to safety.

Unfortunately, right at the end, one final wave broke against the side of the ship. This spilled spores across the deck. Violent. Scarlet. Thirsty. Enough to overwhelm the silver protections for a few seconds. And Tress wasn't the only one who had been ill.

It happened with a burst of red on red. A flash of spikes on the main deck, near the steps up to the quarterdeck. In the blink of an eye, one of the Dougs had been nailed to the wood outside the captain's cabin. I'll leave off crass comparisons to pincushions and just say this: I've never seen a man bleed out so quickly. But I've also never seen a man with so many places for the blood to escape.

Everyone stared at the terrible scene, and Tress groaned, turning back to her bucket for a second unmealing. Then the Dougs—remembering their training—scrambled for the emergency towels to sop up the blood and prevent any from leaking over the side of the ship. In the Verdant, a stream of blood over the side could have immobilized them. Here it would rip the ship to pieces.

Fortunately, ships on the spore seas are built to prevent this, with all seams pitched and sealed. The silver eventually did its job—and everyone walked across dead grey spores, grinding them against the wood.

In the midst of this dreary scene, the ship ground to a halt. The stilling had arrived.

I'll admit to feeling uneasy, even now, about those days crossing the Crimson. I know the cosmology and arcanum of Tress's planet quite well, and I'm confident that no entity directs its storms.

And yet. Knowing is not always believing.

The two dozen of us on deck turned, as one, to watch the rains veer and inexplicably bear down on us again. Relentless. Water in front leading a charge of violent aethers behind, wide as three ships beside one another.

A storm *is* a living thing, even when not specifically Invested. Because "life," as a concept, is a human construct. *We* define it. Nature doesn't care; it sees everything as a chemical process. It couldn't care in the slightest that a bunch of carbon, hydrogen, and oxygen one day decided it would really prefer to sit on a sofa rather than a bench.

Therefore, something lives if we decide it does. To us on that ship, that day, the rains *were* alive. They had to be. And I know for a fact Tress was shaken not only physically, but emotionally as she looked up from her bucket to see the rain coming again. Captain Crow was powerless to do anything. Not even Salay could save the ship during the stilling.

The line of water missed us by a few hundred yards.

What had seemed, in our horrified eyes, a direct attempt to kill us had instead been random chance. So we watched as the rain vanished into the distance, leaving a persistent wall of red thorns. They towered high, a barricade that would only sink once the seethe began again.

The rain danced around in circles in the distance, then vanished. A capricious god taunting us? A natural process, given autonomy only by our brains as they searched for patterns, meaning, and volition?

I know what I believed that day.

44

THE FALLEN

I implied that I didn't remember the names of the Dougs. That was a lie—I wanted to keep your focus on the main players of this particular story.

But every person has a story, Dougs included. The one who died was named Pakson; both he and his sister were Dougs on the *Crow's Song*. Pakson was tall and awkward on land—the type of man who seemed to have been born with legs a size too large for his torso. He was bald, despite his relative youth, and his neck kind of merged with his chin—to the point that after meeting him, you'd inexplicably get a hankering for a baguette.

He was also unaccountably kind. He was the man who had kept checking on Tress as she clung to the side of the ship. He'd held the rope with several others as Fort pulled her up.

He'd always laughed at meals and thanked Fort for the food, no matter how bad it had tasted. He loved music, but couldn't play, and had always secretly regretted never learning. I wish I'd been in a state of mind to give him lessons.

Now he had fallen. We gave his corpse to the spores and sailed onward.

Tress felt responsible. Maybe if the ship had waited a few more months out in the Verdant, they wouldn't have encountered the rains that day. She was terrified that Pakson wouldn't be the only casualty of her recklessness. So she sought her room—and the distracting comfort of her spores.

As always, Huck was there. Talking to her about life as a rat. His voice distracted her from her problems. The ratty tales were relaxing; even when he spoke of fears and challenges among the rat community, she found herself soothed. Because those events had happened far away. They were personal, yet somehow abstract at the same time.

"It's really interesting," he was telling her, "how much we can smell of the world that you don't seem to be able to. Everyone's *shoes* smell different. Did you know that?"

"I'd have thought they all smelled the same."

"Not to a rat!" Huck said, sitting on the table next to where she was working. He launched into a story about how he'd been able to follow a human through a crowd by sniffing for the distinctive scent of his boots.

Tress half listened, half worked. She was tinkering with the other flares for her augmented flare gun. In each, she adjusted the amounts of the various types of spores, then recorded them in a notebook so she could see which experiment worked the best.

Up above, gulls called in the air. The Dougs, perhaps needing something to take their own minds off what had happened to Pakson, were fishing the air to catch meat for upcoming meals. Plus, birds were very rare on the Crimson, so you moved when you had the chance.

Tress soon had four different flares alongside four different charges. Each flare would theoretically release verdant aether upon hitting, but how much each released was different, which would help her iterate the design. And the charges each had differing amounts of zephyr spores.

She told herself this work would help the other crewmembers. The sooner she found a way to disable Crow, the sooner they could all point the prow out of the Crimson. Regrettably, this argument found a hostile audience, even though she made it only to herself. She *was* planning, after all, on trying to get the crew to sail the Midnight next—and it was said to be even *more* dangerous.

How many lives was she willing to risk to save one man? At what point did the good of her crew outweigh that of Charlie?

You might think this an unfair moral problem to force upon a simple window washer, but there's a certain arrogance in that kind of reasoning. A window washer can think, same as anyone else, and their lives are no less complex. And as I've warned you, "simple" labor often leaves plenty of time for thought.

Yes, intellectuals and scholars are *paid* to think deep thoughts— but those thoughts are often owned by others. It is a great irony that society tends to look down on those who sell their bodies, but not on those who lease out their minds.

As Tress set the final flare in the row, Huck trailed off.

"So . . . I guess now we have to test them," he said. "Any thoughts on how to do that?"

"Well," she said, "the Dougs have mostly been staying on the upper deck lately. And the hold is empty of goods."

Huck nodded; it was the most obvious choice. She set him on her shoulder, then packed her flares, gun, and notebook in her bag. She went and explained to Laggart that she wanted to inspect the handiwork Ann had done patching the hull down below. It might, Tress explained, help her understand how to make better roseite patches in the future.

It was an unremarkable lie, but if Laggart saw through it, he likely thought she was trying to make work to stay busy. The cannonmaster gave his permission and said he'd keep anyone from bothering her. The exchange was so relatively pleasant, Tress briefly wondered if something was wrong with him.

On her way down, a Doug called from the rigging, pointing into the distance. Another rainline had been spotted. Tress's breath caught, but the rain—this time—swerved away from the ship and vanished soon after.

Tress tore her eyes away and hastened down to the ship's cavernous hold. She latched the trap door at the top of the steps for a little extra security, then set out her three oil lamps—something denied to common sailors. It was unwise to leave too many things burning when you lived in what was essentially a giant dry, hollow piece of firewood.

The hold was half empty, having disgorged its goods at the last stop before the Crimson. Foodstuffs and water supplies made up her audience as she loaded a charge, then a flare, into her weapon. She then turned and raised the gun toward the empty aft portion of the hold.

Huck, to his credit, didn't run, though he did cower a bit in her hair, which she left unbraided more often these days—in a tail or just unrestrained, waving free. She paid for that with the brush at nights, but it felt . . . liberating. At home, she'd always been embarrassed for how her hair behaved. But out here, there were so many more pressing things to worry about.

Tress pulled the trigger—which caused the gun's hammer to hit the flare with enough force to break the tiny glass vial in the charge. Zephyr spores exploded, releasing air, faintly blue. The flare popped out the front of the gun . . .

. . . then flew approximately a foot before nose-diving into the floor. She probably should have used a tad more zephyr.

Unfortunately for Tress, the rest of her work had been meticulous. She'd fundamentally grasped the nature of the mechanisms from the schematics. And so, her design functioned perfectly. When the flare hit the deck nose-first, the shock pushed the silver point inside into the sphere of roseite, releasing the water.

Verdant vines exploded outward, seizing Tress and enwrapping her with dizzying speed. She felt an initial spike of fear and some discomfort as the vines constricted, lifting her up a good two feet. But there was no actual pain, and once it was over she felt more humiliated than frightened.

"Tress!" Huck said. "Oh, Tress! Are you all right?" He scampered off her shoulder and onto the vines.

She wiggled her fingers, then started laughing.

Tress's laugh was a silly thing, involving snorts and hiccups. It was an honest laugh, validated by its ridiculous nature.

In that moment, the last vestiges of Tress's spore fear died away. She'd made a mistake, and she *would* be careful in future experiments. But today, her mistake had merely cost her a little dignity—traded away for the pleasure of knowing what it felt like to be a grape trellis.

"In my bag," Tress said, still chuckling. "Fetch me the silver knife."

As Huck scrambled to obey, Tress noticed the ends of the vines were still growing. As before, when she thought about them, they turned toward her. In this particular case, she didn't want them to constrict her further, and so she thought of them pulling away. Remarkably, they did.

It wasn't perfect control. Plus, she couldn't do anything about the already grown vines and had to use the knife to cut herself free. But it left her wondering how far her control could go.

She carefully added more zephyr spores to each of her charges. The next experiments were less amusing. All three flew as she wanted, though one of the flares bounced free without releasing vines.

The other two exploded with vines just as she'd hoped. During the last experiment, she tried thinking about the vines as they grew, willing them to not grab onto anything. This time, instead of taking hold of the wall and the ribs of the ship, the vines stretched toward her—then the entire mass fell to the floor.

She spent the rest of the afternoon cutting the vines down and taking them up to dump out her window. She hid everything incriminating in her room with Huck—chastising herself for forgetting to lock the door on her way out earlier—and rushed to help Fort with the day's dinner. He found her a distracted helper, as her mind was elsewhere. Why had one of her flares failed to release vines? What if she fired a dud when she was facing Crow?

She'd need to do more testing before initiating a confrontation. But she finally had a weapon. A surprise.

Crow was looking for someone who didn't fear the spores. And that was just what she was going to get.

45

THE PROTECTOR

The captain authorized opening a keg of something intoxicating after dinner, which Tress considered a nice gesture. It proved the captain wasn't completely heartless. (Granted, that meant Crow *did* have a conscience, but ignored it most of the time. Which is verifiably worse.)

Tress did not partake of the brew. She'd only been drunk once in her life, two years before at a holiday gathering when she hadn't realized how much punch was in the punch. That day, she'd blathered endlessly about her favorite recipes. While Charlie had found it endearing, she worried a little alcoholic grease today might make her plans slip out as freely.

Instead she gathered up a plate of the night's meal: biscuits and a strong meaty gravy with vegetables. It was basically stew you ate with your fingers, but it at least gave the illusion of variety. There was only so much she could do with the ingredients at her disposal.

The crew loved it anyway. After months of meals that bore an uncomfortable kinship with tile grout, one did not complain at a little repetition on a delicious theme. And—though one might not believe it after experiencing the variegated ways the Dougs could assault a language—the crew was not stupid. They saw that Tress was helping Fort. And suddenly their meals contained food rather than something merely—by the strictest definition of the word—edible. So when they cheered her as she left, it wasn't only because they were mildly inebriated.

She felt undeserving of this attention, particularly considering how her actions had put them all in such danger. So she hurried to Salay's cabin with a plate of food. Salay hadn't made an appearance at dinner, and Tress worried about her.

Tress knew the right door only because of the number on it; she'd never visited Salay. Tress knocked hesitantly, and thought she heard someone blow their nose on the other side. A moment later, Salay opened the door, and though her darker skin tone masked things like a red nose and cheeks, her eyes made it clear she'd been crying.

"Oh, Tress," Salay said, her voice as clipped and stern as always. "Is something wrong?"

"I brought you dinner," Tress said, uncomfortable. She'd never seen Salay in anything other than her naval outfit, with stiff trousers and coat. It felt wrong somehow to be barging in on her when she was wearing a robe over a nightgown.

Still, the woman gestured for Tress to enter and put the plate on the desk. Tress slipped in, shocked to discover how small the room was. It was barely half the size of her own quarters. As helmswoman, Salay was the ship's third in command. Surely she deserved more space than this closet.

"I appreciate the meal," Salay said. "It was inefficient of me to make you bring it. I need to maintain my strength, of course. Today only proved that more . . ."

She pushed past Tress and settled down at the desk, taking the plate. Tress wondered if she should go, but Salay kept speaking, so she lingered.

"I keep thinking there has to be a way to avoid the rains," Salay explained. She absently pushed the plate of food aside, then pointed at the unrolled chart on her desk. "There's no *pattern* to them though. People have sailed the seas for centuries, and *still* there is no known safe passage through the Crimson. If it hasn't been found by now . . ."

Salay stopped, then looked back at Tress. "You know of one, don't you? A way to protect the crew? You wouldn't have brought us here if you hadn't known of a method, right?"

"I . . ." Tress said, then swallowed. "I'm sorry, Salay. For what happened to Pakson."

"It's my job to do what the captain and first officer cannot," Salay said. "Or . . . or will not. Someone has to look out for the crew." She pounded the table, then put her hand to her head, staring at the chart.

Tress settled down on the narrow bed beside the wall, sitting with her hands in her lap, feeling as if she were intruding. The room was remarkably bare of personalization. Some maps in tubes in a bin by the wall. Neat and organized chests for items under the bed. And a picture hanging above the porthole, lit by a flickering desk lamp.

It was a drawing; these people hadn't discovered photography yet. But it was a good one, drawn expertly but quickly by a street artist in the zephyr capital. It depicted a tall, smiling man and a young girl who bore a striking resemblance to Salay.

"Your father?" Tress asked, pointing.

Salay looked up, then nodded. "I promised him I'd pay his creditors. But when I returned, he was gone. Pressed into labor by the king's collectors. By the time I caught up to the ship, they'd left him at a debtor's prison at some port, but couldn't remember which one."

"That's awful."

"Trouble is, when royal ships need an extra hand, they can always press men from the debtor's prisons onto their crews. So tracking him proved impossible. He must have bounced around the islands, being pressed and dropped off a dozen times.

"I keep telling myself, and promising Mother via letter, that our only hope is for me to keep sailing. Keep visiting new ports and asking. He's out there somewhere, Tress. Either that . . . or he died in one of the conflicts , forced onto the crew of a warship. If that's the case, I guess I'm too late. I've already failed him, like I failed Pakson."

"Salay," Tress said, "you mustn't give up hope."

"Why not?" Salay asked, turning toward her. "Is it true? Do you have a way to get us out of this? Do you have a secret from the king that will let us survive the Crimson? Please. *Please* tell me you have a plan."

"I . . ." What could she say? Did she try again to protest she wasn't what Salay thought? Now, when she'd just told the woman to keep hope?

Hope in a lie—hope in me—is not true hope, Tress thought.

Unless she could do something. Unless there *was* a way to help. Tress remembered with stark clarity watching the rains approach, knowing there was nothing she could do to stop them. Knowing her life was now subject to random chance.

She'd almost begun feeling like she was in control. Like she could shape her own destiny. Then the rain had come, a hammer sent by the moons to deliver humility to her via a firm blow to the forehead.

Salay turned away. "It's not fair of me to ask you to protect them, is it? I don't know your mission here, your *true* mission. It's possible your duty was simply to get us out of the kingdom. We had become dead-runners, dangerous to all we encountered. I can't blame you for steering us toward our deaths, to protect the innocent. I let it happen. I failed there too." She smoothed the edges of her map of the Crimson Sea. "If only we knew where the captain was taking us. Then at least I could plan for how long we'd be in here."

"Oh," Tress said. "Salay, I know that."

"You do?"

"Yes. Er, I should probably have told you earlier. The captain is taking us to see the dragon."

"Xisis?" Salay said, spinning again in her seat. "Is he *real*?"

"Ulaam says he is. And the captain has books that claim the legends are real."

"Well, Ulaam would probably know," Salay said, rubbing her chin. "But why visit the dragon . . . Oh, she's looking for a way out of her affliction, isn't she? I had assumed Crow was so stubborn, she'd bullied the spores in her blood to submit. She's lived longer than anyone should as a spore eater. But what would she trade . . . ?"

They locked eyes.

"Oh," Salay said. Then she laughed. "She thinks you're going to let her trade *you* for her life? Ha!"

"Yes, um, it's very funny."

"Well, I suppose that's one thing to look forward to," Salay said. "It's going to be rich watching her discover what you really are. But tell me. I know you can't confirm or deny your true mission, but is there any hint you can give me for what to expect after Crow is dealt with?"

"Well," Tress said, "I will need your support. If I do deal with Crow—

if—then I wouldn't want the crew to free her. I would need to ... um ... take her to face justice, you see."

"Of course!" Salay said, looking hopeful for the first time today. "Yes, I can arrange that. Once you have her, we leave the Crimson, then?"

"Yes," Tress said. "Though ... well, this is a little awkward ... but I have business with the Sorceress in the Midnight Sea next. And I was hoping ..."

Salay's eyes went wide. Then she laughed again. Her laugh was like a bell calling sailors to arms. Sharp, excited, yet somehow controlled. "Of course you do. Why was I worried? If you are going to sail the Midnight ... well, dealing with the *Crimson* is nothing to someone like you."

Then her expression turned more serious. "But could you help me protect the crew? I know a bunch of pirates are worthless to the king, but nobody else is going to look out for them. Even their captain doesn't care about them. Please, *please* don't let us lose another friend."

In that moment, Tress felt like something Fort had cooked. Grimy, crusty, and barely able to fulfill its intended purpose. She shrank down before the weight of Salay's hope. What could Tress do? She was a fake. A liar. A ...

Wait.

A very strange, very desperate idea occurred to her. Probably nothing. Probably a useless whim.

Notably, strange desperation is exactly the state that often leads to genius.

"Be ready," Tress told her. "There *is* something I can try."

46

THE INFORMANT

Tress spent the next few days in a fervor of panicked studying and studious panicking. Her budding plan was far, far more dangerous than her work with the flares. And in this instance, she didn't have anyone else's schematics to lean upon.

She spent much of that time experimenting with verdant spores. The fruit of the Emerald Sea itself, which she'd never understood in her youth. She wasn't alone—nor was it surprising that the more she learned, the less afraid she had become. It is that way with most topics, as fear and knowledge often play on different sides of the net.

There are obviously exceptions. Certain individual humans, like certain sausages, break this convention. While neither larger group is collectively terrifying, they contain remarkable individuals that absolutely *should* frighten you. The more you learn about these individuals, the more worried you should become. But for humans at large, knowledge usually equates to empathy, and empathy leads to understanding.

Tress found verdant aether to be almost *playful*, eager to respond to her mental commands in exchange for water. Over the days of study, she grew proficient at making the vines grow in spirals, to stretch tall and strong, and even to grow slowly—holding back much of their strength.

She could feel, as always, a sensation beyond the vines. Nothing so distinct as a mind. An impression. One that she thought might be the moon itself—or the always-growing maternal vines that lived upon it.

Other than necessities like sleep, Tress only broke from her studies when she had to go help Fort prepare dinners. Each time, seeing the faces of the crewmembers made her more concerned.

Three days after her meeting with Salay, she sat in her chambers, encouraging a few verdant vines to grow delicately around her fingers without squeezing too hard. The ship was currently tacking in such a way that she could see the sporefall out her porthole. The sporefall had grown bigger and bigger with each passing day, and it had become increasingly obvious that this was the captain's destination. The dragon's lair must be near it. Or perhaps inside it.

It's not immediately obvious in most of the seas, but at the lunagree, falling spores make a pile—like the sand on the bottom of an hourglass. The sea was actually a mountain the size of a kingdom, though the incline was incredibly shallow, and therefore imperceptible. But the closer they sailed, the *higher* they needed to go.

Currently, items on Tress's desk were in danger of sliding off, and everything felt askew compared to the horizon—as if we were seeing through the lens of a student who had just discovered experimental film.

Huck periodically dripped more water onto the vines for her, using a small spoon and a cup of water (wooden, with a good smooth finish from long years of use) stuck to the desk with wax.

"What if," Tress said, "I learned to sail the ship *myself*."

"The entire ship?" Huck asked.

"Maybe not this one. A smaller one. Surely there are sailboats that a single person can crew. I could take one of those into the Midnight Sea, so I don't risk any other lives."

"And how long do you think it would take you to learn to sail on your own?" he asked. "Particularly in such dangerous seas? You could spend *years*."

"Maybe that's what I need to do."

"Or maybe," he said, "you need to acknowledge something far harder, Tress. That your friend is out of your reach. That you should give up on this quest and take care of yourself."

She didn't respond, though the anger she felt at his words manifested in the vines tightening on her fingers—as if they too were frustrated.

She forced herself to relax as Huck dribbled another spoonful of water on the vines. He was getting better at balancing on two legs as he assisted her—he'd needed to do that far more often with her than he had in his past.

"Tress," he said, "I don't like to see you sad, but I'd *hate* to see you get hurt. What you've done here on the *Crow's Song* is incredible, but it's still *leagues* away from the dangers you'd face on the Midnight Sea."

"Is it? Nobody knows! I've asked Fort, Salay, and even Ulaam. They all tell me that the Midnight Sea is dangerous, but nobody can say why. They just know that the 'Sorceress watches' those spores. Ships that go there vanish. There's maybe something about monsters? Nobody can say for certain."

Huck dribbled more water. Then he sighed softly. "Remember how I went ashore at the last port?"

"How could I forget? You've told me six stories about it so far."

"I . . . left out the most important one."

Tress glanced up. The four vines curling around her fingers turned their tips, like heads, to regard Huck.

"I went looking for the rat population," Huck explained, setting down the spoon and wringing his paws. "There are some of us on most islands these days. Talking rats, I mean. With a little work, I found one who had visited the Sorceress's island. Before you ask, he didn't know the way. He simply happened to be on a ship that visited. But . . . he did relate to me the dangers they faced."

"And you weren't going to tell me?" Tress said, her four vines growing upward with a sharp, sudden motion, like spikes.

"I didn't want to encourage you!" Huck said. "I'm worried about you, Tress. But maybe if you know the dangers, you'll see how difficult it's going to be."

(Fun tip: Being told "I kept you in the dark to protect you" is not only frustrating, but condescending as well. It's a truly economical way to demean someone; if you're looking to fit more denigration into an already busy schedule, give it a try.)

Tress was able, with effort, to appreciate Huck's sentiment. And fortunately—like the girl who asked the suddenly quiet room of people if they wanted to see her tattoo—he realized that there was no turning back now.

"There are three trials one needs to face to reach the Sorceress," Huck said. "I guess she likes things to be dramatic. Anyway, the first is the most obvious. You have to cross the Midnight Sea."

"Which we can do," Tress said, "now that Hoid has pointed out the way for us to go."

"You know where to go, yes," Huck said, "but Tress, don't you understand? Rain falls in the Midnight Sea like everywhere else. The Sorceress has rigged up some way to continuously feed the creatures that pop out of the spores. They roam and rove the oceans—midnight monsters the size of ships. You remember that thing you created to watch Crow? You think you could fight a hundred of those attacking the ship?"

That . . . did seem daunting. The vines on Tress's fingers wriggled down, hiding behind her palm.

"If you survive that," Huck said, "you have to face the Sorceress's guardians: a force of metal men that live on her island. They're completely indestructible, impervious to all kinds of weapon fire, and are relentless.

"They capture anyone who sets foot on the island, then imprison them. Captives don't even get to meet the Sorceress—so don't think that's a way to get her attention. I'm told she thinks anyone foolish enough to get captured by the guardians is beneath her notice."

Huh. Getting captured on purpose had been one of the plans Tress was considering.

"And if you *somehow* escape them," Huck said, "you'll never reach the Sorceress. She lives in a tower made of an indestructible metal. It is so slick it cannot be scaled, and nothing will stick to it. She stands atop it in the evenings to commune with the moons, but there are only two ways in. Through doors locked by mysterious means, or through the small window where her ravens travel in and out, doing her bidding.

"Tress, if you attempt to go to that island, you'll get eaten by Midnight Essence monsters. If by some miracle you survive and make it to the island, you'll get locked away forever by the guardians. And even if you escape them, you'll end up sitting in front of the tower and screaming to be heard until you lose your voice. There's *no way* to accomplish what you want."

"Hoid did it," she said. "He saw her. And so did Charlie."

"Charlie," Huck said, "was specifically kidnapped because she hoped to be able to ransom him to the king! Who knows what happened with Hoid. It could have been the same thing."

She sat back, and to some extent Huck's information did as he hoped. It revealed exactly how difficult her task was.

Well, she couldn't focus on it at the moment. She had other problems to deal with. She wouldn't be around to get cursed by the Sorceress if she ended up imprisoned by a dragon first. And she'd never have a chance to be imprisoned by a dragon if she was killed by rainfall on the Crimson.

So, Tress returned to her practice with the vines.

47

THE POET

The flare burst at Ulaam's feet. A writhing, twisting mass of vines subsumed the surgeon, wrapping him all the way up to his neck. He tried to free himself, but the best he could achieve was a cross between a convulsion and a dry heave.

"What do you think?" Tress said, hurrying through the hold to stand next to him. "Will it work to capture Crow?"

Ulaam struggled to shrug. "From my understanding of her ailment and her powers, this should be sufficient. Her vines intercept physical danger, but they don't care if she's immobilized. Their needs and hers do not entirely align, hmmm? So long as she keeps living to provide them with water, they don't care what happens to her."

"Do you think it's overkill?" Tress asked. "If what you say is true, we could jump her in the night while she's sleeping."

"Her vines would *surely* react to that," Ulaam said. "The spores inside her have no way of judging your intent. They would assume the worst and fight you off.

"The brilliance of this mechanism you've devised is that you don't have to fire it directly at the captain. The vines will judge your shot off-target, and therefore might not respond. Once she's wrapped tight, be certain not to make any threatening moves, and the spores should be satisfied."

"Thank you," Tress said. "Oh! Let me get you out." She reached for her silver knife.

"No need," Ulaam said. "This is quite pleasant. Tell me, where did you find those flares?"

"I made them," Tress said, digging through her bag—which was on the floor of the hold near where I was sitting. She'd taken the chance to explain her plan in detail to Ulaam and me.

I had, of course, responded by asking what she thought of my mullet. Please stop trying to imagine that. It would be best for both of us.

"You made them?" Ulaam said. "Yourself?"

"I had some of Weev's schematics, explaining how cannonballs worked," she explained. "It wasn't so hard to extrapolate."

"Remarkable. I say, young lady, I *must* have your brain. Once you are through with it, naturally. Hmmmm?"

"I'm sorry, Ulaam," she said as she hunted in her bag. Where had she put her notebook? She wanted to record that this design worked better than her previous one. Ten shots, and so far no duds. "Talk like that still makes me queasy."

"You haven't the nerves of a pirate yet, I'm afraid."

"I know."

"I could insert some. It's a thirty-five percent agony-free process!"

"No thank you," she said, pulling out the notebook and turning. She jumped as she found Ulaam standing next to her. The vines lay in a heap where he'd been standing.

"How?" she asked.

"I digested them," he explained, "in a few key places."

". . . Digested?" Tress asked.

"He's extra gross!" I said. "I envy him."

"As you should, my friend," Ulaam said. "By definition, I can do anything a human can—plus more. I see you are taking notes on your experiments, Tress. Interesting, interesting. You know, I could certainly—"

"My *brain* is *not* for *sale*," Tress said.

"I was going to ask about your hands this time. Such excellent penmanship. My, my." He smiled, showing a literally inhuman number of teeth. He says he does it because he figures an extra big smile should be extra comforting to humans. I can never tell if he's joking or not.

"Hands," she said. "Not for sale. Nor my knees. Or my ears. No body parts for sale, Ulaam. Ever."

"Well, that's quite definitive," he said. "You've grown rather forceful, hmmmm? I remember when you first arrived, and you seemed embarrassed to turn me down."

"I'm not any different now. I'm simply more desperate."

"More desperate than those first few days on the ship?" he asked.

Tress hesitated, thinking back to those first awful days. Well, yes, she'd been desperate then too. She'd *assumed* herself to be as desperate as was possible.

Perhaps it was like lifting weights—her capacity for desperation was increasing with time. And there just wasn't room for other emotions, like embarrassment.

"Regardless," Ulaam said, "we shall move on. No more offers for now. Your plan with the captain. You're certain the others will join you in this mutiny?"

"Pretty sure," Tress said. "I . . . may have led Salay and the other officers to think I am a King's Mask . . ."

"Oh my," Ulaam said. "How did you manage that?"

"Accidentally," Tress said with a grimace. "Somehow I seem to be best at lying when I tell the truth."

"Wise words, wise words," I said. "But tell me, have you heard my latest poem?"

"Excuse me," Ulaam said, "I'm disconnecting my ears for the next two minutes."

"What?" Tress said. Unfortunately, she was limited by her anatomy. She couldn't disconnect *her* ears unless she wanted it to be permanent.

"There once was a farmer with a tulip bulb," I said. "Who had nowhere to plant it. He found a place to sit. He then threw a fit. And accidentally mashed it into pulp. The end."

Oh, gods.

Oh, Shards within.

What had I become?

"That's . . . nice," Tress said. And for a girl who claimed she was bad at lying, she pulled that one off swimmingly.

Ulaam returned to sensibility a short time later. "Ah!" he said. "You're not bleeding from your ears, Tress? Remarkable. Is that all you'll be needing from me today?"

"I suppose," Tress said. "But . . . are you sure you won't help? In our mutiny?"

"Alas," Ulaam said. "I can offer only medical attention, should you require it. More interference would not be proper."

"If we don't get out of the Crimson soon," Tress said, "the ship could end up sinking. That would kill you too."

"Assumptions, assumptions," Ulaam said, walking to the steps. "Hoid is immortal, and I am nearly so. While I don't relish the idea of walking across the bottom of the spore sea to reach safety—particularly with him tagging along in his current state—that is not outside my abilities."

I stood up to go after him, as a part of me—that piece that was slightly self-aware—kept trying to ambush him with bad poems.

I stopped next to Tress, however, who now sat with her flare gun in her lap. Staring at the floor. Outside, the soft hiss of spores rubbing along the hull was a steady companion. A reminder that we were moving inevitably toward the dragon's lair.

Captain Crow estimated it was only two days away.

"I'm worried," Tress said softly, looking up at me. "I'm . . . I'm terrified."

I put my hand on her shoulder and managed to keep myself from vomiting forth another poem. She must have seen something in my eyes, the fragment of lucidity I still possessed.

"I'm terrified," she repeated. "Not only for everyone else, though I do feel that. I'm scared for myself and what Crow is going to do to me. I can't beat her. Deep down, I *know* it."

I raised my other hand, lifting a single finger. "You have," I whispered, "everything you need, Tress."

"The flare gun? But what if I fail?"

"You have *everything* you need." I squeezed her on the arm, then started up after Ulaam. Then I slowed. Something was wrong, wasn't it?

Other than the fact that I wasn't currently launching into an epic ode to the beauty of calluses?

Oh. The hissing on the hull had stopped. The seethe had paused, and the ship was slowing. Well, nothing to worry about there. That happened all the time, and wasn't dangerous.

Unless rain was near.

You can probably guess what happened next.

48

THE NIGHTMARE

I have nightmares. My unique state of being doesn't prevent that, though I don't need sleep nearly as much as ordinary humans do.

My worst recurring nightmare—the one that grabs me by the throat and shakes me until I wake, raw and steaming in my own sweat—is not that I am being chased by a monster. It's not that I'm lost, or that I'm unloved.

No, my greatest nightmare is the one where I learn I've been repeating myself for years, telling the same tired jokes, the same stories—energetically wearing a path through people's patience and fondness until even the weeds upon it are dead.

So I'll refrain from repeating my suspicions and fears regarding the rains upon the Crimson. But if ever there were proof that Fate herself had placed long odds against the *Crow's Song*, it would be the fact that there were not one, but *two* separate rainlines heading straight for the ship.

Two at once. With the ship dead on the slopes of the vast crimson mountain, prow pointed toward the column of particles streaming from the angry moon.

When Tress reached the upper deck, she saw Salay standing on the quarterdeck, holding firm at her post in case the seethe began again and she had a chance to steer them to safety. The ship remained still, damningly so. All her skill, all her passion, meant nothing when the ship was sporelocked. She was helpless.

Dougs shouted ideas at one another, several suggesting they run across the spores to safety. That was, of course, stupidity. If the ship were destroyed, they'd die the moment the seethe began again. There were two lifeboats, yes, but what would that offer? Slow death by dehydration. They were upon the Crimson. Few sailed here.

With very, *very* good reason.

Salay looked past the Dougs and met Tress's eyes.

It's time, she mouthed. *Please.*

Tress grabbed one of the Dougs, a lanky woman with her hair in a long tail. "Go to Salay!" Tress shouted at her. "Tell her I need two very long ropes and the barrel of water from the cannon station. Go! *Go!*"

Tress went running for her room, shoving past Laggart on the steps. He bellowed after her, but she wasn't of a mind to listen. She had minutes, maybe, until the rain arrived and their story ended. Unless Tress could add another chapter through sheer force of will.

Heroism is a remarkable thing, oft misunderstood. We all think we understand it because we want to see its seed inside ourselves. That is part of the secret, really.

If you gather together stories of heroes—those who have risked their lives for others, those who have stood against overwhelming odds, those who have barreled heedlessly into danger with the aplomb of a champion diver leaping from the highest platform—you find patterns. Two of them, in fact.

The first is that heroes can be trained. Not by a government or a military, but by the people themselves. Heroes are the ones who have *thought* about what they're going to do, and who have trained to do it. Heroism is often the seemingly spontaneous result of a lifetime of preparation.

But if you ask these heroes why they risked their lives, don't do it on a stand in front of a crowd while you give them their medal. Because the truth is, they likely didn't do it for their country. Or even for their ideals. Consistently, across cultures, eras, and ideologies, war heroes report the same simple motivation. They did it for their friends.

In the frenzied anarchy of destruction, loyalty to causes and kingdoms alike tends to fall to the chaos. But the bond between people, well, that's stronger than steel. If you want to create heroes, don't give them something to fight for. Give them some*one* to fight for.

Tress unlocked the door to her quarters and slammed it open, sending Huck scrambling under the bed. She rushed to her desk, where she found a large ball of roseite, grown and shaped over the last few days. It was the size of a child's head and was waxed on the outside, and it was filled with an enormous charge of verdant spores, colored faintly violet by the roseite around it.

Tress barely had time to note that she'd apparently spilled a couple midnight spores on the desk, a sloppy move on her part. She heaved the roseite "cannonball" off the desk, then dashed out into the hallway.

On the deck, the Dougs had gathered around Salay. Captain Crow was out of her cabin, standing on the quarterdeck and drinking from her canteen with an air of fatalism. She had hoped not to die here, of course, but she was already terminal. There was only so much a new form of demise could move the proverbial needle, once you've stared down your own mortality every day for over a year.

Salay broke through the Dougs and gestured to the rope and the barrel of water. "We got it, Tress. What now?"

"Tie one rope to the barrel," Tress said, "and lower it *carefully* over the side to the spores." She took a deep breath. "Then tie the other rope around me and do the same."

Everyone in the group turned, pointedly, and stared at her.

Then Salay barked orders, and the crew saw it done. Ann personally lowered the barrel, while Fort and a few Dougs gingerly lowered Tress. She touched down, feeling again the soft scrunch of spores beneath her feet. Being so close to the Crimson, she felt as if she'd stumbled upon some mythological land where the ground had somehow rusted and the sky looked a strange cast of blue by contrast.

Spores ground against wood in a familiar sound as the barrel touched down beside her. Ann waved from above, and dozens of eyes followed Tress as she untied the barrel and rolled it up next to the hull of the ship.

Then she pried off the top—her hands trembling—and stared at the dark water. What she was about to do went against everything she'd ever been told.

"The rain is almost here, Tress!" Salay shouted from above. "Oh, moons. It's coming!"

Tress could hear the crunching and clattering of the crimson spores as they grew in a frenzy. Like thousands of raised spears. Trembling, she reached into the pocket of her red coat and removed a spike, tipped with silver. With her other hand, she held the roseite cannonball.

Grab hold, she thought. *Just grab. Don't destroy the barrel. Out, then grab.*

With the spike, she drilled a hole into the top of the sphere, revealing the green spores within. Then she dropped it into the barrel.

Vines *exploded* forth, thick as arms, spiraling around one another. A small charge of verdant could create enough vines to entangle a person— and she'd packed this with many, many times that. Tentacles surged out of the barrel and slammed against the ship. Drinking eagerly of the water, the vines continued to grow, thicker, stronger.

The twisting, fulminating mass shoved the *Crow's Song,* tipping it and causing the crew to shout. Tress initially backed away, but no. No, she'd made this. She couldn't run from it. She was *part* of it.

She pressed both hands against the still-growing vines, feeling the taut verdant—like sinew—undulate beneath her fingers. *Up,* she thought. *Please, PLEASE.*

UP.

The ship rocked further. Then it began to rise into the air. The mass of verdant vines reoriented and *lifted,* like a many-fingered hand. Without the seethe, the ocean surface was a sturdy enough footing, so long as the vines—having fully burst from the barrel—spread out.

The rising motion caught Tress, who was still tied around the chest by the rope. She spared a moment to hope that Fort wouldn't let go of her, but kept most of her attention on the growing vines. For she could hear the rain getting closer, announcing itself with the sound of water pelting something hard: the snarls of crimson spines they created, then bathed.

I've talked to many a sailor, and this—across dozens of worlds—was *their* nightmare. The sound of the rain, the howl of the wind, and the embrace of the abyss. On Tress's world, it's not the water below that is the danger, but the water above. However, the nightmare is the same, born of the sure knowledge that the very thing you sail, the very thing that carries you and gives your life meaning, will someday try to kill you.

Twin streams of rain intersected at the *Crow's Song*, washing the deck clean of dead spores, soaking the sailors—from the lowest cabin boy to the captain in her plumed hat. Nightmare manifest. A ship caught alone in a storm, rain making a thunder on the wood.

In every story, warning, and song, this meant death.

Except that day. On that ship.

Crow waited for the awful moment—waited for the spikes to shred her ship from all sides, impaling her crew, snapping boards. It never happened. She only felt the rain, hitting like a thousand tiny punches. The water was colder than she'd imagined.

Dougs crowded the side of the ship, and Crow pushed her way through, cursing for them to make room. What was going on? She'd seen Tress go over the side and had assumed she was running, though to where she had no idea. The ship had rocked, yes, but . . .

She didn't understand until she looked down and found a colossal *tree* had grown under the ship. That was the only word to properly define it: a tree made of interweaving vines. A spreading finger-fan of vine-roots braced it, and vine-branches had latched onto the *Crow's Song*.

The tree had lifted the ship some forty feet into the air—right above the thicket of spikes that had grown beneath. The spikes had pierced the trunk, but verdant vines were elastic. And besides, they had still been growing. If anything, the network of spikes helped *stabilize* the vines.

Hanging over the side of the ship, dangling from the rope that Fort held firm, was a shivering, soaking-wet girl, her face hidden behind a mess of damp hair.

It was then that, belatedly, the Dougs started cheering. I don't blame their delayed reaction. They'd gone from certainly dead to very much alive, and that kind of existential whiplash requires a few heartbeats—thumping in your ears to tell you yes, this was real—to recover from.

"Help us pull her up, you louts!" Salay said, grabbing the rope with

Fort. He stood with one foot against the rail, holding the rope with hands that—though crooked—were as solid as bricks. His quick thinking—hauling Tress up a few feet as the vines grew—had saved the girl's life. As it was, the tips of the crimson spikes had touched her shoes.

Everyone helped haul Tress up, and doubtless many of them were thinking of how they'd done this once before—weeks ago when they'd first brought her on board. They cheered again as Fort lifted her gingerly onto the deck.

Crow watched it all, silent. She didn't dare say anything in the face of such a remarkable salvation. Indeed, the vines didn't appear to have harmed the ship at all. With the silver-edged axes, the Dougs would be able to loosen the vessel, then cut them free once the seethe returned and the tree sank. They'd practiced it as a way to escape being tangled up during a cannon battle.

So Crow wasn't worried about the ship. Or about reaching the dragon, as the lair was very close now. She'd told everyone that their destination was two days away, as she didn't want them to panic, thinking she'd take them into the sporefall itself. That wouldn't be necessary.

Today, Crow's fear was of a completely different breed. For though she had spent her entire life instilling fear in her crew so they would obey her, she knew there was another emotion that made people even *more* loyal. Unfortunately, it was an emotion she had never truly understood.

And if Crow had a nightmare, it was standing before her now. In the form of a small shivering girl who had somehow earned the love that Crow had never known.

THE MARTYR

A few hours later, Tress sat in the quartermaster's office with Fort, Salay, and Ann—who conversed in hushed tones.

Tress said very little, instead holding a cup (her one with the butterfly) with tea from Fort's personal store. It said a great deal that he hadn't even *mentioned* a trade as he handed it to her. What Tress had done for them all had incurred a debt Fort feared he'd never pay off.

He *did* intend to try nevertheless.

We have to act quickly, he wrote. **If what Tress says is true, and the captain is planning to trade her to the dragon, we haven't much time. Crow said our destination was only two days away.**

"She said that this morning," Ann agreed. "I can guess we ate up a good chunk of that today, before the rainfall."

Tress sipped the tea. She hadn't stopped trembling since the event, and she actually liked that this tea was warm. It chased the chill from her soul.

Outside, the calming sound of spores on wood had resumed. Though she'd feared her stunt would cause permanent damage to the ship, the crew had efficiently cut the vines free once the seethe returned. The trunk had been pulled into the depths by the spines of the many crimson aethers, leaving the *Crow's Song* to float serenely onward.

Was it odd that Tress felt *guilty* about using the aether tree, then abandoning it? Would the aethers be sad down there? What happened to the ones that sank, anyway?

Perhaps instead of ruminating on such things, she should have been more worried about her looming date with a dragon. She just felt so bare, like a broom worn by good work down to its last few bristles. Following the tension of the day, she found it difficult to summon more fear.

"Then we need to strike," Salay said from beside the door. "Tomorrow morning. Are we agreed?"

"Agreed," Ann said.

Yes, Fort said, holding up his board. **With a King's Mask on our side, we cannot fail.**

They looked to Tress. She wished she could wither away before their expectations. They could use her flaking soul to brew some more tea.

"Maybe we shouldn't," Tress said softly.

"What?" Ann said. "Girl, she's going to *trade you.*"

"I'm not losing another crewmember," Salay said.

Fort studied her, thoughtful.

"The crew is alive by a miracle," Tress said. "I'm worried about what will happen to you if we try to fight Crow. She's dangerous. I feel it."

So you'd let her trade you? Fort said. **Willingly?**

"It's not death to serve a dragon," Tress said. "I don't think so, at least. And maybe I can find a way to escape. Or . . . or buy my freedom . . ."

She knew she wasn't making much sense. She'd spent frantic days trying to devise a weapon against the captain. Tress *did* want to escape. And really, shouldn't she feel excited? Optimistic? Her plan to save the *Crow's Song* had worked, after all.

But lies have a way of diluting a person. The longer you live them, the more you become a bucket of mixed paint, steadily veering toward generic brown. That has never stopped me, mind you, but I'm not the person Tress was.

"We can't lose to Crow," Salay said, "as long as we have you, Tress. You're a—"

"I'm not, Salay," Tress said, exhausted. "I'm not a King's Mask. I didn't even know what one was until you mentioned them to me." She shook her head. "Please believe me."

They didn't, of course. A boring truth will always have difficulty competing with an exciting lie.

"Look, Tress," Ann said, "you think our problems will go away once the cap'n has talked to the dragon? We'll still be under her thumb."

"You'd be able to fight her," Tress said. "She won't have the spores to protect her. If you let her trade me, you have a much better chance of succeeding."

Fort rested his hand on hers, then tipped his sign toward her. **But we'd have to live with it, Tress. Crow forced us into this life. We didn't know she intended to kill. But if we don't stand up to her now, we don't get to use that excuse anymore. We know what she is now.**

Tress read the words through twice. And . . . though her first instinct was still to protest . . . something else was growing. She'd have called it arrogance, and it frightened her. But arrogance and self-worth are two sides to a coin, and it will spend either way.

That day, she met Fort's eyes and nodded. "All right."

"Mutiny," Salay said. "Tomorrow morning. I'll make certain the Dougs are with us."

"I'll distract Laggart," Ann said. "If I'm firing the cannon, he'll come scold me again."

I have a key to the captain's quarters, Fort said. **She doesn't know. We will go in while she's asleep and take her captive. Then we sail for the Verdant Sea and turn her in to the king's officials in exchange for our lives.**

Tress took a deep breath. "Capturing her won't be that easy, Fort. The spores inside her will react to someone trying to restrain her. Fortunately, I've devised a weapon that might work. It . . ."

What was that?

"It . . ."

Tress shivered. She felt something. A familiar itch, distinct as the scent of her mother's bread. Without thinking, she reached to the side, into the shadows underneath the overhang of Fort's counter.

Some of the darkness there resisted her fingers. It felt like a filled waterskin.

Midnight Essence.

Tress felt another mind controlling it, but it was distant and she was near. Working by instinct, she seized control. Immediately her tongue felt dry. She coughed, and—panicking—somehow severed the connection completely. The Midnight Essence puffed away, becoming dark smoke.

That other mind.

That had been Crow.

Crow had been listening to them with Midnight Essence.

"Oh . . . oh *moons*," Tress rasped. "Crow knows."

50

THE MURDERER

The ship's bell rang a series of unceasing sharp notes.

"All hands on deck," Ann said. "How . . . how could she know, Tress?"

"Spores," Tress said. "It's hard to explain."

The bell continued to ring, and each peal seemed a threat: Die. Die. Die.

"What do we do?" Ann asked. "She'll execute us, same as she did with Weev."

"We fight," Salay said. "We were going to do it tomorrow. We'll have to start early. Tress, you said you have a weapon we can use?"

Though she wanted nothing more than to sleep, Tress nodded. They were committed now. She stood and threw open the door, intending to run down the hallway to her room to get the flare gun. However, as soon as she opened the door, she found a pistol leveled at her forehead.

"Well now," Laggart said, "captain wants to see you four most of all. How . . . convenient to find you all together."

Tress's trembling returned, then redoubled, trying to make up for lost time. She stared down the barrel of that gun and found her mouth had gone dry again, for a different reason. She forced out some words anyway.

"You can't hurt me," she said. "Captain needs me."

"True, I'm afraid," Laggart said. Then he turned the gun and shot Salay in the thigh.

Ann screamed and Fort lunged forward to try to grab Laggart—but he stopped short when he saw a second pistol pointed right at him.

"Captain didn't say anything about bringing the other three of you up alive," Laggart said. "So now, Fort. Can you read what I'm saying, or does the gun speak loudly enough for you?"

The large man froze, but Ann ignored the gun, kneeling and using her handkerchief to bind Salay's wound.

Tress felt helpless. Ann finished the binding, but then looked up, uncertain. They needed Ulaam. It was bleeding so much . . .

"Up on deck," Laggart said to them, backing away and gesturing toward the steps. A few gawking Dougs hurried past, feet thumping on the wood.

"She's bleeding!" Tress said.

"Not as much as she would be with another hole in her," Laggart said. "*Up.*"

Fort gently pushed Ann to the side, then lifted Salay, who put her arms around his neck. She nodded to Tress, grimacing at the pain. Ann glared at Laggart, her hands bloody. He just smiled and wagged the pistol's tip.

Reluctantly, Tress led the way, and the five of them emerged on deck. The Crimson Moon hung ominous in the night sky, pouring spores down in a vast haze—like the misty sheet of rain you might get beneath clouds on another planet. Here, the bright moonlight made them shimmer like tiny drops of glistening blood.

Crow stood framed beneath the moon, her shadow breaking the red light. Dougs gathered on either side of the deck, leaving an open space in the center for the captain—and the four mutineers. Fort settled Salay down, and she held a firm hand on her bound wound. The other three huddled around her. Laggart came up behind them, then climbed up onto the quarterdeck where he had a good view of—and line of sight on—all of them.

"So," Crow said, "you lot want to take my ship away from me, do you? Mutiny against your own?"

None of the four responded.

"Honestly," Crow said, "I didn't think you had it in you—considering how I had to force you lot into this life." She waved, and a Doug hurried forward, setting a small table onto the deck between them.

"I'm impressed," Crow said, slipping a pistol out of her belt and setting it on the table. A second followed. Then a third. "Consider me a . . . proud parent. But it makes me wonder. How many on this ship truly respect their captain?"

Fort was watching his board. He tapped a few words on the back. **No one respects you, Crow. They do what you say because they fear the spores in your blood.**

"Now, I thought you were the smart one, Fort," Crow said. "It's not the spores they fear. It's *me*. Isn't that right, crew?" She scanned the Dougs, most of whom backed away beneath her glare. "I do have to hand it to you, Tress. I—"

"Hand?" Dr. Ulaam said, perking up at the back of the crowd. "I have—"

"Shut up, Ulaam," Crow growled, not turning toward him. She kept Tress's eyes. "I knew I'd eventually have to deal with Salay, maybe Fort. But you gave me all of them in a neat package, with proof of their treachery." She gestured toward the table. "Well, let's get on with it. An old-fashioned duel. Three pistols. The four of you—well, three, as I see Salay is grappling with the result of her arrogance—against me."

"Hardly fair," Ann said. "Your spores will stop any bullets we fire at you."

"Don't fire them at me then," Crow said, gesturing toward the quarterdeck. "Kill Laggart before I deal with the three of you, and I'll step down as captain."

"Captain?" Laggart said, stepping to the edge of the rail.

"Put your pistol away, Laggart," Crow shouted. "And stand there like a good target."

"But . . ." He trailed off as he realized that yes, she *was* that callous. He slowly put away his pistol.

"Well?" Crow said. "This wasn't a negotiation. I'm not making an offer. It's an ultimatum."

Fort moved first, leaping for the guns. Crow kicked the leg out from the table—scattering the weapons to the deck—then surged forward and *slammed* her elbow into Fort's face. Tress had never heard anything quite like the *crunch* that made. The sharp crack of breaking cinnamon sticks mixed with the dull thud of tenderizing a gull's breast.

The sound shocked her, made her acknowledge what was happening. She'd been in a daze, but now she leaped for the deck, trying to snatch one of the guns. In the chaos, she lost track of what was happening—though I had an excellent view. Crow vaulted over Fort as he held his face, then slapped Salay's hand—she'd tried crawling to one of the guns.

Crow snatched up that pistol, then nonchalantly tossed it overboard. She spun around and rammed her fist into Tress's stomach, throwing her full weight and momentum into the swing. Tress's breath, drive, and hope were rammed forcibly out her mouth as she crumpled around the fist.

There's no hands-off way to prepare to take a punch. No conceptual training, no schoolhouse theory. When you get hit, yes, a part of you panics. But a bigger part of you is dumbfounded. The mind cannot *accept* that such a thing could happen, for nothing in life has prepared it for such brutality. It's hard to internalize the truth that someone was actually willing to hurt you—even murder you.

That is an edge a person like Crow will always have over others. Her mind accepts these facts easily. She will hurt, and she will kill. She enjoys both.

She was grinning madly as she grabbed the table and slammed it into Fort's face. It didn't break, like they sometimes do in stories of bar fights. It was good solid wood, and it *thumped* against his arms—which were sheltering his broken nose—and sent him sprawling.

Crow tossed the second gun overboard, then looked for the third. It was in Ann's hands, pointed at Laggart.

Crow's grin widened, then she gestured as if to say, "Be my guest."

Laggart started to back away.

"Leave your post, Cannonmaster," Crow said, "and I'll shoot you myself. Think very carefully about which bullet you'd rather risk."

He remained in place. Ann's arm started to shake. She looked at Crow and saw a woman with nothing to lose. In that moment Ann was the smart one, because she realized that no matter what she did—whether she hit or not—Crow wasn't going to let herself lose this fight. She'd go back on her word if she had to. What were the Dougs going to do? Tell the king's marshals?

But at least if she shot Laggart, they would have one fewer enemy to worry about. Ann steadied her arm. She aimed. She fired.

And she missed by at least half a boat length.

Crow laughed, then shoved Ann aside. The scrappy woman came back up with a knife and death in her eyes.

Crow chuckled and slipped something from her pocket. A stubby gun with a very wide barrel.

Tress's flare gun.

Through the tears in her eyes—still stunned from the punch—Tress saw the captain fire it and hit Ann in the chest. The flare connected with a thump, and her body cushioned the trigger enough to prevent it from going off. So it fell to the deck, and there—hitting tip-down—it released its explosion of vines to wrap around Ann.

"For cheating," the captain said, tucking the flare gun away. She absently slammed her heel into Salay's wounded leg, making the woman scream in pain. Crow checked on Fort last—his face was a mess of blood, and he still seemed dazed.

After making sure he wasn't going to come up swinging, Crow walked over to where he'd dropped his strange magical writing board. Her heel took this next, snapping it in half with a crunch.

Fort cried out. It was the only time I've heard him speak, other than to laugh. It was a mournful cry full of primal human grief. He slumped forward, putting bloody hands to bloody face, heaving as he sobbed.

Tress finally understood Crow's purpose. Killing the four of them might have inspired rebellion among the Dougs; she'd learned from her execution of Weev. Death made martyrs. Humiliation made servants.

The Dougs lowered their eyes when she scanned the deck. Fort's sorrow turned silent and personal. The ship fell quiet—but it wasn't the quiet of a night of falling snow. It was the quiet of a hospital room after a loved one died.

Crow had defeated the four best officers on the ship, and hadn't even *needed* her strange spore blood. Ulaam was surprised it hadn't manifested, he told me later. Crow had better control of her ailment than any of us had realized. She'd purposefully kept the vines in, so no one would wonder later whether she was less dangerous without them.

There would be no crossing the captain again after today.

"Cannonmaster," Crow barked. "Lower anchor."

"Captain?" Laggart said. "But you said we needed to keep sailing to reach the lair . . ."

"We've arrived."

"But—"

"A quick piece of advice, Laggart," Crow said. "If you suspect mutiny, always tell people the trip will end a few days after it actually will. Human nature compels cowards to wait until the last possible moment before they try anything."

The anchor went down with a rattle of its chain. Crow wasn't bluffing—we'd gotten close enough, though there wasn't a precise location one needed to reach to get the dragon's attention. You simply needed to be within the region he watched. Crow proved this by tossing a letter overboard, held in the traditional glass case, as her books instructed.

Then she hauled Tress to her feet, restraining the girl by means of a death grip on her shoulder. "You," Crow said, "are going to go with me quietly and willingly, or I'll have Laggart start executing your friends. This is another ultimatum."

Tress nodded, because she still hadn't gotten her breath back. Her first real fight, and she'd lasted exactly one punch. Her eyes were *still* watering, her stomach aching. She felt useless—at least until she saw Salay looking at her.

Then Tress felt worthless instead.

Salay was holding her thigh, where blood was seeping through the makeshift bandage. Through her pain, she was looking to Tress, pleadingly.

Tress turned away.

At that moment, Salay finally understood. She finally believed. "You were never one, were you?"

"No," Tress whispered. "I . . . tried to tell you . . ."

Salay slumped to the deck, defeated.

Beyond the ship, the spores began to undulate, then spin in a whirlpool as if draining from below. The Dougs and I rushed to the side, watching as a large tunnel appeared in the spores, the sides of it solid despite the seethe. It led down into darkness. Xisis had received the message.

"Prepare the launch," Crow shouted. Once the small rowboat was ready, hanging beside the deck, she forced Tress in.

Crow climbed in next and nodded to Laggart, who held a pistol on Ann. "If we don't come back in an hour," Crow shouted, "kill one of them."

Tress slumped down into her seat. Then she felt a hand on her shoulder. She looked to see me reaching across the railing to her.

"You still have," I whispered, "everything you need."

I backed away at a bark from the captain, and the Dougs lowered the boat like a makeshift elevator to get them down to sea level.

Crow pushed Tress in front as they stepped out onto the strangely firm spores, then started down into the tunnel.

51

THE DRAGON

The spore seas aren't that deep, relatively speaking. Compared, for example, to the depth of the Lilting Abyss on Threnody, the spore seas are practically ponds.

But when you have to *hike* to the bottom—all the while being cuffed and shoved by an impatient pirate with a terminal disease—a few hundred yards can feel far, far longer. Nonetheless, it did beat the traditional method of reaching the bottom of an ocean.

Crow carried a lantern, and the way the light glistened off the crimson tunnel made it seem as if they were climbing down the dragon's own gullet. Tress wondered what would happen if the stiff walls were exposed to water. Would spikes grow out of them, or did the dragon's strange power prevent the aether from expressing itself? It says more than I could ever explain about the changes in Tress that she briefly considered licking the wall, just to see.

Eventually the tunnel leveled out, then opened into a vast chamber—also made completely out of solidified spores. Tress had been expecting to reach the bottom and find out what was down there. Was it stone, soil, or merely piles and piles of aether spines sunken from thousands of years of rain? She supposed she would have a lifetime down here to learn.

That was when the true weight of it all hit her. She'd spend her *life*

down here. She had failed Charlie. Equally bad, and somehow more terrifying in the moment, she might never see the moons again. The prospect of never again seeing the sky, never again feeling the sunlight, never being bathed in the Verdant Moon's glow . . . it made her knees grow weak.

Crow shoved her forward anyway, causing Tress to stumble into the vast crimson chamber, then fall to her knees. She choked back her emotions, as tears could be fatal if those spores could indeed express their aethers. But she couldn't help curling up, trembling. For a time, she was insensate to Crow's cursing, even her none-too-gentle kicks.

It was all so very much to carry. The weight of the day's emotions stacked upon Tress in a heap, heavy as the ocean itself. Had it only been earlier that afternoon when she'd felt vibrant, relieved, and triumphant as she was pulled up through the rain?

Could a day contain too many moments? Yes, the hours and minutes had been the same today as every day, but each of the moments inside had been fat, like a wineskin filled to bursting. Tress felt as if she were going to leak it all out, vomit emotion all over the place—there wasn't enough Tress to contain it.

You still have everything you need . . .

Did he mean the flare gun? Crow was carrying that, wasn't she? But Tress could not best Crow in a physical contest; she had conclusive empirical evidence of that.

"On your feet, girl," Crow said, hauling her up, then shoving her forward.

The chamber ahead of them appeared empty, save for enormous spore columns wrapped in black ribbons of cloth. Braziers burned at the corners—revealing a large corridor leading away to the right—but they didn't completely dispel the chamber's darkness. Indeed, shadow dominated, as if the lights existed only by its forbearance.

"Dragon?" Crow called, her voice echoing. "I have come, as stipulated, with the proper sacrifice! Show yourself!"

The word "dragon" has filtered its way into nearly every society I've visited, but unlike the name "Doug," this wasn't the result of natural linguistics. Rather, the dragons have made certain that they are known and remembered—a feat often accomplished by interacting with said societies during their formative years.

Like a child learning her name, cultures learn to respect and fear the dragons. It's a matter of convenience, really. Though the vast majority of the people in the cosmere will never meet a dragon—let alone see one in their natural form—dragons do like to interact with mortals. Like a grandmother tucking away that bit of string that wrapped her package, the dragons want to know they have a certain number of easily influenced cultures around, for the proverbial rainy day.

All of this is to explain that when Tress and Crow saw the shadow moving down the large hall to the right, they *kind of* knew what to expect. Indeed, it had a sinuous neck, a reptilian body, and two vast wings, formed as if to block out the sky.

Other details were unexpected. For instance, the mane of silvery hair that adorned the dragon's head, continuing down under the neck and chin as a beard. Or the metallic silver ridges that split the dragon's otherwise onyx hide, outlining his features. This silver ran down the sides of all six limbs, up the sides of the neck, and formed two burnished horns, accompanied by a line of spikes down the back—more subdued, the subjects to the regal majesty of those horns.

There were other mortals in the dragon's house, though they were not allowed in the entry hall when supplicants arrived. Xisis did not want his servants to be tainted by things like reminders of the world outside. They had important work to do, after all: serving him and his research into the complex ecosystem at the bottom of the spore seas.

It is commonly presumed that dragons collect hoards of wealth, and I've often wondered if that tale began because of the otherworldly metal left behind on their corpses. I've never known a dragon to be fond of riches. Ideas though . . . those they *do* hoard, and in this area they are misers fit for legend.

The dragon did not make the ground shake, despite his enormous size. (He was easily as tall as four humans standing on one another's shoulders.) Indeed, he seemed to glide as he approached, flowing around columns, entering the shadows at the center of the room. Firelight reflected off his dragonsteel, making it seem like liquid metal as he loomed over the two women. Tress gasped; even Crow cringed back.

When Xisis didn't speak, Crow found her courage—it had only gotten a step or two away—and spoke. "Dragon Xisis, I have come to initiate your ancient pact of promise." She gestured to Tress. "To this end, I have brought you this slave to work in your domain."

The dragon leaned down, his breath like burned hickory wood, and eyed Tress. She looked into those eyes, which were a shimmering mother-of-pearl, and thought she saw into infinity. Then, reflected, she saw herself. And Crow.

You have everything you need . . .

Tress's courage had never gotten away, though it had been pounded flat by all the other emotions. As it began to shine through, a certain whimsy struck Tress. Crow had nothing to lose . . . but Tress had *everything* to lose. And in that moment, she bet it all on a desperate ploy.

"Dragon Xisis," Tress said, her voice ragged, "I have come to initiate your ancient pact of promise. To this end, I have brought you this slave to work in your domain." Then Tress gestured to Crow.

52

THE SACRIFICE

What?" the dragon said.

"...*What!*" Crow said.

"She will make a good slave," Tress explained. "She's very strong—I can show you the bruise on my stomach as proof. And she's not in the least afraid of spores. She used midnight aether earlier tonight."

Crow grabbed Tress, reaching as if to forcibly shut her up. The dragon interrupted this by very deliberately moving his forearm forward, letting five silver claws—each as long as Crow's leg—click against the crimson ground.

"I will not have you harming one another in my house," he said in a deep voice. "One of you shall be my servant, and I do not like damaged property."

Crow looked at her reflection in the dragonsteel claws, then let go of Tress.

"Great dragon," Crow said, "this girl is the servant brought to be your payment. I am the captain of the ship!"

"So you're saying you're the more valuable prize," Tress said, rubbing at her throat where Crow's nails had scored her.

"I do prefer my servants to be of a certain quality," Xisis said. His voice was deep not in a musical sense, more in the way that the ground might vibrate with a profound resonance during a quake.

"But you would also prefer a young servant, wouldn't you?" Crow said, realizing that she would have to argue her case. "I am old and calcified, stubborn. She is young, easy to mold. Why, she hasn't even been off her home island for a month yet!"

The dragon settled down, folding his arms. To the horror of both women, he looked *amused*.

"Go on," he said to Tress. "You have a response to that?"

"Um," Tress said, "you seem like someone who enjoys a challenge. Which would be more interesting to train? A girl who knows nothing, or a vibrant sea captain, full of skills you could unlock?"

"I prefer not to make too much effort in training my servants, girl," the dragon said. "You argue against your interests."

"Yes," Crow said, "and besides, she is more expert in spores. She has been building devices of ingenious make. She designed a kind of verdant bomb that raised our ship up high above the sea, so rains didn't destroy us! And she made a gun that fires spores. This girl is some kind of spore prodigy. She will serve you well."

"Is it true?" the dragon asked Tress. "Did you make those things?"

"I did," Tress admitted. "I'm not very smart though. I merely took some designs I found and tweaked them."

"Humble too," Crow noted. "Who wants an arrogant servant?"

"Crow has experience leading people, sir," Tress said. "She would make an excellent overseer for your servants."

"Ha!" Crow said. "Tell him honestly what my crew thinks of me! They *hate* me, don't they, Tress? Admit it."

The dragon rested his head on his forearms, looking almost like a dog with its head on its paws, and grinned at the exchange.

"Powerful Xisis," Crow said, "this girl is *beloved* of the people of my ship. She's earned their hearts after only a short time sailing with us. She is an excellent cook, and is nauseatingly selfless. When she heard her friends were going to mutiny to prevent me from trading her, she offered to go willingly, to save them from danger."

"Is this so?" the dragon asked Tress.

"I . . ." Tress said. "Great dragon, Crow needs you to take her as a servant. She's dying of the spores in her blood. Only by living with you could she be healed. It would be magnanimous and wise of you to take her."

"Ha!" Crow said, pointing at Tress. "He knows I'll ask for healing in trade for you! I will live just fine after this."

"True," the dragon said. "Child, you are losing ground quickly." He gestured to Crow. "I cannot see a reason why I'd want this piece of filth in my domain when I could have someone even-tempered, well-liked, and skilled."

"You should have tried to be more awful, girl," Crow said. "I warned you that this life was not for you."

"I . . ." Tress took a deep breath, looking up at the dragon. "I think I'd make a bad servant, great dragon. Because I really, *really* don't want to be one."

"And I do?" Crow said. "I—"

The dragon hushed her with a click of his claw. He narrowed iridescent eyes at Tress. "Tell me, why is it you do not wish to serve me? Contrary to what you might have been told, my servants are treated well. You shall know no disease while you are here. You shall have engaging work, regular meals, and books in your off hours to read at your leisure."

"But dragon, sir," Tress said, "there is someone I must rescue. The man I love is held captive. I need to free him."

"I don't care for the hearts of mortals," the dragon said. "Except for how they taste. Do you have any other argument for why I shouldn't take you right now and put you to work in the kitchens?"

"Because . . . because . . ." The Tress she had been might have accepted her fate. The Tress she had been would have wanted to please him. That Tress was dead.

She was now the Tress she had become.

"Because I won't stay," Tress said. "No matter what you do. I will not give up what I want for you, dragon."

"No one has ever escaped my domain."

"Then I will be the first," Tress said, growing louder as she continued. "Because I can promise you this, great dragon. You will *never* be able to trust me alone. I will dedicate everything I have—every thought, every moment, every *waking breath*—to escaping you! I will not calm down. I will not grow complacent! I will not lose my resolve!

"I *will* find a way out. Even if I have to collapse your entire cave! Even if I have to walk through the spores! Even if it takes fifty years, I will never relent. And you, dragon, will eventually have to *kill* me to stop me. Because I *will* get to the Midnight Sea, and I *will* find the Sorceress, and I *will save the man I love!*"

Her voice echoed in the cavernous room. The dragon let it fade, watching her with ancient eyes.

"The Sorceress?" Xisis said. "You are going to try to confront the *Sorceress*?"

Tress nodded.

"Then perhaps taking you captive now would be a mercy."

"Exactly!" Crow said. "Just as I've been—"

"Oh, hush." The dragon waved a clawed hand in her direction. The cloth enveloping the nearest pillar suddenly wiggled as if alive. It whipped forward, wrapping around Crow's face and gagging her.

Xisis studied Tress, watching her with those incomprehensible swirling eyes. "I believe you," he finally said. "You are too driven to make a useful servant."

"Thank you," Tress said.

Crow, in turn, began to claw at the gag, her eyes wide. The strange black cloth wrapped her further, then pulled her back tight against the pillar.

"She really is awful, isn't she?" the dragon said.

"I'm afraid so, sir," Tress said.

"Well, I suppose I do need someone to scrub floors, now that I've promoted Lili." The dragon stretched, rising up and arching his back like a cat—one that was over twenty feet tall and covered in scales. "I make it a point not to interfere too much in the workings of the society above. If you really have made the discoveries she mentioned, then by taking you, I'd be interrupting the planet's technological progress. I'll pick that as my excuse for letting you go."

"Excuse, sir?" Tress asked.

"Yes, excuse," he said, making it clear he would explain no further. "What is the payment you request?"

"...Payment?" Tress looked at Crow. "Oh! I hadn't gotten that far, sir. And...I don't know that I can take payment for selling a person..."

"If she really is a spore eater," Xisis said, "then you've saved her life. I can heal the disease, yes, but I wouldn't have mentioned to her that the healing only lasts a year or two at most. The infestation will return, so long as she is away from me. Her only path toward long-term survival is to remain here."

Tress considered that, and thought that if he was lying—and the cure *was* permanent—this would be an excellent way to make certain Crow remained with him willingly. And so, Tress wisely remained silent on the matter.

"Regardless," the dragon said, "the deal has been struck. I must pay you, however little I think the trade was worth. So ask your boon. Be quick with it."

"Can you remove a curse that the Sorceress bestowed?"

"No," he said. "Nor will I do anything to help your quest. There is precisely one being I fear on this planet—and no, your friend Cephandrius doesn't count."

Rude.

"I don't know if there's anything I want..." Tress said, feeling exhausted. "My life is enough." She hesitated. "Unless..."

"Yes?"

"Would you consider three small boons instead of one large one?"

53

THE SURVIVOR

A short time later, a very tired Tress hiked the last few feet up out of the tunnel, holding three cloth-wrapped packages—one larger, two smaller.

She was greeted by the sight of Laggart, standing watch at the ship's rail. The two stood, facing one another while his brain caught up to his eyes, then his common sense came huffing up behind with an ache in its side. He lowered his gun and backed away.

This allowed a crowd of more friendly faces to appear. They cheered as Tress sluggishly settled into the ship's launch. The tunnel collapsed in on itself as soon as the Dougs began hoisting her up to the deck. At the top, she was greeted by an ecstatic Ann.

"How?" she demanded. "How?"

"The captain probably should have gagged me," Tress said. "Take note, Ann. If you ever go to make an important deal, make certain your payment can't speak for itself."

You'd be surprised how often that advice has been relevant during my travels.

"Here," Tress said, handing one of the small packages to Ann. "The dragon couldn't help me with my problem, so I got this for you."

The woman took it, frowning. But Tress was too tired to explain at the moment. The crew, realizing this, gave her a little space as she picked her way over to where Dr. Ulaam was tending Fort and Salay. Their wounds were already being treated by one of his fantastic salves—they didn't heal a person immediately, but they did speed it up and left one feeling in much better shape.

Ulaam was explaining the benefits of the various noses he could provide (I've always wanted to try the one that can't smell cheeses), but Fort just slumped against the rail, staring ahead as if dazed.

Tress knelt, then delicately unwrapped the larger of the two remaining packages. Inside was another board like the one Crow had destroyed. Fort sat up immediately. He looked from her to the board, then back at her.

Then he hugged her. No words needed to be said. Ann walked up holding the pair of spectacles she'd unwrapped, one end dangling from her fingers as if she were holding a dead mouse by the tail.

"The dragon," Tress explained, "says you have something called micropsia. He gave a technical explanation, but I didn't understand it. I don't know if that disease could have caused you to somehow hit someone standing *behind* you, but . . . well, those spectacles should help."

Tress handed the final package—more an envelope—to Salay, then stood and walked to the steps up to the quarterdeck. She settled on the steps and tried to process everything.

The others left her alone for the time being, so Tress wasn't interrupted until Salay came limping over, using a crutch.

"You should probably stay off that leg," Tress noted.

Salay shrugged, settling down with some effort next to Tress. She carried a folded piece of paper.

"Filistrate City," Salay said. "I *searched* Filistrate City."

"The dragon says your father arrived there six months ago."

"Damn," Salay said. "Right after I left. I'd have kept hunting, never knowing he was behind me . . ." Then she reached over and gave Tress a hug.

It was exactly what Tress needed right then. When emotions start leaking, it's best to give the body a good squeeze and force them right on out. Like lancing a boil.

When their emotions were thoroughly lanced for the moment, Salay forced herself to stand up. Crutch under her arm, she saluted. "It will take us about a week to reach the Midnight Sea, Captain. But supplies should hold out just fine. We bought plenty at that last port."

"Salay . . ." Tress said, "you should be captain."

"Can't be captain," Salay said. "It's my job to make certain the captain is making good decisions. That's what a first mate is for."

"But—"

"You're trying to make a bad decision, *Captain,*" Salay said. "See? I'm good at the job."

"The Midnight is dangerous," Tress said. "The dragon wasn't willing to give me any help. Even *he* fears the Sorceress."

"Well," Salay said, "we'll just have to figure out how to cross the Midnight like we did the Crimson, Captain. Do we set sail now, or wait for the morning?"

Other objections died before Tress could get them out.

This was what *she* wanted.

"We sail tonight, Helmswoman," Tress said. "And if I'm the captain, then I'm going to go claim Crow's bed. Don't wake me up unless Death himself has shown up, nails in his eyes. Even then, see if you can stall."

PART

6

54

THE VALET

People want to imagine that time is consistent, steady, stable. They define the day, create tools to measure it, chop it up into hours, minutes, seconds. They pretend each one is equal to the others—when in fact some are clearly prime cuts, and others are full of gristle.

Tress understood this now, as she'd known a hearty day thick with meat and fat. But the next few were lean and limber, passing quickly. While not the diaphane days of a vacation, they were ephemeral nonetheless—for all their increasing tension. The ship drew steadily closer to the Midnight Sea, interrupted only once when Tress had to lift them during a stilling.

The rain missed them on that occasion, but none of the crew had complained about the hassle of chopping vines off the ship. If anything, this near miss was a reminder that they—by all reasonable accounts—should not be alive.

Tress felt a momentum to her travel, a phantom tailwind. Encouraging, but also relentless. After so much wandering, so many detours, it was happening. She was sailing to confront the Sorceress. This was perhaps what made the days pass with such elasticity—if the first part of her voyage had been the bow being drawn, now the arrow had been released.

She also decided to cast off a little emotional ballast. She was tired of lies and deception. With a frankness that was honestly somewhat inconvenient when trying to create a story, she gathered Salay, Ann, and Fort—then introduced them to Huck.

He'd agreed to it reluctantly, and perhaps only because he'd been so elated when Tress had stumbled into the captain's cabin that first night after confronting the dragon—and discovered him in a little cage, the cat pawing at the bars. Despite everything, Tress found room within her to feel guilty for not thinking of him. In her defense, she'd assumed him safe in her cabin—though the knowledge that Crow had ransacked the place should have raised if not a red flag, at least a fuchsia streamer.

Still, his excitement to hear of her exploits had washed that guilt away like grime off a window. And now he sat on her palm, introducing himself to the ship's officers, explaining how he and Tress had met. That done, he and Tress both waited for their reactions.

You did so much to help, Huck! Fort wrote. **Moons! We need to tell the Dougs. We can't have anyone stepping on you! You're a hero!**

The rat perked up.

"Yeah," Ann said. "And we've got to do something about that cat— can't let it roam free! I'll build a cage or something for it, keep it in my room until the next port."

All turned to Salay, who did her best to look calm and commanding despite her crutch. She rubbed her chin. "A rat on the crew," she said. "Tell me . . . what is your opinion on tiny pirate hats?"

Spoiler: he turned out to be quite fond of them. It was honestly a little distracting.

The second thing Tress did in the name of abject honesty was explain the challenges that would face them in the Midnight Sea. This, in turn, led her to explain who she was, why she'd left her home, and what she was trying to do.

Afterward, Ann did ask what was so great about this guy she loved. Tress did her best to explain, though she was certain world-traveled people like them would find her love plain and unremarkable.

She underestimated the power of simple words spoken with passion. No one questioned her after that.

So, the days faded behind her like the setting Crimson Moon. And ahead, a jet-black moon broke the horizon. It reflected no light, and seemed more a void than an object. A tunnel to nothing. As it emerged from the horizon Tress feared, irrationally, that it would keep growing—that the Midnight Moon wouldn't be the size of the others, but would turn out to be a vast darkness that consumed the entirety of the sky.

To escape it, she spent time in her new quarters. The captain had far more space than Tress had been assigned, though she still used her old room for spore experiments. She filled page after page of the captain's notebook with discarded ideas for how to protect the ship as it crossed the Midnight Sea.

Trouble was, her mind didn't seem to work right anymore. Where it had once seized upon ideas with a predatory vigor, now it seemed trapped in a room, scratching uselessly at the walls with nothing to show for the effort.

What had happened to her ingenuity? Her self-defining thoughtfulness? She grew more and more frustrated as each day slipped away from her, leaving no further progress than frazzled hair and another scribbled-out page in the notebook. What was wrong with her?

Nothing.

Nothing was wrong with Tress. Her mind was functioning properly. She hadn't lost her creativity. She hadn't run out of ideas. She was simply tired.

We want to imagine that people are consistent, steady, stable. We define who they are, create descriptions to lock them on a page, divide them up by their likes, talents, beliefs. Then we pretend some—perhaps most— are better than we are, because they stick to their definitions, while we never quite fit ours.

Truth is, people are as fluid as time is. We adapt to our situation like water in a strangely shaped jug, though it might take us a little while to ooze into all the little nooks. Because we adapt, we sometimes don't recognize how twisted, uncomfortable, or downright wrong the container is that we've been told to inhabit.

We can keep going that way for a while. We *can* pretend we fit that jug, awkward nooks and all. But the longer we do, the worse it gets. The more it wears on us. The more exhausted we become. Even if we're doing nothing at all, because simply holding the shape can take all the effort in the world. More, if we want to make it look natural.

There was a lot about being a pirate that *did* suit Tress. She'd learned and grown a great deal—but it had still been a relatively short time since she'd left the Rock. She was tired in a way that a good night's sleep—or ten of them—couldn't cure. Her mind didn't have any more to give. She needed to allow herself a chance to catch up to the person she'd become.

She was now only three days away from the Midnight Sea, and she was no closer to thinking of a way through it. And pounding her head against the page wasn't accomplishing anything more than getting ink on her forehead.

Tress was dreading what would happen next. And indeed, it arrived with a polite knock on her door. She nodded to Huck, who had—for some strange reason—decided she needed a valet. Did captains have valets? She thought those were for gentlemen with so many pairs of shoes they needed someone to organize them all.

Huck scampered over to the table beside the entry and called, "The captain bids you come in!"

Tress figured she could have done that herself. She was not yet accustomed to the finer points of being in charge, which often involve being too important to do things the sensible way.

Salay, Ann, and Fort entered. Tress steeled herself for their recrimination. Here, today, they would see the truth. That she had no plan. That she was an unfit captain.

In actuality, all they saw was that she had very nice penmanship. Even written backward on her forehead.

"All right, Captain," Salay said. "We've been giving this voyage some thought. And the protections around the Sorceress seem almost impossible to overcome."

"I know," Tress said, bracing herself. "Salay, I . . . I don't . . ."

"Therefore," Salay continued, getting out some papers, "we've been working hard on ways to overcome them. We've got some pretty good suggestions here, if you want to see them."

Tress blinked.

Well, she often blinked, as people do. In this case, it was a meaningful blink. It was the kind that said, *Wait. What did I just hear?*

"You have . . . suggestions?" Tress asked.

"Here, let's get to it," Salay said, each of them grabbing a chair and settling down next to Tress's meeting table.

Tress drifted over, then looked with amazement as Salay laid out the first set of plans. "This was Fort's idea," she said. "He should explain."

Huck says, he wrote on his board, **that the island is protected by machine men, an entire legion of them, who can't be harmed in any way. I started working on a way to distract them, until I realized you already solved this problem, Tress.**

The new sign was an improvement over the other. Lines of text disappeared at the top, replaced with new ones at the bottom, so he didn't have to stop—he could keep tapping words on the back for them, speaking more in real time.

Also, it could do different fonts.

"I . . . solved the problem?" Tress asked, taking the chair that Huck was trying to push over for her. Once she sat, he dusted his paws off as if he'd done an excellent job, then went to count her pairs of shoes.

You did, Fort said. **With your flare gun modifications! You were already prepared to face someone we can't kill. We just need to expand what you came up with! I figure, a legion of mechanical men can't hurt us if they're wrapped in vines.**

See, here's a schematic for a cannonball using the ideas you came up with. We could lure out the metal men, bombard the beach with verdant, and tie them all up. Then you slip right past!

She took the diagram. It had several parts that said "sprouter mumbo-jumbo" on it, so he obviously didn't grasp the finer details of what she'd done. Yet, the idea was sound. Excellent, even. They already had cannonballs made to explode on a timer—she could build ones that burst with vines instead of spraying water.

"This is brilliant, Fort!" she said.

Fair trade! he said, tapping the board. **Once you have your friend back, then we'll be even. Not before.**

She didn't point out that he'd only lost his original board because of her—and so giving one back to him was already a fair trade. She was too amazed.

They'd solved her problem. Instead of being angry at her for not having the solution, they had worked out one themselves. She . . . didn't need to do this all on her own. That shouldn't have been such a revelation for her. But after spending ages walking around with everyone piling bricks in your arms, it can throw you off balance when someone removes a brick to carry for you.

"Thank you," Tress whispered, trying to maintain her composure. She wasn't certain if captains should cry in front of their crew. Seemed like there'd be a maritime law against it. "Thank you so much! I've been trying and *trying* to think of a way through this."

We're here for you, Fort said. **We're your crew, Tress. Your friends. Let us help.**

"Yes, of course," Tress said. "But . . . thank you."

She looked at them each in turn, beaming.

"I'm trying to figure out why it says 'Ask nicely' on your forehead, Tress," Ann said.

Technically, Fort added, **it says "ʎləɔiu ʞsA."**

"Actually it says neither," Salay said. "Because it's crossed out. See?"

"Oh yeah," Ann said. "Anyway, we might have a solution to the other problem on the island: getting into the tower. You gave us the clue to this one too."

"Growing a tree of verdant vines?" Tress said. "To reach the top, and get in that way? I thought of that, Ann, but *surely* the Sorceress keeps the door locked."

But not the window, Fort said. **Where she lets out her ravens.**

"Far too small."

For a human, he wrote.

Their eyes turned toward Huck, who stood before the room's wardrobe. He'd finished counting the shoes Tress owned. That hadn't been difficult, as she was wearing both of them presently. So he'd moved on to making a mental list of the different types she'd need to buy.

He felt the stares. It's a thing rats learn. So he turned, feeling like the only piece of cheese left in the larder. "What?" he said.

"We need someone small," Salay said, "to sneak into the Sorceress's tower through her raven window."

"Tricky," Huck said, "since I don't think any human could fit through . . . Oh. Rat. Right." He wrung his paws together.

We need to do this for the captain, Fort said. **And the debt we owe her.**

"Huck owes me no debt," Tress said. "He wouldn't be on this ship except for me."

Which means he'd be on the bottom of the Verdant Sea.

I doubt he'd have made it to the bottom. Rats are rather low in body mass. He'd almost certainly have ended up wrapped in a vine ball, drifting through the middle depths of the ocean until he decomposed. But as no one in the room was versed in spore depth density and relative fluidized viscosity, they took Fort's words as fact.

"It's all right," Tress said to Huck. "You don't need to do it if you don't want to. I'd hate to force you into anything. But . . . it *is* a good solution. You're good at sneaking, Huck."

"But how will I reach the window?"

"On verdant vines, which I'll grow upward for you."

"No good," he said. "The tower is coated in silver. Didn't I tell you that?"

He hadn't. And that *would* cause a problem. Tress sat back, her face falling. Something in that expression pained Huck. He couldn't stand how gloomy she'd been feeling lately. Like smog over an island, he thought. So something slipped out.

"I can get you through the door," Huck said. "I . . . have a way we rats know about. If you somehow got me to the tower, I could open it. But Tress, isn't all of this irrelevant? We would have to cross the Midnight Sea first. And we shouldn't do that. We've barely survived the Crimson!"

He was, unfortunately, correct. Tress looked to her friends, hoping they knew a quick solution to this problem as they had the first two. No one spoke up. The other three might not have been marked, both literally and literately, by the fruits of their frustration on this point, but they were equally stymied.

Curiously though, there is a feature of collaboration that is often misunderstood. Two heads are not necessarily better than one (no matter what Dr. Ulaam might say). That rather depends on the heads in question.

However, when someone tries, it makes *others* more willing to try. And when you taste a little success—even vicariously—it can act as a mental laxative.

Or if you prefer, a little success is the metaphoric bang on the front of the mental vending machine that jostles loose the stuck ideas.

Tress's eyes went wide.

55

THE HYPOCRITE

Tress placed exactly two midnight spores on the table. The other officers shied back noticeably, though there wasn't a lot of room in the captain's cabin for shying. She'd spent a little while preparing this experiment, which had given Huck time to scamper off, not wanting to be in the room with more active midnight spores.

Tress put her silver knife on the table, then got out an eyedropper full of water. "Midnight spores behave differently than the others. The others all have an immediate, almost *chemical* reaction to water. But these spores, they seem almost alive. Like they want something."

"What . . . what do they want, Cap'n?" Ann asked.

"Water," Tress said, leaning down to eye level at the table, holding her eye dropper. "It's like . . . a trade. I give them water, and they obey me for a time." She raised the eyedropper, causing Salay to gasp despite herself. "This should be safe. But in case it's not, be ready to sever my bond to the spores with that knife."

Sever it how? Fort asked, leaning forward. He was the only one in the room who didn't seem positively terrified. Something about this entire conversation (and if you've been paying attention, you'll know what) intrigued him—overcoming his natural fear.

"Black lines," Tress said, glancing at his board. "Cut them with the knife. But I'm hoping that won't be necessary this time."

She released a single drop of water. Like before, the midnight spores bubbled and merged, becoming something not unlike an undulating pustule. Or (and please forgive me) a boiling boil.

As before, Tress felt a connection to it immediately. A tugging at her mind. She could initiate the link, could offer the water and make the bond. But for now she resisted.

"I feel something," Ann said. "Like it's yanking on my brain!"

"It's looking for a host," Tress said. "Or . . . a buyer. The monsters that roam the Midnight Sea? This is what they are. Creations of the Sorceress, bound to her. I wonder how she feeds so many . . ."

The globule lurched toward Fort, then took on the shape of a cup—specifically, the large metal tankard that was the heaviest and largest of Tress's collection. The midnight cup then grew legs and moved toward Fort. He'd bonded it inadvertently, as evidenced by him suddenly putting his hand to his mouth—which would inevitably have begun to feel dry. A small black line began to move between him and it.

Tress seized control.

When Captain Crow had used the midnight spores, Tress had been able to take control of the thing, destroying it in the process. This time it was far easier. She pushed her mind against the spores and offered water. More water. A bribe.

The thing immediately moved to her instead, and let her take over. She was closer to it, which Tress thought was key. She took complete control, then severed the bond before she could be drawn into the thing's eyes and experience life as if she were a midnight cup.

It popped and evaporated, leaving smoke, then nothing.

Fort gasped, then took a long drink from a red ceramic mug of water Tress offered him.

"What happened?" Salay asked, stepping forward.

"I took control of the thing," Tress said. "I bribed it with my water instead—offering that in trade, giving it more freely than it could take from an unwilling subject. Once it accepted, I took control, then dismissed it."

"And . . . you think you can do this with the ones guarding the Midnight Sea?" Ann asked.

"We are going to find out," Tress said, standing up. "How long until—"

A pounding came at the door. Tress hesitated, then nodded. Ann moved to open it, and they were confronted by Laggart.

Hell. I forgot to tell you about Laggart. Tress let Laggart stay on the *Crow's Song*. She rightly figured that without Crow around to impress, he wouldn't try anything funny.

(Not that he could, mind you. Laggart was to funny what liquid nitrogen is to a healthy set of lungs.)

He'd spent the last few days strutting back and forth up and down the deck. Ornery. Confused. Uncertain. "I need to speak to you in private, Captain," he said.

Tress was unsure about this, so she rested her hand on her flare gun. But she nodded to the others, indicating they should leave. They did so, closing the door behind them as Laggart stepped inside.

They regarded one another for a short time. Then Laggart drew himself up—looking like a buzzard that forgot to put on its feathers after its morning shave—and met Tress's gaze. "I demand," he said, "that you shoot me."

"Shoot you?" she said.

"For what I've done to you!"

"I told you that you were forgiven for that."

"I know!" he said, and began to pace. "Captain, I can't take the lies. I *know* what you're really doing. I *know* you're waiting until I'm calm and comfortable, so you can toss me over *then*. It's cruel, waiting to kill a man until he's sure you won't. I figured you for someone better than that."

He spun on her. "I demand to be shot. Get it over with. Be forthright. Shoot me."

Tress sighed, rubbing her forehead. "Laggart, I'm not going to shoot you."

"But—"

"Look, I'm far too tired to pretend to understand what your mind is doing to you right now. I'm not going to shoot you, but if you insist, I can throw you in the brig or something."

He perked up, then craned his neck. "Really?"

"Really."

"You'd do that for me? Imprison me instead of kill me?"

"Laggart," she said. "I'm not going to kill you. I was *never* going to kill you. I didn't even kill Crow."

He chewed on that. Then chewed on it some more. Then a little more. Those were words with gristle.

Laggart was not a smart man. True, the things he lectured people on could fill a dictionary—but what he *actually* knew would barely fill a postcard. That said, he wasn't an idiot either. He settled somewhere between smart and stupid, perched on the very peak of the bell curve and assuming that it was the right place to be, as highest has to be best.

In that moment though, he understood.

Tress was willing to throw him in the brig. But . . . she wasn't going to shoot him.

She wasn't going to toss him overboard. She *hadn't* been playing tricks on him. She had been *honest*.

She'd been *kind* to him.

This was the most difficult idea he'd ever been forced to swallow. You see, Laggart hadn't known much kindness during his existence, and it's a sorry truth that people often live what they know. He didn't view himself as mean or callous. He thought the way he acted was normal, because that was how he'd always been treated. In the land where everyone screams, everyone is also slightly deaf.

Now, it should be said that there *are* people who escape such a cycle of cruelty. When you find them, cherish them. Because unfortunately, many continue like Laggart, never realizing the way they are. Until perhaps they experience a moment like the one that happened on that ship. Where Tress showed him pure kindness, forgiving his actions.

Yes, he was no longer confused. Instead he was horrified. Because he'd realized at long last that there were people who *felt* the things they said.

There were genuine people in the world. To a determined hypocrite like him, that changed everything. He stumbled to the door, shoved it open, and fled.

Tress, in turn, watched him with her head cocked. Blissfully unaware of the war happening inside the man's heart. She didn't demand he be thrown in the brig. If he wasn't going to press the issue, she wouldn't either. Instead she carefully tucked away her box of midnight spores.

And honestly, she felt a growing elation. She had a plan for dealing with the monsters. If she could defeat them, she would have overcome the final obstacle between her and the Sorceress.

She was close. Truly *close*. She felt like celebrating.

That lasted about as long as it took her to find out what I'd been up to the past few days.

56

THE TRAITOR

Tress expected a certain sense of reverberation from the officers as she left her cabin. She felt enthusiasm, relief, excitement. They had an answer to each of the problems they needed to face in order to reach the Sorceress. The other officers, naturally, should have returned similar emotions to harmonize with her own, making the music of shared success.

So she was confused as she saw Salay running up to her with a concerned expression. Apparently Dr. Ulaam's treatment had run its course, but Tress hoped Salay had not grown any extra toes.

"What?" Tress asked, her sense of dread returning. "What's wrong?"

Salay led her to the hold of the ship, where I sat in chains, happily thinking of great conversation starters like politics, religion, and your uncle's overtly racist views. I experienced my tawdry ruminations among the remnants of the ship's food stores. An alarmingly small collection now, as I'd happily dumped the rest of the stores overboard.

"We caught him with three jugs of water," Salay said. "He was preparing to toss them out the rear porthole of the middle deck—where it appears he's been throwing out our food stores for days now."

Tress let out a groan. "How much do we have left?"

"Plenty of water," Salay said. "But less than half of our food. Roughly enough to reach the Verdant Sea, should we leave now. And Captain . . .

we saw birds on the Crimson only twice, and they don't live in the Midnight at all. We can't forage out here."

They looked at me.

"I had to throw the jugs out," I explained, "as the food is lonely on the bottom of the sea. Also, Tress, how does your uncle feel about seagulls taking his jobs and/or sandwiches?"

Tress looked at the gathered officers, then all of them turned to Ulaam, expecting him to have an answer. They foolishly assumed he could grasp the complex network of motivations, loyalties, and historical failures that made up the ever-changing web of my psyche.

"He is currently way too stupid to have done this on his own," Ulaam said. "See how the ones he was going to toss out are marked with chalk?"

Well, all right then. Points to Ulaam, I suppose.

"The rat said my mission was absolutely *vital*," I told them. "It's also secret. So please don't tell Tress."

A short time later, Tress approached Huck in his quarters—her former ones, which she'd assigned to him. His very own room. Yes, it didn't have silver, but it was more than most rats ever got. He'd been sitting there making a list of all the hats she owned. It only had one item so far, but he was an optimistic type of rat valet. What's more, he'd been so nervous that he'd needed something to pass the time.

He looked at her. "Did the test with the midnight spores work?" he said, dropping the pencil and scurrying over. "I would have come back to watch. Should have. But . . . that's not something a valet has to do, right? Be around midnight spores? They give me chills, Tress."

"I . . ." She didn't know what to say. It is an affliction that I've never known, but I hear it can be quite debilitating.

"Tress?" Huck asked. "I feel like you should be excited. Maybe enthusiastic. Certainly relieved. Yet . . ."

"I've discovered," she said, "that our food stores are frighteningly low. Somehow, we lost count of how much we had. It seems . . . we have barely enough to make it to the Verdant Sea, should we turn back now."

"Oh!" Huck said. "Well, that's dreadful news, but I suppose with everything that has been happening, it's not too surprising that something slipped through the cracks! We must make sail for the Verdant Sea, restock, then . . ." He trailed off, meeting her eyes. He wilted. "Hoid talked, didn't he?"

"You're remarkably good at reading human emotions," she said. "For a rat."

"Well, emotions are emotions," he said. "Doesn't matter the species. Fear, concern, anxiousness."

"Betrayal?" she asked. "Is that emotion the same for both human and rat?"

"So far as I can tell," he said, his voice growing very soft. "I'm sorry, Tress. I can't let you face the Sorceress. I *can't*. For your own good, you see."

Ah, those words.

I've heard those words. I've said those words. The words that proclaim, in bald-faced arrogance, "I don't trust you to make your own decisions." The words we pretend will soften the blow, yet instead layer condescension on top of already existent pain. Like dirt on a corpse.

Oh yes. I've said those words. I said them with sixteen other people, in fact.

"It hurts that you don't trust me, Huck," she said. "But you know, it hurts more that I can't trust *you* now."

"I get that," he said. "You deserve better."

She found a cage for him. It felt appropriate that she should put him back in one, and Crow had a couple of the appropriate size for keeping messenger birds.

It broke Tress's heart to leave Huck inside, huddled against the bars, refusing to face her. But she had a crew to protect, and she couldn't risk Huck doing something even more drastic to stop them. As it was, she barely contained her frustration. They were so close. Now they'd have to sail across the entire Crimson and restock.

Moons . . . could they afford to restock? How was she going to pay the crew? Would they continue as pirates? And if she did find Charlie, what then? Disband the crew? Give the ship to Salay and go home? Her focus on reaching the Sorceress had let her, so far, procrastinate addressing these questions. Payroll didn't seem so pressing when you expected to get captured and turned into a marmoset the next week.

These thoughts weighed on her as she opened the door and found a collection of Dougs waiting outside.

By now, Tress knew them all personally. The one at the front, holding her cap, was a good-natured woman who had once explained that she thought birds were the souls of the dead, watching over sailors as they traveled. It had been awkward, considering Tress had been serving pigeon pie that night; the Doug had just laughed and said that *was* a way of helping.

They all had quirks like that. Personalities, dreams, lives. Human beings are like the shorelines of continents. The closer you look, the more detail you see, basically into infinity. If I didn't practice narrative triage, you'd be here all week listening to how a Doug once got so drunk, she ended up as queen.

Today, fortunately for us, they acted in concert—and in service of the story. Because they had something to tell Tress.

"Let's keep going, Captain," the lead Doug said. "If you don't mind. Let's keep sailing, and go save that man of yours."

"But, the food . . ." Tress said.

"Pardon, Captain," another Doug said, "but we can eat verdant for a little while."

"Agreed," said another. "If it helps you, we can eat weeds for a few weeks."

"Wait. You can *eat* verdant vines?" Tress asked.

The Dougs were shocked to hear she didn't know this. You might be too, as it was mentioned earlier in the story as clever foreshadowing. But Tress had been distracted during that conversation, and had missed the point. Besides, few people who had grown up on islands had to know that the vines were technically edible. Because on islands, there was so much better food you could grow with far less danger, assuming you had access to soil or compost vats.

Even her family, poor though it had been, had always had normal food to eat. Regardless, people *could* survive on verdant vines, provided they were fully grown, a process that involved soaking them for a day. They provided some few calories and nutrients. Do it too long without supplemental protein and you'll have a rough time, but they could manage to get to the Sorceress's island and back on vines, plus what they had remaining.

Behind her, Huck looked at his feet. He was realizing that in the end, his betrayal hadn't even accomplished anything.

"Thank you," Tress said to the Dougs.

"Captain," the one at the front said, "we spent a *month* eating Fort's food. Then you started cooking dinners that didn't taste like they were scraped off the bottom of a shoe and . . . well, we can survive a little verdant."

"Besides," another added, "it's worth continuing. After this, we're gonna be the only pirates who ever robbed the *Sorceress herself*!"

57

THE MALIGNED
FASHION EXPERT

About that.

Tress knew that there was a hole in her plans. In fact, there were exceedingly more holes in her plan than there were wholes. For example, she couldn't be certain she'd correctly guessed the island's location. Even if she had, there was no guarantee their plans would work. She might not be able to get past the Sorceress's defenses.

All of those issues, however, were secondary to the biggest one. Lurking like a shadow beneath the ocean. Her focus so far had revolved around getting *to* the island, then *into* the tower.

But what *then*?

How under the moons was she going to find, then rescue Charlie? How would Tress deal with the Sorceress? Their plan involved firing cannons at the metal servants on the beach. That would make a ruckus and certainly draw attention.

How would Tress, after making so much noise, secretly get to the tower so that . . .

So that Huck could let them in.

Her confidence wavered. Well, it had been wavering for days—not unexpectedly, considering its flimsy foundation. Now it threatened to topple right over. Their plans had relied on Huck letting them into the tower. Now that obviously wasn't an option.

Tress felt sick about this, but no solutions revealed themselves over the next few days. The ship sailed inexorably toward the terrible Midnight Moon, until it reached the border. That place where spores mingled, like a scar that was festering and black on one side. A limb that had suffered full necrosis.

Black spores, stretching to infinity. Tress watched from the quarterdeck, feeling an unnatural quiet as the Dougs stilled and even the sails seemed to hold their breaths. It was here, the Midnight Sea.

Salay looked to Tress.

"Drop anchor, Helmswoman," Tress said. "It's nearly night. I shouldn't like to sail that sea in darkness."

"Agreed," Salay said.

"Keep a double watch tonight," Tress suggested. "I don't fancy being taken by surprise—either by rain, or by something else coming up through that darkness."

Salay nodded, visibly uncomfortable.

Tress moved to go down to her cabin, then paused. "Salay. Have you ever heard of anyone sailing it successfully?"

"The Verdant King keeps sending fleets to try to capture the Sorceress," Salay said. "Some ships do survive the Crimson. That's random luck, after all. I've never heard of one coming back from the Midnight though. They sail out into that, and are almost instantly overrun by dark creations of foul spores."

Tress shivered. Did she really think she could do what those capable sailors had failed to do? What was she thinking? Why was she even here? She was a sham of a captain, playing dress-up.

Granted, Tress wasn't giving herself enough credit—please act surprised—as she'd come quite far, all things considered. And it's true that numerous members of the king's court hadn't managed to survive their first encounter upon the Midnight Sea. But then, you've met at least one member of the king's court: he was the handsome fellow in the early part of the story with both the jaw and the intellect of a marble bust. So, you know, maybe they didn't set the highest standard.

Regardless, Tress was suddenly very uncertain of herself. She fled below, to the familiar hallway of the middle deck. She passed her old room, and found herself *nostalgic* for a couple weeks earlier. Days when she'd sat reading about spores while listening to the comforting footsteps above. Those footfalls had sounded so confident. Random, but somehow still rhythmic. Beats indicating a song the crew all knew and played together.

Now she was in charge. The one everybody was confident in was *her*.

She approached Dr. Ulaam's office and was let in after a quick knock. She found him inspecting his hand, which had grown a sixth finger. Tress sighed in relief. Finally a normal and familiar sight.

"Tress!" he said, trying out a ring on the finger. "I'm pleased by the visit! Have you reconsidered my offer?"

"Thank you, but no," she said. "I'm rather attached to all of my toes."

"Everyone is, dear. That's why the Father invented scalpels. But now, you look distraught. Here, sit. Let me boil some water." She sat down as he used some odd device that worked like a hot plate, but without fire or spores to warm it up. He set a kettle on top, then turned and regarded her, grey-skinned fingers laced in front of him as he leaned against the counter. "Speak, please."

"Ulaam," she said, "I can't defeat the Sorceress."

"No, of course you can't," he said.

"All of the others are expecting me to. And . . . I'm increasingly terrified I'll let them down."

"Ah, well then," he said, "can I help you with this anxiety, hmmm? I don't even have to give you a sedative. You needn't worry."

"I needn't?" she said. "Really?"

"Yes. You see, no one expects you to defeat the Sorceress. I believe they're all expecting to die. And so, you won't disappoint them, child, when the Sorceress inevitably murders the entire crew!"

She groaned.

"That was a joke," he noted. "I doubt she's capable of killing me—though she thinks she can. Even if she is right, she *certainly* can't kill Hoid, even in his current state. So it will only be most of the crew she murders."

Tress felt dizzy.

Ulaam, it should be noted, is not known for his bedside manner—as

I've pointed out, his people lost something when they stopped being forced to imitate actual humans. I can genuinely say that without that burden, they've all become increasingly themselves over the decades.

That said, Ulaam is legitimately the best doctor I've ever met. If you are easily stressed, but need his help, I suggest you ask him to sew his mouth shut before he visits. He'll probably find the idea novel enough that he'll try it.

That day, however, he realized he'd said too much. Even Ulaam, a creature with the empathic talents of an angry emu, could occasionally realize when someone was in emotional distress.

"Child," he said, "I—"

"How *could* you?" Tress snapped at him. "How can you *sit there* and not care? What is *wrong* with you?"

"Oh!" he said. "Hm. Ha ha. Well, no need to bite my head off. I have several saws for the purpose right over—"

"Jokes don't *help*, Ulaam!" she said, standing up.

It hadn't been a joke, mind you. He actually had three. He let her pace for a little bit, and when the teakettle began to whistle, he didn't move to get it.

As she paced, one point stuck in her brain. He'd mentioned Hoid again. The drooling cabin boy. Ulaam was a creature of strange powers, but he saw *me* as someone even greater.

It wasn't the first time Ulaam had said something like that. But this time it actually struck her.

Finally she took a deep breath. "I shouldn't have snapped at you," she said. "You've been helpful in the past, Ulaam, telling me things you didn't have to. I shouldn't get angry at you for not doing more. I . . . I don't know what's wrong with me. I never would have acted that way in the past."

"I think," Ulaam said, "that perhaps nothing is wrong. Maybe you *should* snap at me more often. I forget sometimes what I've been told about the stresses mortals live under."

"You're right though," she said, pacing the other direction in the small room. "We *are* going to die. This quest is foolishness! When it was only *me* who was risking my life for Charlie, that was bad enough. I can't force the rest to join me."

"You aren't forcing them, Tress," Ulaam said. He finally rose and began to make the tea. "Have you seen how they walk these days? How they hold their heads? They know they're partially to blame for the people Crow killed.

"You're not bullying them. You're offering them a chance at reclaiming their humanity. They *want* to try to rescue your friend. They *want* to prove to themselves that even though they might not be first-rate men and women of valor, they at least possess a secondhand variety."

He turned, handing her a cup and gesturing toward the seat. It was a nice cup. Tin, but dinged up with the respectable scars of favorite use, and shined along the handle from the caress of fingers. She sighed, taking the seat and the tea, though she put the latter aside to let it cool.

"Look," she said, "*Huck* was willing to move against me. Perhaps I should see his point. Even if I don't, I can't use him to get into the tower now. So the mission is a bust."

"You still have Midnight Essence," Ulaam said. "Maybe you can make a creature that can sneak in and unlock the door."

"The tower is coated with silver," Tress said. "So I wouldn't be able to touch it as a midnight creature. At least that's what Huck said. I don't know if that's true, or what to trust from him, but either way we have a bigger problem. Ulaam, I can't beat the Sorceress. She's going to know I'm coming."

"She knows already, I suspect," Ulaam said. "From what I know of her, she is probably looking forward to seeing how you deal with her defenses."

"Is it . . . possible to impress her so much with what we do that she lets Charlie go?"

"Unlikely," he said. "Best you can hope for is that she finds you amusing and sends you away with a particularly creative curse."

"So there's no hope."

"Well . . ."

Tress looked up.

"I am supposed to remain neutral, you see," he said, "in the actions of certain individuals such as the Sorceress. But there is someone who never follows those rules. He's on this ship. And he has a pair of bright red sequined briefs."

"Hoid," she said. "You've mentioned that he's . . . not what I think he is. Is he truly something greater than the Sorceress?"

"Well, these things are famously difficult to judge," Ulaam said. "But I should say yes. I wish you could know the real Hoid. As amusing as it has been to watch his current incarnation in all its splendor, he is normally quite different from the person you know."

"And that person is . . . less embarrassing?"

"Well, usually more embarrassing. But also quite adept at certain things. If there is a single person on the entire planet who can defeat the Sorceress and get you and yours out alive, it is that man. I tell no joke or exaggeration in this, Tress. When he wants to, there are few people in the entire cosmere who can influence events like our dear friend with the inappropriate undergarments."

I'll have you know I owned those briefs before the curse, and I stand by the purchase.

Tress considered that. Then she finally tried her tea, which alone proved her bravery. I never drink anything Ulaam gives me without first seeing what it does to the houseplants.

"If he's so powerful," Tress said, "how did the Sorceress end up cursing him?"

"I have no idea," Ulaam said. "But it's not *that* surprising. For how capable he is, Tress, he often overreaches in some way. It doesn't matter how powerful a person is, if they believe they are slightly *more* powerful than they truly are, there's room between those margins for big errors. Hmmmm?"

Yeah, that one was fair.

"Regardless," Ulaam said, "I think in this case, what happened to him wasn't an accident. If I were to lay down money—or, more valuable, my favorite set of fingernails—I'd guess he got cursed on purpose. And is now having more trouble than expected getting out of it."

"Why?" Tress said. "Why would he get cursed on *purpose*?"

"I haven't been able to decide," Ulaam replied.

Tress was skeptical. But in this case, Ulaam was (unfortunately) right. I had honestly thought I would have sorted through this by now. It was . . . proving more difficult than I'd anticipated.

Fortunately, I was close. Closer than ever. Because Tress hit on the most important idea right then.

"So . . ." Tress said, "maybe I *don't* have to defeat the Sorceress. Maybe I just have to find a way to get *Hoid* to do it."

"Perhaps. Yes, perhaps indeed."

Tress excused herself, then wandered to her quarters. There she dug under the bed and brought out her collection of cups. It had been so long since she'd admired them. The part of her that enjoyed them hadn't changed, but she just . . . didn't have the time she'd once had. Really, these days she'd only been using the big metal one. It was the one that wouldn't break if it dropped off the table when the ship swayed.

Still, she took them out one at a time and placed them on the counter. Last of all she got out the ones Charlie had sent her. She stared in particular at the one with the butterfly soaring across the ocean. She'd originally assumed the butterfly had to be forced into such a terrible situation. Why else would it fly out over the spores?

She saw it differently now. Perhaps it was simply a butterfly who knew what it wanted—and was willing to try to get it, no matter how impossible.

It wasn't a suicidal butterfly. It was a determined one.

She put away the other cups, but kept this one out, along with the pewter tankard. These were her two favorites. One a symbol of determination. The other a solid and heavy practical device—almost a weapon.

I, she thought, *am these two cups.* One side utilitarian, one side dreaming. Opposites. Yet both served the same function. Remarkable.

That butterfly, though, had gone out on the ocean alone. It hadn't brought an entire crew with it to die. She took a deep breath and tied her hair back, then took the two cups and stalked out onto the deck.

"Salay," she said to the helmswoman, "I've changed my mind. I want you to set down the launch. I'm going to take it into the Midnight Sea. Alone."

58

THE MONSTER

The objections were mountainous.

"Alone?" Salay said. "Captain, what moon gave you such a lunatic idea?"

"I'll go with you," Ann said. "I can keep you safe. I've got six pistols on me, and four eyes to aim them with now!"

Even Laggart, hovering about the back of the group of officers, seemed concerned.

Fort just held up his board. **Why?** he asked.

"I want to try the experiment with the Midnight Essence," Tress said. "See if I can actually control or destroy the monsters—because if I can't, there's no moving forward and all of this is moot. I will try it alone, as there's no reason to bring the rest of you. There's nothing you can do."

"I think this is a bad idea, Captain," Salay said, folding her arms. "I won't let you go into another sea alone."

"Am I not the captain?" Tress asked. "Can I not make this decision?"

"You can," Salay said. "But you *shouldn't*."

Irony is a curious concept. Specifically, I mean the classical definition: that of a choice leading to an opposite outcome from what is intended. Many grammarians bemoan the word's near-constant misuse—second only in dictional assassination to the way some people use the word "literally." (Their use of which is ironic.)

I'm not one of those people who care if you use words wrong. I prefer it when words change meaning. The imprecision of our language is a feature; it best represents the superlative fact of human existence: that our own emotions—even our souls—are themselves imprecise. Our words, like our hearts, are weapons still hot from the forging, beating themselves into new shapes each time we swing them.

Yet irony is an intriguing concept. It exists only where we want to find it, because for true irony, expectation is key. Irony must be noticed to exist. We create it from nothing when we find it. But unlike other things we create, like art, irony is about creating *tragedy*.

Irony is reversal. Set up, then collapse.

A perfect bit of irony is a beautiful thing.

So watch. Enjoy.

"I cannot let myself create more hardship for any of you," Tress said. "I need to do this next part alone."

Salay sighed softly—the kind of sigh you make when you're trying not to yell, but need to give your lungs something to do. She nodded to the side. "Can we speak in private a moment, Captain?"

Tress nodded, and the two of them stepped away.

"I have another suggestion," Salay said. "We sail the *Crow's Song* in a little way and skirt the edge of the border for a while. Try to attract one of these monsters. Then we trap it with verdant spores and haul it on board. From there, we can retreat to the Crimson and take our time experimenting on it."

"Too dangerous," Tress said.

"More dangerous than you going in alone?"

"Too dangerous," Tress revised, "for all of *you*. This is something I have to do, but I can't let you keep risking yourselves."

"Captain," Salay said, her tone softening, "Tress. My entire life changed when you returned from the dragon's den. I've been searching for Father for . . . for so long. I hoped for such a long time that hope started to wither. I was simply doing what I'd done because I was afraid to let it fully die.

"It's alive again now. Watered by you, nurtured back to life. He's *alive*.

And I know where he is. I *need* to survive what's coming next so I can get to him."

"Then go," Tress said softly. "You need to live to save him. You can't take risks."

"I need a good crew to get through these seas," Salay said.

"This *is* a good crew."

"It was one," Salay said, "and can be one again. But Tress, do you know what it does to a person's soul to serve someone like Crow? You build up a black crust. Like toast left too long in the oven." She nodded to the crew gathered on deck. "I put you in charge for several reasons. One is that I think you'll be a good captain. But another is that they need someone to lead them who can set things right again. Someone who didn't agree to Crow's demands. They need *you*."

Tress nodded, understanding a shade better. Salay taking over would be a little like a team taking a time-out to reassess their strategy. Giving the ship to Tress was like tearing down the stadium to build a new one.

"Ever since you came on this ship," Salay said, "you've done nothing but try to protect and help us. The crew knows it. They'll follow you. *I'll* follow you. But I can't save my father yet. Can't save . . . myself yet. Not until I help you and this crew. So, I'm asking. Let me help you right now."

"Why ask?" Tress said. "Why not demand?"

Salay shook her head. "We mutinied against Crow. We can't afford to let that kind of behavior be seen as normal. We have to make it clear that disobeying Crow was an extreme exception.

"So we'll follow you. Exactly. The officers and I, we'll model for the others, because we know if we don't . . . well, that's when things on ships can go extra poorly. When exceptions become habits. So if you tell us to let you do this alone, we *will* let you, Tress. We have to."

She met Tress's eyes with one of those looks full of implication.

That never works as well as you think it might.

Because Tress had learned the wrong lesson. She'd heard the part about helping the crew. About protecting them. And so, she doubled down.

"Thank you, Salay," Tress said. "Now, please prepare the launch. I will be going alone into the Midnight Sea to test my theories about controlling the spore monsters there."

The sigh this time was accompanied by a barely contained growl, like Salay had swallowed something angry and furry.

Speaking of which.

Tress returned to her cabin to grab her hat before heading out for her experiment. And when she did, a voice spoke from the corner.

"Take me," Huck said.

Tress froze, then turned toward his cage.

"Bring me," he said. "I heard you speaking. Take me in the cage, if you must. But *bring me with you*, Tress. On that boat. You might need me."

She nearly dismissed him. But something about his voice . . . the tone of it perhaps . . . She pulled on her hat, wavered for a moment, but then decided. As she left, she grabbed his cage by the handle on the top and carried it with her as she swept out onto the deck.

And so, soon afterward, Tress found herself in a rowboat, the Midnight Sea surrounding her in all directions. Accompanied by only a caged rat, a keg of water, and a couple of free-range cups. It was time to see if she could get past the Sorceress's first line of defense. To see if she could conquer the terrible tar monsters that roamed the Midnight Sea. It was a tense, dramatic moment—that unfortunately the terrible monsters forgot to attend.

Surely they'd be along any moment now.

Tress continued to drift alone in all that blackness. The sea was *warm*, gorged on sunlight as it was. Somehow it felt even more alien than the Crimson Sea. She might have thought black spores would be more familiar. The world turned black for roughly half the day, every day. It was a natural color.

Yet sitting there, she felt as if her tiny boat were hanging in a void. A vast nothing. Even the sound of the seethe making the spores ripple wasn't comforting. It *sounded* wrong here. Upon this persistent night. Upon this gluttonous expanse that ate the very sunlight.

And now the sun was going down. Tress turned and looked backward longingly—but she had rowed herself out here for a good hour or so. Her arms were burning as proof.

The *Crow's Song* wasn't even visible, nor was the Crimson Sea. She was alone. Except for Huck, who huddled in his cage, quiet and terrified—despite having demanded he be brought along. To pass the time, Tress tried writing a little in her notebook. But she was too worried, too distracted. It wasn't only the thought of the Midnight Essence, but the fact that the spores were so close. Churning and bubbling right outside the hull of her boat.

She tried looking up at the sky, but as she did, the sun sank behind the moon on the horizon. The Midnight Moon, like a hole in reality.

So she waited. There are few things worse than stressful—yet empty—time. Free time that you can't use in any way always feels like nature itself is mocking you.

Finally though, Tress spotted movement.

The Midnight Essence had gotten alarmingly close to her without being noticed. Perhaps because it was black upon black, though the fact that it was moving *through* the spores also helped hide its approach. Once she spotted it though, she tracked it easily—for it reflected the light of her lamp like oil.

Her breath caught. She stopped worrying about the spores, fixated only upon this approaching horror. What kind of beast moved *through* the spores? Bathing in them? Or . . . swimming? Was that the right term?

Tress knew the word from one of Charlie's stories, though she found the idea remarkable. There were places with so much water that you could go in over your head? Wouldn't you sink and drown?

Whatever the word, the creature approaching was doing it. You might have recognized the Midnight Essence as resembling some kind of eel or sea serpent, perhaps half as long as the *Crow's Song* was. But you come from a world where things live in the water; that idea was wholly alien to Tress, and so she found the beast's movements unnatural, unnerving. A spine should not move in such a way, like a piece of string, bending with supple contours.

It circled her boat, predatory. Also confused.

Why was this human sitting out here alone in a little boat? You'd have felt similar if you'd been strolling through the woods and found a warm steak dinner chilling on a stump. What kind of trick was this?

To this day, I can't completely say if Midnight Essence is alive or not. The Luhel bond is an odd one, to be certain. For the context of the story though, pretend that the thing slinking along outside her boat was functionally self-aware. At the very least, it had been given a specific set of commands that approximated life.

And so, it knew to be cautious. This gave Tress the opening she needed. With a trembling hand, she reached out and touched the thing as it swam past.

This was, in the thing's perception, deeply unsettling. There it was, an eldritch monster of nefarious design, imbued with a hatred for all life. It had spent its entire existence seeking out ships, then growing legs to slip on board and consume those inside. When people saw it, they made all kinds of noises—though each one ended up as a painful gurgle. That was the sound of a job well done, an existence fulfilled.

People feared it. They *didn't* reach out to touch it. That was basically like a salami standing up and trying to jump into your mouth. It isn't that you don't like a good salami, but you should at least have to work for it.

Also, there was the mind control.

Tress had bet everything on being able to do what she had earlier—and seize control of this thing.

It was more credible a plan than you might think. You see, there was too much sea to cover for the Sorceress to pay attention to each creature individually. She made them in batches, then sent them out with orders, maintaining only a loose control. Indeed, if she'd tried to actively direct all of these things, even she would have been quickly dehydrated and killed.

Beyond that, the creatures had just enough self-awareness to make decisions. To choose. That's a dangerous feature to build into your roaming minions, but again, the Sorceress didn't have another option. She had to give them a measure of autonomy, lest they be incapable of doing the job for which she'd designed them.

So yes. Tress's plan could have worked.

If she'd been sprouting for more than a couple of weeks.

Tress tried to seize control as she'd done earlier, pressing her mind against it. The thing reared up out of the spores, pulling away from her hand, and looked at her with midnight eyes. A question came into her head, like . . . it wanted something. She tried to offer water, hoping it was more than the Sorceress was giving.

The thing rebuffed her. Naturally, the Sorceress knew of this possibility. She understood the weakness inherent in her creations. And she'd built them, with complex mechanisms, to recognize an outside attempt at control. Tress was tenaciously talented and demonstrably determined. But she was still new.

And the Sorceress, it should be noted, was *not*.

The thing reared up with a hiss, opening its mouth, anticipating its feast. Tress threw herself to the bottom of the boat, terrified.

When a small, high-pitched voice spoke.

"Stop," Huck said. Then, sounding reluctant, he continued, "Take us to your mistress. I . . . have free passage."

The creature swayed its head, the complex sets of commands that guided it converging on the owner of that voice. One it had been instructed not to eat. One it was to bring to its master when commanded.

Huck the rat had returned to the place where he'd been created, as instructed by the Sorceress.

59

THE PRISONER

The next morning, Tress arrived at the Sorceress's island.

She'd been allowed a drink and the use of the facilities (a chamber pot) on the little rowboat. But otherwise she'd spent the trip wrapped in the coils of the Midnight Essence. Immobile. Two others just like it had emerged from the spores to push the boat, with incredible speed, to its destination.

Huck refused to answer her demands for explanations of what he'd done, or why the creatures listened to him. But Tress had her suspicions.

So it was that after an incredible journey, Tress finally arrived at the Sorceress's island. And found it smaller than she'd envisioned. This is notable, as the island Tress came from was already small by the standards of most worlds. So her surprise was akin to a four-year-old remarking, "You know, I expected you to be more mature."

As the spore seas lack the fine carbonates derived from coral refined by ichthyological digestive processes (yes, your favorite beaches are fish poop), the Sorceress's island was merely another pile of rocks rising from the spores. In this case, the slate-grey stone skerry was suspiciously circular, and perhaps two hundred yards wide.

A few trees tried to spruce up the landscape but failed, both by being too intermittent and by not being the right species. Instead they were spindly, gnarled things with tufts of leaves growing only at the very tips of their branches. As if they knew the concept of "trees" only by description, and were doing their best, all things considered.

Tress had spent the trip alternating between hating Huck and hating herself. With the most generous helping heaped on herself. Now she sat, wrapped in the coils of the Midnight Essence, watching with dread as they approached the island. The Midnight Essence, it should be noted, now looked less like an eel and more like a pile of verdant vines.

The boat had a line of silver in the hull, which left dead spores trailing them in a dissipating wake. The creature took care not to touch the silver, but—like Tress had noticed when she'd seen through the eyes of the Midnight Essence rat—could get close to it without being destroyed.

It had unlocked Huck's cage. He sat on one of the plank seats, near the front of the boat. Spores crunched and rustled as the two midnight creatures pushed the little craft steadily forward.

"You *have* been here before," Tress said, voicing her guesses. "All that talk of growing up in a community of rats—that was all lies, wasn't it?"

"Yes," Huck whispered.

"You belong to her," Tress said. "You're a familiar of the Sorceress, or something like that. You've *always* belonged to her."

"Yes," he said, even softer.

Each answer hit like an arrow. The barbed kind that hurt going in—but also rip and tear going out. The kind that make you want to leave them in, walking around with wounds that can never heal, for fear of the worse pain of removal.

Still, as much as that stung, she forced herself to admit something. Huck had done everything he could—short of abandoning the ship at port—to keep her from coming this way. To protect her from the Sorceress.

He had lied, yes, but he was obviously terrified of the Sorceress. She couldn't blame him too much for how he acted, now that she'd unwittingly brought him back here. She could, however, blame herself.

She should have been smarter, come up with another plan. Maybe she should have taken Salay's advice, and let the crew help with the problem? Tress wavered on a precipice as she thought about that.

Change has an illusory aspect to it. We pretend that big changes hang on single decisions, single moments. And they do. But single decisions and single moments, in turn, have a mountain of smaller decisions behind them. You can't have an avalanche without a mountain of snow, even if it begins with one bit starting to tumble.

Don't ignore the mountains of minutes that heap up behind important decisions. That was happening to Tress right at that moment. Full realization hadn't dawned yet, but the glow was on the horizon.

The midnight monsters steered the boat in an odd way as they approached the island, and Tress soon observed why. Long, jagged lines of stone cut up through the sea here, like sandbars with teeth. The Sorceress had chosen her island deliberately; the approach to the place was exceptionally treacherous. Hidden rocks lay like mines, barely peeking through the seething spores, giving almost no hint to their locations.

Approaching, then, was nearly impossible. As the boat made a sequence of expert maneuvers—steered by monsters who knew the correct path by magical gift—Tress felt her stomach drop. This was a protection to the island they hadn't known about. Huck hadn't told them of it, perhaps with nefarious intent. (In fact he simply forgot, but that's beside the point.)

If the *Crow's Song* had arrived and tried to sail up to the island, it would have surely ripped its hull to pieces and died upon the spores. Her mission here had been doomed all along.

Eventually their little boat—a lone speck of color skimming the top of the void—navigated to shore. Here Tress could make out the legion of golden metal men standing in ranks around the Sorceress's tower. Outfitted with spears and shields, Tress could almost imagine them as men in armor with lowered faceplates. If only they hadn't stood so unnaturally still.

Other than the lonely trees and the hundred metal men, the island's only feature was the tower itself. This, in contrast to the size of the island, was much larger than Tress had anticipated. Wide and tall, with a peaked top, Tress was too modest to say out loud what it resembled. I, of course, don't know what modesty feels like—so when *I* mentioned what it looked like, the Sorceress asked me if I'd like a large yonic symbol splitting my forehead.

Tress had hoped for a way to escape once the boat landed, but the creature kept her wrapped tightly, lifting her and carrying her before it-self as Huck hopped off the boat. On the stone ground, he looked toward Tress. The first time he had looked directly at her since they'd gotten on the little boat.

She glared back at him. He wilted visibly, like a vine without enough water. Then, however, he perked up—as if deciding something. "Yes. Yes, that's it," he said. "Not doing what she asked at all."

He eyed the monster, then scampered forward before Tress could berate him again. They crossed the ground to the tower itself, the metal men letting them pass. The things seemed to be asleep at the moment, in Tress's estimation. Merely statues.

The tower soon took her attention. It was an awe-inspiring sight, more silver in one place than she'd ever seen before. There was so much of it, in fact, that it would destroy spores at an incredible rate. Protection against enemy sprouters.

A door was built into the side of the tower, apparently also made of silver. Huck stood up in front of it, and in a loud voice, spoke. "As I was commanded, I've returned to the tower with a captive to present to the Sorceress. Magic door, please open! Uh, I was told—"

The door swung open on its own.

"Right," he said. "Good." He scurried in, then looked down at himself, then back at Tress. Uncertain what would happen next.

The midnight monster—now looking like a large centipede with tentacles for feet—let Tress go and shoved her through the door into the tower. It couldn't follow, because of the silver. Instead it tossed her something. Her cups. The pewter one and the one with the butter-fly. It had brought them—because it had found them in the boat and didn't know if they were important or not.

As Tress fumbled to catch her cups, the door slid shut. Locking her inside and leaving her with only one choice.

To proceed. And meet her destiny.

THE SORCERESS

Tress took a moment to reorient herself, taking a deep breath, rubbing her arms—and trying to brush free the touch of the strange midnight creature. She thought of grabbing Huck, but he was quickly vanishing up a set of steps—using the running board alongside them as a ramp.

Tress stayed still for the moment. She'd entered an all-metal corridor, decorated only by a red carpet down the middle like a tongue. It was inlaid with symbols that a well-traveled person would recognize as Aonic, but that Tress saw as some kind of arcane rune. Which wasn't too far off.

The walls—instead of being lined with pictures or tapestries—bore several panels that reminded Tress of Fort's writing board. Now, many storytellers would describe such a hallway with words like cold and sterile. That's mostly due to past association. The calm, pure white lights in the ceiling—diffused through a plastic filter—might remind you of an office building, while the unadorned metallic finish might remind you of a hospital operating room.

To Tress, the room wasn't cold. It wasn't stoic, or bleak, or stern—or any words that might describe a politician at his trial after he escapes the dumpster.

"It's beautiful," she whispered. "So clean and so radiant. Like I imagine the afterlife."

Her words echoed in the corridor. Finally, she took a long breath. She was here. She wasn't dead. Perhaps ... perhaps she could find a way to rescue Charlie. Despite everything. This *was* where she'd been pointed her entire voyage, after all.

So, scraping together what was left of her determination, she strode forward and up the steps. At the top, a door opened on its own, sliding to the side. Because the Sorceress had very particular ideas about what the interior of this kind of vessel should be like.

Beyond the door, Tress entered a large, circular room with doors at the sides. The chamber had a lived-in look, decorated with the kinds of things that would make a mess if the Sorceress had to leave in haste. Furniture, bookshelves. The floor was still metal—inscribed with a map of the planet—and the lights were still industrial, but she made it look cozy.

The woman herself sat at her desk near the bookshelves, holding a fluffy white cat and idly doing something on her laptop. Or, I mean, her "magical seeing board" that let her watch events outside, as well as occasionally play a mystical card game to pass the time.

Her skin glowed, and she had a silvery effervescence to her. She was maybe in her fifties—rather, that was how old she'd been when she'd stopped aging—and she'd come a long way from the withered husk she'd once been. Short, a little plump, she liked keeping her hair in a bun for convenience and abhorred makeup. I mean, I would too, if I literally glowed. Her kind tended to prefer clothing and other accents that didn't distract from their luminous nature.

Though she was a long, long way from home, she was extremely powerful. She rotated in her chair, setting her mystical board on the table, then shooing her cat off her lap. It hopped onto the floor, then eyed Huck—who cowered on the desk. The Sorceress pointed, and the cat slunk toward the door, slipping past Tress and out.

Tress was paying little heed, as she was mesmerized by the various seeing boards on the desk. One showed a view of the hallway where Tress had entered. Several other panels on her desk showed things like shots of the island—but one of them depicted the deck of the *Crow's Song*.

"Ah!" the Sorceress said, standing up. She glanced at Huck, who shied down before her gaze. "So this is her. Your offering. I have to say, I'm not impressed. She seems scrawny. And that hair! Girl, I know your planet is rather unimportant, but surely your people have invented *hairbrushes*."

Tress swallowed. To her, the woman looked deific. It was the glowing skin. Really helps you land a good first impression. I've been envious of that look for centuries now, and have been aiming to adopt it.

In fact, that is what this has all been about. But I get ahead of myself.

Tress shoved down her awe and cobbled together her ramshackle plan. She drew herself up, clutching her cups for strength, and spoke. "Sorceress! You have taken captive someone I love. I have come to demand his return."

"Demand?" she asked. "What makes you think you can demand anything of me?"

"Because I," Tress proclaimed, "have defeated you."

"Defeated me?" the woman asked, amused, glancing at Huck.

"I've crossed your ocean," Tress said, "approached your island, passed your metal army, and gained entrance to your lair. I have overcome the four trials you've put before me, and have obtained your presence."

"Ha!" the Sorceress said. "My four trials? I love it. You've been listening to Hoid. Tell me, how is Ulaam?"

"Er . . ." Tress looked at Huck, who was wringing his paws. "He's . . . fine, my lady. He seems happy on the *Song*, at least."

"All this time," she said, "and he's never come to see me. Wise, I suppose. He knows I keep a vat of acid just for him. It's one of the only ways to be sure about them, you know. That or a good fire."

The Sorceress strolled through the center of the circular room, walking across the map of the world inscribed on the floor. Offworlders called the place Lumar, which is a pretty good translation of the name used by several native languages. Tress had never seen a map of it so detailed, but there was a lot to take in, so she didn't spare much thought for it.

The Sorceress stepped right up to Tress. Obviously unafraid of physical altercation.

"So," Tress said. "I've defeated you . . ."

The Sorceress grinned. "Did you *really* think that would work, dear? Pretending you got captured on purpose to get past my defenses?"

Tress swallowed, then went for her backup idea. "I . . . um . . . I want to make a trade with you. I have a flare gun. It shoots bullets that create explosions of spores."

"Yes, I've seen," the Sorceress said, gesturing to her viewing boards. One of which still depicted the *Crow's Song*—and the image was wobbling, moving . . . and there were some fingers at the side of the image, gripping it . . .

Fort's board, Tress realized. *That's a view from his board, facing outward. The Sorceress has been using it to spy on us.*

Indeed she had. If I'd been in my right mind, I'd have realized ages ago that the security protocols were off by default, letting the things be hacked quite easily. The Sorceress had been watching this entire time, save for the short period where Fort had been between boards. She'd stopped paying quite so much attention to the *Crow's Song* once Tress left.

"My gun," Tress continued. "It's a design I made, known nowhere in the rest of the seas. I want to trade you the designs. In exchange for the return of Charlie, the man I love."

"You think," the Sorceress asked, "that with all the advanced technology at my disposal, I'd be interested in your spore gun? A type of weapon that is already being manufactured in several seas on this very planet, which simply hasn't made its way to your ocean yet?"

Tress's resolve had already been crumbling. Now it all-out collapsed. She looked to Huck, who—strangely—raised a paw toward her in a little fist. Encouraging her.

Something else was going on here, Tress realized. Something she hadn't grasped yet. She began thinking back through the events that had led her to this point. Huck had been able to demand the midnight monster bring her to the island. The Sorceress seemed intrigued by her and her crew. They were worth noticing and watching. Why?

Hoid, Tress thought. *Hoid can defeat her. She's been watching* him.

So how did Huck fit into this? And why was the Sorceress chatting with Tress instead of locking her away?

Tress hadn't known what to anticipate in a confrontation with this woman. But a civil conversation certainly hadn't been it. It made Tress feel terribly *un*certain.

The Sorceress turned and walked toward her desk. "Well, child, I don't need your technology, but I find you intriguing. Seslo, please open the bridge's holding chamber."

"As you wish," a monotone voice said. It was the spirit that inhabited this place, you see, obeying the will of its owner. Yes, like the speaking minds inhabiting the ships you've seen landing on your planet.

One of the doors at the side of the room clicked audibly, then swung open. Behind it was Charlie.

He looked a little worse for wear. He had on one of his formal outfits, one Tress had seen him in when making appearances with his father, but it was rumpled and torn in a few places. Otherwise, he looked exactly as she remembered him, with hair that didn't comb straight and a wide grin.

"I knew you'd come," he said, rushing over to Tress. "I knew you would! Oh, Tress. You've saved me!"

At this moment, Tress's emotions were complicated. Like that rope you always swear you put away neatly, but which comes out of storage looking like someone used it to invent new theoretical types of knots that bend space-time.

It was Charlie. Seeing him was incredible. That made her happy, and also relieved. Celebratory, overwhelmed, excited, grateful—yes, all of that. All the emotions you would expect were present and accounted for.

But she also felt a sadness she couldn't explain. (We'll get to it.) And in addition, confusion. Suspicion. That was it? Was she truly just going to get what she wanted?

"I will trade him," the Sorceress said, "for those two cups."

"What, really?" Tress asked.

"Really," the Sorceress said. "Simply leave them on the shelf by the door."

"Is he . . . ensorcelled in any way?" Tress asked.

"Oh, that. I should play the part, shouldn't I? Ahem.

"Under shining bulb,
With mighty gulp,
I make it felt
That I break this spell."

Barbarian. She does that to annoy me.

It was exactly the sort of thing that Tress expected to hear though. Arcane nonsense—comfortingly mystical. Charlie put his hand to his head, then leaned down and gave her a brief kiss.

That made Tress's emotions twist even further.

"See, rat?" the Sorceress said. "I told you, didn't I?"

Huck, on the desk, bowed his head.

"Say it," the Sorceress continued. "Say it, rat."

"You were right," he whispered, almost inaudibly. He slunk away from the desk, dropping to the floor. Vanishing.

Tress took hold of her emotions, slapped them sensible, and sent them to stand in an orderly line. There would be time to deal with them later. For the moment, she made a decision.

It was time to leave. She grabbed Charlie by the hand, put her two cups on the shelf by the door, then hurried out and onto the stairs.

Charlie took it all in stride, starting a rather boring story about his days in captivity that I won't tediously repeat here. Particularly since he soon moved on to other comments. "Oh, Tress," he said, "won't it be so nice to get back to our normal lives on the Rock again? Won't it be so nice to go back to pies, and window washing, and gardening?"

It was here—right at the bottom of the steps, listening to those questions from Charlie—that Tress's sadness assaulted her. It fought dirty, you see, as sadness usually does. Going for the kidneys. Or the heart.

Charlie didn't seem like he'd changed at all. That was good. She'd worried his captivity would have left him mentally scarred. But here he was, perky and excitable as always. He could have given lessons to puppies on how to be properly enthusiastic. Good old Charlie. Same as ever.

Tress was not the same.

She'd changed *so* much in the course of her time away from the Rock. She found she didn't care about pies, or window washing, or even cups in the same way. She cared about spores, and what she could do with them. About sailing, and her crew.

All of this . . . all of this meant she couldn't go back to being the same person. She, you see, *had* been scarred.

There it is! Irony. The very journey she'd taken to find what she wanted had transformed her into a person who could no longer enjoy that victory. She looked into Charlie's eyes, and her emotions parted asunder, bowing before her building sense of melancholy. Crowning it queen.

In that moment, looking into Charlie's eyes, she thought of someone else. Someone Tress shouldn't have cared for, on paper. That's one thing we get wrong far too often in stories. We pretend that love is rational, if we can only see the pieces, the motivations.

Charlie grinned. It was such a familiar grin. Perfectly like him.

She didn't believe it. That smile was one step too far. Because she *knew* Charlie.

Tress turned, ran up the steps, and burst into the main room, startling the Sorceress—who was settling down into her seat. Full of electric defiance, Tress shouted, "That is *not* Charlie."

The Sorceress hesitated.

"You like to torment people," Tress said, pointing at the Sorceress and stalking forward. "You curse them with the worst curses you can imagine, *tailored* to the individual and their pains. You didn't keep Charlie here."

"And what," the Sorceress said, "do you think I did with him?"

"You turned him into a rat," Tress said.

Ha! Finally.

61

THE MAN

Tress kept striding forward, step by step, toward the Sorceress. "Each time I tried to get Huck to talk about this place, or you, he stammered. He searched for words. Because a spell was preventing him from speaking things that would let me know he was Charlie, cursed."

"If that is so," the Sorceress said, "then how could he have told you about the defenses here? I know he did. I know many things, child."

Tress stopped, and her eyes widened. "Because when he told me . . . he was trying to get me to stay away . . ." She focused on the Sorceress. "Because me coming here is the way to break the curse, isn't it? Moons! You cursed him, and said the only way to break it was for *him* to bring *me* here, to you! That's why he tried *everything* to stop me. Because . . . because he loves me."

The room fell still save for one sound. Sniffling.

Tress approached the desk and found Huck the rat behind it. He looked up at her, his eyes red. Unlike the doppelganger she'd been given, Huck was a mess. Shivering and crying as he curled up in a ball.

Tress knelt. "Charlie . . ."

"I'm sorry," he whispered. "I didn't want her to be right. She told me I'd end up bringing you here so she could play with you. I tried not to follow her prophecy, but I'm stupid, Tress. Stupid and worthless. You deserve so much better. Look at all you've done, and I couldn't even manage one thing to keep you safe . . ."

"Oh, Charlie," she whispered, picking up the rat, cradling him. He trembled, his eyes squeezed shut.

The desk rolled to the side at an offhand whim of the Sorceress. She now stood in the dead center of the room. The fake Charlie had walked up to the doorway, and the Lightweaving had fallen away, revealing a creature that only resembled a human—reptilian with golden eyes and a toothy grin.

My best guess is that she wanted to plant someone on the *Crow's Song* to deal with me more permanently. I suspect she was beginning to worry about our bet. And the fact that someone so close to me had been able to get into her fortress, even as a captive.

The Sorceress showed none of these emotions. Instead she tossed aside her amiable air. Her eyes grew hard as stones. Her lips drew to a line. She didn't like that Tress had seen through this ruse. In addition, something else bothered her. Something that might be obvious to you. If not, it will be revealed in a moment.

Tress was oblivious as she cradled Charlie the rat. He'd indeed tried to tell her, several times. When he couldn't say his name was Charlie, he'd tried "Chuck." But the curse had only let "Huck" come out.

"Charlie," Tress whispered. "You sent me cups."

He looked at her. "That was a lifetime ago, Tress."

"I love them. Particularly the one with the butterfly on the sea. Like us, Charlie. Soaring over places we never thought to go. And the one made of pewter. Like us, Charlie. Stronger and more straightforward than we have a right to be."

"She has us though," he said. "Because of me, she has us both. She told me . . . the only way to be free was to bring her the person I loved, then give them to her to curse. She said she'd make me watch. Moons, it was excruciating, watching you sail ever closer. I should have tossed myself overboard. Then you'd have never learned how to get in . . ."

He trailed off as she held him up before her, meeting his eyes. "Charlie," she whispered. "I want this."

"I . . ."

"You remember what you told me? Before we parted?"

"Always," he whispered. "Always . . . what you want."

"I want *this*," she said. "To be with you."

He met her eyes, and found in them strength enough for two. Then his head cocked. The same thought occurred to the two of them simultaneously.

"Charlie," she said, "if the way to break your curse was to bring the person you love to the Sorceress, why are you still a rat? Is it because . . . Is there someone else you love?"

"No!" he said. "It's you. But . . ."

"It's because," the Sorceress said from behind them, "I haven't cursed you yet. His torment can only be ended if he brings you to me for that specific purpose."

Tress rose, holding Charlie in her palm, looking toward the Sorceress—who seemed to be another person. Same shape. Different soul. No jovial playfulness. Instead a cold monster. Some scholars say that when you become an immortal like the Sorceress or me, your soul gets replaced with something new. Like the fossilization process.

In her case, in lieu of a soul, the woman had pure ice. Kept cold and frozen by her heart.

In the face of this, Charlie—who had himself been changing, day by day, on this journey—spoke. "You're wrong," he said softly. "I'm still a rat, and will remain one. Because for my curse to be broken, I have to bring her to your home in trade for my freedom. I realized on the way in that I *haven't* done that. I brought her, Sorceress, but not in trade. Not to get cursed. I brought her to *defeat* you."

"Remarkable," the Sorceress said. "I didn't give you the intelligence of a rat, but it seems you've adopted it willingly. I can't be defeated by—"

A red light appeared on her desk.

Several other lights appeared on the wall. Then several more. The Sorceress spun, surprised, commanding the soul of her building to show her what had tripped her alarms. A large screen appeared in the air beside one wall, depicting a ship crashing through the seething midnight spores.

As I said, she hadn't been paying enough attention. If she had, she would have seen this coming.

Because the *Crow's Song* had arrived.

62

THE HUNTER

How?

Let's jump back a day. To the crew, who had been waiting for Tress's safe return. A Doug posted on duty high atop the main mast had been able to see—through a spyglass—when Tress was taken. He'd scampered down to explain.

This put the crew in a bind. What did they do? They couldn't give chase through the Midnight Sea, could they? The very monsters that had taken Tress would claim them as well. They perhaps should have turned and tried to escape through the Crimson to safer spores. It was what Tress had said she wanted.

Instead they'd held an emergency meeting. And a solution had been offered. By Fort.

It was a chance for him to claim the title of the greatest hunter his people had ever known. A chance to hunt monsters made from midnight spores. The others had listened to his plan, then gone to the Dougs to propose it. The crew had voted unanimously in favor, save for Laggart.

So they'd sailed the Midnight Sea. Fifteen minutes in, the first midnight monsters had appeared. Three of them slithered up on deck, completely impervious to normal weapons, looking for warm bodies and blood to feast upon. For liquid, for water. For death.

Instead they found a large man standing at the center of the deck surrounded by barrels of water. Each with a keg of spores suspended above it by a rope.

Welcome, he wrote to the three monsters—with Ann saying the words out loud in case the creatures couldn't read. **I have quite the deal for you today.**

The things slithered forward, making for him. In turn, Fort moved to cut one of the kegs free.

Careful, he warned as Dougs moved to do likewise. **We'll feed all this water to these other spores, leaving none for you, unless you take care.**

The midnight monsters stopped. They didn't need the words, as they could sense what a person was saying or meaning. Their essence reached out to people, seeking the Luhel bond. And so what Fort said registered on some level with them.

They communicated with one another by wiggling tentacles. And Fort . . . well, he understood. Not because he knew another sign language, but because of that same bond. They *did* want the water. But there were sources of blood on the ship, and that would do as well.

Warning, he said, gesturing to the rest of the crew, who had gathered with guns at the back of the ship. **If you don't stop, they're going to throw themselves overboard and feed their water to the spores. Other spores. Not you.**

This finally got through to the creatures. It was a conundrum. So much water. But . . . if they weren't careful . . . it would all go to someone else.

Fort rammed his hand into one of the barrels of water, then made signs with the other—signs the creatures understood because of the bond.

I can feed you all of this, he said. **All for you three.**

How? they signed back. **What will it take to be able to eat and drink and thrive and drink and drink and drink?**

Protect us, Fort said, **as we sail farther into the sea here.**

As I said, there's a flaw in using self-aware magical creatures as guards. This process was efficient, allowing the Sorceress to send them out in large numbers, although she couldn't spare much attention for them.

But midnight aethers are insatiable. And their inherent nature is to trade. To do a human's bidding in exchange for water and form. That left them highly susceptible to someone who understood the mechanics of the magic—and had a mind for a good trade.

And thus, using the coordinates on the map that Tress had gotten out of me, the *Crow's Song* arrived at the island only half an hour after Tress had. Ready to rescue their captain.

It provided the exact distraction Tress needed in the moment. Because the Sorceress, reorienting to these new arrivals, needed to awaken her defenses. She began shouting orders—for the moment ignoring Tress and Charlie.

"They came for me," Tress said. "Those beautiful fools. They should have stayed away!"

"Like you should have stayed away?" Charlie said. "Instead of coming for me?"

Tress looked at him sitting in her palm, tears in her eyes. And the avalanche started to tremble. She realized that she was the fool. Not for coming to save Charlie—but for trying to keep others from following their own hearts in the same way.

"We have to do something," she whispered. "I need to warn them about the rocks under the spores. There has to be a way to talk to them."

Both of them looked at the Sorceress's desk—in particular, the magical board that displayed the image from Fort's similar one. Then, as the Sorceress was waking up her armies, Tress and Charlie grabbed the board and stared at it. Trying to figure out how to operate it.

"Uh," Charlie said. "Board? Can you please let us talk to the people you're showing us?"

"Video conferencing engaged!" the board said, happy to be of service.

Fort, who had been holding the board, stood up from his chair. He'd spent the entire night drinking water and feeding it—via the bond—to the three monsters. So he was both tired and feeling a little odd, as he'd been able to drink multiple barrels' worth but didn't feel full.

Still, their arrival had made him alert, and he'd sent the midnight monsters—now fully under his control by the strengthening of the bond—swimming away to fight others that had tried to get onto the ship.

His always won those fights, of course, having far more water to build new body parts from the spores around them if wounded.

Regardless, he had a moment of peace. And could cock his head, frowning as the back of his board—which used to display words for him—now showed Tress and the rat, huddled up close to the camera on their side.

"Fort?" Tress asked. "Can you see us?"

The words scrolled across the screen, obscuring the view a little.

I can! he typed, the words appearing underneath theirs but from the other side. He waved to the others, and in a moment Ann and Salay had joined him. Even I huddled up with them, curious.

"Captain?" Salay asked. "Captain! Are you well?"

"We're in the tower," Tress whispered. "How did you survive the spores? No, never mind that now. Explain later. Salay, you need to watch out. The sea here is full of rocks under the spores. They're extremely treacherous!"

"I'll watch for those," Salay said. "Thank you."

"You shouldn't have come here," Tress said. "If you try to sail through those rocks, you'll sink."

The three of them frowned. Then Salay asked simply, "Do you order us to turn around?"

Did she?

Could she?

Dared she?

In that moment, the decision was made. The rock tipped and the avalanche of change that had been building in Tress started tumbling down.

"No," Tress whispered. "Please help me."

The three of them grinned. I scratched my head. Because something about the place where Tress was standing, visible behind her, was familiar to me.

"We'll do it," Salay said. "We're coming."

"Don't get yourselves hurt!" Tress said.

"Captain," Ann said, "we're going to save you. Because you deserve it. You remember, you once told me somethin' that made me see the world in an entirely new way."

"And that was?" Tress asked.

"'Here, try on these spectacles.'"

Ann, Fort wrote, **that was almost as bad as one of Hoid's jokes.**

"It isn't just a joke though," Ann said, tapping her spectacles. "It's true. I see a new world. A world where we aren't condemned people any longer. A world where we've got ourselves a future."

"You know I'm not a King's Mask," Tress said. "I can't get him to pardon us."

"We'll find another way," Ann said, looking to the others, who nodded. "Because once we saunter up to the Sorceress herself and get away . . . well, I figure after we do that, we'll be able to do *anything*."

The three of them nodded to her, and she felt overwhelmed. By their loyalty, by her own (at long last) willingness to accept help. By . . .

Wait.

Within Tress's avalanche of emotions, something stood out. Prompted by how I, standing there with the other three, was trying to use my tongue to pick my nose.

Her thoughts were a curiosity, you might say.

A revelation, *I'd* say.

"Hoid," Tress said. "Hoid couldn't point out the way to the Sorceress. We had to guess the location by pointing to places other than this one. He could talk about all of those . . ."

And? Fort said.

"And I assumed the reason was because he couldn't talk about his curse," Tress said. "But the solution to Charlie's curse involved him returning to her. If Hoid couldn't show us the way here, at least not intentionally, then maybe the solution to his curse involves *him* coming here too."

She looked down at the floor.

A map of the world.

You must bring me to your planet, Tress.

"Yes . . ." Charlie whispered. "Hoid could talk about being cursed, once you knew about what had happened to him. He should have been able to easily mention the Sorceress and her island. But if he couldn't? That implies that doing so would help *break* the curse. His solution must involve getting back into the Sorceress's tower. Passing her tests . . . Tress, it makes sense!"

She looked up toward the others again, her eyes widening. "You need to bring him here. Into this room."

"The cabin boy?" Ann asked, frowning.

"Captain?" Salay said. "Are you sure?"

"Yes," Tress said. "Please. Bring him to me. I know it's hard, but *please.*"

"Well, if you order it . . ." Salay said .

"Don't do it because I order it," Tress said. "Do it because you trust me."

The others nodded. They did trust her. Which was good, since the Sorceress had noticed what Tress was doing. Eyes wide with fury, the woman barked an order, shutting off their communication. She thrust her hands into the air, her fingers leaving trails of light as she constructed powerful runes. As she finished them with a flourish, a blast of light erupted from them and crossed the room, slamming Tress back against the wall and holding her there.

A crash and a clank sounded as two cups tumbled free of their perches. The one with the butterfly shattered. The other bounced, gaining a new dent.

The Sorceress turned back to mobilizing her armies. Charlie—who had been dropped as Tress slammed into the wall—picked himself up and scampered over to her, climbing her clothing. He tried to nibble at the lines of light to free her. It worked about as poorly as you might imagine.

"Charlie," Tress whispered.

He looked up at her, frustrated that glowing lines of light could be so strong. "I . . . I'm sorry, Tress. You can't rely on me. I'm useless. I'm failing again. I . . ."

"Charlie," she said, "there's something I've been meaning to tell you. I wish I'd said it earlier, so I'm going to say it now, although it's probably a terrible time for it. I love you."

"I feel the same," he said. "I love you too."

"Good. It would be very awkward if that turned out not to be the case." She struggled, then looked over at the *Crow's Song* on the screen, sailing toward the island. "Please, Charlie. I hate to impose. But if they fight through the defenses, they'll never get into the tower to rescue us."

Realization hit him. "I . . . I can open the door for them, Tress. *I can do that.*"

"If it's not too much trouble," she said.

Yes, she'd changed. But even big events change us only a little at a time, and she *was* still Tress.

Charlie looked toward the room's open door, leading to the steps down to the outer door. Where the Sorceress's cat was prowling.

"It might be too frightening for Huck the rat," he said. "But I think perhaps Charlie the gardener is made of something stronger." He nuzzled up against Tress's cheek. "Thank you," he said, softer. "For coming to get me. I wish I could have told you earlier."

Then he leaped down to begin his quest.

THE PILOT

The Sorceress was not angry. Not yet.

Not even frightened. Not yet.

She was mostly annoyed. And admittedly a little worried.

She had thought I was handled. When I'd started across the Crimson, she'd watched not because she was afraid I'd actually reach her tower, but because she enjoyed seeing me inconvenienced. She thought maybe I'd get sent to the bottom of the ocean, and she figured that would be a delight to watch.

Now, somehow here I was. Surely I couldn't get past her defenses, not on a common boat. Yet she hadn't thought I'd pass the Crimson, or sail the Midnight. She now assumed I had somehow, despite my enormous hindrances, been behind the ship's survival of those dangers. She didn't realize that my true advantage has never been my uncommon intellect.

It's been my ability to find the right people and stick close to them.

Right then, I clung to the side of the *Crow's Song*—up on the quarterdeck, near the helmswoman's station. I had stolen Huck's tiny pirate hat, thinking he didn't deserve it. Which, strictly speaking, was wrong. Can you really be mad at a pirate for stabbing you in the back?

It looked much worse on me. So of course I wore it clipped in place. I was grinning wildly, wind in my hair, eyes wide—because I figured they might dry out that way, and then I could stop blinking.

Salay spun the ship's wheel. She shouted orders to the Dougs, who worked their magic on the sails. The Sorceress was extremely confident in her defenses. Certain that no one could sail the passage between the rocks to her island.

She hadn't counted on a woman like Salay. Sailing with her father's final letter in her pocket, knowing that if she died on this sea, he would remain imprisoned by his debts forever. A woman who had just discovered a renewed purpose in life. A woman who had taken a bet on Tress, and had earned the lives of the crew in return.

A woman who would not back down when the lives of her friends were at stake. Pray you meet such a woman at least once in your life. Then pray you get out of her way quickly enough.

She held to the wheel as wood groaned, her will against that of the spores, and steered the ship past stones. Unblinking. I was impressed by that part.

"Why?" Ann said, holding the banister and walking up the steps toward me. "Hoid, why does Tress have this strange idea that you can be savin' her?"

"Probably," I shouted over the rush of wind and spore, "because I just realized I should take up painting! And the Sorceress will be scared of my talent!"

"You are so aggravating!" Ann said.

"Nonsense," I replied. "Your cabin, Ann! Feels like it could use something to spruce it up. Or, if trees won't fit, maybe some paintings of dogs wearing hats. Oh!" I looked at her, my eyes wild as a spray of black spores crashed up beside me while the ship navigated a near-impossible curve. "Oh, I've just had the *best* idea. I could paint the pictures on *velvet*."

"Why in the name of the Verdant Moon's own backside would you do somethin' like that?"

"To give them texture when you lick them, obviously," I said. "Really, you should think about things more before you ask stupid questions, Ann."

And she *should* have known better. She might not have been asking a stupid question, but asking a question of stupid is nearly as futile.

Salay was so far into her zone of focus, she didn't hear the conversation. Back in the tower, the Sorceress paused to watch as the ship slipped among the rocks, drawing ever closer. A sailing ship is a strange thing to control—I'm sure some of you know. You often don't steer so much as ride the waves, winds, and currents. You need speed to maneuver, but motion is always both your enemy and your ally all at once. Too little, and you can't complete your turns. Too much, and you end up kissing the rocks.

That day though, the ship appeared to obey neither wave nor wind, spore nor shoal. The ship obeyed Salay, and for a short transcendent moment, we seemed not on a ship at all. We rode upon her willpower made manifest, dodging rocks by inches, leaning so far to the sides at times I thought for sure we'd capsize. She had an instinct for where those rocks were, based on how the spores churned. And she did it all with eyes straight forward, focused on her goal.

To the Sorceress's astonishment, we broke through the rocks into the island's small bay. She shook her head, moving from annoyance to genuine concern. Behind her, Lacy—the cat—screeched and pounced, causing the worried Charlie to retreat into the room. He tried to race down the stairs again, but was chased back.

The Sorceress gave another order, and her group of metal men marched forward, ready for battle. They, surely, would put an end to this farce. They'd always been her most secure form of defense.

"Cannonmaster!" Salay said on the ship. "Prepare arms!"

That meant Ann. She hurried to the front of the ship to her cannon. It was her chance at last. To prove herself, one way or another, a bespectacled spectacle.

She'd been practicing these last few days, enough to be worried. She didn't seem to be supernaturally bad at aiming any longer, but that didn't mean she was good. She was really, *really* worried about that. And about how, despite years of dreaming of this day, everything suddenly came down to her.

On the shore, the metal men marched in ranks, responding immediately to the Sorceress's orders. The color of burnished brass, each one seven feet tall and carrying a spear with a glistening tip, they were an intimidating sight. Their instructions (carefully conveyed by the Sorceress when Breathing life into them) were complex, careful, and meticulous.

They were far better servants than the scouts made from Midnight Essence. While they were on duty, they would form a barrier to prevent any kind of landing. Even from the deck, wet firing rod in hand, Ann could see why the king's forces had never had any luck against them. Musket balls would bounce off them, and cannonballs . . . well, those might knock one of the creatures down and leave a dent. But they'd be up again soon after.

Tress's designs though—they would work. Ann's hand trembled anyway as she rammed the firing stick into the cannon and launched a cannonball. The metal men didn't flinch. In part because the cannonball went wide, smashing through a tree, bouncing along the stones, then vanishing into the spores in the near distance.

Sweating profusely from the stress, Ann loaded another cannonball. She didn't turn around and look at the crew. She knew what they were thinking. It wasn't only eyesight that had been Ann's problem. Something else was wrong with her.

And she was right.

But it wasn't bad luck, or some mystical curse. It was something far more mundane, but equally pernicious. Ann didn't miss just because she had poor eyesight. She missed because of *momentum*.

There's an opposite force in life to the avalanche Tress was feeling. There's always an opposition, you see. A Push for every Pull, an old adversary of mine always says. Sometimes the moments in our life pile up and become an unstoppable force that makes us change. But at other times they become a mountain impossible to surmount.

Everyone misses shots now and then. But if you become known as the person who misses—if you internalize it—well, suddenly every miss becomes another rock in that pile. While every hit gets ignored. Eventually you become Ann: arm shaking, sweat pouring down your face, clutched by the invisible but very real claws of self-fulfilling determination. Then you start missing not because your aim is bad, or your eyesight is poor, but *because* your arm is shaking and sweat is pouring down your face.

And because missing is what you do.

Dreading what she'd once loved, Ann raised the stick to the side of the cannon. A calm voice interrupted her.

"Hold your fire, shipmate Ann," Laggart said, one hand on the forestay rope to keep his balance as he squinted at the shore.

Ann hesitated.

"Three degrees to aft and one up, shipmate Ann," Laggart said, his voice calm and firm.

She hesitated only a moment, then began cranking the cannon as he indicated. The ship continued to rock in the shallow waves of the bay, moving alongside the shore.

"Hold," Laggart said as she put the firing rod in place. "Hold. *FIRE!*"

An explosion of spores and force blasted the cannonball on its way. As she'd imagined, it hit one of the metal men in the chest and knocked it down, but didn't destroy it. However, the vines that burst out grabbed and enveloped all the metal men nearby.

They, in turn, were completely flummoxed. On the ship, Ann took one step toward her mountain and found it quite a bit smaller than she'd imagined.

"Reload and reset," Laggart said.

"Reloading and resetting, sir!" Ann said, moving with an efficiency that would have impressed any naval officer.

"Two degrees up," Laggart said.

"Two degrees up!" she said. "And one to port!"

"Aye," Laggart said, surprised. "And one to port. Now hold. Hold . . ."

"Fire!" Ann said at the exact same moment he did.

This shot flew true as well, catching another group of metal men.

"Reloading and resetting, sir!" Ann cried before he could give the order. She had the next blast off in quick succession. She looked to him, breathing quickly.

"Damn fine shooting," Laggart said, with a nod. "*Damn* fine. Assistant Cannonmaster."

And standing there on the summit of her mountain, Ann wondered at how tiny it suddenly seemed.

64

THE HERO

Back in the tower, Tress was still a captive.

It was humiliating, yes, but somehow . . . also gratifying? In that this was what she had expected to happen.

From the moment she'd launched from the Rock, she'd anticipated grand failure. She had gone not because she'd assumed she would succeed, but because something had to be done. And though many things had gone wrong on her quest, she'd somehow always managed to make them go right too.

She had found her repeated success almost *uncomfortably* consistent. In the same way that if you keep rolling sixes, you start to worry that something is wrong with the dice. Failing here, getting captured, being immobilized and unable to help . . .

Well, she wasn't *happy* about it. But a part of her *was* relieved. It had finally happened. As it should have. She wasn't a King's Mask or a pirate. She was a window washer. With hair that really needed to be pulled back into its tail, because she could barely see through it at the moment. Unfortunately, the Sorceress's bonds had locked her hands in those glowing bands of light, pressed to the wall.

Through her hair, she was able to watch the Sorceress's annoyance as the cannons completely immobilized her troops. This wasn't supposed to happen. She had designed the men to withstand cannon fire. She'd designed them to be unstoppable. They could march right out into the ocean, and even had grappling hooks that let them climb aboard ships—often spearing them from underneath first, puncturing the hulls.

They were impervious to basically every weapon available to a pre-industrial culture. Fearsome, destructive, deadly.

They didn't know what to do about vines though.

Even a semi-self-aware construct like an Awakened soldier relies on its instructions. They're far more versatile than something running on a traditional computer program, but they're also not fully alive. And these, confronted by vines holding them down, were baffled.

Their instructions told them not to be afraid of weapons brandished by interlopers. So they kept trying to march forward. The cannonballs continued to explode around them, causing more vines to spring out. When immobilized, the metal men had instructions to call for support. Normally that was a valid line of programming.

In this case though, it sent the entire group into chaos. They'd alternate from trying to march on the ship to trying to free one another, to locking up as they tried to decide what to do when neither was possible.

In short, the cannonballs worked.

Blessed moons, they *worked*.

Despite her situation, Tress couldn't help grinning as she saw *her* designs incapacitating an entire legion of supposedly unstoppable foes.

Charlie climbed up her leg, clinging to her trousers as the cat prowled below. He was puffing from exertion. "I . . . am having a little trouble with the beast."

"It's all right, Charlie," Tress said, still watching the cannon fire.

"Hey," he said, "don't you cry. There's a maritime law against that."

"Sorry," she said as another cannonball exploded, vines reaching out like some unholy hybrid of an octopus and a bag of lawn clippings. "It's just . . . they're beautiful."

A short time later the crew was on shore, running past the immobilized troops—Fort leading the charge, and carrying me overhead. I'll pretend it was in a dignified fashion.

But if Charlie didn't open the door, they'd be trapped outside the tower. And the story would end there.

Tress looked to Charlie. "I'm sorry. That in the end, we got captured. It's like we said would happen, isn't it?"

He nodded. "But Tress," he said, "I remember another part of that conversation. Something about shining armor."

"I don't think they make armor in rat sizes, Charlie."

Charlie saw something on the floor. His eyes narrowed. "Distract her," he said. Then he drew upon every ounce of courage he had remaining—it wasn't much, but when you're in such a small body, courage (like booze) goes further than you expect.

Charlie leaped. The cat gave chase immediately, bearing down on him as he dashed for something lying on the floor near the stairs.

A large pewter tankard.

The Sorceress was turning her attention to the tower's defenses. She might well have figured out what was happening if Tress hadn't done as Charlie asked.

"Sorceress," she said, "have you heard those stories? About the fare maiden who gets captured?"

"Thinking about your fate?" the Sorceress said, never one to pass on inflicting a little misery. "Thinking about how you traveled all this way only to end up in chains?"

"Yes," Tress said. "And thinking that . . . well, it's not that bad, actually."

"Not that bad!" the Sorceress said, stalking forward, ignoring the clinking sound from behind—like something metal going down the steps. "Dear, you're powerless! You wanted to save your love, but can't even save your own self! You thought yourself a powerful pirate, yet here you are. At the end of your quest. You've ended up like every girl from any story. Needing to be rescued."

Freeze that moment.

Imagine it: Charlie the rat, spinning in the air within a pewter cup, bouncing down the stairs. Observed by a bemused cat from above, who had given the swat that sent the cup tumbling.

Fort, Ann, and Salay reaching the tower with me hoisted high over-head.

Tress. Bound by glowing bonds. Held to the wall.

Confident.

"Those stories always leave something out," Tress said. "It's really not a problem that someone needs to be saved. Everyone needs help. It's hard to be the person who makes trouble, but the thing is, *everyone* makes trouble. How would we help anyone if nobody ever needed help?"

"And you?" the Sorceress asked, starting to draw runes in the air. "You're going to have quite the curse, I'll tell you. I've been saving this one for a *special* occasion. You will spend the next several decades in misery, child."

Down below, a tiny voice echoed up from the hallway. "Magic door, please open!"

"The part the stories leave out," Tress said as the Sorceress's runes formed into a vibrant wall, "is everything that comes before. You see, I've discovered that it's all right to need help. So long as you've lived your life as the kind of person who deserves to be rescued."

The Sorceress released her curse, a blast of light and energy meant to enwrap Tress and transform her. Instead, the runes exploded in a blinding shower of light. Filling the room with white energy that momentarily blotted out all possible sensation.

When it faded, I stood between Tress and the Sorceress—with the key officers of the *Crow's Song* behind me and a little rat on my shoulder— my hands pressed forward, having created an Invested shield of light to shelter Tress. It was constructed of Aons. Which I could now draw. The mechanics might bore you. The results, though, were spectacular.

I was wearing a floral buttoned shirt, shorts that were way too short, and sandals.

With socks.

"Hello, Riina," I said. "I hope your last few years have been *exactly* as lovely as *you* are."

She lowered her hands, her jaw dropping.

"Why, yes," I said, gesturing to my current clothing, "I *do* know this outfit is awful. I realize one should never bring up politics at dinner with one's in-laws. And I know that you, my dear, are living proof that someone doesn't need to be the least bit funny to be an *utter clown*."

A deep glow pulsed beneath my skin. *Finally.*

Turns out that to get this particular set of powers to work, you couldn't simply fake Connection. You needed an invitation and adoption into a very select group. My only chance had been to find one smart enough to be a member of that group, stupid enough for me to toy with, and sadistic enough to trade membership for the opportunity to see me cursed.

"Damn you," she muttered.

My curse was broken. My senses restored. She could see it as easily as I could.

I'd won.

"Excellent work, cabin boy," Tress said, still attached to the wall. "We're going to have to promote you after this."

"Wait . . . we won?" Salay asked. "Hoid, you're . . . um . . . What are you?"

"The term 'sorcerer' will do," I told her. "I have won our bet."

"Wait," Charlie said from my shoulder. "It was really a bet? You let her curse you for a simple *bet*?"

"Please," I said. "Was *anything* about what we just did simple?"

The Sorceress waved her hand, dropping Tress from the wall. "Go," she said. "Before I change my mind."

Fort helped Tress as she stumbled, and she nodded in thanks. Then she turned to the Sorceress. "First," she said, "end Charlie's curse."

"I can't," the Sorceress said. "I can't break a curse unless the terms are met. It's impossible."

Tress looked to me. There were ways, but the Sorceress probably wasn't capable of them. So I nodded. It was true enough.

Tress took a deep breath, then looked back at the Sorceress, her face becoming like steel. "We're not leaving," Tress said. "*You are.*"

"Excuse me?" the Sorceress snapped.

"You've cursed people who only wanted to talk to you," Tress said. "You've taken prisoners, robbed merchants, and destroyed fleets. You are a scourge upon this sea. This planet." She drew herself up, partially to intimidate the side of her that was shocked by her own audacity. "I demand that you leave this world. Go away, and never return."

"Oh please," the Sorceress said. "Who are *you* to make demands of *me*?"

In response, Salay and Fort pulled pistols on her. Ann somehow got out three at once. Charlie growled. It wasn't very intimidating, but it made him feel good to contribute.

Tress didn't bother with a gun. She nudged me. "Cabin boy," she said, "zap her or something."

"You're giving *me* orders?" I said softly.

"You're on my crew, aren't you?" she said. At least she had the good graces to blush about it.

I sighed and, as ordered, stepped forward and raised my hands. I met the Sorceress's eyes, and knew what she was thinking. She, like most of her kind, was very good at something we call risk/reward projections. She'd come to this planet because nothing here could threaten her. Then she'd found a dragon living here. Then I'd arrived.

She might have been able to beat me. Curse me again. But she might *not* have been able to. Even if the odds were only one in five that she'd lose, you didn't live long by frequently taking one-in-five chances that you'll die. And Riina had lived a very, *very* long time.

A short time later, we all stood on the deck of the *Crow's Song*, looking up at a twinkling speck of light as it vanished in the sky. The tower was gone, taking the Sorceress with it.

I have that effect on people. Stay around too long, and you'll inevitably envy those who have never met me.

Behind us, the Dougs started to whoop and cheer. Fort rolled out something wonderful to drink, which he'd been saving for such an occasion. Ann decided their cannons needed names, much to Laggart's lamentation. Salay put her hand to her pocket—and the letter from her father—and suffered it all for now. She even let herself enjoy the celebration.

Tress stepped up to me, holding Charlie. Who was still a rat. "Is there . . . nothing you can do?" she asked. "No way to break the curse?" Both of them looked to me with hope in their eyes.

"I can't undo the curse," I said. "Not at my current skill with the arts. No one can."

"Oh," Charlie said.

"But perhaps," I said, inspecting the runes I could make out surrounding him, "I *can* change the parameters a little . . ."

EPILOGUE

Five months later, a ship arrived at the Rock that was not a rock. That ship bumped the docks as it slowed, on account of its new apprentice helmsman being inexperienced. Salay's father looked chagrined, but Salay merely smiled and gave him a few pointers.

The ship was not the *Crow's Song*. The crew had decided that a fresh start would help them in their new lives, and besides, the captain had wanted a few extra cabins. So after receiving their pardons, they'd sold the old ship and bought a new one. With a brand-new name.

The captain soon emerged onto the deck of the *Two Cups* sporting a long captain's jacket and a hat with a plume. She made a few hand signs toward the helm—some of the ones Fort had been teaching the crew. Turns out, it's handy for multiple reasons to be able to communicate with signs on a ship: you can talk to sailors on the rigging or give a direction to the helm without needing to yell over the sounds of the spores or wind. In this case, she congratulated the apprentice helmsman on his first steer into port. Bumps notwithstanding.

After that, Tress walked to the rail and took a sip from her cup. One with a butterfly, which had obviously been glued back together after being shattered into many pieces. The captain didn't mind the breaks. Cups with chips, or dings, or even cracks had stories. She particularly liked the one this cup told.

The dockmaster and dock inspector arrived, and Salay soon presented them with *quite* the royal writ detailing the important nature of this vessel. Single-handedly stopping the Sorceress had earned Tress and the crew a tad more than a pardon. Plus there was the matter of their exclusive ability to trade through the Crimson and Midnight Seas, opening new opportunities with once-distant seas. Every person on that ship would, within a few years, become fantastically wealthy. (I knew them when they were all just Dougs.)

The king had of course insisted that he'd always intended for this to happen—that he'd believed in Charlie, and his chosen bride, from the beginning. If that sounds like hypocrisy to you, well, we prefer to call it politics.

While the dockmaster and inspector were rereading the writ, Charlie finally emerged on deck.

Fully human again.

The curse had said he needed to bring the person he loved most to the Sorceress's home, to be cursed, in exchange for his freedom. My modifications allowed him instead to bring the person he loved to *her* home, to be versed, in exchange for his freedom. A good, sensible, *non-slant* rhyme.

Tress had left their cabin at his request so he could transform in private. Now he strode out, holding the poem he'd written for her, a stupid grin on his face.

She loved that one.

Also, the only thing he was wearing was a tiny pirate hat. As he stepped up beside her, she leaned in. "Love," she whispered, "clothing. Humans wear *clothing*."

He looked down. "That is going to take getting used to," he said. "Um . . . excuse me."

Yes, they stayed together. The two of them had both been changed by their journeys—but in complementary ways. Tress remained captain and expert sprouter, while Charlie turned out to be an extremely capable valet and a passable ship's storyteller and musician, a well-versed man indeed.

With a few tips, he wasn't so boring after all. Secretly, I'll tell you that you aren't either. Anyone who tells you otherwise is trying to lower your value. Don't trust them. They know they can't afford you otherwise.

The crew began to climb from the ship, excited for some shore leave, even if it *was* on the Rock. They all made an appearance, except for Laggart, who was currently in the brig for starting a bar fight at the last port.

You'll be happy to know that, as I've kept track of the crew over the years, even he has shown some growth. It's beginning to look like instead of following his family's tradition of being an unpleasant snarl of misery until you get yourself killed, he's on track to do . . . well, basically anything else.

As Charlie was getting dressed, Tress read his poem, the verse that broke the curse.

It is only for her. I'm sorry.

Once she looked up, she spotted something exhilarating. Her parents were stumbling down toward the docks, her little brother in tow. Tress's mother had spent most nights since she'd left watching the sea for any signs, but even with the eventual letters Tress had been able to send, she hadn't quite believed Tress would return. Neither of them had, until they saw her standing there.

Tress strode down onto the dock, then onto the once-familiar stone ground—salty and black. Odd, how foreign the place felt. How could something feel both familiar *and* foreign? As her family arrived to embrace her though, she discovered that was exquisitely familiar. Not foreign in the least.

They'd brought their luggage. And their cabin was ready. She ushered them toward the ship, but was interrupted as the duke arrived at last. Red faced. Bearing his scowl. He had only one, Tress had decided. For while you needed a smile for every occasion, a scowl needed no variety.

"What is this?" he said, slapping the writ in his hand. "What have you done?"

"I've rescued your son. The real one. Not the walking chin with a six-word vocabulary."

"I meant what have you done to the island!" the duke said, gesturing at the king's words. "Anyone can leave if they want? The island will soon be completely depopulated."

"Read the next part," she said, and took a sip of her tea, then walked off, not waiting for him.

He had to read it several times to put it together. The king had proclaimed that a generous stipend would be paid to anyone who lived and worked on the Rock for twenty years. If you're so lucky as to get a job on Diggen's Point, you'll retire with a sizable nest egg.

But be warned, positions there are hard to come by these days. No one wants to leave. The beer is great, the company passable, and the pay . . . well, it makes up for the rest.

Tress stepped back onto the deck of her ship, meeting a newly beclothed Charlie. She nodded down toward his father on the dock. "Want to say hello?"

"No thank you," Charlie said. "Did you leave Mother's letter?" (The duchess, it should be noted, had moved away from the island—and more importantly from her husband—several months before. Turns out that abandoning your only son to certain doom is not a path to a healthy marriage.)

"It's in the stack," Tress said. "He'll find it, assuming he bothers to keep reading. Ah, look. He's scowling again."

"Life is easier for him that way," Charlie said. "He only has to maintain one expression." He wrapped his arms around her and put his head on her shoulder. "It's going to be annoying to no longer have fur, but the other perks are certainly going to outweigh that loss."

"I wonder," she said idly, resting her hand on his as he held her, "if there's a maritime law against a captain dating her valet. What will people say?"

"They will say," he replied softly, "what a lucky, lucky man he is."

They didn't stay long. Just enough time to gather some supplies and for Tress to give another thanks to those who had helped her escape all those months ago.

And then the ship left to sail the ocean with a girl and a rat on board.

The rat, it turns out, was not actually a rat. In more ways than one.

The girl, you may have discovered, was not actually a girl. She was seven ways a woman, regardless of her age.

The ocean, however, was now as you hopefully imagine it. Assuming you imagine it as emerald green, made up of spores, and bearing endless possibilities.

THE END

POSTSCRIPT

I'm certain this Kickstarter campaign will become a defining moment of my career. So it's strange to think of how humble its beginnings were.

As is usual for me, the book was born out of a mashup of a couple of ideas. Stories grow out of the friction points between thoughts, like mountains being pushed up by tectonic movement. The first idea for this one is probably obvious: I wanted to do a full-length story told in Hoid's voice.

Someday I'm going to write Hoid's backstory, and I wanted to get fluent and practiced at writing from his viewpoint. I don't think this voice (the way he tells a story like this) will be where I land for his own story—that will need to be more raw, less whimsical. However, I wanted to start with a book that felt like one he'd tell—a full-length version of something like "Wandersail" or "The Dog and the Dragon."

So, I knew this book would have one foot in a whimsical space. I didn't want a fairy tale, but I wanted something adjacent. However, I also didn't want it to be too childlike. I wanted something my fans would enjoy: a grown-up fairy tale, so to speak. And so, my mind went to William Goldman's incredible book *The Princess Bride*. It's the closest thing I know of to the tone I was trying for. (Though *Good Omens* by the late Sir Terry Pratchett and Neil Gaiman is another really good comparison book for what I wanted to accomplish.)

I showed the film of *The Princess Bride* to my family during the COVID-19 lockdown. I didn't know at the time that I'd end up writing this book; I wasn't really even thinking about doing so. I was just tinkering in the back of my head with ideas—as I often do. Usually they take years or decades to mature.

The film holds up wonderfully, of course, though one thing has always bothered me. The princess who the book and film are both named after just . . . doesn't get to do much. My wife, Emily, noticed the same thing, and mentioned after the film something along the lines of, "What would that story have been like if Buttercup had gone searching for Westley, instead of immediately giving him up for dead?"

And that was my seed. The idea that started worming about and growing like verdant aether in my brain.

Oh, I should mention the aethers. For years, I'd been thinking of a world where people sailed on oceans of something that wasn't water. (Non-liquid oceans are something my brain keeps going to.) I started with people just skidding across the surface, pulled by kites. That wasn't working, but then I remembered the process of fluidization, where sand becomes like a liquid when air is pushed through it from below. This landed me on my oceans.

But for a worldbuilding element like this, I want it to be more relevant than just a substance swap. If there are oceans of spores, but they behave exactly like water, then what's the point? It's a cool visual—and that is sometimes enough. But I wanted something that really affected the story.

So, I reached back to an idea I'd had some twenty-five years ago—a group of primal elements known as aethers. I'd hinted at their existence in the Cosmere; mentions or Easter eggs about them show up in other Cosmere novels. This felt like the right time to introduce them, and their explosive potential. There will be more talk of aethers in the future, as this isn't the primary planet they originate upon.

The idea of spores that react to water in dangerous ways making up these oceans gave me just the hook I needed for the setting. And thus I had three pieces. A magic system, evoking an entire setting. A tone, as a story told by Hoid. And a plot: a quest to save a loved one who had vanished at sea.

But what about the character? Well, in this case I did what I often do. I started writing. And I explored who this young woman would be. I like to discover characters, and build the story around their choices.

I probably shouldn't have done what I did, which was start writing this book in secret. Telling nobody, even saving the files in a hidden place on the cloud where my team couldn't see them. But I wanted something that was just for me and for my wife. Something I could share with her, and not worry about deadlines or expectations. I just wanted to write, free of business constraints or fan expectations. To see where the story took me, and build something like I did long ago, in the days before I had quite so many constraints.

I kept it hidden for almost two years, shared only with Emily. But now I have given it to you as well. I hope that you enjoyed the journey, and will join me for the next three of these projects—which are each unique in their own way.

Brandon Sanderson